The
EWINGS

The

EWINGS

by JOHN O'HARA

Random House · New York

To Graham Watson

The
EWINGS

O<small>N</small> the fifteenth day of January, 1913, in the presence of both families and about two hundred invited guests, William Bloodgood Ewing and Edna Everett became man and wife. The ceremony took place in the First Presbyterian Church of Wingate, Michigan, and the reception was held at the home of the bride. Not everybody who was invited to the church was invited to the reception. There were perhaps fifty fewer people at the reception. According to the custom of the times, servants and tradespeople were not invited to the reception and were not expected to give wedding presents. It was a four o'clock wedding, which gave the bride plenty of time to change her clothes and make the eight-fifteen train to Detroit, which made connection with the nine-fifty to New York. But instead of taking the nine-fifty to New York, the couple took the train for Chicago, which left fifteen minutes later, and meant that they did not have to spend their wedding night on a train.

They arrived at the Palmer House without having been to bed, but that was Bill Ewing's plan. "Nobody knows we'll be in Chicago," he said. "This way we'll have a better chance to get acquainted." He did not say, because he did not have to say, that they could postpone their wedding night and all its vulgar implications until the second night. With this implication Edna concurred, and so it was that on their second night, Bill and Edna performed the sexual act, having had dinner in their room and become better acquainted. Two days later they went to New York and occupied a room in the Waldorf-Astoria, the Thirty-third Street side, and there it could be said that their marriage really began. The strain and the awkwardness of Chicago were behind them. There was something in the atmosphere of New York, the foreignness of it, that brought them together and relaxed them, and Edna even had her first bowel movement in four days. They went shopping together and took in some shows and the opera, for which Bill put on his full-dress suit, and except for a visit to Wall Street, they were together all the time. The visit to Wall Street was for the purpose of telling a law firm that Bill had decided to stay in Cleveland. "I owe them that courtesy," Bill said. "You don't mind, do you?"

"Not at all. I'll get an appointment with the hairdresser," said Edna.

"It isn't every day that a firm like Edwards-Clendenning makes you an offer. They even offered to pay my fare to New York. But my future is in Cleveland, so you don't mind, do you?"

"No, I think you're doing the right thing," said Edna. "Cleveland is the place for you."

"I think so. I'd rather be a king among monkeys than a monkey among kings," said Bill.

"You a monkey among kings? What a thing to say!"

"Well, I'll go down and have a talk with Mr. Clendenning. I

have an appointment with him for eleven o'clock."

"You'd have kept the appointment no matter what I said," said Edna.

"I knew you wouldn't mind," said Bill.

"But you'll be back for lunch?"

"In plenty of time for lunch."

"I'll be through with the hairdresser by twelve."

"And I'll be here no later than twelve-fifteen," said Bill. "The subway gets you there fast, and gets you back just as fast. Give us a kiss, Edna."

"Just a kiss," said Edna.

"That's all I asked for, now," said Bill.

They spent two weeks in New York. "Think of going to our own home. It'll be so strange not going back to Wingate, and yet it won't be. I could never go back to Wingate again. I don't mean that I didn't like Wingate. But Cleveland is my home, our home," said Edna on the train.

"Yes, I hope you like our house," said Bill.

"Well, I more or less picked it," said Edna.

"With the help of my mother and father and your mother and father. We'll live there for five years, then sell it."

"Let's not talk about selling it when we haven't even spent the night there," said Edna.

"You know where I want to live," said Bill. "I want a big house in the country, with three or four children and three or four horses."

"In five years?"

"Well, not all at once, but we can plan with that in mind," said Bill.

"You could be President of the United States if you set your mind to it."

"Maybe," said Bill. "If I wanted to be. President of the United States isn't the be-all and end-all of everything. A college professor made it, and God knows he isn't so much."

"Do you really mean that, Bill?"

"That I could be President, or that Wilson isn't so much? I mean both."

"I never heard you talk this way before," said Edna.

"I don't talk this way often, but a man can talk this way to his wife. And you are my wife, Edna. Aren't you?"

"For better, for worse. For richer, for poorer. Until death us do part."

"That's good. Because I have a lot of things to say to you that I won't say to anyone else," said Bill.

"There's only one thing I want you to say to me that you won't say to anyone else."

"That I love you," said Bill.

"That's right," said Edna. "I wish we were home right now."

"So do I," said Bill.

They were met at the station by Walter, the family chauffeur, in the family Pierce-Arrow. "Walter, how goes it with you?" said Bill.

"Goes all right with me. Don't go so good with your Daddy," said Walter. "How do, Mrs. Ewing?"

"What's the matter with my father?" said Bill.

"He's poorly. He had another of them heart attacks. I'm not supposed to say anything, but he's very poorly."

"Then take us to his house. You don't mind, do you, Edna?"

"Certainly not," said Edna.

"They took him to the hospital day before yesterday. I'll drive you there," said Walter.

They got in the car. "This is the second heart attack for my father," said Bill. "A fine homecoming for you."

"Where is Mrs. Ewing, Walter?" said Edna.

"Hospital. At his bedside," said Walter.

"Is Dr. Fogel in charge?" said Bill.

"Dr. Fogel and Dr. Hendricks, both in charge," said Walter. "I don't like that Dr. Hendricks."

"He's the heart specialist," said Bill.

"He's a cold man, cold," said Walter.

"Yes, he is that," said Bill.

"He don't think your father's going to live," said Walter. "He says it like he was pleased. He says it like if your father had any sense, he'd have come to the great Dr. Hendricks, but now it's too late. A cold man."

"That's just his manner," said Bill, but in a whisper he said to Edna: "Walter's right."

Dr. Fogel was with Bill's mother in a room adjoining Mr. Ewing's. "You just come from the train?" said Mrs. Ewing. "It was nice of you to come, Edna." She kissed Edna and burst into tears when she kissed Bill.

"You can go in now, Bill," said Dr. Fogel. "One at a time."

Bill went in the sickroom, and was shocked at the appearance of his father after two weeks. "Hello, Father. How're you feeling?"

"Hello, son. You got here in time," said Mr. Ewing. "Is Edna with you?"

"Of course. Do you want to see her? She's with Mother, in the next room."

"They better both . . ." His words were lost forever in death. The nurse summoned Dr. Fogel, who bent over Mr. Ewing, then said, "He's gone. He had just enough strength to wait for you, Bill. He's gone, Mrs. Ewing, both Mrs. Ewings." He left Bill and the two Mrs. Ewings alone with the senior Mr. Ewing. "Goodbye, Father," said Bill. "Let's leave Mother with him."

"What for? He's gone," said Mrs. Ewing. "Your Aunt Esther is waiting down the hall for me, Bill. I'll be all right. You two take Walter and go on home. I insist. Maybe I'll be out to see you later, but I insist on your going home now."

"If you insist," said Edna.

In the car later Edna said, "Your mother was right, insisting that we go home."

"I don't know why you think so," said Bill.

"I know you don't, but what's more important? To grieve over your dead father, or to get started on our marriage? Your mother knew, she understood. A very wise woman, your mother."

The house that was to be their home was two stories high, with an attic and a cellar, and a garage in back and a lawn in front. It was, if anything, on the formal side and was built of white brick. It was a new house, had never been lived in before, and there was a new face at the door, greeting Mr. and Mrs. William B. Ewing. She was Martha Buck, the colored maid. "Welcome to your new residence," said Martha. "I hope you will be happy here." It was a set speech, but it was accompanied by a smile. Walter, the chauffeur, sniffed.

"Shall I tell her?" said Walter.

"No, don't," said Edna. "Thank you, Martha. I'm sure we will be."

"You just in time for lunch," said Martha. "Calves liver, like you said."

"That will be fine," said Edna.

"Bring our bags inside, and then go back to Mother," said Bill. "I might as well tell Martha about Father."

"You don't have to, I know," said Martha. "Your mother phoned me. Said I wasn't to let on. I'm sorry for your trouble, Mr. Ewing, Mrs. Ewing. I'm very sorry. But you have to eat, don't you?"

"Yes, we have to eat," said Bill. "Let's go up and see how everything looks. We'll be down in about ten minutes, Martha."

Bill and Edna went upstairs. "Those flowers must be from your mother," said Edna. She looked at the card. "Yes, they are. She says, 'May these flowers bring you many years of continued happiness,' and signed Ada Ewing. That was thoughtful. I suppose my parents didn't know when we'd arrive, or they'd have sent some. At least I think they would have."

"You better let me shed my tears now, Edna," said Bill.

"I know, Bill," said Edna. "I'll leave you alone."

"I don't want to be left alone. I didn't mean that. I just want to—

I don't know what I want. Too much has happened all at once. I'd planned to carry you over the threshold, but I forgot."

"Carry me over this threshold," said Edna. "Martha can wait."

"You knew what I wanted better than I did," said Bill.

"I wanted you," said Edna.

She took off her clothes and he took off his and they stood together, admiring each other until the moment came when she was ready for him and they were ready for each other. Then she lay on the bed and he mounted her. "Is it all right?" he said.

"Yes, I think so," she said. "Can you wait a minute?"

"I'm afraid I can't," he said.

"Then go ahead," she said. "It'll be all right."

"I can't wait," he said.

"You don't have to," she said.

"I'm coming. I'm coming," he said, and did so. "I couldn't wait."

"Neither could I," she said.

"Did you come?" he said.

"Yes," she said.

"Are you sure?" he said.

"Yes, couldn't you tell?"

"I wasn't sure," he said.

"I was. It hurt at first, but I'm getting used to it. I take longer than you do. But once you're inside me, it's all right. It's lovely. I can't tell you how lovely it is."

"That's good," he said.

She lay in his arms. "What are you thinking?" she said.

"How wonderful you are," he said.

"What else?" she said.

"That's all," he said.

"You weren't thinking of calves liver and bacon?"

"Were you?" he said.

"And Martha. I must have been," she said. "I'm going to take a quick bath. You can take one in the other bathroom."

"Let me look at you," he said.

"Now?"

"Now," he said. "You're perfect, Edna. Perfect."

"Except for my appendicitis scar," she said.

"You always say that," he said.

"Take your bath, Bill," she said.

He kissed her appendicitis scar. "That's to make it well again."

"My husband," she said. "My darling husband."

He put on the same clothes he had taken off, and she unpacked a dress she had taken to New York. "I don't think we're going to fool Martha," she said.

"Probably not," he said. They descended to the dining-room and ate their lunch.

"I guess we ought to go out and see Mother," said Bill.

"She was thinking of coming here," said Edna.

"Not really," said Bill. "She'll go home and stay there till after the funeral. I know Mother."

It turned out that Bill was right. His mother did not leave the house until it was time to go to the church for Francis Ewing's funeral, when she had as her escort her brother, Asa Bloodgood.

"I hope you stay sober till after the funeral," said Ada Ewing.

"Now what kind of talk is that, Ada?" said Asa Bloodgood.

"I know you," said Ada Ewing. "If you're not going to stay sober, I'll get someone else to walk with me. Jim Williams, or one of his other law partners."

"I promise you I'll stay sober," said Asa Bloodgood. "But my goodness, Ada."

It was noticed that Asa Bloodgood was making the effort. He wore his frock coat and his high silk hat, and he offered his arm to his sister when it was needed, at such times as when they entered the funeral coach, and walked up and down the steps of the church. They shared the funeral coach with Bill and Edna Ewing, and the women, in veils and black gloves, made small talk while the men maintained a silence. "It was nice of your father and mother to make the trip," said Ada Ewing.

"They wouldn't have thought otherwise," said Edna.

"I would have put them up if I'd known they were coming," said Ada Ewing. "But I suppose they'll be more comfortable at the hotel."

"We offered to put them up," said Bill Ewing. "We had plenty of room. But they wouldn't hear of it."

"No, I don't blame them," said Ada Ewing. "A newly married couple shouldn't be reminded of a death in the family."

"That's what Daddy said," said Edna Ewing.

"I notice the governor was here," said Asa Bloodgood.

"Why shouldn't he be?" said Bill Ewing. "Why the hell shouldn't he be?"

"Well, that's true. Why shouldn't he be?" said Asa Bloodgood. It was all the conversation that went on between uncle and nephew.

"The governor's coming back to the house after the services," said Ada Ewing.

"What for? Is he running again?" said Bill.

"Oh, now that wasn't fair," said Ada Ewing. "He had great respect for your father. Well, here's the church."

"And here's the steeple. Open the door and here's all the people," said Bill. "Are you all right, Mother?"

"Yes, I'm all right. As all right as I'll ever be," said Ada Ewing.

"You get some rest after this is over," said Bill.

"I'll have plenty of time for all the rest I need," said Ada Ewing.

The service was conducted according to the Episcopal book, with the hymns chosen by the widow. "A Mighty Fortress Is Our God" and "Oh God Our Help in Ages Past," and played, but not sung, "Merrily Sing We All to D. K. E.," which was a choice of Francis Ewing's. "I wonder how many recognized the Deke song?" said Bill. "It was practically the only song my father ever sang. He wasn't much of a singer." After the service they all returned to the Francis Ewing house for lunch, and Asa Bloodgood said to his sister, "Is it all right if I have a drink now?"

"Yes, and thank you for staying sober," said Ada Ewing.

"It was an effort," said Asa Bloodgood. "I hope Francis appreciates it."

"I did, if he didn't," said Ada Ewing.

"It was very cold at the cemetery. I could have used a nip there."

"I appreciate that, Asa. Now go talk to the governor. He may have a job for you, even if you are a Democrat," said Ada Ewing.

"Fat chance," said Asa Bloodgood. "I'll talk to Louise Fuller."

"Oh, is she here?"

"You know damn well she's here, Ada."

"I invited her, but I didn't think she'd have the nerve to come," said Ada Ewing.

"She's here, all right," said Asa Bloodgood. "She has as much right to be here as you have. With those parting words, I take my leave of you."

"Goodbye, brother," said Ada Ewing.

The Everetts, the parents of Edna Ewing, were ill at ease in Cleveland, where they knew only a few people and those were friends of their son-in-law. They had met Francis Ewing only in connection with parties incidental to the wedding of their daughter, and a year ago they had been unaware that Francis Ewing, his wife, and son existed. Paul Everett was a man of means, but nowhere near the kind of means that were on display at the funeral of Francis Ewing. The Ewings, for instance, had a butler and two or three maids, all colored. Paul Everett owned a furniture factory, which was doing well, with the vogue for Mission furniture, but the governor of Michigan would not make the trip from Lansing to attend the funeral of Paul Everett, that was certain. "They gave your father a nice turn-out," said Paul Everett. "I understand the governor came up from Columbus."

"Yes, we know the governor," said Bill Ewing. "Can I get you anything?"

"Who is Mr. Bloodgood?" said Mrs. Everett.

"He's my mother's brother," said Bill Ewing.

"Oh, then he was at the wedding. He acted like he knew us but for the life of me I couldn't remember his name. Bloodgood. Is he married?"

"No," said Bill Ewing.

"He walked with your mother at the funeral, didn't he?" said Paul Everett.

"Oh, that's why he looked familiar," said Mrs. Everett.

"And we'd seen him at the wedding," said Paul Everett.

"That's right, we had," said Mrs. Everett. "So many new people these last couple of weeks. Well, it's going to be quiet in Wingate with Edna moved to Cleveland. You must come up and visit us."

"The trout season'll be along before you know it," said Paul Everett. "Are you a trout fisherman, Bill?"

"No, I used to go gunning with my father, but that was all," said Bill Ewing.

"I'll have to get you to go fishing with me. I used to take Edna trout fishing."

"I didn't know that," said Bill Ewing.

"Oh, yes. Didn't she ever tell you?" said Paul Everett.

"No, I don't believe she ever did," said Bill Ewing. "You must excuse me. I have to say goodbye to the governor."

"It's funny Edna never said anything about going fishing," said Paul Everett.

"I guess we had other things to talk about," said Bill. "Excuse me, Mr. Everett, Mrs. Everett."

"Fine boy," said Paul Everett.

"Fine boy. We were very lucky.

"You mean Eddie Noisrander. I never thought that was serious with Edna, not after she met Bill Ewing."

"Well, I guess not what you'd call serious, but he was around a lot," said Mrs. Everett.

"Enough to introduce Edna to Bill," said Paul Everett. "Edna knew what she wanted, I'll have to give her that. She had a good head on her shoulders. Well, let's get started back to Wingate. We can get the five-twenty to Detroit and the eight-twenty to Wingate. I don't want to spend another night in that hotel."

"East, west, home's best," said Mrs. Everett. "Let's say goodbye to the two Mrs. Ewings."

The two Mrs. Ewings had finished saying goodbye to the governor and some members of his cabinet, and were momentarily alone. "You're not leaving already?" said Ada Ewing.

"Paul has to leave," said Mrs. Everett. "It was all he could do to get away. The factory is so busy."

"May have to work overtime," said Paul Everett.

"Well, I certainly appreciate your coming," said Ada Ewing. "Let me send you off in my car. Edna, tell Walter to drive them to the hotel."

Edna accompanied her parents to the porte-cochere. "Pretty fancy, riding around in a Pierce-Arrow," said Paul Everett. "There isn't a single Pierce-Arrow in the whole of Wingate."

"Don't let it go to your head, Edna," said her mother.

"I'll try not to, Mother," said Edna Ewing. "Here's Bill."

Bill Ewing said, "Mother wanted to thank you for coming. And so do I. I'll take good care of Edna for you."

"You be sure and do that," said Paul Everett. There was handshaking and kissing, and the Pierce-Arrow moved away.

"What's the matter, Edna?" said Bill.

"It's an awful thing to say, but I'm glad to see them go," said Edna. "Let's not go back to Wingate for a year. Thank God you took me out of there."

Edna Everett was generally considered the prettiest girl in Wingate and had been so considered from the time she was fifteen, but beginning at about the time she was fifteen she was also considered to be as disagreeable as it was possible to become at that age. People wondered why. She had had a pony from the time she was twelve, and drove it around in a governess cart or a cutter every afternoon after school, accompanied by a less fortunate friend, who was not allowed to take the reins. This led to a falling-out between Edna and Bertha Linkletter. "Why won't you ever let me drive?" said Bertha.

"Because you don't know how, and besides, it's my pony," said Edna.

"Then let me out," said Bertha.

"All right, good riddance," said Edna.

Ann Collins was a quick successor to Bertha Linkletter in the governess cart. She also made the mistake of wanting to drive, and when she asked Edna if she could take the reins, Edna said, "My father won't let you drive." This was strange, inasmuch as Ann Collins had owned a pony before Edna had Prince, and Ann said so. "Will it be all right if I ask him?" said Ann. "No, it won't be all right," said Edna. "Don't you say a word to my father." But Ann asked Mr. Everett if it would be all right if she drove the pony, and Mr. Everett said he supposed it would be all right with him if it was all right with Edna, and Edna was caught in a lie. It took very little time for Edna's possessiveness to become known among her friends, and the pleasure of driving the pony was lessened by the fact that she could not get another girl to ride with her. "I'm getting tired of Prince," Edna told her father. "I'm too old for a pony." The pony was sold, and to make matters worse, he was sold to Bertha Linkletter's father, who apparently did not think Bertha was too old for a pony, although she was the same age as Edna.

Edna was graduated from Wingate High School when she was sixteen, which her father and mother considered too young for a girl to go to Ann Arbor. "You can take a post-graduate course at Wingate High," said her mother. "We don't want to hurry you."

"Then send me to boarding school," said Edna.

"No, another year at High is what we decided. It won't do you any harm," said Mrs. Everett. "Most girls are eighteen before they go to college, and some are even nineteen. Sixteen is just too young, and that's all there is to it."

Edna spent a miserable year at home until the following spring, when she caught the eye of Eddie Noisrander, a student at Ann Arbor and a graduate of Culver. He asked permission to have her as his guest at the spring dance, but her parents refused. "You're still too young," said Mrs. Everett. "And we hear a lot of things go on at those dances."

"It's Eddie Noisrander, not the things that go on at the dances," said Edna.

"Well, what if it is?" said Mrs. Everett. "Eddie Noisrander ought to know better than to ask a girl not yet seventeen to those dances."

"You never let me do anything," said Edna. "Fishing with Daddy —and that's all."

"You'll be thankful some day that your parents took an interest in you," said Mrs. Everett. "Not like other parents that don't seem to mind how their daughters carry on."

"You don't trust me, that's all," said Edna. "Bertha Linkletter can go to the spring dance, and she's still in high school."

"What Mrs. Linkletter lets Bertha do is her own concern," said Mrs. Everett.

But Paul Everett was inclined to think that he and his wife were being too strict with Edna, and whenever Eddie Noisrander got home on a weekend, he had a date with Edna. "We can't keep her cooped up forever," said Paul Everett.

"More's the pity," said Mrs. Everett.

"What do you mean by that?"

"Nothing now, but you'll see," said Mrs. Everett. "I don't trust that Eddie Noisrander."

"Give me a reason why not," said Paul Everett.

"He has too much money to spend," said Mrs. Everett.

"There isn't much he can do with it in Wingate, not with Edna," said Paul Everett.

"Money is the root of all evil," said Mrs. Everett.

"Well, as the fellow says, 'Give me more of the root,'" said Paul

Everett. "Don't forget, the Noisranders buy a lot of tables and chairs from the Everett Manufacturing Company. It may be only a small brewery, but they buy the best of our bentwood line."

"Well, then I'll shut up," said Mrs. Everett.

Edna Everett accompanied her mother and father to the same summer resort that they had been going to for four or five summers, but this time Eddie Noisrander was a frequent visitor, and his visits were the high points of Edna's vacation. He did not stay with the Everetts. That would have been too much of a commitment, and besides, Edna did not invite him. Instead he would show up at ten o'clock in the morning in his sneakers and white shirt and pants, and they would walk together to the bathhouse and change into their bathing suits and along about eleven o'clock they were ready for the cold dip in the lake. The water was very cold, a daily challenge to both of them, and after their first dip they sat on the float and talked. "What's it like at Ann Arbor?" said Edna.

"You keep asking me that," said Eddie. "It's like any place else, it's not much different. I thought it would be different after Culver, but the only difference is more freedom."

"Freedom is what I want," said Edna. "I've never had any real freedom. My mother and father watch me every minute."

"Yes, I know that," said Eddie. "Why don't you run away?"

"Run away? Where to?"

"You see? You wouldn't know where to run away to," said Eddie.

"I'd run away if I knew where to, but I don't. As soon as I graduate I'm going to Europe, and they'll have a hard time getting me back. I may even go before I graduate."

"You couldn't. You couldn't just go to Europe. You don't know anybody there. Where would you go?"

"Germany. I speak the language," said Eddie. "I'm going to go there because my parents and my grandparents think I'm going to learn about the brewery, but I'm not coming back. I have some cousins over there."

"Did you ever see them?" said Edna.

"An uncle," said Eddie. "He stayed with us a couple of years ago. He convinced my father that they ought to send me over there to learn how to make beer. He was my mother's brother, not a Noisrander. He was the only one of my mother's relations to stay in Germany. My mother and all her brothers and sisters came to this country."

"Why do you think I'm interested in your mother's family?"

"You're interested in me, aren't you?" said Eddie.

"Sometimes, but not in your mother's family. I don't even know them," said Edna.

"Then you'd better get interested in my family," said Eddie.

"Why? Because you think I'm going to marry you? That's a crazy idea," said Edna.

"I'll wait," said Eddie.

"You'll have to wait a good long time," said Edna.

"I still say I'll wait," said Eddie.

"Two years from now you'll fall in love with some German girl and marry her. You'll have a lot of little German Catholics, all speaking German."

"And what will you be doing?"

"Two years from now? I'll be a sophomore at Ann Arbor, dating a Deke," said Edna.

"Why not a Psi U?"

"Because you're a Psi U and you'll blackball me. No Psi U will ever have a date with me. Isn't that true?"

"As true as the other nonsense you talk about fraternities," said Eddie.

"But I'm learning," said Edna.

They would sit on the float until it was time to eat their lunch, getting a good sunburn, and then they would swim for five or ten minutes and Edna would have to be home for lunch. Eddie would have lunch with some of the boys from Ann Arbor, a sandwich or something, and then go to Edna's house and wait for her to go canoeing with him. Sometimes they would take the canoe—Edna's

—and be gone far out of sight, but they always had to be back in time for supper. Mr. and Mrs. Everett were strict about that. In the evenings there was a movie show from eight o'clock until nine, and the same show from nine until ten, provided it did not rain and provided nothing had happened to the*films. There was a pavilion where dancing was held on some nights, usually Friday or Saturday nights, but Edna would take a look at the crowd, and if her father and mother were not there, they would not stay. They would go instead to one of several places they knew, and there they would make love.

Edna was extremely careful about the limits of her love-making. Eddie was permitted to kiss her and to press her breasts on the outside of her clothing, but he dared not touch her bare breasts or the skin of her legs. No boy was expected to violate this rule. Some of the boys were known to have violated the rule, but not with the girls who enforced them, and who were just as strict with the other girls as they were with the boys. A girl who did not make it understood that she did not permit liberties with a boy was punished by ostracism, and she and her male companion were left out of things. The boys who had dates with girls who violated the rules could not get dates with the girls who observed the rules, and as they were the most desirable girls, their rules were enforced.

Some of the boys had had experiences that they liked to talk about among boys, but for the most part this was boasting, exaggerating. And a boy's boasting was liable to be held against him. "I don't want a lumberjack to have a date with my sister," said one boy. "And what's more, no lumberjack *gets* a date with my sister." In these words a fraternity brother of Eddie Noisrander's made clear that he had heard a bit of boasting, and that it was too late to do anything about it. The boasting boy did not get a date with the girl and she never knew why.

As it was, the liberties the girls permitted were far and away greater than their parents permitted. A goodnight kiss was reserved for couples who had announced their engagement, and was not approved of for the others. Mr. and Mrs. Everett pretended not to know that Eddie kissed Edna at the conclusion of an evening together, and care was taken to maintain the pretense. "I'm sure Eddie kisses Edna," said Paul Everett.

"He probably does," said Mrs. Everett. "But I never let you kiss me till we were as good as engaged. And that's the way we'll try to have it with Eddie and Edna. Time enough for those familiarities when they're engaged."

"And that will be never, if you have your way about it," said Paul Everett.

"Well, it'll be a long time ahead," said Mrs. Everett. "I'll do all I can to discourage it. Eddie Noisrander is a Catholic, and that's enough. I don't say he's a good Catholic, but he'd make Edna turn. They all try."

"Yes, I guess they do," said Paul Everett. "Well, I'd oppose it. However, we don't have to worry about that now. It's the kissing and hugging we have to watch out for. A girl can find herself in a pretty predicament before she knows it."

"That's exactly what I'm going to guard against. Fortunately I don't see Edna as that kind of a girl. She's too level-headed," said Mrs. Everett. "But Eddie Noisrander would take advantage of her."

"We could stop him from seeing her," said Paul Everett.

"Oh, I thought of that," said Mrs. Everett. "But it's too late now, and besides, we have no excuse. If we caught them hugging and kissing, it'd be different. But here at the Lake they don't get much chance to be off by themselves. I watch them pretty carefully, and I account for just about every minute of their time."

And so Eddie and Edna managed to steal their moments of limited love-making under Mrs. Everett's more or less watchful eye. The last night the two were together, Eddie put his hand under Edna's skirt but Edna resisted him. "You spoiled everything," she said. "I never thought you'd spoil everything our last night together."

"I couldn't help it," said Eddie. "I wanted you so much."

"You realize I'll never be able to see you again. Why did you have to go spoil everything? Take me home, take me home right away."

"We can't go home till the dance is finished," said Eddie.

"Yes we can, or I'll go home by myself, and my parents will know something's wrong. Oh, Eddie, you did spoil everything. I have a notion not to go to Ann Arbor."

"You wouldn't do that," said Eddie.

"Yes, I would. I would too," said Edna. "I thought we were going to have such good times together there, but this makes everything different."

Upon Eddie's solemn promise not to put his hand under her skirt again, Edna agreed to go to Ann Arbor and to more or less be his girl.

But at Ann Arbor, Edna was a fresh face, dressed well, had money to spend, and did not take seriously her promise to be Eddie's girl. The disagreeable side of her nature seemed to have vanished with her effort to be well liked at Ann Arbor. She was not one of the richest girls at the university, but as the only child of a furniture manufacturer she had money to spend and she spent it. She joined the Kappa Gamma Theta sorority, the newest on campus, because she would be a founding member and possibly because the Tri-Betas had had a letter from a woman in Wingate urging them not to pledge so disagreeable a girl. The other Tri-Betas could not see that side of her nature, but they went along with the blackball because home-town letters were strongly influential, and the Tri-Betas thus lost a class president. As president of the freshman class Edna was decorative and little else, but she was that, and on the few occasions when she made an official appearance her beauty was outstanding. It was so seldom that a girl was chosen for her looks, and Edna moreover had good marks. Mr. and Mrs. Everett had made a wise decision in keeping Edna in high school for the extra year. It did a girl no harm to repeat her

fourth year in French and math, especially math, which she understood better the second time around. The fact was that Edna was
impatient to learn, and her eagerness showed in her aptitude.
"Everything comes so easy to you," said a classmate.

The truth was that Edna was happy at Ann Arbor. "I could
hardly wait to come here," said Edna. "I had to repeat most of my
senior High because I was too young, or my parents thought I was.
Maybe I wasn't, at that. Anyway, here I am."

The classmate, who was flunking nearly everything, said, "But
what did you do about boys? You had to see the same boys for two
years."

"No, I didn't. I didn't date high school boys. The year I took
post-graduate I began seeing a sophomore from Ann Arbor. He was
a Psi U."

"Is he still here?"

"His name is Eddie Noisrander," said Edna. "Do you know
him?"

"Eddie Noisrander? Everybody knows Eddie Noisrander. Do
you mean to say you went out with Eddie Noisrander?"

"All the time. Why?"

"I don't know, but from what I've heard, a girl isn't safe with
Eddie," said the classmate.

"That's not true," said Edna. "He never got fresh with me. Only
once."

"He's just like the rest of those Psi U's."

"But how do you know if you never went out with him?" said
Edna.

"A Psi U is a Psi U. They're all alike. They're as bad as the Betas.
And you know how *they* talk. A girl's reputation isn't safe with
them."

"I never went out with a Beta, but I went out with Eddie Noisrander. I think you're exaggerating."

"Not from what I hear," said the classmate.

"Oh, you hear the same thing about any fraternity," said Edna.

"But mostly about the Psi U's and the Betas."

"You hear it about the Kappa Sigs and the Phi Gams," said Edna.

"No, I never heard it about the Phi Gams," said the classmate.

"That's because you date a Phi Gam," said Edna. "But *I've* heard it about the Phi Gams, just as bad."

"What did you hear about the Phi Gams?"

"The same things you heard about the Psi U's and the Betas," said Edna.

"What?"

"That a girl's reputation wasn't safe with them," said Edna.

"Well, it isn't," said the classmate.

"I'd sooner trust a Psi U than one of your Phi Gams," said Edna.

"That's because you know a Psi U," said the classmate.

"Exactly," said Edna. "Boys are all alike. They all want the same thing."

"Well, I guess that's true," said the classmate. "I guess there's a lot of truth in that."

There was a continual state of excitement produced by the football games at Ann Arbor, the rushing season of the sororities and fraternities, the Indian summer, the early autumn, the first snowfall, the class elections, and suddenly the knowledge that the Christmas holidays were just around the corner. Edna's roommate was the daughter of a missionary in China, who would not be seeing her parents until the following summer, and was dividing her holiday between Edna and another Kappa Gamma Theta whose home was on the Peninsula. She was a rather plain girl, who was not looking forward to her first Christmas away from her parents, and Edna in turn did not look forward to the task of entertaining her. Wingate was small, and Faith McCracken was not interested in boys. She had not had a date with a boy since coming to Ann Arbor, and her romantic life consisted of a weekly exchange of letters with a boy who was a sophomore at Amherst, likewise the son of a missionary. Frank Carlson, the missionary's son, could not be induced to come to Wingate; he was earning some extra money at the post office in

Amherst and would be there throughout the holidays. Nevertheless Edna was determined to show Faith a good time. There was a Christmas dance at the tennis club and Edna would give a dinner before that, and there was a New Year's Eve party at the Elks' club, which was not as bad as it sounded. "But I won't be in Wingate New Year's Eve," said Faith.

"In case you change your mind," said Edna. "They hire a good orchestra from Detroit, and maybe I could persuade you to stay over."

"I don't think so," said Faith. "You'll be sick of me by then."

Mr. and Mrs. Everett met the girls at the train in Mr. Everett's brand-new Hudson. "You'll be plenty warm enough with the side curtains," said Paul Everett. "And you can put the top down in the summer."

"Not me," said Mrs. Everett. "It's nice to have you visit us, Faith."

"It's nice of you to have me," said Faith.

"What do you hear from China?" said Paul Everett.

"From China? I had a letter from my mother. My father's on his annual visit to the interior. He ought to be back by now. It takes so long for a letter to reach me."

"Yes, I guess it does," said Paul Everett. "Two, three weeks about."

"Sometimes longer than that," said Faith.

"My, it must be strange," said Mrs. Everett. "Think of a letter taking three weeks to get here."

"Or longer," said Faith.

"I don't know what I'd do without a letter from Edna, every Tuesday on the dot," said Mrs. Everett.

"Oh, stop talking about it!" said Faith, and burst into tears.

The Everetts, shocked, could not find anything to say for the moment. "You're right, Faith," said Paul Everett. "We're so glad to have our little chicken home to roost, we forgot about you."

"I'm sorry, I apologize. I really apologize," said Faith.

"That's all right," said Paul Everett. "It's perfectly natural."

"Why don't you drive around and show Faith the sights," said Mrs. Everett. "Beginning with the Everett Manufacturing Company."

"Well, I don't know. Would you like to see that, Faith?" said Paul Everett.

"*I* would. I haven't seen the new addition," said Edna.

"We'll have a look while it's still daylight," said Paul Everett.

"I'd like to very much," said Faith. She had recovered from her outburst as rapidly as it had come on, and the embarrassing moment was over by the time they drove slowly past the factory. But Mrs. Everett was not used to such behavior.

"What came over Faith in the car?" she asked Edna when they got to their separate rooms.

"Oh, nothing, Mother. She just got homesick," said Edna. "All that talk about letters."

"But does she often get like that?" said Mrs. Everett.

"No, it was very unusual," said Edna.

"Well, I should hope so. I wouldn't want you rooming with a girl that flew off the handle like that," said Mrs. Everett.

"It was nothing, Mother. Really it was."

"It was pretty darn rude," said Mrs. Everett. "It gave me a bad impression."

Faith and Edna busied themselves the next few days with preparations for the dance at the tennis club, seeing friends like Bertha Linkletter and Ann Collins, and having Eddie Noisrander and a fraternity brother in for tea. Meals and shopping took up a good deal of their time, and it was well they did; there was so little to do, otherwise. There was a heavy fall of snow that threatened to call off the tennis club dance, but in four days Wingate got used to it, and since the tennis club was within walking distance of the partygoers, a little thing like four inches of snow was not taken seriously. They were used to snow in Michigan. Four-buckle arctics would take care of that, and there was actually a festive spirit prevailing on the night of the dance.

Edna's guests for dinner were Eddie Noisrander and his friend, Pat Boyle; Bertha Linkletter and her date, Ann Collins and her date, Emily Noisrander and her date, and Clare Shipstead and her date. Eddie Noisrander and Pat Boyle owned their own Tuxedos; the other boys hired theirs at Kauffman's or the Outlet. Clare Shipstead's date wore a pair of high-button shoes belonging to his father, but at least they were black. Eddie Noisrander and Pat Boyle wore the badge of the Psi Upsilon fraternity on their waistcoats; Bertha Linkletter's date wore the pledge pin of Sigma Chi in his lapel, and Ann Collins's date wore not only the Delta Tau Delta badge on his waistcoat but the key of Kappa Beta Phi on his watchchain. Naturally there was a good deal of good-natured raillery over the Kappa Beta key, and it helped to break the ice. The girls wore dresses from the Bon-Ton, Wingate, except Edna and Faith, who wore dresses from Hudson's. Faith borrowed hers from Edna.

It was the first time Mrs. Everett had had to put all the leaves in the dining-room table, for which she required the expert assistance of her husband. They had a table cover large enough for the table, but it had never been used, and Mrs. Everett decided to save it for Edna's wedding, and use doilies instead. "I'd hate to see cigarette ashes ruin our good table cover," said Mrs. Everett.

"How many of the girls smoke?" said Paul Everett.

"None of them, I hope, but the boys all do," said Mrs. Everett.

"That's entirely up to you," said Paul Everett. "Do you want to have candles on the table?"

"I think it would be nice, Christmassy," said Mrs. Everett.

"Well, I have to go and put on my Tux," said Paul Everett. "You finish setting the table and then come help me with my bow tie. We have to be at the Wendells' by eight."

"I don't think I'll put candles on the table after all. It's too dim," said Mrs. Everett.

[26]

"Suit yourself, but remember the Wendells. I'll be ready for a snort by the time we get there," said Paul Everett.

"You and your snort," said Mrs. Everett. "Harry Wendell doesn't want one any more than you do, but you think because it's Christmas you have to have one."

"Well, we're going to," said Paul Everett.

There were no snorts for the guests at Edna Everett's party, and they began to arrive past the hour when Paul Everett and his wife had taken off for the Wendells', thereby depriving the Paul Everetts of the pleasure of greeting them. "I wanted to see what Bertha Linkletter would be wearing," said Mrs. Everett. "Some outlandish thing, I'm sure."

"You'll see her at the dance," said Paul Everett.

"That isn't the same," said Mrs. Everett, without explaining why.

Edna and Faith said goodbye to Mr. and Mrs. Everett and fifteen minutes was expended in the necessary introductions, and dinner was announced at eight-thirty. Place cards directed the guests to their seats, and the soup was served by Olga, the Everetts' maid, assisted by Gretta, who was helping Olga for the evening. Gretta was more accustomed to serving traveling salesmen at the Hotel Wingate, but she had the night off because the Hotel Wingate was empty during the Christmas season, and working at the Everetts' gave her a chance to pick up an extra two dollars. She also supplied her own uniform, which Olga did not have, and which added a certain elegance to the occasion. Gretta, who called Edna "dear," was the hit of the evening, and exchanged pleasantries with all the boys until about halfway through the meal. Olga then took over the serving chore; Gretta had passed out, having discovered a bottle of whiskey that Mr. Everett reserved for a cold. Aside from that, the dinner proceeded according to plan. The main course was roast chicken, with chestnut stuffing, followed by plum pudding with hard sauce, and at ten o'clock the partygoers were ready to put on their arctics and brave the slush and snow on the two-block walk to the Wingate Tennis Club.

They were all to meet at the club, where a table had been held for them. "How did it go?" said Mrs. Everett.

"Gretta got intoxicated. Otherwise it went fine," said Edna.

"I was afraid of something like that. Just wait till she comes around for her pay," said Mrs. Everett. "But all the others had a good time? What did you talk about?"

"Oh, I don't know, Mother," said Edna.

"Did Faith have a good time?" said Mrs. Everett. "The party was in her honor."

"I guess she did. I haven't had a chance to ask her," said Edna. "The party isn't over yet. It's just beginning. This dance goes on till one o'clock, and is it all right if I ask them back to the house after?"

"All of them? What will we give them?" said Mrs. Everett.

"Oh, scrambled eggs," said Edna.

"I hope we have enough eggs," said Mrs. Everett. "Is that the thing to do?"

"Some will come and some won't, but I have to invite them all," said Edna. "I must get back to my guests."

The fox trot was just catching on in Michigan, the one-step had already arrived, the maxixe had come and gone, the waltz was the waltz. But Faith McCracken had never learned to dance, and had not told Edna. "Oh, everybody can do the waltz," said Edna. "Go on and try. You and Pat, go on."

Pat Boyle was an excellent dancer, and he made a try, but Faith was a hopeless partner. She gave up, and halfway through the first waltz she sat down, determined not to move out of her chair again. "I *told* you I couldn't dance," said Faith.

"Well, if you can't, you can't," said Edna. "I just wish you had told me beforehand. I thought everybody could waltz."

"Everybody but me," said Faith. "In China I never learned. It was sort of against our religion."

"Well, do you mind if I do?" said Edna.

[28]

"No, you go ahead," said Faith.

All the others fox-trotted and one-stepped and waltzed as the evening went on, and several times Faith was left alone at the table as the extra man found a partner from another table. At one o'clock the orchestra played "Good Night, Ladies," and there was an abortive effort to keep the orchestra for an extra hour, but the older people had had enough. "Let's all go back to my house for some scrambled eggs," said Edna. But excuses were made, and Edna finally realized that her party had been a failure. Eddie Noisrander and Pat Boyle escorted the girls home and left them at the front door.

"If it's all the same to you, I think I'll go to bed," said Edna. "I'm more tired than I thought."

"I'm sorry I spoiled your party," said Faith.

"Oh, that's all right. Sleep as late as you like," said Edna.

"I'm really sorry," said Faith. "I've been a terrible house guest."

"Not at all. Goodnight," said Edna. "Don't lock up. My parents aren't home yet." She retired to her room, took off her dress, and lay on the bed. She must have fallen asleep; at any rate she came to and the house was deathly quiet and she put on her wrapper and found the lights off downstairs and her parents' bedroom door closed. And she smelled gas coming from the guest-room bathroom.

Faith McCracken lay naked on the bathroom floor, and she was dead. It was a little after four in the morning.

It was not her fault. She kept telling herself it was not her fault. Her mother told her it was not her fault. Her father not only did not consider it her fault, but he had not even bothered to pass a judgment on her. Her father knew something that neither she nor her mother knew: at the coroner's autopsy it transpired that Faith McCracken was three months pregnant, and Paul Everett kept that fact to himself. According to his reckoning, the father of the unborn child was most likely the boy who worked in the post office at

Amherst. But what was the use of adding that bit of scandal to the already abundant disgrace? "Do you have to say that?" said Paul Everett. "Her parents are missionaries in China thousands of miles away from here. Maybe she didn't even know she was pregnant. She certainly didn't look it. And I'm not sure the young man at Amherst was the father. It could have been anybody."

The coroner, who was a good friend of Paul Everett's and a brother Mason, was inclined to agree with Paul. "There's no doubt about her committing suicide," said the coroner. "Can you th... any reason for it?"

"Yes, I can. She was homesick. Homesick and miserable. Th... why Edna invited her to spend Christmas with us," said Paul Everett. "We'll bury her as soon as the ground gets soft enough, and we'll bury her secret with her."

"You're a kind man, Paul," said the coroner. "I'm willing, if you are."

"If I am?" said Paul Everett.

"If you don't say anything to your wife."

"Oh, I see," said Paul Everett. "No, I don't think it'll be necessary to tell her."

Edna returned to Ann Arbor in the expectation of a battery of questions, but Faith McCracken was soon forgotten. She was that kind of girl. Edna wrote a letter to Frank Carlson at Amherst, telling him of Faith's suicide and returning unopened two letters from him, but she never had an answer from him, not even an acknowledgment of her communications. The midyear examinations occupied her attention, and she found that she too had come to forget Faith McCracken. The truth was she had never known her. Faith's clothes and her personal possessions became a bit of a nuisance until Edna turned them all over to the dean of women to dispose of them. "I've written to her mother in China," said Edna.

"A very difficult letter to write, I'm sure," said the dean.

"Yes, it was," said Edna. "The most difficult letter I've ever had to write. But will you write and tell her that I've given you all her things?"

"Of course," said the dean.

"Then that's taken care of," said Edna. And truly it was. At last she faced the fact that she had never really liked Faith McCracken. was a great relief.

Eddie Noisrander and Faith McCracken got out of Edna's life it the same time and with almost equal positiveness. One on campus Eddie introduced Edna and Bill Ewing, and there ever any doubt from that moment on that it was a match. ill Ewing, a fourth-year man in the law school, had not paid much attention to the pretty freshman, had not even spoken to her. There were plenty of pretty freshmen who knew about Bill Ewing, whose father was a prominent lawyer in Cleveland, and who was himself nicknamed The Judge. "I know you, you're The Judge," said Edna. "Why do they call you that?"

"Ask Eddie," said Bill Ewing. "Eddie, why do they call me The Judge?"

"I guess because you're sober as a judge," said Eddie.

"Are you?" said Edna.

"I probably am," said Bill Ewing. "At least I am compared with Eddie."

"Oh, come on," said Eddie. "I may take a snort now and then, but Edna knows I'm not a drunk."

"I've never even known Eddie to take a snort," said Edna. "He's never taken one when he was with me."

"Thanks, Edna," said Eddie. "I have to rush. I have an eleven o'clock." He left them.

"So long," said Bill Ewing. "Do you mind if I walk the rest of the way with you?"

"My name is Edna Everett. No, I don't mind. I'm only going to the drug store."

"I'll buy you a soda."

"You don't have to buy me a soda," said Edna.

"I'd like to," said Bill. "I liked the way you came to Eddie's defense just now."

"Oh, I get sick and tired of people accusing Eddie of being a drunk. I've never known him to take a drink," said Edna.

"That's what I mean. Eddie drinks, but who doesn't?"

"That's what I mean," said Edna. "I guess it's because his family own a brewery."

"And I'm called The Judge because my father is a lawyer and I'm studying law."

"You might as well call me The Joiner. My father owns a furniture factory, and a joiner is another word for a man who makes furniture."

"Yes, I knew that," said Bill Ewing. "Are you from Wingate? Is that how you happened to know Eddie?"

"Yes, we're both from Wingate," said Edna.

"You're very pretty. I guess you've heard that a thousand times," said Bill Ewing.

"Not quite a thousand, but I've heard it," said Edna. "It's still nice to hear it."

"That's good. I was afraid you'd think me fresh."

"No, I don't think you're fresh," said Edna.

By accident he saw her again the same day and she smiled at him and he smiled at her. Miss Everett, Mr. Ewing, were the exchange of words, but they had been thinking of each other, and for the next couple of days they continued to think of each other, and when next they met on the street Bill said, "I was wondering whether you ever go to the basketball games?"

"Occasionally," said Edna. "I'm not crazy about the game, the way some girls are, but I go occasionally."

"Will you go to the game with me Saturday night? I confess I don't even know who we're playing. Butler, I think."

"Yes, it's Butler," said Edna.

"You don't sound very enthusiastic," said Bill Ewing.

"I told you I wasn't very crazy about basketball," said Edna.

"Then how about going for a spin in my car? I have a Saxon I just bought. It has no top."

"I've seen you driving around in it. I'd rather do that than go to the basketball game," said Edna.

"What'll we do if it snows?"

"We'll just have to let it snow," said Edna. "What time will you stop for me?"

"Seven o'clock? Will that be all right?"

"Yes. I live at the Kappa Gamma Theta house. Do you know where it is?" said Edna.

"I know you do," said Bill Ewing. "I've found out quite a bit about you."

"You have?"

"Yes, and I intend to find out a lot more," said Bill Ewing. "I'll see you Saturday at seven o'clock. Oh, I forgot to ask you to dinner. You can have dinner with me, can't you?"

"That will be very nice," said Edna.

They went to a place about twenty miles from Ann Arbor. "This is Paul's. Did you ever hear of it? It's where the Dekes had their banquet this year."

"Looks nice," said Edna.

"Paul is a Frenchman and he knows how to cook, if you like French food. I made a reservation, so he's expecting us. Otherwise you have to wait, especially Saturday. Ah, good evening, Paul."

"Good evening, Mr. Ewing. I have a nice table for you. Good evening, mademoiselle."

"Good evening. Is there a place where I can fix my hair?" said Edna.

"Of course, mademoiselle," said Paul. "This way."

When she returned to the table and they had ordered the filet mignon on Paul's recommendation, Edna folded her hands and said, "You told me the other day that you know a lot about me, and then announced that you were going to find out a lot more. Proceed."

"Proceed? All right. First of all, is Eddie Noisrander the Number One man in your life?"

"Eddie Noisrander? Yes, I suppose he is. I've dated Eddie more than anyone else, so I suppose that makes him the Number One man. Next question."

"I took very careful notice, and I noticed that Eddie still wears his fraternity pin," said Bill Ewing.

"Yes," said Edna.

"Isn't that, to say the least, unusual?" said Bill.

"You mean why don't I wear his Psi U pin? I'll tell you why. Fraternity pins don't mean a thing. A girl wears a boy's fraternity pin, and it's supposed to mean something, but what does it mean? It should mean that they're engaged, but I know a girl who has four pins and she changes them all the time. When I get ready to wear a boy's pin it'll be that boy's pin and no one else's. And the boy will be ready to buy me an engagement ring, which does mean something."

"That makes sense," said Bill.

"Does it answer your second question? It should answer your first. Eddie Noisrander is the boy I've dated the most, but I'm not ready to be serious with him. I'll never be. There's only one boy I could be serious with."

"Is he at Ann Arbor?"

"Yes, he's at Ann Arbor," said Edna. "It's you."

"*Me?*"

"Oh, yes. I could be serious with you. But don't let it alarm you. I have three more years at Ann Arbor, and I may change. On the other hand, I may not, and meanwhile you may fall in love with some other girl and marry her. That would be awful for me, but I'll just have to bear it."

"I think you're pulling my leg, Edna," said Bill.

"It may sound that way, but I'm not. Just because I haven't even kissed you, just because this is our first date, doesn't mean I haven't made up my mind. But I may change. There's always that."

"The shrimp cocktail for mademoiselle?" said Paul.

"*S'il vous plait*," said Edna. "That's the first time I've spoken French to a Frenchman."

"*Mademoiselle parle Français*," said Paul.

"*Un peu*," said Edna. "As long as you understand it."

"*Je comprends votre Français très bien, mademoiselle*," said Paul.

"Where did you learn French?" said Bill.

"I had three years in high school and one year at Ann Arbor," said Edna. "No, two years in high school and one at Ann Arbor. I finished high school in three years and then my parents made me stay another year because I was too young for college."

"I wasn't trying to change the subject, but Paul interrupted," said Bill.

"I'd finished what I was saying," said Edna. "Do you want to talk about something else? I'd as soon. I was telling you how serious I was about you, but there'll be plenty of time for that. I just want you to know, Bill Ewing, that I *am* serious about you. No fraternity-pin stuff. I've made up my mind that you're the man I'm going to marry—if you don't marry someone else first. But I don't really think you will."

"Will you please tell me why? You haven't fallen in love with me."

"Maybe I have, in a way," said Edna. "Not romantically, not the fraternity-pin kind of love. But I think I always knew who I'd want to spend the rest of my life with. The boy would have to be serious about what he was doing—I used to think it would be a doctor, but a lawyer's just as good. He'd have to know what he wanted to do by the time he went to college, not just a boy who wanted to waste a lot of time deciding. My father isn't a doctor or a lawyer, but he made up his mind about two things. One, he was going to marry my mother, and two, he was going to take over the business he started out in. He married my mother when he was twenty-one and they didn't have much money, and he started up the Everett Manufacturing Company when it was Harvey Brothers carpenter shop, and he changed the name. That's one and two. Three, he was never going to leave Wingate. That was a matter of pride with him. His father was born in Wingate and went away to the Civil War, but he came back and took to drink and never amounted to anything, but my father was different. I can remember my father saying to my mother that he was going to be one Everett that the town would be proud of. And now it is."

"Proud of your father?"

"Yes. He did something for that town. Not much, maybe, but he did more for it than anyone else," said Edna. "I'm proud of my father—although he may not know it. Are you proud of your father?"

"Very," said Bill Ewing.

"Not just because he made a lot of money?" said Edna.

"That too, but the things he did for Cleveland."

"What did he do for Cleveland?" said Edna.

"Well, for one thing, he didn't go to New York when he had the chance," said Bill Ewing. "One man who believes in a town can make the town believe in itself. It's hard to explain, but I know a lot of people that felt that Cleveland was all right if it was good enough for my father. I suppose it's much the same as Wingate and your father."

"Yes, I understand that," said Edna.

"New York isn't everything," said Bill Ewing. "My father wanted to send me East to school. I'd have gone to Andover or Exeter, and then probably to Yale. But I decided to come to Ann Arbor. I went to day school in Cleveland and then I came here. I may regret it later, not getting a Harvard Law School degree, but right now I see myself as a Middle Western lawyer, with a Middle Western background, marrying a Middle Western girl."

"Who? Me?"

"Yes, you. Who else?" said Bill Ewing.

"That's nice," said Edna.

"Is that all you have to say? 'That's nice'?" said Bill Ewing.

"That's all for the present. Here's Paul with my filet mignon," said Edna.

Later, in Bill's Saxon, she kissed him. "I won't hold you to your proposal," she said. "You have to have time to think it over."

"Do you have to think it over?" he said.

"Not really, but we both have to think it over."

"Didn't you like the way I kissed you?" he said.

"Well, I have to think that over, too," said Edna. "Did I like the way you kissed me? Yes, I did. Although I was really the one who kissed you. I had to do everything tonight. The proposing, the kissing."

"You know that's not true," said Bill Ewing.

"I know it *is* true, but I guess that's the way we are," said Edna.

From that time on there was no one else for Edna, no one else for Bill Ewing. It was a campus romance, neither of them revealing it as such to their parents, but Paul Everett made a special trip to Ann Arbor to have a talk with his daughter. "What's this I hear about you and the Ewing boy?"

"I don't know. What do you hear about me and the Ewing boy?"

"You're going steady?" said Paul Everett.

"Where did you ever get that expression? That sounds like something Olga would say," said Edna. "Nevertheless, I suppose it's true."

"We kept you in high school an extra year because we thought you were too young. I hope you're not planning to do anything foolish now," he said.

"I'll do whatever Bill wants me to do. I'm not going to do anything that you'd call foolish, Father."

"Sometimes you call me Father, sometimes Daddy," he said.

"Sometimes you're Father, sometimes you're Daddy," said Edna.

"I'm Father now. This boy, all I know about him is that he comes

from Cleveland and his father's a lawyer. That's little enough to
know."

"What else do you want to know? I'm in love with him, if that's
important."

"It's the most important thing I have to know," said Paul Everett.
"Your mother hasn't heard about this, by the way. I came here on
my own. I had business in Detroit and I told her I might see you,
but I didn't say why."

"Don't tell her," said Edna.

"No, I guess I won't," said Paul Everett. "She thinks you're
tucked away for three more years."

"But you know better?"

"I guess I do," said Paul Everett. "The matter-of-fact way you
said you were in love with him. I'd like to meet this boy, but I
guess it's out of the question now."

"Out of the question," said Edna.

"I didn't find out much, did I?"

"You found out all there is to know," said Edna. "Tell me, how
did *you* know about Bill Ewing. Who told you about him?"

"A customer of mine," said Paul Everett. "Here in Ann Arbor.
You bought a chair from him last fall, remember?"

"I remember buying a chair," said Edna. "But it wasn't one of
your chairs."

"There are other good chairs," said Paul Everett. "This was a
second-hand chair, and when you gave him your name, naturally
he remembered and he asked me if I had a daughter here and I
asked him to keep an eye on you. Not the way that sounds, but
in case you wanted a cheque cashed or anything like that. Harry
Gibson. A pretty good customer and a heck of a nice fellow. He's
getting on now, must be pretty close to seventy. Anyway, he wrote
me a letter about a month ago and said he didn't have anything to
report except that you were seeing a lot of a fellow by the name of
Ewing, from down Cleveland way. How he found that out I have

no idea, but local gossip, I guess. Ann Arbor's a small town, and if you have nothing better to do, all you have to do is make a few inquiries."

"So you had me spied on," said Edna.

"You mustn't think that, Edna."

"I don't think it, Daddy, honestly I don't," said Edna.

"If you knew Harry Gibson you'd know he wasn't the kind of man who'd spy on anybody."

"I know you, that's better," said Edna. "Just don't tell Mother about this."

"I won't," said Paul Everett. "When you're ready is time enough, and I'm not worried about you."

Eddie Noisrander had another girl to take the place of Edna, a Pi Phi sophomore from Detroit who could not conceal her distaste for Edna. Her name was Ruth Velie and she was the daughter of a woman who was an acquaintance of Edna's mother. Mrs. Everett, anxious to assure Edna of every possible success at Ann Arbor, had written to Mrs. Velie, asking her to look up Edna when she entered the freshman class. Mrs. Velie, who did not know Edna except as the daughter of an acquaintance, turned the matter over to her own daughter, which meant that Ruth Velie was to see that Edna got invited to have tea at the Pi Phi house. But Edna pledged herself to Kappa Gamma Theta, the newest sorority on the campus, without letting the Pi Phis have a look at her, and Ruth Velie felt snubbed. The fact that Edna was pretty did not make it any better, and the fact that Eddie Noisrander came from the same town and had dated Edna, made it even worse. The two girls could not stand the sight of each other, an animosity that grew each time they double-dated with Eddie Noisrander and Bill Ewing. "Why don't you like Ruth Velie?" said Bill Ewing. "She seems all right to me."

"I don't like her perfume," said Edna.

"I never noticed it," said Bill Ewing.

"Neither did I," said Edna. "As far as I know, she doesn't wear any. But if she did wear some, I wouldn't like it. That's just a way of saying she affects me unpleasantly."

"Oh," said Bill Ewing. "You women have funny ways of putting things, if you don't mind my saying so."

"I don't mind your saying so. You can say what you please," said Edna.

"If Ruth affects you this way, we don't have to go out with them. It isn't any treat, you know. You and Ruth snapping at each other, making sarcastic remarks every chance you get."

"It suits me. I'd just as soon not go out with them," said Edna.

"Well, we won't have to go out with them any more. Vacation starts soon. Which reminds me, Eddie has invited me to Wingate. Shall I go?"

"If you want to meet my family, yes. It seems like a good opportunity. If you think it's too soon, no. Theoretically I have three more years here."

"Theoretically," said Bill.

"That's what I said, theoretically."

"Do you believe in long engagements?" said Bill. "I don't."

"Right now, I don't know what I believe. I think you have a case on Ruth Velie."

"Me a case on Ruth Velie?" said Bill. "How could you say such a thing? Ruth is Eddie Noisrander's girl."

"That wouldn't stop you from having a case on her," said Edna.

"Well, all right. I dated Eddie before I ever dated you, and I can date him again any time I want to. He still likes me."

"You'd have to do more than you used to do with Eddie," said Bill.

"What do you mean?"

"Just what I said. You wouldn't stop at kissing Eddie," said Bill.

"Doesn't Ruth?"

"No, she doesn't," said Bill.

"She *doesn't?* You mean she goes all the way? I don't believe it," said Edna.

"Ask Eddie."

"He wouldn't tell me," said Edna. "You mean they go all the way? Did Eddie tell you?"

"Yes, and I believe him. It wouldn't be the first time. Eddie has a pretty bad reputation. And if you start dating him again, I'll know what to think."

"Eddie goes all the way with Ruth Velie," said Edna. "I can't believe it. I just can't believe it. You mean he uses one of those rubber things? Otherwise she'd get pregnant."

"He didn't tell me what he uses. One of those rubber things, I guess."

"What if it breaks?"

"Then I guess she gets pregnant," said Bill.

"Where do they do it?"

"I don't know where they do it. How should I know? There are plenty of places," said Bill.

"Ruth Velie," said Edna. "She'll never look the same to me again."

"And you thought I had a case on her," said Bill.

"I don't now."

"And you were going to start dating Eddie again," said Bill. "Are you still going to?"

"I only said that," said Edna.

"The very thought of you dating Eddie is—abhorrent to me. It's abhorrent, that's all."

"It is to me, too. I couldn't let anybody touch me but you. I'd rather die," said Edna. "I haven't even kissed anybody since the first time you kissed me—or I kissed you. I think of us together, how it's going to be, and how it's going to be worth waiting for."

"Do you think about us together, Edna?"

"All the time. When I least expect to, I find myself thinking about us. I can be walking along the street and all of a sudden I'll be thinking about us. Together. I have to put such thoughts out of my mind or I'd be like Ruth Velie."

"You'd never be like Ruth Velie."

"You don't know the temptation," said Edna..

"Oh, yes I do. I think of you that way. It's only natural."

"Yes, I suppose it is," said Edna. "Oh, Bill, kiss me."

He kissed her, and he kissed her again.

"You'd better stop or I'll be like Ruth," she said. "We must save it. Bill, take your hand away."

"No," he said.

"Please take your hand away," said Edna. "Please. Please."

"Let me touch you," said Bill. "Just let me touch you."

"No, no."

But he touched her between her legs and she let him, then she said: "Stop it, Bill. You've got to stop," and she crossed her legs. "You won't have any respect for me."

"I'm sorry, Edna."

"It was that talk about Ruth. It was on your mind and on mine," said Edna.

"Ruth didn't have anything to do with it. It was you and me," said Bill.

"Whatever it was, you mustn't do that again," said Edna. "I'm only human."

"So am I," said Bill.

"I have desires, the same as anybody else," said Edna.

"You wouldn't think so," said Bill.

"Somebody has to know when to stop," said Edna. "If I didn't, we'd go all the way, and I mean all the way. And then where would we be?"

"But we were meant to go all the way."

"I'll go all the way with you when the time comes and not before."

"You mean when we're married?" said Bill.

"Yes."

"How long will it be before that?" said Bill.

"If I can wait, so can you," said Edna.

"You mustn't let on that I told you about Ruth and Eddie," said Bill.

"How could I?" said Edna. "How could I?"

"You might."

"You're sorry you told me," said Edna.

"Very sorry," he said.

"Well, you needn't be. I think I'd have known anyway. There's something in her face, something about the way she looks at you."

"At me?"

"At everybody," said Edna.

"Oh, come on, Edna," said Bill. "You can tell whether a girl's gone all the way? I don't believe that."

"I don't care whether you believe it or not, it's so."

"Do you expect something to show in your face when you've gone all the way?"

"Yes, I do," said Edna.

"What?"

"I don't know what, but it'll show," said Edna.

"If it shows on a girl, why doesn't it show on a man?"

"Oh, but it does show on a man. I've always known it about Eddie."

"Do you know it about me?" said Bill.

"Yes. I know you *haven't*."

"Well, I haven't, but I don't see how you know," said Bill. "Unless Eddie told you about himself."

"Eddie didn't tell me, I just knew," said Edna. "The way he is with a girl. I wouldn't be surprised if he started early. Sixteen or even fifteen."

"Then how did he know when to stop with you?" said Bill.

"He went as far as he could, and then I stopped him," she said.

"How far was that?"

"He never did what you did," said Edna. "He never put his hand there. But Ruth and I are different, and she let him go on. She probably couldn't help herself."

"No, I guess she couldn't. Because Eddie isn't the only one that's gone all the way with Ruth."

"Oh, I knew that," said Edna.

"No, you didn't. Not till I told you," said Bill.

"Yes, I did, really. You only confirmed my suspicions. I could tell you about some other girls too, but I won't."

"You mean girls in your sorority?" said Bill.

"Oh, I wouldn't believe them. They're all virgins, or so they say."

"But you can tell those that aren't simply by looking at them?" said Bill.

"Pretty much," said Edna.

"What did you know about Faith McCracken?" said Bill.

"Practically nothing," said Edna. "It's an awful thing to say, but I didn't want to know any more about her than I did know. She was a strange girl. She took off all her clothes the night she committed suicide. That must have meant something but I'm not sure what."

"I never knew her," said Bill.

"Neither did I, really. She was my roommate and a Kappa Gamma Theta and outside of that I hardly knew her. What made you ask about her?" said Edna.

"I don't know. We had a letter from Frank Carlson, her beau at Amherst, asking for information about her. He was a Deke, and he wrote to John Draper, the king of our chapter, but John had to tell him that nobody knew her. I guess that was before I knew you. I never bothered to tell you, and I don't know why I bother to tell you now. I guess your mentioning Kappa Gamma Theta reminded me of her."

"She was one who didn't claim to be a virgin, but I thought

she was pretending not to be. Whether she was or not didn't interest me."

"Do you think she was?"

"Search me. But she took off her clothes to commit suicide, and that may mean something or it may not," said Edna.

"I'd be inclined to say it meant a lot, one way or another," said Bill.

"Yes, but what? Except that she had a good figure and didn't mind showing it, at least when she was dead. She was very modest about it when she was alive. I never saw her fully undressed before I found her on the bathroom floor."

"I wonder if Frank Carlson ever saw her that way," said Bill.

"Yes, I think he did," said Edna. "Don't ask me why, but I think he did. Let's not talk about her any more. It's very depressing."

"I can see how it would be," said Bill.

College was over in June and after the Fourth of July Bill Ewing accepted Eddie Noisrander's invitation to visit him in Wingate. "I happen to know Edna will be up at the Lake in August. Maybe you happen to know it, too," said Eddie.

"I happen to," said Bill.

"So July will be your last chance to see her—unless you get invited to the Everetts', and I doubt that," said Eddie.

"You seem to know an awful lot about the Everetts' plans," said Bill.

"I guess I do," said Eddie. "I know the Everetts. By the way, I'm not going up to the Lake this August. I'm going to Germany to have a look at my cousin's brewery. Six weeks I'll be gone. The last week in July, all of August, and the first week in September. I thought I'd tell you, I'll be out of the way."

"Because of Edna?"

"Because of Edna," said Eddie. "Last summer she was kind of my girl, but that was before you entered the picture. She never had much use for me after you entered the picture."

"Don't be modest, Eddie. Ruth Velie entered the picture too," said Bill.

"Ruth would be out of the picture if Edna would have me. But Edna is too pure. Are you planning to marry Edna?" said Eddie.

"Yes, eventually," said Bill.

"You'll make a good couple."

"Why do you say that?" said Bill.

"Don't you know it? You're both Protestants, you're both pure, you both have money. I'm not the kind of a fellow for Edna," said Eddie.

"Is Ruth Velie a Catholic?"

"She certainly is not," said Eddie. "She was sore as hell when she found out she'd been screwing a Catholic. But it was too late then. One Saturday night I told her I had to be up for early Mass, and she said, 'Don't tell me you're one of *those*,' and I said I was. But it was too late then. She'd gotten used to humping me. She was good humping, too."

"Are you planning to marry Ruth?" said Bill.

"Me marry Ruth? She's not *that* good humping—or maybe she is. Maybe she's too good, with too many other guys. It'd be funny if she ended up marrying a Catholic, but it won't be me. Some football player, like Stanley Nork. He's a Catholic, but I don't think she knows it, although he comes from Hamtramck, along with the other Polacks. I guess she thinks all Catholics are named Murphy or O'Brien."

"Well, most of them are," said Bill.

"Except those that are named Noisrander or Nork," said Eddie.

"Does Stanley Nork know about you?"

"Christ, no! He'd kill me. He'd kill her, too, if he knew about me. Did you ever see those hands of Stanley's? I think his old man's a blacksmith at Ford's, and Stanley could be one too, except he's smart."

"I know. He's studying law," said Bill.

"I know, and he'll be the smartest dumb Polack in Detroit one of these days. Ruth could do a lot worse than marry him, even if she had to turn Catholic. But I don't know if she's that smart. She's too fond of her humping."

"How do you come across a girl like Ruth Velie?" said Bill.

"By accident," said Eddie. "Purely by accident. She was carrying a heavy suitcase and out of the kindness of my heart I offered to carry it for her, first noticing that she had good legs. But when she said she lived at the Pi Phi house I said, 'Let's take a taxi.' Which we did. And I made a date with her that night to go to the movies and I gave her a little feel. She objected to that, but not very strenuously, and when I took her home that night I tried again and this time I had more success. She let me feel her cunt while she played with my dingus, and the next date we had she was all prepared. In other words, she wasn't wearing any bloomers, and I was ready, too. In other words, a rubber. All because I carried her heavy suitcase. At least as far as the taxi."

His parents were surprised that Bill was going to visit Eddie Noisrander, who was not a fraternity brother and therefore not known as a particularly close friend of Bill's; but Mrs. Ewing thought there might be a girl behind the visit, and Mr. Ewing thought it was about time. "As long as she's a nice girl," said Mr. Ewing. "He'll tell us about her when he's ready." Bill was not taking the Saxon. Too long a trip and Eddie Noisrander had a car of his own, a new Lozier phaeton that his father had given him for passing all his exams. The Ewings had to look up Wingate on the map of Michigan and found that it was roughly a hundred and twenty miles from Cleveland, more or less in the vicinity of Grand Rapids, the furniture town. Beyond that they knew nothing about Wingate or Bill's visit, except that Eddie Noisrander had a dog called Fido. "What a ridiculous name for a dog," said Mrs. Ewing. But as Mr. Ewing pointed out, it would have been a more ridiculous name for a horse.

Fido was a Weimaraner, too large a dog to keep at Ann Arbor, but he knew whose pet he was. He was devoted to Eddie. "You'd think he'd forget you between vacations," said Bill.

"Not Fido," said Eddie. "I'm taking him to Germany with me. He was born in Germany. I had him all the time I was at Culver, and he remembered me. I think he thinks I'm an officer in the German army and have to be away from him while I'm on maneuvers. But as soon as I come home it's just as if I'd never been away. He's very fond of Edna and she of him. She says he's the only dog she ever liked. Of course she never had a dog. Mrs. Everett doesn't like dogs. Edna could have anything she wanted, even a pony, but she really wanted a dog. Anyway, a Weimaraner."

"I'm going to propose to Edna."

"I thought you had."

"This is going to be a real proposal. I'm going to ask her to quit college and marry me. Will you be my best man?"

"I'm counting on it," said Eddie. "When do you plan to get married?"

"First I have to tell my father and mother. *First* I have to get Edna's consent, I should say."

"That's a foregone conclusion," said Eddie. "There was never any doubt about you two."

"No, I guess not," said Bill. "Take me around and show me Edna's house."

"All right, I will," said Eddie.

The Lozier was a big car and rather a noisy one, and it could be heard approaching Midland Avenue, where Edna lived. "Take a look at your future mother-in-law," said Eddie. "She's sitting on the porch, hidden by the screen, but you can see her." Eddie raised his hat in salute to Mrs. Everett. "Good afternoon, you old goat," he said. "She was always against me. She's wondering who you are, but I won't stop now. Say hello to the old goat, Bill,"

Bill raised his hat and bowed. "Good afternoon, you old goat. I'm going to marry your daughter," he said. "You made me do that."

"You'll do it on your own when you get to know her," said Eddie. "He's not so bad, Mr. Everett, but she's an old goat. She's a Protestant old goat. You won't like her. But remember I warned you."

"I ought to stick up for her if she's a Protestant," said Bill.

"You'll see," said Eddie.

That night, shortly after eight o'clock, Eddie and Bill paid a call on the Everett family. Edna knew they were coming, but she pretended it was a surprise, and she introduced Bill to her father and mother as a friend of Eddie's. "Where are you from?" said Mrs. Everett.

"Cleveland," said Bill.

"Cleveland, Ohio. Well, that's a nice place," said Mrs. Everett. "I don't know many people there but I know a few. Edna has cousins living there named Schultz."

"I didn't know that, Mother," said Edna.

"You never met them, but Paul Schultz is married to my first cousin, Adeline Brockway, and I visited them when you were about six or seven years of age. Your father had some business there and they put us up for four or five days. Paul Schultz was the Lutheran minister."

"That's correct," said Paul Everett.

"Well, I ought to know it's correct. It was my cousin he was married to," said Mrs. Everett.

"Who took care of me while you were in Cleveland?" said Edna.

"Olga did," said Mrs. Everett.

"No, that was before we had Olga," said Paul Everett. "You stayed with the Linkletters."

"That's right, I remember," said Edna.

"Yes, come to think of it, you did," said Mrs. Everett. "Olga took care of you later, when your father and I spent a week in Detroit."

"Correct," said Paul Everett. "That was when I'd just about taken full possession of the old Harvey Brothers business. The turning-point in my life, if you remember."

"How well we do remember," said Mrs. Everett. "That was

when Mr. Everett went into business for himself. What business are you in, Mr. Ewing?"

"I just finished getting my law degree," said Bill.

"Oh, so you're going to be a lawyer?" said Mrs. Everett. "That should be interesting."

"Bill is nicknamed The Judge," said Edna.

"Well, isn't that interesting?" said Mrs. Everett.

"I hope it will be," said Bill.

"Oh, I'm sure it will be," said Mrs. Everett. "Eddie, didn't I hear you were off to Germany to learn the brewery business?"

"I suppose you did," said Eddie. "Those things get around."

Edna had had enough of this conversation. "Eddie, take me for a ride in your new car. Let's go out to the Park."

"All right," said Eddie.

"They tell me your father bought you a Lozier," said Paul Everett. "Does it use much gas?"

"I haven't kept track," said Eddie.

"I get about ten miles to the gallon on the Hudson. They told me I'd get more, but I've yet to see it. What kind of a car do you drive, Mr. Ewing?"

"Well, sir, my father has a Pierce-Arrow," said Bill.

"A Pierce-Arrow. Nobody in Wingate owns a Pierce-Arrow," said Paul Everett. "That's a car built to last. Seven main bearings."

"I don't know. I haven't had much chance to drive it," said Bill.

"Well, are we going or aren't we?" said Edna.

"Don't be out too late, Edna," said Mrs. Everett. "The Park is no place for a young girl. A lot of the riff-raff go there."

"I'll be fully protected, Mother," said Edna.

They got in the Lozier. "How does your mother know about the riff-raff at the Park?" said Eddie.

"Oh, just an idea she's got," said Edna. "I don't think she's ever been there."

"I thought not. Somebody ought to tell her the Park is owned by the Noisrander Brewery. It's very respectable," said Eddie.

"Oh, well, you know Mother," said Edna.

"By this time I ought to," said Eddie. "Bill, can you drive a Lozier?"

"I guess so. Why?" said Bill.

"Then let me out at home and you and Edna take the car. You have something to say to Edna," said Eddie.

"I have? What?"

"You know what," said Eddie.

"Oh, *that?* All right," said Bill.

"She's waiting to be asked, you damn fool," said Eddie.

They let Eddie out at the Noisrander house, and Bill took the wheel. "That was nice of Eddie," said Edna.

"Yes, it was," said Bill.

"Aren't you going to ask me?" said Edna.

"All right," said Bill. "First of all, will you marry me?"

"You know the answer to that. What else?"

"Will you resign from college and marry me in the fall?"

"I guess so. I don't see why not. Any other questions? I have to meet your father and mother," said Edna.

"That can be arranged," said Bill. He stopped the car on the edge of town.

"What are you stopping for?" said Edna.

"Doesn't a man usually kiss the girl when she says she'll marry him?" said Bill.

"I believe it's customary," said Edna.

"That's why I'm stopping," said Bill.

"Then turn off the motor," said Edna.

"The trouble is, I don't know how to start it again," said Bill.

"Hasn't it got a self-starter?" said Edna.

"The hell with it. I'll kiss you while the motor's running," said Bill.

"It won't be a very long kiss," said Edna.

"If it was the Saxon I could crank it, but these expensive cars— I can't crank this car."

"Just give me a kiss, a short kiss," said Edna. "You might at least have gotten instructions on how to start the car."

"How did I know I was going to stop here?"

"I don't think you planned this very carefully," said Edna.

"Well, I didn't. It was Eddie's idea."

"Then let's go back and ask him how to start the car," said Edna.

"I know. You push down on this thing."

"Let's go back and ask Eddie and be sure," said Edna.

"I wouldn't do that."

"You will so do that," said Edna.

"What shall I tell him?"

"Tell him you forgot to ask him how to start the car."

"I can't tell him that now," said Bill.

"I have a notion not to marry you," said Edna.

"I think you have to crank it," said Bill.

"You're not paying any attention to what I say," said Edna.

"The important thing is you said you'd marry me," said Bill.

Bill had a job in his father's law office that summer. He went back to Cleveland after Wingate and told his father, then his mother, that he was going to marry Edna. "But what if she's only a sophomore?" said his mother.

"I'm going to persuade her to quit college," said Bill. "I want to get married on the fifteenth of January."

"Why the fifteenth of January?" said his mother.

"It's your anniversary. It worked out pretty well for you," said Bill.

"I didn't think you knew," said his mother, but she was touched. "I take it Mr. and Mrs. Everett have given their consent."

"No, but they will."

"Edna must be used to having her own way," said Mrs. Ewing.

"She is, but so am I."

"Yes, I've noticed that," said Mrs. Ewing. "Your father is too."

"Somebody has to," said Bill.

"We'll have to meet the Everetts."

"They're nice people. Mr. Everett is a self-made man, owns a furniture factory in Wingate. He's well off. Mrs. Everett is inclined to be bossy, but since we'll be living in Cleveland, I don't expect much trouble from that direction. As soon as I get their consent, we'll have them down here for a couple of days, and I suppose we'll have to go up there. You and Father, that is."

Edna made the announcement to her parents at the Lake. "I'm not going back to Ann Arbor," she said. "I'm going to marry Bill Ewing."

"You are? When?" said her mother.

"On the fifteenth of January," said Edna.

"Isn't this rather sudden?" said her mother.

"No. I've been seeing a lot of Bill at Ann Arbor and we've made up our minds. We love each other, and there's no use postponing it any longer."

"Not even to ask your parents' consent?" said her mother. "I think we ought to have some say in the matter."

"Just say yes. I'm the one that's getting married, Mother."

"You haven't even met the Ewings," said her mother.

"The same thing goes for them," said Edna. "Bill has told them he's going to marry me, and Bill's a man who knows what he's doing."

"Doing, Ewing," said Mr. Everett. "Well, I happen to know who the Ewings are, even if I haven't met them. Mr. Ewing is a very prominent lawyer in Cleveland, very well thought of."

"I seem to be the only one that's been kept in the dark," said Mrs. Everett. "Did you know about this, Paul?"

"I had some idea, especially after Bill visited Eddie Noisrander. Let's cut out the nonsense and give our consent. Edna's in love with this young man, who comes of a very good family in Cleveland. It isn't as if she were going to marry some hunky. Even if she were, Edna would go ahead and marry him, if I know Edna. You married me when I wasn't even a master carpenter, and we've done all right considering."

"That's all you think of, is money," said Mrs. Everett.

"No, it isn't, but I give a hell of a lot of thought to it when it comes to my daughter getting married. So do you."

And so, in the autumn of that year, the parents exchanged visits. Mr. and Mrs. Everett went to see the Ewings in September, Mr. and Mrs. Ewing went to see the Everetts in October. The Everetts spent two nights at the Ewings'; the Ewings spent one night at the Everetts'. The Ewings gave a dinner party for the Everetts, the Everetts gave one for the Ewings. Mrs. Ewing, who was more accustomed to the role of hostess, took Mrs. Everett to a fashion show at Halle Brothers department store and to a Junior League luncheon at some women's club. Bill Ewing, in his Dodge, showed the Everetts several houses he was thinking of buying for himself and Edna. Mr. Ewing, who was not free in the daytime, arranged for Paul Everett to visit several furniture factories in the neighborhood, and Paul, on his own, arranged to make appointments with several furniture dealers in the Cleveland area.

"Well, what did you think of them?" said Mr. Ewing the day after the Everetts returned to Wingate.

"Let's put it this way," said his wife. "She tried."

"Yes, I guess she tried. What did you think of him?"

"Well, he doesn't contribute much to the conversation, unless you happen to be in the furniture game," said his wife. "I never thought of it as a game, did you?"

"Not the way he plays it," said her husband. "However, I like him better than her. She's too refined. She wanted to be buddies with you, and she never could be as long as she lived. Thank God they live in Wingate and not in Cleveland."

"We'll have to visit them in Wingate, you know."

"We can go up to Ann Arbor for a football game and break the journey that way. We can have Bill and Edna go to the game with us, and I'll be able to see some of my old Deke friends. We can have dinner with the Everetts the night before, and that will be enough."

"This sounds more like a Deke reunion than a visit to the Everetts, but I'm for it," said his wife. "After all, we'll have to visit them again for the wedding."

"I was thinking of just that," said Mr. Ewing. "The less we see of Mrs. Everett, the better I like it."

The Ewings' visit to the Everetts consisted of Ada Ewing's having tea with a few of Mrs. Everett's friends, Francis Ewing visiting the furniture factory, and a dinner party for the Ewings. "Well, what do you think of them now?" said Francis Ewing, as they got ready for bed.

"As I told you before, she tried," said Ada Ewing. "There was one nice woman at dinner, a Mrs. Linkletter. She told me a story about Edna and her pony cart that explains a lot about Edna. That girl's used to having her own way. I hope Bill realizes that."

"Yes, because Bill's used to having his," said Francis Ewing.

"Well, so are you."

"I wouldn't be much good if I didn't, and neither would Bill," said Francis Ewing. "Well, tomorrow we're off to Ann Arbor."

"As you planned," said his wife.

"As I planned," said Francis Ewing. "Bill and Edna will be at the Deke house, where I haven't been since Bill was initiated. It'll be a relief to get away from the Everetts."

"Francis Ewing, you're a snob."

"Yes, I am, but don't let on," said Francis Ewing. "They'd kick me out of D. K. E. if they knew. I'd have to join Psi U." In his cracked voice he sang a few measures of the Deke song, and Ada knew that he was feeling good, alone with her and free from the Everetts, looking forward to the trip to Ann Arbor. "Ada, did you know that D. K. E. was the mother of jollity?"

"Yes, Francis, I knew it," she said. "Come to bed." She also knew that his physician, Leonard Fogel, had told him to take it easy, and what did you do with a man who had been told to take it easy? You did what he wanted you to do, and you hoped that this time it would be all right. The mother of jollity indeed.

Edna Everett Ewing, being the daughter of a furniture manufacturer, was more or less compelled to permit her father to fill the new house with samples of his product. It pleased her that Bill Ewing liked the Mission line and it delighted Paul Everett, but Everett Chippendale and Everett Duncan Phyfe, no matter how well built, embarrassed her. "Why should that embarrass you?" said Bill Ewing. "Because it's fake? Who's likely to know the difference? How many of our friends can tell a Duncan Phyfe reproduction from an original? Besides, when we start having kids we won't want them scuffing up originals. I want chairs that you can sit in, not just admire. I don't want to be afraid that our kids will ruin a museum piece when they come home from school and throw their books every which way."

"I think you enjoy the Mission line to please Daddy," said Edna.

"No, I like it because it's comfortable," said Bill. "I might get tired of it if the whole house were filled with it, but don't forget I want to live on a farm."

"It'll be all right for that, goodness knows," said Edna. "Speaking of children, I think I'm having a baby."

"For God's sake, Edna. What a way to tell me."

"Would you rather I started knitting tiny garments? For one thing, I can't knit. For another, I'm not sure, but I'm almost sure. Dr. Fogel is, but—"

"What more do you want? If Dr. Fogel is sure, this calls for a celebration. Who else knows?"

"Nobody. I'm two months late, but that isn't proof positive. I could be wrong, and so could Dr. Fogel. It could be one of those phantom pregnancies."

"Not the way we've been behaving," said Bill. "Notice I said behaving, not misbehaving. I feel like buying you a present. What do you want?"

"Let's wait and be sure before you go buying me presents," said Edna.

"I'm sure," said Bill.

"How many periods have you missed?"

"Two," said Bill. "No, I was serious. I noticed you weren't having your period when the time came, and I began to wonder. I didn't say anything, but it's closer to three months."

"Well, I guess you can stop counting," said Edna. "At least you can stop counting how long it's been since I had a period and start counting months. According to Dr. Fogel I have about six months to go. It'll be some time early in 1914, probably February. Is anybody's birthday in February? I mean besides Washington and Lincoln and St. Valentine's Day? I don't want the baby to be born on somebody's day that I hate. Wouldn't that be awful, to have the baby born on the same day as somebody I didn't like?"

"It'd be nice if it was born in March, my birthday, or May, yours," said Bill.

"When is your mother's birthday?" said Edna.

"September, I think. The seventeenth. My father was born in October," said Bill.

"My father was born in October and my mother in July. My mother was born on the Fourth of July. Imagine having a baby when everybody's setting off firecrackers."

"It doesn't seem to have affected you. I think the worst birthday to have is Christmas Day or the day after. Nobody gives you any presents," said Bill.

"I've decided you can give me a present now. I want you to give me your Deke pin."

"My Deke pin? You could have had that any time," said Bill. "Why do you want that now?"

"Because now it really means something," said Edna.

"It's upstairs in my bureau drawer. I'll get it."

"You don't have to. I took it," said Edna. "I wish your father could see me wearing it. I think he'd be pleased. Put it on."

Bill took the pin and pinned it on her dress. "There," he said. He fondled her breast. "Let's go upstairs," he said.

"I'm ready," she said.

"I know you are," he said. "So am I."

She undressed and stood naked beside the bed and looked down at herself. "He's somewhere in there, the baby. *There,* do you think?" She put her hand over her navel.

"Farther down, I should imagine," said Bill. "If it's only three months."

"I can't remember whether a boy's supposed to be high or low," said Edna. "Maybe it's too early to tell. But I know it's in there."

"If it isn't, it will be," said Bill. "But I feel sure it is."

The news that Edna was having a baby was received by Mrs. Everett as something of a shock. She was not quite ready to believe that Edna had had intercourse with Bill, although they had been married since January. She wanted to know whether Bill had hurt her the first time he entered her, and Edna refused to tell her. "It was six months before your father could do it without hurting me. I was very small, and your father was very big," said Mrs. Everett.

"I don't want to talk about it," said Edna. Her mother had taken the first train to Cleveland when she heard the news. "And please, Mother, don't act as if this were the first baby ever born. I wouldn't have told you if I thought you'd come right down to Cleveland. I haven't even told Mrs. Ewing."

"Well, I should hope you'd tell me first."

"Yes, but now I'll have to tell Mrs. Ewing, and I wouldn't have had to if you hadn't come all the way to Cleveland," said Edna.

"It'll begin to show before long. How is Mrs. Ewing? I had a nice letter from her a month or so ago. She wrote me on that nice heavy writing paper. It's very formal, but she's that way. I mean the writing paper, not the letter. It's almost the kind of paper you get wedding invitations on. Ada Ewing. Her maiden name was Bloodgood, but you knew that. That's Bill's middle name, too. The Bloodgoods were an old Cleveland family. I found that out from your cousin that I visited a long time ago, Adeline Brockway Schultz, the wife of Paul Schultz, the Lutheran minister. She took to writing to me after you married Bill. I ought to go see her while I'm in Cleveland."

"You didn't invite them to our wedding," said Edna.

"Well, no, I didn't. I didn't know if they were still alive and you lose track. But she saw in the paper where you'd married Bill, and she wrote me a letter, and I answered it and that led to this correspondence. She told me all about Bill's uncle, Mrs. Ewing's brother. I gather the Ewings didn't think much of him. He's been having an affair with some woman in Cleveland."

"Uncle Asa," said Edna.

"That's right, Asa Bloodgood. He came to your wedding, and we saw him at Mr. Ewing's funeral. He drinks like a fish. Do you ever see him?"

"Now and then," said Edna.

"They say it's a good thing he has money or the nice people in Cleveland wouldn't pay any attention to him," said her mother.

"You mean Cousin Adeline Brockway Schultz says that."

"Yes, that's what I said," said her mother. "She's my only source of information in Cleveland. By the way, Eddie Noisrander's back. He's been in Germany for almost a year."

"Not that long, Mother. He was an usher at my wedding, and that was only in January. What made you think of him?"

"Asa Bloodgood. The two are very much alike."

"Yes, they both have the same kind of car, a Lozier," said Edna.

"That's not exactly what I meant, but you're not fooling me, Edna," said her mother. "I hear tell he's going back to Germany to live."

"Well, why not? He has relations there."

"You always had a soft spot in your heart for Eddie, I never knew why."

"You weren't supposed to know," said Edna.

"I mean even before he introduced you to Bill. You always had a soft spot for him. Well, there's no accounting for tastes."

"Truer word was never spoken," said Edna. "If you don't mind, Mother, I'm going to take a nap."

"That's right, get your rest," said her mother. "When I was carrying you I used to often wish I could take a nap. I put on twenty pounds when I was having you, although you only weighed seven and a half pounds at birth. Get all the rest you can."

"I intend to," said Edna. It was harsh to think of her mother as a bore, and it was snobbish to admire Mrs. Ewing for all the things her mother was not, but that was the way it was—and had been for a long time. Her mother was a small-town gossip who thrived on bits of misinformation and half truths, made to seem more vicious by the fact that they could not be completely denied, nor, for that matter, wholly admitted. In her small-town way she was masterful at innuendo.

The next day Mrs. Everett took the noon train back to Detroit and proceeded to Wingate. She told her husband how glad Edna had been to see her, how pleased Edna was that she was having a baby, and how sorry Bill had been not to have been able to have dinner with her. Bill, it appeared, was having dinner with a client from Dayton and had to spend the evening with him. But he had had breakfast with Mrs. Everett, and looked fine, and sent his regards to Paul Everett. He hoped she would let Edna and Bill know when she was coming to Cleveland again. That would be sometime around the birth of the baby, probably February, although you never could tell with a first child. "I was thinking we might go to Cleveland for Christmas," said Paul Everett.

"No, let them have their first Christmas together," said his wife. "Edna's very particular about that. I was too."

"You were? I thought we spent our first Christmas with your parents," said Paul Everett.

"Oh, no. We only had Christmas dinner with them. Don't you remember?"

"I guess so," said Paul Everett. He always said "I guess so" when his wife made a positive statement that he had some reason to doubt. It saved argument, or argufying. Argufying was generally a waste of time, whether with a customer or your wife. The point was that Edna wanted to be alone with Bill on this, their first, Christmas, and that spoke well for their marriage. He could sneak in a trip to Cleveland to call on one of those furniture dealers he had met when he and his wife had visited Francis and Ada Ewing. It might not be necessary to take his wife along. After all, she had gone to Cleveland without him.

Edna's baby was born on the first of February, and it was a boy. She was in labor about four hours and Dr. Fogel was with her all the time, urging her to bear down and keeping up a running conversation with her to divert her from the pain without giving her an anaesthetic. "You can do it, you can do it," he kept saying. "It won't be much longer now. If the pain gets too bad I'll put you to sleep, but it's better this way. It's better for Baby. It's always better for Baby this way. You're a good girl, Edna, and I want you to have a fine baby."

"Please put me to sleep, Doctor," said Edna. "I can't stand any more."

"All right, I will, in just a moment," said Dr. Fogel. But he waited until the baby was born and the cord was cut and the water-break occurred, and natural exhaustion set in.

"Let me see my baby," she said, and then she slept, and when she awoke Bill was at the foot of the bed. "I was expecting to be in the hospital, but I'm not," she said.

"No, you're not," said Bill.

"Why aren't I in the hospital?" said Edna.

"We changed our minds, don't you remember?" said Bill.

"Now I do. Have you seen the baby? It's a boy," said Edna. "I think it's a fine baby, but I don't know. Is it all right? I mean, nothing wrong with it."

"You have a fine baby, Edna," said Dr. Fogel.

"I want Bill to tell me," said Edna.

"It's a fine baby, a great baby," said Bill. "Did he give you much trouble?"

"I guess not. Ask Dr. Fogel. I forgot to say thank you, Doctor."

"If all the mothers were as little trouble as you, I'd be satisfied," said Dr. Fogel. "Your pelvic structure was just right."

"Did you hear that, Bill? My pelvic structure is just right," said Edna. "What are we going to call the baby? Francis, after your father?"

"No, not Francis, and not Paul, and not Bill. I'm for calling him John."

"John?"

"My grandfather was named John. John Stewart Ewing. He was a United States senator from Ohio, and a good man."

"Oh, I remember John Stewart Ewing," said Dr. Fogel. "He certainly was a good man. Without him there'd have been no Nickel Plate railroad."

"I wasn't thinking of that so much as other things he did," said Bill. "He did a lot for Western Reserve, including going there. He sent my father to Ann Arbor, but that was really my father's choice. What are we talking about? A name for the baby. You haven't said what you'd like to call him, Edna."

"John Stewart Ewing, of course," she said.

"Thank you, Edna," said Bill.

"I think it's time you got some more rest, Edna," said Dr. Fogel. "Your husband and I will be back this evening."

"Thank you, Doctor," said Edna.

The baby progressed from extreme infancy and helplessness to crawling and falling and in between the usual amount of bawling, and for Bill and Edna the resumption of the sex relationship when the baby was three months old. "Dr. Fogel says three months will be all right," said Edna. "Some women wait six months, but they haven't got the pelvic structure I have. You're lucky. I'll bet Ruth Velie didn't have my pelvic structure."

"Ruth Velie? What on earth made you think of her?" said Bill.

"Oh, ever since the baby was born I've been thinking of girls and their pelvic structure."

"Then tell me what it means," said Bill.

"I guess it means wide hips," said Edna.

"Then why don't they say wide hips? Your hips aren't so wide. I think it means something else," said Bill. "I wonder what ever happened to Ruth Velie, by the way."

"She married Stanley Nork."

"The Polack football player? Did she turn Catholic?"

"She must have. We got an announcement of the wedding, in St. Somebody's Church, Hamtramck."

"Why didn't you tell me?" said Bill.

"It slipped my mind. We only got an announcement of the wedding, not an invitation. I didn't invite her to our wedding. I didn't invite Stanley Nork either."

"There's no reason why you should have invited him, but she was sort of a friend of yours, wasn't she?" said Bill.

"She *was* not," said Edna.

"I was kidding," said Bill. "Well, I guess Stanley Nork knows all about her pelvic structure by now—if he didn't know before."

"A lot of people knew about her pelvic structure, including Eddie Noisrander."

"Did Eddie Noisrander ever know anything about your pelvic structure?" said Bill.

"How could you ask such a question? How could you *ask* such a question?"

"I always wanted to know, so I thought I'd ask," said Bill.

"Well, this was no time to ask," said Edna.

"I'm sorry, Edna. I had to ask you."

"No you didn't," she said. "Just when I was glad about our three months being up you had to go and ask a question like that."

"You're not going to?"

"Not going to what?"

"You know what," said Bill.

"No, I don't feel like it," said Edna.

"Then I'm going to sleep," said Bill. "Goodnight." He turned out the light and they lay there in the dark for ten minutes, twenty minutes. Then she spoke.

"Bill?"

"What?"

"The three months are up," she said.

He got into bed with her and she made him glad, and she was glad.

There was no more talk about Eddie Noisrander and there would be no more until late that summer, and this time Edna brought up Eddie's name. "I heard the most extraordinary thing about Eddie Noisrander," she said. "I had a letter from Mother today, and Eddie has joined the German army. Do you believe it?"

"He's in Germany, so I don't see why not," said Bill. "He could have joined the German army. He's an American citizen, but they take American citizens, or I guess they do." On that point it developed that Eddie had changed his citizenship some mont⸱ ⸱ "I don't quite see Eddie Noisrander in a spiked helmet, b⸱ ⸱ see him going after those Belgian girls. Eddie went to Cu⸱ ⸱ know, and I suppose there's always been a strong militaris⸱ in him."

"Yes, come to think of it, he always wore his Culver uniform at Christmas vacation. He looked well in it, too. I'd forgotten that," said Edna. "I hope we're not going to send John to a military school. Are we?"

"Andover, or Exeter."

"And Ann Arbor?"

"We'll wait and see," said Bill. "He's not yet a year old. He may want to go to M.I.T."

"Well, I'm glad he's not going to a military school," she said.

"I liked the Black Horse Troop, but that's because I like horses," said Bill. "And who knows? John may not even like horses. My father liked them, but he didn't have the time to enjoy them. He spent all that money on the farm, but just about the time he was getting ready to enjoy it he died. That's not going to happen to me "

The farm was about ten miles from Cleveland, accessible by motorcar only, therefore not accessible in bad weather, when the storms came down from Lake Erie and the winds came out of the West. Francis Ewing had always been a city boy, with a city boy's fondness for farm life, and the Ewing farm had grown from 160 acres to twice that, through the purchase of neighboring land. The manager of the farm, Lloyd Sharpe, had gone to work for Francis Ewing when it became a 200-acre establishment, and Lloyd was just out of Ohio State. "Hiring Lloyd was the smartest thing I ever did," said Francis Ewing. "I won't say he saved me any money, but maybe he did in the long run. I'm not a farmer, and Lloyd is. I'm a lawyer with an expensive hobby, and Lloyd keeps me from letting it get out of hand. What's more, I can sleep at night without worrying about the farm as long as Lloyd is in charge."

Ada Ewing was a city girl without the city boy's fondness for farm life until Francis Ewing gave her permission to build a house on the farm. The roads were getting better, and Francis Ewing farm more frequent visits to the country when Ada had a place to show her friends.

"How much can I spend?" said Ada.

"I made twenty-five thousand dollars from the cash register people," said Francis Ewing.

"And I can have that? Twenty-five thousand?" said Ada.

"That sounds like a lot of money, but not when you're building a house in the country. You'll spend it," said Francis Ewing.

"What kind of a house shall I build?"

"I'll leave that entirely up to you. Just remember that it's to be a farmhouse, not a stone mansion," said Francis Ewing.

"You couldn't build a stone mansion for twenty-five thousand," said Ada Ewing.

She chose the site, not far from a stream, and she chose an architect whom Francis had never heard of. He was a young Pole, a serious-minded man whom she had met at concerts of the orchestra and who she had thought was a musician. On her second meeting with him she learned that he was an architect, and on her third meeting with him she told him of her plan to build a house. Would he do as she said, and not try to force his ideas on her? "You're paying me—and besides, you don't know what my ideas are," he said. His name was Anthony New. "That doesn't sound Polish, but I'm Polish. My real name is too full of c's and z's, and you wouldn't remember it," he said. "Who's going to live in this house?"

"My husband and my son and I. The boy is getting ready to go to Ann Arbor the year after next, to study law."

"Oh, you're *that* Ewing. I wasn't sure," said Anthony New.

"You could have asked me," said Ada.

"I didn't want to ask too many questions, and I needed the job," said Anthony New.

"Well, you have it," said Ada Ewing.

They drove out to the site in her Pierce-Arrow, the predecessor of the succession of Pierce-Arrows in the Ewing family, and she told him what she wanted. "We're going to build a dam when the house gets finished," she said.

"Why not start building it now?"

"I suppose that makes sense," said Ada.

"Everything I say makes sense, Mrs. Ewing. I hope you're not going to cut down those sycamores."

"Not any more than I can help," said Ada Ewing.

"That's good," he said. "Can you read blueprints?"

"Yes, I suppose so."

"I'll have blueprints for you in two weeks."

"Two weeks? Isn't that an awfully short time?"

"We're not very busy, Mrs. Ewing," he said. "Why did you think I was a musician?"

"I saw you at the concerts, and I was introduced to you by a musician. Isn't that logical?" said Ada Ewing.

"I guess so. I should have known who you were. Mrs. Francis Ewing. But somehow I never connected you with the lawyer. I never connected you with anybody. I thought you were just a lady who liked to go to the concerts by herself."

"I don't always go by myself," said Ada.

"I never saw you with anybody, except that one time with George Barr, and he wasn't sitting with you. It was a lucky thing for me you knew George, otherwise I wouldn't have got this job."

"Well, let's hope it will be lucky for both of us. You say you'll have the blueprints in two weeks?"

"I'll have them. Could you advance me fifty dollars?"

"Of course."

"I hate to ask you for this, but I'm short of cash," said Anthony New.

He brought the blueprints to her in two weeks, and they were what she wanted. "These are exactly what I wanted. How did you know?"

"I studied you," he said.

"I'm very pleased. I thought it would take months. I have a few changes I want made, but they won't be drastic."

"I expected *some* changes, Mrs. Ewing. Could I have another fifty dollars?"

"Certainly. More, if you like," said Ada Ewing.

It was decided that they would drive out to the site every day, five days a week, in the afternoon, and this they did. Within a month the house was taking shape. Even the plumbing and wiring were progressing, and within two months the house was ready for occupancy. "I don't see how we did it in such a short time, but you were there to keep an eye on the workmen, and that helped," said Ada.

"And they knew their jobs," said Anthony New. "The building contractor didn't give me any trouble, and I hope I didn't give you any trouble."

"You didn't. I'm very grateful to you. My husband will be too. He was sure it would take a lot longer."

"It probably would have if he'd been around giving orders."

"I made him stay away," said Ada Ewing.

They were walking through the house, its walls and floors bare, and there was not even a campstool for her to sit on. The sound of their slow footsteps echoed as they walked, but they were alone in the house. "What's your husband like?" said Anthony New.

"What's he like? I've been married to him for eighteen years and I've never been asked that question," said Ada Ewing.

"How often do you go to bed with him?"

"Well, that *is* a question, isn't it? And I don't think I'll answer it," said Ada Ewing.

"Why? Are you afraid to answer it? I used to wonder why you went to concerts by yourself. It's unusual for a pretty woman—or handsome. I'd call you handsome rather than pretty."

"Suddenly the conversation has taken a decidedly personal turn."

"Why not? There are a lot of things I want to ask you, and I won't get much more chance to."

"Not after this conversation you won't," said Ada.

"I've always liked older women. I guess you must be around thirty-eight or forty, but you have a young figure. Did you have any feelings for me? Don't answer that. You'll lie to me. But I know you have had desires for me. I've had them for you."

"It's a pity you couldn't keep them to yourself. Anthony, it's time we were leaving."

"No, I don't want to leave. I want to fuck you. I want to be the first to fuck you in this house," he said.

"Don't use that word," said Ada.

He put his arms around her, trying to force her to kiss him. "Somebody'll see you," she said, resisting him, but he was strong. He put his hand on her breasts, and when she fought him off there he put his hand under her skirt. "Anthony, stop. Stop it, I tell you." She broke away from him and went to a corner of the bare room. "We can't do it here anyway," she said.

"Where can we?"

"I don't know, but we can't here," she said. "Walter will see us. The painters."

"Then play with my cock," he said.

"They'll still see us," she said.

"We can go in a closet. They won't see us there," said Anthony New. It was better to do as he wished than to continue the struggle, and she went with him to the closet. She had never known a man like him, but she knew that nothing would stop him now.

"What do you want me to do?" she said, when the closet door was closed. "What *can* we do?"

He opened his trousers, and his penis was hard and large. "Play with it," he said. "Put it in your mouth."

"No," she said. "I'll play with it, but I won't put it in my mouth."

"Then jerk me off," he said.

She put her hand on his penis and stood beside him and pulled it back and forth as they both watched. When finally he came he would not let her stop until the penis became limp. "Is that all?" she said.

"That's all, you cunt," he said.

She used her handkerchief to wipe away his juice, but it was not a large handkerchief and the juice was everywhere. "Give me your handkerchief," she said. "You've made a mess."

"I didn't make it, you made it," he said.

"Are we finished now?" she said. "If we are, let's go back to the car. I have to go home." She picked up the handkerchiefs, sticky with his juice, and put them in her pocket.

"What are you going to do with them?" he said.

"Don't speak to me," she said. "I have nothing to say to you. I'll let you out at your office and I'll mail you a cheque."

On the ten-mile ride back to Cleveland she maintained her silence, and he broke it to say, "What about the fence? Shall I send you some sketches?" She did not answer him. At his office he got out of the car and she did not say goodbye. "All right, Walter. We'll go home now."

"Yes, ma'am," said Walter. "He wasn't very talkative today. He usually talks a blue streak."

Francis Ewing was home when she got there. "Come on upstairs," she said. It was an invitation to bed.

"Upstairs? All right. I'm feeling a little that way myself," he said. "*Cinq à sept,* as the French say."

"I'll be with you in a minute," she said. There were some handkerchiefs she had to rinse out, and a curious feeling of guilt that she hoped to absolve. None of what had happened at the farm was her fault, but Anthony New had called her handsome and she had accepted the compliment. There was a certain obligation for an accepted compliment. In bed, with Francis, she was willing to do what she had refused to do with New, who had paid her the compliment in the first place, but Francis Ewing, who loved her, was entitled to the reward. He suspected nothing, and what was there to suspect? What was there to suspect? She had resisted New, and successfully. The young man had not really touched her, had not even seen her breasts nor the other part of her that counted. But how would Francis Ewing behave if he were to know what she had actually done? It was almost worse than if she had got down on the floor and permitted Anthony New to go inside her. There was a degree of intimacy to what she had actually done that was somehow worse than if she had gone the limit, as though the pleasure she had given New had been a peculiar pleasure for her. And therein lay the feeling of guilt, for there had been pleasure in it for her. No one could know this, least of all Anthony New, but in the weeks that they had been working together the young man's presence was vital and real. It had to end with some such contact as the incident in the closet. She gave everything to Francis Ewing, as she nearly always had, but there was room inside her mind for thoughts of Anthony New. "Oh, that was good," said Francis Ewing.

"I enjoyed it," said Ada.

"Better than a cup of tea, any time," said her husband. He was cheerful and totally unsuspecting.

The next day she telephoned Anthony New. "This is Ada Ewing," she said.

"I'm sorry for what happened yesterday," he said.

"Then let's forget it. I want you to send me the drawings of the fence," she said. "Put them in the mail as soon as they're finished."

"Does that mean you're not going to see me again?" said Anthony New.

"It just means we still have work to do," she said.

"You forgive me, then?"

"I don't think I can ever forgive you, but we have work to do. Put the drawings in the mail, please, and I'll be in touch with you," she said. Now she had a strong desire for him and the best part of it was that the desire would last as long as she wanted it to, and she could not tell how long that would be.

The farmhouse was completed and the furniture installed, and Francis Ewing suggested that they give a party, a housewarming, which seemed like a good idea to Ada. But she had second thoughts on the housewarming, and she postponed the party until time passed and they had lived in the house so long that the immediacy of a housewarming slowly vanished and Francis Ewing forgot about it. One day, months after the habit of going to the farm was well upon them, he remembered. "We were going to give a housewarming at the farm," he said. "It's too late now, but what ever happened to that idea?"

"Oh, I thought of it," said Ada. "I even made a tentative list for it. But I decided against it. Too much show, especially for a simple house in the country."

"I think you're right," said Francis Ewing. "Well, it's too late now."

"People would think they had to bring presents, and they'd be the wrong kind of presents," continued Ada.

The truth was she had not wanted to invite Anthony New to the housewarming, and she had not seen a way to have a housewarming without inviting the architect. She mailed him his final cheque, with a note informing him of that fact, and carefully refraining from any personal touch. With that note she hoped that there would be an end to her memories of the incident in the closet, and to make sure, she stopped going to the concerts. It was perhaps a year later that she had a carpenter knock out the walls of the closet to make more room for the grand piano in the livingroom. *Now* Anthony New could come back to the house and not even find the closet.

Except for the closet and its unpleasant memories Ada was fond of the farm, and when Lloyd Sharpe was hired as the manager she took a greater interest in it. Lloyd Sharpe was the son of a downstate farmer, a husky man with a small wife he had met at Ohio State, who raised Plymouth Rocks. There was a lot of paper work to be done by the Sharpes; Lloyd kept notes on everything, so that at night he was often up as late as ten o'clock with the never-ending records of planting and fertilizing and harvesting of the crops, while his wife Beulah was busy with the records of her poultry and her truck garden. The Sharpes were the true farmers on the property, and Francis Ewing had the good sense to stay out of their way.

Ada Ewing would often go out to the farm unaccompanied by Francis, and she wondered why. She had come to know the names of the stock—those that had names—and she followed the progress of their breeding habits. Francis Ewing had bought a prize bull named Nobleman of St. Mary's, a handsome Jersey that he intended to use as the founder of his herd, and when the bull sired his first calf it was an important event. "Nobleman had a heifer," she said. "He should have had a young bull."

"Heifers turn into cows, Mrs. Ewing," said Lloyd Sharpe. "And we want to see how rich this heifer's milk's going to be."

"Oh, I was thinking how pleased Mr. Ewing would have been," said Ada.

"I'm more interested in the cow's butterfat," said Lloyd Sharpe. "Bulls are all right, but you need cows for milk. Mr. Ewing is the only Jersey breeder in the Valley, and he's anxious to make a showing with this heifer. It's his first, and it'd be nice if this heifer turned out well."

"That's true," said Ada. She looked at Lloyd Sharpe and thought of Anthony New, and she began to understand why she came to the farm without Francis Ewing. Lloyd Sharpe, with his broad back and overalls, was the picture of virility, but he would never dream of doing to her what Anthony New had done. But the presence of so much vigor renewed her desire for a man, any man, and she would return to Cleveland and Francis Ewing re-stimulated. She had been married to Francis Ewing for many years when the scene in the closet with Anthony New took place, and their love-making depended on Francis Ewing's need but not on hers. Twice a week—usually on Sunday morning was a predictable time —Francis Ewing would come into her bed and fondle her breasts, and if her pessary was not in place he would wait for her to put it in. But passion and spontaneity had been lacking. But then they almost always were lacking for her; passion had come slowly to Ada Ewing, and experimentation was limited to Francis Ewing's sucking of her breasts. Fellatio and cunnilingus were never attempted by Francis and Ada Ewing, and the episode in the closet had a lasting, disturbing effect on her. She had never seen a penis except that of her husband and that of her son in his extreme youth when she bathed him. During her menstrual periods Francis Ewing stayed away from her, consequently the incident with Anthony New was a new experience to her. She did not know, for instance, whether it was an experience that other women had frequently or at all. Francis had never told her, and she certainly was not going to tell him about Anthony New. They never talked about such things. And yet this Polish architect, the one time he had taken any liberties with her, had had a desire for her that he showed her how to satisfy, and she wondered what she had done to invite the desire. For as the years passed she became convinced that she had done something, said something, that led Anthony New to believe that she would satisfy him. Long after her desire for Anthony New had vanished she blamed herself. Well, at least she was safe with Lloyd Sharpe.

Before Bill Ewing's parents bought the farm he was very much the city boy, with city friends and city habits and interests. But his friends and habits and interests were formed at a time when the country influence was strong, especially upon the children of the rich. Back of the stone house that was his home stood a stable, which had four box stalls and space for two standing stalls. There was room for the victoria, the landau, the two-horse sleigh, the cutter, the runabout, and the buckboard. There were pegs for the saddles and bridles, and the various sets of single and double harness hung from the ceiling. On the second floor were the living quarters for the coachman-chauffeur, and a hayloft. The whole stable was lighted by electricity, and there was an iron bathtub in the toilet. It was a city stable, and in its way luxurious. Bill Ewing grew up in the final stage of the horse age, and there was even a period when his father had a cow in the stable to provide milk for him, but Walter complained about the cow manure and Ada objected to the non-pasteurized milk, and the cow did not last. Nevertheless the horses and the experiment of the cow familiarized Bill Ewing with the use of animals and the existence of non-urban life. He was not entirely a city boy, dependent on the trolley car for transportation and on the fire department for his knowledge of the horse. The horse was part of his life. For the years between five and ten he had a Shetland pony, coincidentally named Prince like the pony driven by Edna in Wingate, and he too had a governess cart and a cutter, as well as a dog cart. But the pony, being a Shetland, was not for riding; under the saddle he would put his head down and bear out or otherwise misbehave, and it was not until Bill was ten and his father bought him a larger pony that Bill learned to ride. Rex was a hackney, bought for his looks and not for the hackney action, but Bill loved him and rode him for six years until he outgrew him and retired him to the newly purchased farm. Bill had grown tall rather suddenly, had long pants and stopped wearing an Eton collar, and had taken up tennis. His friend at University School, Halsey Brodbent, was not a horseman, nor was he tall, but Bill saw him every day and sought to earn his approval. If that meant retiring Rex to the farm, so be it. There was more fun to be had with Halsey and his comments on people and his game of tennis.

Halsey Brodbent was the son of a history professor at Western Reserve and as such had to watch his pennies. Halsey had three older sisters, all of whom had graduated from Bryn Mawr; and Halsey was on his way to Harvard. "The only thing I can wear that belonged to my sisters is sweaters," said Halsey. "That's why I have so many sweaters. Well, I can wear Judith's sneakers, but they have holes in them, so they're not much good." The Brodbents were seldom all together at home. Marian, the eldest, was married to a man who taught English at Haverford; Barbara, the second sister, was an instructor in French at the Brearley School in New York; Judith, the only one at home, was an assistant to the dean of women at Western Reserve, and was the prettiest one.

"Do you want to see Judith take a bath?" said Halsey.

"Sure," said Bill. "How can I?"

"She won't mind. At least she doesn't when I watch her."

"Yes, but you're her brother," said Bill.

[75]

"What's the difference? I'm a member of the male sex. Come to my house on Sunday morning. She spends all Sunday morning in the tub. She hardly ever goes to church, and you can just walk in the bathroom."

At ten o'clock on Sunday morning Bill showed up at the Brodbents' house and Halsey said, "She's been in the bathroom about fifteen minutes. She went in right after my father and mother went to church."

"What shall I do? I can't just walk in," said Bill.

"Pretend you're going in to take a pee," said Halsey.

"But the door will be closed," said Bill.

"What if it is? She's seen me take a pee," said Halsey. "I know what you can do. You can knock on the door and pretend you didn't hear her."

Bill accordingly knocked on the bathroom door and opened it without waiting for a response. Judith, her hair covered with lather, was in the tub. "Oh, hello, Bill," she said.

"Oh, I beg your pardon," said Bill. "I didn't know you were in here."

"The hell you didn't, but go ahead and have a *good* look," said Judith. "It won't do you any harm." She stretched out in the tub and watched Bill's expression. "Is that all you want, a good look? My little brother put you up to this, didn't he?"

"Yes," said Bill. "I mean, no."

"All right, you've had your look. Now go tell Halsey you've seen me naked," said Judith.

"Gosh, you're pretty," said Bill.

"Please close the door," said Judith.

He went out and down the stairs and without a word to Halsey continued on his way home. He went to his own bathroom and tried to recapture the ecstasy of seeing Judith Brodbent in her tub, and for a moment he succeeded, but then it got shameful and messy.

"Say, you didn't stay up there very long," said Halsey, the next day.

"Long enough," said Bill. "Let's not talk about it."

"O.K., I just thought you'd like to see Judith taking a bath," said Halsey.

"I *said,* let's not talk about it. Isn't that enough for you?"

"All right, don't bite my head off," said Halsey.

Halsey Brodbent remained his friend until Harvard separated them, Ann Arbor separated them. New England and the Middle West separated them. Bill wrote to Halsey, inviting him to be an usher at his wedding and offering to furnish his railway ticket to Wingate. It came as no surprise when Halsey declined. "I will be otherwise occupied on the 15th of Jan.," Halsey wrote. "I will not even get home for Christmas with my family. It would be easy for me to say that I am working for my master's degree, which would be true, or that I could not afford the railway fare, which your generous offer makes untrue. But the fact is that there is a deeper reason for not wishing to be an usher at your wedding, which has nothing to do with my M.A. or my straitened finances. I have become a socialist. I do not see myself putting on a cutaway and marching up the aisle with you and enjoying the parties that will no doubt be part of the festivities. I cast my first vote for Eugene Debs and Emil Seidel in November and I do not consider it a wasted vote. Time is on our side." There were a few socialists at Ann Arbor, but they were mostly Jews and Bill hardly knew them. They were not in Deke or Psi U, the principal source of Bill's friendships. If he had gone to Harvard, would he have turned socialist? He thought not, not even under Halsey's influence, strong and subtle though it was. His father's influence was stronger and his mother's too, and Edna's was strongest of all.

By the simple act of giving him a baby Edna established herself as his breeding partner, his successful breeding partner and more than simply his wife. She possessed the magic of reproduction, and John Stewart Ewing was there to prove it. The infant child at his mother's breast—Edna had milk for him—was a source of never-ending delight for Bill. He would try to get home from the office every afternoon to watch the baby being fed, and he would sit silent during the ceremony, thinking fatherly thoughts. "Dr. Fogel says I ought to give up nursing him pretty soon," said Edna. "In a few weeks he'll start on formula."

"Save a few drops for me," said Bill.

"No, you don't need it," said Edna. "You're a big boy now."

"There was some saint that got his milk from the breast," said Bill. "He was in prison, and the women used to feed him that way."

"Well, you're not a saint—thank God," said Edna.

"You let me suck you when you didn't have any milk."

"That was pleasure. I'll let you suck me again, but not while I have milk. This milk belongs to John-Stewart and nobody else. Do you really want to?"

"No, not if it belongs to John-Stewart. I wouldn't deprive him of any nourishment."

"Besides, I'm superstitious about it," said Edna. "I don't know why, but I am."

"Well, I was there before John-Stewart was, and I'll be there again," said Bill. "I wouldn't want to take a single drop of milk that belongs to him. He has to grow up big and strong."

"Like his father," said Edna. "Oh, I hope he'll be like you, Bill."

"I think he will be. It may be a little too early to tell, but he has my good disposition, don't you think? He doesn't cry much."

"The only time I've seen you cry was when your father died."

"I cried when Rex died, my pony, but that was before I knew you," said Bill. "I'm going to get John-Stewart a pony like Rex. Not a Shetland. They're mean and stubborn. But Rex was just right for me."

"There, that's all for you, young man," said Edna. She removed the baby from her breast and held him until he burped. "I'll miss

feeding him, but Dr. Fogel thinks I've nursed him long enough.
I don't know what we'd have done without Dr. Fogel."

That summer and all that autumn Bill and Edna were more
interested in one tiny life and the formula that Dr. Fogel recommended to sustain it than in the destruction and blood-letting
that was reported from Europe. "What do you say we go up to
Ann Arbor for a game?" said Bill. "We haven't been there since
graduation."

"If we go to a game, we'll have to go to Wingate," said Edna.
"We haven't been there, either."

"Then I guess that rules out Ann Arbor," said Bill. "I just
thought it would be fun to see my old friends at D. K. E. I don't
care about the game. Which reminds me, I wonder how Eddie
Noisrander is getting along in the war."

"I suppose his parents would know," said Edna. "Do you want
me to find out for you?"

"Not really," said Bill. "Do you realize that of all the thousands
of people fighting in Europe, Eddie Noisrander is the only one
we know on either side?"

"Not surprising. It's not our war, thank God."

"Well, that's not quite true. There was a man here in Cleveland
named Joplin, Philip Joplin. He was a few years ahead of me at
University School, and I understand he was killed with the
British. I never knew him very well, and of course you never
knew him at all. He went to Oxford, or maybe it was Cambridge.
One or the other. His father is getting up a memorial fund in his
memory, so I gave ten dollars, but this time I'm with Wilson. I'm
neutral. If I'd have had time to think, I wouldn't have given the
ten dollars."

"Oh, well, he was a schoolmate," said Edna.

"But a fund in his memory, in memory of a British soldier, is
British propaganda. I'll know better the next time. And there'll
be a next time. Two more boys from University School have

joined the Canadians. One boy was in my class, the other a class behind me. The boy from my class went to Williams but he didn't graduate. I wonder how Halsey Brodbent feels about the war. Socialists are against war unless it happens to suit them, and then they don't call it a war. I don't like socialists."

"But you do like Halsey Brodbent. You asked him to be an usher at our wedding," said Edna.

"Yes. I asked a socialist to be an usher at our wedding and he turned me down. And I asked Eddie Noisrander, and he's a German officer."

"Well, you had four other ushers and a best man, and they all turned out all right," said Edna.

"My marriage turned out all right, that's what matters," said Bill. "My best man and four of my ushers were Dekes, that's why."

"That's why," said Edna.

"It's probably as good a reason as any," said Bill.

"I'll hit you," said Edna.

"If you do, I'll cry," said Bill.

"If you did, *I'd* cry," said Edna.

"Then don't hit me. Would you ever hit me, really?"

"If you deserved it. If you had relations with another woman I would," said Edna.

"What ever made you think that?"

"I don't know. I guess because I'm so happy with you and John-Stewart. My mother is fearfully jealous of my father, and he never gave her any reason to be, at least as far as I know."

"Well, don't you go start getting jealous," said Bill. "I never look at another woman. Oh, I *look* at them, but I never have any evil intentions toward them."

"Who do you look at—without evil intentions?" said Edna.

"Who do I look at?" said Bill. "Be hard to say. You know Mrs. Auerbach. She was Judith Brodbent before she was married, Halsey's sister."

"I've met her. She's a little old for you, but she's good-looking in a bespectacled way."

"I saw her take a bath," said Bill.

"You mean in the tub? Naked?"

"When I was about fifteen. One Sunday morning I went in the bathroom and there she was, lying in the tub and washing her hair. She told me to go ahead and have a good look, and I was so excited I went home and masturbated."

"I'd say you had evil intentions there," said Edna.

"I didn't do anything to her."

"You sure you didn't masturbate in front of her?" said Edna.

"I probably would have if I'd thought of it, and had the nerve."

"Didn't she ever make any effort to see you naked? She didn't know what she was missing," said Edna.

"I've told you the whole story. She was the first woman I ever saw naked, with hair down below and breasts. She was beautiful. When I was about ten or eleven a little girl used to come to the stable and if Walter wasn't there she'd put it in her mouth. I'd hate to tell you who that little girl turned out to be."

"Who was it?"

"None other than Alice Minzer."

"Alice Minzer? That fat girl that's always hanging around your mother?"

"The same," said Bill. "She was a very unattractive little girl and she hasn't gotten any more attractive. But Mother puts up with her, I don't know why. Mother puts up with a lot of unattractive people since my father died. I guess she's lonely."

"Yes, she doesn't seem to care any more," said Edna. "She spends a lot of time on the farm."

"With the Jerseys," said Bill. "At that, the Jerseys are more attractive than Alice Minzer. How old would you say Mother was?"

"In her forties, I guess. She's never told me, and I wouldn't dare ask her."

"Do you think she's going through change of life?" said Bill.

"I guess she must have. That's another thing I wouldn't dare ask her."

"What exactly *is* change of life?" said Bill.

"I was hoping you wouldn't ask me. I don't know, and I was counting on you to inform me. You stop menstruating, and you have these hot flashes, and I *have* heard that you lose all sexual desire, but on the other hand, I've heard that when it's over your sexual desire is as great as ever."

"You're a woman. I thought you could help me."

"Women don't talk much about change of life," said Edna. "They talk about childbirth and pregnancy, and how they got pregnant. But change of life is a sort of forbidden topic. I'm sure my mother has had it, but I wouldn't know it from her. Their poor husbands know, God knows. Women get depressed and have those hot flashes and take to their beds—without their husbands. They even get suicidal. Life is over for them, some of them. On the other hand, there was a Mrs. Latham in Wingate, close to seventy, and she went right on menstruating. She had hardly a grey hair in her head. She got married for the second time when she was sixty-some, to a man in his forties. Everybody said her second husband was after her money, and he may have been. But whatever they did, they died happy. They were both killed in a train wreck, somewhere in the South."

"How did you know so much about Mrs. Latham?" said Bill.

"Well, Wingate's a small town, and Mr. Latham was a foreman in my father's plant, and my mother never missed a trick."

"She couldn't have if she knew about Mrs. Latham menstruating," said Bill.

"Oh, that was common knowledge," said Edna. "Everybody knew that. I remember hearing about it when I was in high school. I was just starting to menstruate and I asked Bertha Linkletter how long it went on, and she told me Mrs. Latham was still doing it at sixty-some. How she knew about Mrs. Latham I can't say, but she knew."

Their conversations were all like that. They had not known a thing about each other until Ann Arbor, and the first eighteen years of their lives was pristine. Nearly all of Bill's memories were of Cleveland, nearly all of Edna's were of Wingate. In the beginning of their romance they talked about each other, whom they saw the day before, whom they were seeing that night, immediate topics. It was not until they had been married for a year or so that their conversational pace permitted them to reminisce, and then they discovered how much they did not know about each other, the years of childhood and adolescence. "I was very unpopular when I was fourteen," said Edna. "The worst of it was, I knew it, and I didn't try to change myself. I'd never let Bertha Linkletter drive my pony, although she was dying to. She used to beg me to let her take the reins, but I wouldn't let her. In fact, we had a falling out for that reason, and Ann Collins would ride with me. But when Ann asked to drive Prince I told her a lie, I said Daddy had forbidden me to let anyone else drive. Right away Ann asked Daddy if it was all right if she drove, and he said of course. I hated to be caught in a lie."

"That's the trouble with ponies. Everyone else wants to drive," said Bill.

"I've often wondered why I was so mean," said Edna. "I wasn't that mean about clothes when I went up to Ann Arbor. I had a squirrel coat that I let everybody wear, and I loved that coat. I had a blue evening dress that I spent forty-five dollars for, and by the time I got to wear it everybody thought it was borrowed. But believe me, I was the only one that could touch the reins of my pony. I guess I was more sure of myself at Ann Arbor than I ever was in Wingate. We weren't the richest people in Wingate. There was a family there named Mr. and Mrs. J. Clinton Whitehill and he owned a lot of timberland and some copper mines, and she was the social leader of the town. It was a great disappointment to me they didn't come to our wedding. They were traveling in Europe. But at least they sent us a wedding present, that silver tea service, the one from Tiffany's in New York. So I guess Mrs. Whitehill approved of me. Mr. Whitehill liked my father, but I never heard Daddy call him anything but Mr. Whitehill. The Whitehills of Wingate. They gave a party every Fourth of July and nobody missed that. The first year I was invited I couldn't go because we were married and living in Cleveland and I'd just gotten pregnant, but my mother made sure people knew we were invited. Mr. Whitehill was the only Yale man in Wingate. He had a son graduated from Yale, but J. Clinton Junior lived in New York City. He was a lot older than I was, at least ten years. J. Clinton Junior went to the St. Paul's School, somewhere in New Hampshire, and I can't say I ever knew him. He married a girl from Long Island right after he got out of Yale, and they have a country estate there. It's funny how New York attracts some people from the Middle West. The only thing that would get me to live there is if you had taken that job with Mr Clendenning."

"Are you glad I didn't take that job?" said Bill.

"I would have been miserable in New York."

"But you're not miserable in Cleveland, I hope," said Bill.

"No, here there aren't a lot of people dropping their r's and talking in that affected way. I'll bet that was one of the reasons why you turned it down."

"It may have been. I never thought of that," said Bill. "I know I'm better off where I am. Four or five years from now I'll be taken into the firm. They'll have to change the letterhead. My name is in small type now, to distinguish me from my father, the original Ewing of Hotchkiss, Ewing and Kelley. Bob Hotchkiss is in small type too, to distinguish him from his father, Arthur Hotchkiss. And Clarence Kelley is the only original partner still alive. He outlived both his partners."

"You never hear of Mr. Kelley," said Edna.

"Oh, yes you do. Other lawyers hear of old Clarence. They hear about him plenty, and that's where it counts. It's about time you had Mr. Kelley for dinner. I think he's lonely. Ever since his wife died, which must have been ten years ago at least, he's been living at the Union Club, and that must be pretty lonely. His two daughters are married. One lives in Pittsburgh, married to a doctor, and the other is married to a theatrical producer and lives in New York. I hear they're not getting along so well, and that worries Mr. Kelley, but there's nothing he can do about it. She has taken to drink, so I'm told, and that's bad because Mr. Kelley's wife died of it. Mrs. Kelley was a loud-mouthed woman, the exact opposite of Mr. Kelley, and my mother couldn't stand her. She said awful things about my father and of course they all got back to him. I was in the office one day, waiting for my father to take me to the ball game, and Mr. Kelley came in and said he owed my father an apology. My father tried to stop him because I was there, but Mr. Kelley said I was old enough to understand. I didn't quite understand but he went on anyway. Apparently Mrs. Kelley had blamed my father for losing a lawsuit that involved a case in the Supreme Court—the case of U.S. versus Ingersoll, which became famous, and which my father defended. I won't go into it now, because it was a complicated case, but the Court ruled against my father by one vote, and Mr. Justice Holmes wrote one of his dissenting opinions on it, which would seem to show that my father had made a good case. Be that as it may, Mr. Kelley was there to apologize for something his wife had said the night before, and my father hadn't even heard about it. He would have in time, but he hadn't then. I will never forget how upset Mr. Kelley was. 'If you want my resignation, you have it,' Mr. Kelley said. And my father said, 'Well, Clarence, I lost the case, so maybe I'm the one to resign.' My father was like that. Never a word about Mrs. Kelley or her foolish accusation. 'You have to excuse me now,' he said. 'I'm taking Bill to the ball game.' Mr. Kelley remembered that at my father's funeral. He really loved my father."

"When shall we have him for dinner?" said Edna.

"Friday'd be all right. He eats meat on Friday," said Bill.

"Why don't I ask your mother and maybe one other couple?" said Edna.

Ada Ewing, though considerably younger than Clarence Kelley, was delighted to join him for dinner, along with the Bob Hotchkisses. The men wore their Tuxedos, the women dressed accordingly, and it was rather a festive gathering, with cocktails and wine. "I was just thinking as I sat down, what good-looking women the firm of Hotchkiss, Ewing and Kelley have picked for wives," said Clarence Kelley. "Beginning with Ada, and then there was Frannie Hotchkiss and my wife, Doro. And now we have Edna and Priscilla Hotchkiss. I venture to say we'd stack up against any other law firm in the country in that regard."

"Hear, hear," said Bill Ewing.

"I therefore propose a toast: to the ladies of Hotchkiss, Ewing and Kelley."

"The ladies," said Bill and Bob Hotchkiss.

"And I too propose a toast," said Ada Ewing. "To Clarence Kelley, for what he is and always has been, a gentleman and a scholar and a heck of a man to oppose in a lawsuit."

"Hear, hear," said they all.

Priscilla Hotchkiss stood up.

"You, Priscilla?" said her husband.

"Yes, me. I thought you were leaving out two men that I think ought to be mentioned and that we all love. I refer to Francis Ewing and Arthur Pinkham Hotchkiss, better known as Aph. To them!"

There was not a bit of business discussed all evening, and when eleven o'clock came Clarence Kelley looked at his watch and said, "Ada, I'm sure your faithful Walter is waiting in the Pierce-Arrow, and if you'll give me a lift I'll go quietly. Much as I hate to put an end to this lovely party, old men and infants have to retire early, you know."

He and Ada Ewing said goodnight all around and departed.

"I think the old boy had a good time," said Bill. "It must be lonely as sin at the club."

"It would be if he had nothing to do," said Bob Hotchkiss. "But as soon as he gets to the club he'll get into his pajamas and read till two or three o'clock in the morning. He told me he only needs about four hours' sleep."

"Like Edison," said Bill.

"Yes, the summer I lived at the club he followed more or less the same routine. He used to play bridge or billiards till about ten-thirty or eleven, and then retire. That was when he told me he only needed four hours' sleep. He told me he was reading Caesar's Commentaries in the original Latin. Now he must be reading something else, but it's sure to be something in Latin or the original Greek."

"Greek?" said Priscilla.

"He reads Greek, Latin, and French," said Bob Hotchkiss. "He wakes up about six o'clock in the morning and the night watchman brings him a pot of coffee and he bathes and shaves and walks to the office. He's usually the first there. He won't have a car because he'd be tempted to do without his walk."

"I never knew any of this about Clarence Kelley," said Bill.

"That's because you never spent a summer at the club," said Bob Hotchkiss. "He's an entirely different man there. Friendlier than at the office. At least friendlier then he would be with us young squirts."

"He was friendly enough this evening," said Edna.

"He was indeed," said Bob. "He showed a side of him that I never saw at the club, but that was because there were ladies present."

"He was being courtly, gallant," said Edna. "Bill, was he ever in love with your mother?"

"Not that I know of, but he could have been," said Bill.

"Then I have to tell you something," said Bob. "Yes, he was in love with your mother, but your mother wasn't in love with him. One night at the club he began talking about love. I don't know why or how we got on the subject. Sometimes when we were the only ones having dinner there, which was fairly often during August, he'd launch into a topic that had no connection with legal matters. I had the feeling that he was sounding me out, to see how I felt about this and that. In any event, the topic that night was love, and he started to tell a story about a man he knew in his fifties, who thought that he was all through with romantic interests. The man had had an unhappy marriage, but it was too late for him to get a divorce. He'd been married twenty-five years, and he thought he was through with romance. But he wasn't. The wife of a friend of his, a very close friend, a younger woman, began seeking his advice on something or other, something that her own husband couldn't help her on. The two of them were thrown together fairly frequently, and the man came to the realization that he was in love with the woman. After twenty-five years of marriage to his wife, and maybe ten years that the woman had been married to his friend, he realized that this was the real thing. The only trouble was, the woman was still in love with her husband. That didn't stop him from trying to have an affair with her, and for the next year or two he made a nuisance of himself, asking her to go away with him, things like that. It was l'âge dangereux for the man, and when Clarence Kelley used the French expression I identified the man. It was, of course, Clarence Kelley himself, and the woman was your mother. It all fitted together. That night I went to my room and Clarence Kelley went to his, but along about one o'clock in the morning Kelley knocked on my door. 'I've been thinking about the story I told you tonight,' he said. 'You must have figured out who I was talking about. Myself and Mrs. Ewing. I want you to promise me you'll never repeat anything I told you tonight.' And I promised, and kept my promise, until just now. There's a lot more to the story than what I've told you, but I wonder if he didn't mean that when he told your mother he'd go quietly. It was such an extraordinary thing to say otherwise. I guess it's not much of a story."

"It tells you a lot about Clarence Kelley," said Edna.

"And about Mrs. Ewing," said Priscilla Hotchkiss.

"But more about Mr. Kelley. That poor, lonely man, living in his club and spending his nights reading Greek," said Edna.

"Well, what should my mother have done? Had an affair with him?" said Bill. "She was in love with my father. I don't really like your story, Bob."

"You weren't supposed to."

"Time to go home, Bob," said Priscilla.

"Don't go away mad," said Edna.

"Are you playing golf with me tomorrow?" said Bob Hotchkiss.

"Ten o'clock, but I still didn't like your story," said Bill.

After the Hotchkisses had gone Bill was silent as he undressed.

"What's the matter with you? You might say something nice about my party," said Edna. "It was your idea."

"I honestly believe you think my mother should have had an affair with Clarence Kelley."

"I don't think any such thing, but I feel sorry for him," said Edna.

"If I thought he'd had an affair with my mother, I'm not sure what I'd do," said Bill.

"Well, he didn't have an affair with your mother, so come to bed. You're playing golf in the morning," said Edna.

But the suspicion that Clarence Kelley had once had an affair with Ada Ewing grew, and it affected Bill's work at the office. He was only a clerk there, making slow progress, because that was the way of the firm. He had not yet passed his bar examinations, and his first task of any importance was the drafting of two minor wills. The clients were two young men, friends of his who had not come into any considerable fortunes of their own, but the possibility of their dying intestate was abhorrent to lawyers, and they agreed to make a will despite the small size of their estates. It was also good training for Bill Ewing, who drafted the wills under the supervision of Clarence Kelley. There was an error of omission in the first will which Clarence Kelley quickly pointed out, but the second will had no mistakes. "I see you don't make the same mistake twice," said Clarence Kelley. "You ought to be ready for your bar exams fairly soon. I'm pleased with your progress, Bill." Then a third will contained the same error as the first. "Will you please tell me why you went back to the same mistake you made the first time?" said Clarence Kelley.

"I don't know," said Bill, but he knew: the picture of Clarence Kelley as his mother's lover came between him and the third will, and he thought of resigning his clerkship. He decided to have a talk with his mother, and he dropped in on her after work. "Mother, you and I have always been straightforward with each other, and I have a question to ask you that you may not like."

"That means you want a straightforward answer?" said Ada Ewing. "All right."

"What were your relations with Clarence Kelley?"

"Clarence Kelley? Now let me see. If you're talking about ten or twelve years ago, or maybe fifteen years ago, we went through a period when he thought he was in love with me. Is that what you mean?"

"Yes, that's just what I mean."

"Yes, it was awkward," said Ada Ewing. "Clarence was about fifty then, and fifty is a dangerous age for some men. I was in my thirties then and I don't know what I did to encourage him. I suppose I must have done something, or maybe even *not* done something. One can be as bad as the other in a case like that. You must remember that Clarence was a lonely man, even then. His wife was no help to him at all. She was a noisy woman, who not only drank quantities of gin but used laudanum, a polite way of saying opium. You can imagine what effect that had on Clarence, with his two daughters away at school and Clarence trying to be both mother and father to them. Mrs. Kelley was a mess. I would have put her away. And that's what made him think he was in love with me. He came to me for advice on what to do with her, and I wasn't very good at that because I never liked Mrs. Kelley. She was a handsome woman, although by the time you knew her she'd lost her looks. If ever a man had a cross to bear, it was Clarence Kelley, and he misunderstood my sympathy. Eventually, finally, I had to tell him that your father was beginning to misunderstand it too, and not entirely without reason. I remember your father saying to me, 'Aren't you seeing a little too much of Clarence?' So I stopped seeing him. The other night when we had dinner at your house was the first time I'd been alone with him —on the way home in the car—since I stopped seeing him, fifteen or twenty years ago. I don't know who told you about Clarence Kelley and me—probably Bob Hotchkiss, who probably heard it from his mother. But it doesn't make any difference now. Clarence respected my unwillingness to see him, and that dreadful wife of his lived on till about ten years ago. I think he enjoyed himself the other night. He's old now, and lonely, but he was full of charm. I've often wished I could do more for him, but your father always came first with me, and that didn't leave room for anyone else." She was silent as she thought back on the years past. She did not even make his question a difficult one to answer. "I hadn't really thought of Clarence Kelley until the other night," she said. "I gave him a ride to the club and he held my hand, and when we got to the club he kissed me on the cheek, and that was the first time he'd ever kissed me. I was glad he did. A lonely life, he leads, but I suppose I might as well get used to a lonely life." She looked at her son. "Well, what else is on your mind?"

"I guess that's all, Mother," said Bill.

"Then isn't it time you got home for dinner?" she said.

She saw him to the door and put up her cheek to be kissed, but he was sure she wanted to be alone.

The letter came informing William Bloodgood Ewing that he had passed the bar examinations in the same mail that a letter came from Wingate informing him that Eddie Noisrander had been wounded in action on the Western Front. The letter was signed by Eddie's father, Emil Noisrander. "Knowing you were a friend of Edward's I am passing on this information," it said, and it was typed and had a secretary's initials on the bottom, and obviously it was a form letter. It said nothing about the nature or degree of Eddie's wound or about his condition or the date of his injury. Both letters were at home when Bill returned from work. "You have a letter from Columbus and one from Wingate. The one from Wingate is from Noisrander's Brewery," said Edna. "I don't have to tell you who the one from Columbus is."

"Open it and just tell me, yes or no," said Bill.

She opened it and said, "Yes," and she kissed him. "Congratulations, although I don't think you had a thing to worry about. But you're a lawyer now, a full-fledged lawyer."

"Not quite, but I'm a lawyer in the State of Ohio," said Bill. He opened the letter from Emil Noisrander and handed it over to Edna. She read it carefully.

"Poor Eddie. Such a waste," she said.

"It doesn't say he was killed," said Bill. "It doesn't really say anything except that he was wounded. It doesn't say what hospital he's in or anything about his condition. There isn't anything we can do except write to Mr. Noisrander. I met him when I was staying with Eddie, the summer before I graduated. I met him twice. At Commencement, and then a few weeks later. But he considers me a friend of Eddie's."

"Well, aren't you? He introduced us," said Edna.

"Yes, he's a friend of mine, but with reservations. He joined the German Army when he didn't have to, and the more I think of

what the Germans are doing, the less I'm on their side. As someone said the other day, we're neutral—on the side of the Allies.
The *Lusitania* was just about the last straw. A thousand lives lost,
over a hundred of them Americans."

"But she was supposed to be carrying munitions," said Edna.

"And what if she was? There's a thing called freedom of the
seas. I don't know anything about international law, or maritime
law, but Germany is certainly violating the principle of freedom
of the seas. Torpedoing the *Lusitania* is just that. Did you see
what Teddy Roosevelt said about it? He called it 'damnable and
hellish.'"

"Do you think we'll get into the war?" said Edna.

"A few more *Lusitanias* and we will," said Bill. "Unfortunately,
we're unprepared."

"Would you get in it if we did?" said Edna.

"Of course I would," said Bill.

"Just when you passed your bar exams?" said Edna.

"That wouldn't keep me out. Nothing would," said Bill. "I'm an
able-bodied citizen of the United States, and if my country gets
into the war, I go in with the others."

"Well, let's hope we stay out of it," said Edna.

"It'll be a miracle if we do," said Bill. "Bob Hotchkiss has
joined the National Guard, that's how he feels about it. He drills
one or two nights a week, and all he talks about is the war. And
don't forget, he passed his bar exams."

"I have a feeling Bob won't be as good a lawyer as you'll be,"
said Edna.

"That remains to be seen, but he might make a better soldier,"
said Bill.

"Let's pray for that miracle," said Edna. "What does Clarence
Kelley say about the war?"

"He doesn't say much, but his son-in-law, the theatrical producer who's separated from his wife, has gone abroad to drive an
ambulance for the French."

"To drive an ambulance? Does he speak French?" said Edna.

"I assume he does. I don't know anything about him except that he's married to Clarence Kelley's daughter and produces plays, or did. Offhand I couldn't even tell you his name. And, yes, Clarence likes him. I can tell by the way he speaks of him. He's seen the same thing happening to his son-in-law that happened to him. A drunken wife. His name, by the way, is Fiske, Granville Fiske. I knew it would come to me. I suppose I ought to tell Clarence I've passed the bar exams. He'll be just about at the club now."

He telephoned Clarence Kelley. "Mr. Kelley, I thought you'd like to know that I've passed the bar exams," he said.

"How nice," said Kelley. "I assumed that you would, but it's nice to know. Your mother must be pleased."

"As a matter of fact, I haven't told her yet."

"Oh, you must tell her right away," said Clarence Kelley. "You've told Edna?"

"Yes, Edna knows," said Bill. "She was the first to know. You're the second."

"I'm complimented. Now tell your mother. She'll be very happy to hear the good news. It's a funny thing about exams, Bill. You bone up on things like the Rule in Shelley's Case, and then they don't ask you that, but they ask you some simple question that throws you for a loss because you thought you knew the answer, and you didn't. Probably because you had a cold at the University of Michigan. But I don't suppose you had any colds at the University of Michigan. Well, tell your mother your good news. She'll be pleased that you passed your first time around."

Bill telephoned his mother, but she was on her way home from the farm. "She spends a lot of time at the farm," said Bill.

"Thank goodness she has the farm to go to," said Edna.

Ada Ewing, in her country clothes, had become such a familiar figure on the farm that the workmen would hardly look up when she joined them. "Don't let me disturb you," she had said in the beginning, but she had had to repeat it so often that the only man whom she disturbed was Lloyd Sharpe. A baby had been born to Beulah and Lloyd Sharpe, and another was on the way. The first child, a boy, already looked so much like his father that Ada had said, "I know where the next farm manager's coming from."

"Not Bruce," said Beulah. "Bruce is going to be a doctor when he grows up. I set my heart on a doctor. So has Lloyd, haven't you, Lloyd?"

"That would be nice if he did," said Lloyd. "I'd like if he was a doctor. But it's a little too early to tell what he'll be."

"What if your second is a boy?" said Ada.

"Oh, my second can be a farm manager, just so my first is a doctor. Of course, it may be a girl," said Beulah. "I wouldn't mind if the second was a girl, to keep me company. It's a pretty lonesome life, being a farm manager's wife."

"But you're never far away from your husband," said Ada.

"I don't know. Lloyd spends almost as much time with you as he does with me," said Beulah.

"With me? I hadn't realized that," said Ada.

Later, when she and Lloyd were inspecting the stock, Lloyd said, "You mustn't mind what Beulah said. The truth is she's jealous."

"Of me? Nonsense, she couldn't be."

"Oh, you're pretty, Mrs. Ewing, and you have personality," said Lloyd.

"But I'm old enough to be your mother," said Ada.

"You sure don't look it. You haven't any wrinkles."

"Look closer, Lloyd. They're there," said Ada. But Lloyd Sharpe had paid her a personal compliment, the first he had ever paid her and the first anyone had paid her in a long time. That evening, lying in her tub, she looked at herself in the mirror and was pleased. She was fifty-two and had been a widow for over two years. No man had touched her in that time, no man had seen her, nor was any man likely to get any pleasure out of seeing or touching her, or she out of seeing or touching any man. The pleasure of touching a man had always been confined to the pleasure of touching Francis Ewing, who was dead, or the mixed pleasure of touching Anthony New, who had not even touched her. Her right hand, as she thought these things, lay on her clitoris, a moderately pleasurable experience that she intensified until she discovered that by increasing the pressure and speed of the motion of her hand she approximated a climax. She looked down at herself, half expecting some sort of discharge like the one that she had caused years ago in Anthony New, and when there was none and she felt relaxed, she was relieved. No one in the world would know that she had found a way to get such relief. She got out of the tub and looked at herself in the full-length mirror, and saw that her nipples were erect. She wished that Francis were alive to suck them, but now there would surely be somebody. At least she no longer had the feeling that she was more dead than alive. There would be somebody.

Lloyd Sharpe, the nearest thing to a man in her life, was first to come to mind, and maybe he would be the one. Then she thought of all the things against his being the one: she would have to seduce him, virtually under the eyes of Beulah, and that presented difficulties. But the principal objection to Lloyd Sharpe was Lloyd Sharpe. He was young—and he was a good farm manager, and good farm managers were hard to get. Anthony New, her next thought, was young, but she did not know where he was. New York, the last she heard, working for a big architectural firm. In the years since Francis Ewing died her escorts at dinner parties were few: Clarence Kelley; a man named Ray Bostwick, from Detroit, a recent widower; Walter Finch, a Cleveland resident of whom Francis Ewing had said, "I'll always trust you with Walter Finch. He plays with dolls"; and Peter Hoff, of whom Francis Ewing had said, "He plays with dolls, too, but they're live, baby dolls. Chorus girls and stenographers." Peter Hoff was in the insurance business in Columbus, but he spent a good deal of time in Cleveland, and Ada liked him. In her present lubricious mood she decided to call him. He maintained an apartment at the Cleveland Hotel.

"How lucky I was to find you in," said Ada.

"Five minutes later and I'd have been out. What can I do for you, Ada?"

"Well, you can come to a dinner I'm having a week from Thursday. It'll be only a few people, but I've decided to begin to entertain."

"About time, Ada. It's no use wasting away. A week from Thursday, you say. I'll be in Cleveland that night, and I'll be at your house whenever you say," said Peter Hoff.

Ada immediately invited six more people for dinner a week from Thursday and they all accepted. They were Dr. Hendricks, the heart specialist, and his wife; Priscilla and Bob Hotchkiss; Walter Finch, and Christine Frogg, the sculptor, who wore a Tuxedo and took an instant shine to Priscilla Hotchkiss, as did Peter Hoff. They almost sat down without Dr. and Mrs. Hendricks, who were late. They talked about the war in Europe, which did not interest Walter Finch, who amused Priscilla Hotchkiss with stories about Christine Frogg, told *sotto voce*. Peter Hoff wanted to eavesdrop, but Walter Finch made it difficult. Dr. Hendricks and Bob Hotchkiss dominated the war conversation and Bob Hotchkiss dominated Dr. Hendricks because he knew more about the war. Dr. Hendricks was called to the telephone at ten o'clock and had to go to the hospital, which left only six as his wife departed with him. "Dr. Hendricks always gets a call for ten o'clock," said Walter Finch. "I'll bet if you call him now he'll be at home. It's so convenient being a doctor, and a heart specialist at that." The others remained until midnight, when the Hotchkisses and Christine Frogg decided to go on to Walter Finch's apartment and Peter Hoff decided to go to his hotel.

"Must you go too, Peter?" said Ada.

"No, I just thought it was time I went."

"Then stay awhile," said Ada. The maids had gone to bed and the house was still and empty. "This is the way this house usually is, but I'm going to change that. I'm going to have people in for dinner, like tonight. As you said, there's no use wasting away. Sit here, beside me."

"I'll do just that, Ada. You wouldn't mind if I gave you a little kiss," said Peter.

"Why don't you try it and see?" said Ada.

Peter kissed her once, tentatively, and when the response was good he kissed her again. His hand, again tentatively, moved inside her bosom, and when Ada made no objection he took out her breast and kissed it. The next move, since they were not children, was up to Ada. "You could take off a few clothes," said Peter.

"Must I?" said Ada.

"Well, a few," said Peter. "Your corset."

"I'm afraid the maid will come in," said Ada, but she stood up and unbuckled her corset and hid it under the sofa cushions. "I don't want you to go all the way with me, Peter. I haven't since Francis died. But I'll do anything else you want. I *want* to go all the way with you, but it ought to be in bed."

"I understand," said Peter. "You want to give me a suck?"

"I'll do anything you want," said Ada.

He opened his fly and took out his penis and she held it and looked at it. "I don't think you could have got inside me tonight. Maybe later, but not tonight," she said. With that she put it in her mouth and made him come.

"Oh, that was wonderful," he said. "Superb."

"It was for me, too. Have you got a handkerchief?"

"Was it wonderful for you too? I mean, did you come?" said Peter.

"I think so. Maybe not as much as I would in bed, but almost. I'm still glowing," said Ada. "Thank you, Peter."

"Thank me?"

"For my first experience since Francis died. It meant a lot to me. Thank you for putting my breast in your mouth. That was thrilling, I can't tell you how thrilling it was. Was it to you?"

"Well, not as much as the other," said Peter.

"Maybe not, but it was to me. That can be very exciting to a woman, at least this woman," said Ada. "I hate to say it, Peter, but I have a suspicion my maid is waiting for me. She won't know what's going on."

"Then you'd better not tell her," said Peter. "You're going to have to put your corset on."

"Dear Peter, I might have forgotten, and then she *would* have known," said Ada. "Peter, you know such things. What is a dildo?"

"A dildo? Why, yes, I know what a dildo is. When I took that trip around the world I saw several in Japan. It's a kind of a thing, a device, that women insert in their private parts to make them have an orgasm. Where did you ever hear of a dildo?"

"A little Japanese nurse at the hospital told me about them. She said it was what widows used, but when I went to look her up, she'd gone back to Japan, so I never found out."

"Would you have used one?"

"Peter, the first year I was a widow I'd have used anything, but I was always afraid to ask about a dildo. You have no idea how much I missed Francis. He was the only man in my life, literally, the only man in my life."

The next day, shortly after eleven o'clock in the morning, Dr. Hendricks telephoned Ada Ewing with the sad news that Peter Hoff had died in his sleep at his hotel. "Did you know he had a bad heart?" said Dr. Hendricks. "He'd been a patient of mine for over a year. I thought perhaps that was why you had invited us to dinner with him."

"No, I didn't know anything about his heart except that it was good—not in the medical sense," said Ada. She wondered how much an autopsy would show, but she did not really care. Poor Peter! He had really wanted to go home but she had made him stay, and she blamed her own voluptuousness for what had happened to Peter Hoff. The funeral was to be in Columbus and she thought of attending it until she took into account all those gaping Shriners and the fact that she barely knew his wife. Ada ended up sending neither flowers nor a note of condolence. There was no use leading Mrs. Hoff to believe that there had been more to her acquaintance with Peter than she knew.

But there must be other men in the world, and she was free to help herself to one or even more. She would look elsewhere than Cleveland, and this time she got a thousand miles away. Her friend Sophie Cudlipp said to her, "I don't suppose there's any use asking you to spend a couple of weeks in Palm Beach."

"There might be," said Ada.

"You mean you'd go?" said Sophie.

"It's time I went out of mourning," said Ada.

"Indeed it is," said Sophie. "Can you make the trip in my private car? I leave the fourteenth and I'll be gone till late March. I'd love to have you, Ada, truly I would."

"I think I'd love to visit you for two weeks in February," said Ada. "Is that all right with you?"

"Absolutely any time. You know I'm so glad you're showing signs of life again. I'd begun to despair of ever waking you up. A woman as attractive as you are ought not to let it all go to waste. You really ought to consider getting married again."

"Oh, no, but I'm not going to spend the rest of my life with Walter Finch," said Ada.

"As my late lamented used to say, 'There's no percentage there,'" said Sophie.

Sophie, a widow for about five years, had inherited a trust fund estimated at fifteen million dollars from her husband Dick, and it was no secret that the war in Europe, if it went on as anticipated, might so much as double that. Cuyahoga Iron & Steel, selling at 4 the year Dick died, was now selling at 20, with no telling where it would end. Sophie met Ada at West Palm Beach station in a

Pierce-Arrow brougham, accompanied by a white-haired, deeply tanned man whom she introduced as her house guest, Will Levering, of Philadelphia. Will was in his forties, considerably younger than Sophie, and had beautiful manners and beautiful clothes. He was wearing that day a blue linen suit, a soft-brim Panama, and brown and white wing-tip shoes. He saw to Ada's luggage and got on the box with the chauffeur, allowing the ladies to talk but edging in a word or two through the partition. By the time they reached Lake Worth Ada fully understood the relationship between Sophie and Will. She owned him.

"I'm taking you to a party at the Stotesburys' tonight," said Sophie. "Will knows them. It'll give you a chance to meet a lot of people."

"I met Mr. Stotesbury once, at a party in New York. Doesn't he play the drum?" said Ada.

"Every chance he gets," said Will.

"That's all I remember about him, that he played the drum," said Ada.

"A harmless pastime," said Will. "But don't forget, he's a Morgan partner. He'll undoubtedly play the drum this evening."

Will's room was on the ocean-front adjoining one side of Sophie's, and Ada's was separated from Sophie's by a bathroom. Not a word was spoken about the proximity of Will's room to Sophie's and apparently none would be. Well, more power to Sophie, although it was not quite the arrangement Sophie would have had in her house in Cleveland. They dined that night with a song writer from New York, a comedienne, the comedienne's current husband, and a rather nondescript couple from Philadelphia. It was eleven o'clock when they got to the Stotesburys' ball, and the song writer had made several attacks on Ada's leg. "Did Sol annoy you with his handiwork?" said Sophie.

"Oh, you noticed that?" said Ada.

"He does that to everybody," said Sophie. "The one you have to watch out for is Clem."

"Clem?"

"The man from Philadelphia with the moustache, the quiet one," said Sophie. "He's been known to take it out and hide it under his napkin."

"Good heavens," said Ada.

"His wife thinks it's funny. Well, we won't see any more of them for the rest of the evening. They go home early, presumably to exchange recollections. You're in Palm Beach now, you know."

"I'd thought Palm Beach was full of old ladies cutting coupons."

"Like me," said Sophie. "But there's something invigorating about the air. How do you like Will Levering?"

"Why, he's very pleasant, good manners," said Ada.

"He spends a month with me and a month with Charlotte Ormsbury and then he goes abroad, but because of the European situation he isn't going abroad this winter. He pays his own way, you know, or practically. Of course, he's our house guest for those two months, and that helps considerably, but he's an excellent golfer, and people like to play with him."

"And that's all he does?" said Ada.

"How do you mean?" said Sophie.

"I mean, does he make enough playing golf?"

"If you leave out Charlotte Ormsbury and me, no, but there'd be others to take our places. He wouldn't have any trouble finding them. Let's join him," said Sophie.

Her two weeks in Palm Beach were almost up, an uneventful two weeks except for the overtures that had been made and spurned, and she was lying in bed the next to last day of her visit, thinking what a waste it had been, when Will entered her bedroom. "Shh, quiet," he said, and took off his dressing gown and got into bed with her. "You're leaving tomorrow?" he said in a whisper.

"Yes."

"Then let's make love," he said, whispering. The surprise of it was that she was willing and he had known it, and for that she was grateful. She put her nightgown over her head, and lay there until they both were ready. And then she guided his penis inside her and only half knowing what she was doing, but knowing, she fucked him. "Oh, that was wonderful, Will," she said.

"Shh," he whispered. "I have to go now."

She lay on the bed fulfilled, now quite awake but reluctant to change her position. The thought occurred to her, and would not vanish, that Sophie had sent him in to her. It was a question to which she might never know the answer. But of one thing she was certain: as she walked to the train the next day, there was life in her derrière that had not been there for three years.

Bill Ewing joined the Preparedness League and became very active in it as well as—by coincidence—one of the members of the staff of Hotchkiss, Ewing and Kelley who were assigned to attend to the legal problems of the Cuyahoga Iron & Steel Corporation. It was more or less inevitable that his association with Cuyahoga should affect his views on Preparedness; Cuyahoga *was* Preparedness. Clarence Kelley called Bill into his office, asked him to sit down, and began: "Bill, I think I know your views on the war in Europe pretty well. You're for the Allies, are you not?"

"Yes, I am, and becoming more so," said Bill.

"Good. Now as you know, Cuyahoga Iron & Steel has become one of our most important clients," said Kelley. "From twelfth or thirteenth two years ago, it's mushroomed into second place in amount of fees paid us. Jack McNair is giving Cuyahoga practically his full time, for instance, and I needn't tell you that Jack McNair is one of our most valuable men. I wish we had more like him, but you don't find lawyers like Jack growing on trees, or wherever crackerjack lawyers grow. In point of fact, you find them in a firm like Hotchkiss, Ewing and Kelley. He came with us twenty-odd years ago, fresh from Kenyon College, and he was indentured to me. I taught him all I know about the law, but he had a natural instinct for it that was rare in someone so young. In those days he was inclined to drink too much and we almost had to let him go, but he straightened himself out when he got married. *Sally* straightened him out, is what I *should* say. In any event, Jack McNair can have anything he wants around here. You may wonder why he never became a full partner. The answer is, he was offered a full partnership and turned it down—but he didn't turn down the money. Excuse me, Bill. I have to go to the bathroom. Bladder trouble. But don't move, I'll be right back."

The old man returned refreshed and resumed his seat in the high-backed chair. "That's what keeps me out of court. Some judges would misunderstand my urgency, or my emergency. To continue. We've decided to let you work with Jack McNair on Cuyahoga. You've never worked with Jack before, but you'll find him easy to get along with, as long as you dot every *i* and cross every *t*. And what is most essential to Jack is that you share his views on the war in Europe. That was the first thing he asked me. He said that there would be many occasions when you'd have to work at night and on Sunday, and you might not see the necessity for it, but even in a law firm in Cleveland, Ohio, there is need for haste. Well, how do you feel about it?"

"Pretty darn good," said Bill.

"Good," said Kelley. "This is your first real opportunity with the firm. Up till now you've been doing the sort of routine work that any law clerk would be doing for any law firm, but this is going to be a bit different. There'll be a small raise in pay—ten dollars, I believe is the amount of the raise, although I'm not sure. But it'll be something to help you pay for your golf balls, although when you're going to get time for golf is another matter. Jack McNair hasn't played golf all summer, but he doesn't miss it. I'm going to move your office closer to Jack's. You'll have an office, by the way, not just a desk."

"Clarence, there's only one thing about this—promotion, I suppose you'd call it—"

"You can certainly call it a promotion," said Kelley.

"Isn't Bob Hotchkiss next in line?" said Bill.

"I'm glad you asked that. Yes, Bob is next in line, but as you know, Bob has been made a second lieutenant in the National Guard, and there are rumors that they may be sent to the Mexican Border. I don't know when, and I don't know if the rumors are any more than that, but Bob told me that there's something going on. He wouldn't say what. Bob has seniority over you, and would ordinarily be entitled to the job with Jack McNair, but we can't afford to train Bob in the job, only to have him sent to the Border. We never actually discussed the job with Bob. Naturally he knows you're going to work with Jack McNair. I told him, and he's pleased."

"That's the only thing I was a little worried about," said Bill.

"Oh, you needn't have worried," said Kelley. "Seniority rules in this firm. Or let me put it this way: seniority rules where courtesy is concerned. Now let me take you in to see Jack."

Jack McNair was one of the few lawyers in the firm who worked in shirtsleeves, with a pipe always in his mouth. "Ah, here we are," said Jack. He stood up, Kelley remained standing and said, "I won't keep you gentlemen," and departed, whereupon McNair said to Bill, "Have a seat, Bill."

"Thank you," said Bill.

"You're to have one of the offices next door, and I suggest that the first order of business will be for you to familiarize yourself with the names of the Cuyahoga people. Accordingly, I have got together a list of the men you'll be dealing with there. There are about twenty, to begin with. Some of them are hard names. For instance, there's a man named Czerniewicz, Anton Czerniewicz, a good old Anglo-Saxon name. He doesn't the English speak so good, but you wouldn't know it from his letters. It's just his accent. His letters are masterpieces of English prose. He's in charge of labor relations at Cuyahoga, where they have several thousand Poles. I've prepared you a file of letters to accompany the list of names so that you'll get acquainted with the work that each man does. There's a man named Nork that just joined Cuyahoga from Hamtramck. He went to the University of Michigan around your time there. He's in their legal department."

"I know Nork," said Bill.

"Good. Then there's a whole slew of names that won't mean anything to you at first, but you'll see by their letters that they're important at Cuyahoga. The file's on your desk."

"Already? I haven't even seen my office," said Bill.

"That's the last time you'll be able to say that for the next couple of years," said McNair. "Even if we don't get into the war, there'll be plenty of work to be done, and if we *do* get into it, boy! You're a member of the Preparedness League, are you not?"

"Yes, I just joined," said Bill.

"Get out of it, Bill. I'm all for it in principle, but now that you're so closely identified with Cuyahoga, people will accuse you of being a warmonger," said McNair.

"I'm afraid I'm in too deep," said Bill.

"Well, all right, stay in, but don't make speeches. Leave that to the congressmen. I don't know what you think of Woodrow Wilson, but there are a lot of men in Congress that think he's pussyfooting. I don't happen to think so. I think he's stalling for time, and that we'll get into it sooner or later. So here I am, telling you to get out of the Preparedness League while I support its aims. But public opinion is with Wilson because he's pussyfooting, and it'll change overnight when he decides to declare war. Meanwhile, don't make any speeches."

"I wouldn't be likely to."

"Good. Now you can go read those letters," said McNair. "I hope you'll be happy in your new job."

"Thank you, I'm sure I will be," said Bill.

When he got home from work that day he told Edna about the new job. "It's a promotion, isn't it? How is Bob Hotchkiss going to feel about that?" she said.

"To tell you the truth I don't much care. Bob's a second lieutenant in the National Guard, and he's probably going down to
the Mexican Border to chase bandits. I probably shouldn't say
that. It sounds disagreeable. But maybe I am disagreeable. Bob
joins the National Guard and puts on his uniform, while I stay out
of uniform and do all the work."

"Did you ever stop to think that they may have promoted you
because you're a better lawyer than Bob?" said Edna.

"How can they tell? Bob's been doing the same kind of work
that I've been doing," said Bill.

"But what was it Clarence Kelley said about Jack McNair? That
he had a natural instinct for the law? I don't think Bob Hotchkiss
has that. He has a natural instinct for golf, maybe, but not for the
law," said Edna.

"You're just trying to make me feel good," said Bill. "By the way,
guess who's in the legal department at Cuyahoga? Stanley Nork."

"Stanley Nork, the ex-football player that's married to Ruth
Velie? They're living in Cleveland? How long have they lived
here?"

"At least three months. That's judging by the date of a letter he
wrote," said Bill. "I'll be having to see Stanley in the new job."

"It's funny Ruth didn't look us up," said Edna.

"I'm not even sure she's living here, but I'll undoubtedly find
out," said Bill.

"I'm of course dying to see Ruth," said Edna.

"Yes, I can imagine," said Bill. "Shall we have them for dinner
sometime?"

"Let's give them time to get settled. Say about forty years?"

"Forty years is too long. Let's make it thirty-five?" said Bill.

"Whatever you say, dear," said Edna.

"Mee-yow, mee-yow," said Bill. "Actually, Ruth isn't so bad.
She just got on her back too often for too many people, and she
only did that because they asked her to. At least, I assume they

[107]

asked her. I wonder how she's making out with the football player."

"You could always ask Stanley," said Edna.

"Yes, I could always ask him if he's living with his wife," said Bill. "I'm afraid I'll just have to wait till he brings the subject up."

"Forget the Norks. I'm so pleased about your promotion, Bill. One good thing that's come out of this war in Europe," said Edna.

It was about two weeks before the word reached Stanley Nork that Bill Ewing was working with Jack McNair. "I knew that Hotchkiss, Ewing and Kelley were our lawyers, but I didn't know that you had anything to do with us," said Stanley.

"I didn't until two weeks ago," said Bill. "How are you, Stanley?" Their conversation was taking place over the telephone.

"Pretty good, pretty good."

"I thought you were working in Detroit."

"I was till about six months ago and then I got this offer from Cuyahoga. They wanted a lawyer who could speak Polish and there aren't many of those around, so I got the job. Ruth was tired of living in Hamtramck and she'd have gone anywhere. You knew I married Ruth Velie?"

"Yes, I heard that. How is Ruth?"

"Pretty good. We had a hard time finding a house in Cleveland, but we finally rented one on Ninety-fifth Street. I'll tell her you asked about her."

"Do," said Bill. "Stanley, Mr. McNair would like your office to have another look at the bottom of page twenty-four of the gun-mount contract before it's sent to England. That's page twenty-four of the gun-mount contract."

"Page twenty-four of the gun-mount contract. What's wrong with it, Bill?"

"He wants to be sure you agree with the delivery date, that's all. Are you sure it gives us enough time—meaning Cuyahoga?" said Bill.

"I'll have Mr. Ennis read it this afternoon," said Stanley.

"That's not good enough, Stanley. Have Mr. Ennis read it this morning and call me back by twelve noon."

"I'll try. Mr. Ennis is a pretty busy man," said Stanley.

"So is Mr. McNair, and Mr. McNair doesn't go out to lunch. The contract could be in the hands of the British Purchasing Commission tomorrow instead of Monday, so do what you can, Stanley."

"That McNair is always in a hurry," said Stanley.

"There's a war on," said Bill. "Goodbye, Stanley."

Edgar Ennis, who was head of Cuyahoga's legal department, was a man who liked to take his time, whether it was in having lunch or reading contracts. It was therefore half-past twelve when Jack McNair opened the door of Bill's office and said, "Did you hear anything from Ennis?"

"I'm still waiting to hear from Stanley Nork," said Bill.

"The hell with that. Give me the contract," said McNair. He stormed out of the office and was back by one o'clock. "I went to the Union Club and made Ennis read the contract while he was having his oysters," said McNair. "He could just as easily have been obliging, but he wasn't. Now the purchasing commission will get the contract tomorrow instead of Monday. Ennis is a lazy son of a bitch, but he's Mrs. Cudlipp's brother, so I can't have him fired. However, I gave him an earful at the club. You liking the work?"

"Especially now," said Bill, smiling.

"Think of some way to have Ennis retired," said McNair. "This is no time for him and his snail's pace. You haven't had your lunch, have you? Neither have I. Would you like to have a sandwich with me?"

"I'd love it," said Bill.

Lunch on a tray, with Jack McNair, grew into a habit with Bill, and as Bill was not yet a member of the Union Club, it made small difference to him. Dinner on a tray was another matter, and he had to put a stop to that. "Mr. McNair, Edna is beginning to complain," said Bill.

"What about?" said McNair.

"Two nights in succession I had to tell her I wouldn't be home for dinner, and I haven't really seen my son in three days."

"That's my fault," said McNair. "I'll try to get you home in time for dinner. How is the boy? He's named after John Stewart Ewing, isn't he?"

"Yes, he is," said Bill. "He's coming along fine, thank you."

"I knew his great-grandfather," said McNair. "I knew his great-grandfather, his grandfather, and his father. If he studies law, he'll be the fourth generation of lawyers."

"He won't study law if his mother has anything to say about it. Right now she's rather fed up with lawyers," said Bill. "She says they have no home life."

"I apologize for making you miss dinner," said McNair. "Tell Edna it won't happen again."

"I'd rather you told her," said Bill.

"That would make it official? All right, Bill."

McNair went home with Bill that evening. "Let me see that son of yours. I haven't seen him yet," he said. "John Stewart Ewing. I'd drink a toast to him but I haven't had a drink in twenty years. Say, now, isn't he a fine young man? Who does he look like? He has his father's nose and mouth, but he has his mother's eyes. Look at that smile. He's a healthy young man, isn't he? Oh-oh, he's getting a little damp."

"I'll change him," said Bill. "Give him to me."

"Will you stay for dinner?" said Edna.

"I'm afraid I can't," said McNair. "I have to go back to the office. I only came out here to apologize for keeping your husband, and I'll try not to let it happen again. Mind you, I don't promise, but I realize I've been very unreasonable in my demands on Bill. You're quite right. Lawyers have very little home life, especially when there's a war on."

"Is Bill so indispensable?"

"To me he is," said McNair. "I haven't told him, but we make a team that—it may be too early to tell—but I hope Bill sticks with me. It's a downright pleasure to work with him. Yes, I would say he's indispensable, and I haven't ever said that about anyone else."

Bill returned. "Martha's changing the baby," he said.

"Well, I can get a trolley car at the corner," said McNair. "I'd have to wait too long for a taxi." He said goodnight.

"He looks tired," said Edna.

"He *is* tired."

"I don't want you looking like that when you're fifty. Isn't that about what he is?"

"He's in his late forties," said Bill. "Did he convince you in that short time?"

"Of what?"

"Of whatever he tried to convince you of," said Bill.

"He's a man of great charm, if that's what you mean, and he knows it. I don't usually like men who have charm and know it, but he has enough sincerity to make him irresistible."

"He has a son a Deke at Kenyon, the same way. Young Scotty. He's on the tennis team and hasn't lost a match in intercollegiate competition. Never trains. Just goes out and beats everybody in sight."

"Was Jack a Deke?"

"An Alpha Delt," said Bill.

"Then that isn't Deke charm?" said Edna.

"No. Have I got Deke charm?"

"You sure have, and don't pretend you don't know it," said Edna.

"I was hoping it was just plain old William B. Ewing charm," said Bill.

"Oh, you have that too, but you save that for our intimate moments," said Edna. "I don't want anyone to touch that. Deke charm is different, public. Manners, the right clothes, things like that. The William B. Ewing charm is private."

"So is the Edna Everett charm, very private," said Bill.

"I was hoping you'd say that," said Edna. "We'll go to bed early tonight. But now let's have our dinner. I'll put John-Stewart to bed and he'll be asleep by the time we've had dinner. I love you, Bill. I didn't for the last two nights, but you're just as indispensable to me as you are to Jack McNair. What's more, I can do something for you that Jack McNair can't."

"Or anyone else," said Bill.

There was a farewell party for Bob Hotchkiss when his regiment was sent to the Mexican Border. Bob, in his campaign hat and leather puttees and breeches, had already put away the manners of a civilian and adopted the manner of a second lieutenant. The party was a luncheon at the Union Club, the toastmaster was Clarence Kelley, who remarked that Bob, as an officer in his country's service, had hardly been elected to membership in the club before he got on the non-dues-paying roster. Kelley hoped that Bob would soon be back paying dues, as the club needed the money, and the firm needed Bob. Kelley then introduced Jack McNair, who said that Bob Hotchkiss would be sorely missed at the office, and Edgar Ennis, who spoke too long and declared that Bob's father would be proud of him. They then presented Bob with a set of matched luggage and Bob thanked them. The luncheon was over, and there was a feeling that they had done their patriotic duty to a man who was not headed for the real war. But Bob was the first man in uniform in the office of Hotchkiss, Ewing and Kelley and he was determined to make the most of it. "Most of the men in my platoon have never been out of the State of Ohio," he told Kelley, "and I expect my first big problem will be morale. But they're good men for the most part."

"You'll manage," said Kelley. "You'll manage."

Jack McNair and Bill Ewing walked back to the office together. "I suppose Wilson is right, sending the troops to the Border," said McNair. "What do you think, Bill. You're a young man."

"I don't think many of them will get to Mexico, but maybe that's not the point," said Bill. "Bob looked very snappy in his uniform."

"That *is* the point," said McNair. "Get the people used to seeing men in uniform. My guess is that we'll be in the big show in Europe inside of a year. Have you thought of what you'll do then?"

"Oh, I'll join the army," said Bill.

"What if you're needed here?" said McNair.

"I'll still join the army," said Bill. "As you said, I'm a young man."

"I want to talk to you about that," said McNair.

"All right, when the time comes, but my mind is made up," said Bill.

That night at home Bill said to Edna, "We're not even in the war yet, but Jack McNair's already determined to keep me out of it."

"That sounds as if you were determined to get into it," she said.

"Well, of course I am. Do you want me to be labeled a pacifist?" said Bill.

"You're not going to be labeled a pacifist," said Edna. "Everybody will know you're anything but. Seeing Bob Hotchkiss in uniform was too much for you, wasn't it? What is there about a uniform? Boots and spurs."

"Actually, Bob wore leather puttees, so it wasn't boots and spurs," said Bill.

"Personally, I think the British uniform is much more becoming."

"Well, so do I," said Bill. "Maybe I'll get them to change ours."

"Do they carry swords?"

"I believe the expression is 'wear swords.' I don't believe the British do any more," said Bill. "They did in the beginning of the war, but swords have no place in trench warfare. Swords, or sabres, went out with the horse. There's no such thing as a cavalry charge any more. The uhlans have stopped carrying lances."

"Who on earth are the uhlans?" said Edna.

"German cavalry," said Bill. "Why did you bring up the subject of swords?"

"Swords? I don't know. Yes, I do," said Edna. "I was thinking of Bob and poor Priscilla."

"I don't see the connection," said Bill.

"No, I guess you don't. Priscilla used to refer to Bob's thing as his sword."

"His thing? You mean his pecker? Do you talk about Bob's pecker?"

"Priscilla called it his sword. She had to have some name for it," said Edna.

"I didn't know you ever talked about it at all."

"How do you suppose we ever talked about having babies?"

"I didn't know you ever did," said Bill.

"Priscilla always said 'Bob put his sword in me,' and at first I didn't know what she was talking about. Anyway, it'll be a long time before Bob puts his sword in Priscilla again, and I feel sorry for her. I'd hate that. That's what war does. Separates people, people that should be together, like Bob and Priscilla, like you and me."

Edna and Priscilla, being young wives of young lawyers, in the same firm, had that much in common, and they both had young children. But Priscilla had been the repository for Bob Hotchkiss's growing jealousy of Bill Ewing, and to this was added Bob's petulant superiority over Bill for not joining the National Guard. Bob, in his letters to Priscilla from El Paso, was unable to refrain from commenting on Bill's pacifism, his slacking, his showing the white feather, and Priscilla, always swearing Edna to secrecy, could not always refrain from reading the letters aloud. "Don't tell Bill Bob said this, but Bob resents Bill," said Priscilla.

"Do you resent Bill?" said Edna.

"Of course I don't. Somebody has to stay home," said Priscilla.

"Most people *are* staying home, Priscilla," said Edna.

"Oh, Bob'll get over it."

"I hope he does," said Edna. "They've known each other so long. School together, and their fathers and mothers friends."

"Their fathers were partners, but I don't know how good friends they were," said Priscilla.

"Oh, well now I never knew that. I of course never knew Mr. Hotchkiss, but I took for granted they were friends," said Edna.

"Clarence Kelley was always closer to Mr. Ewing than he was to Mr. Hotchkiss. Mr. Hotchkiss took Mrs. Kelley's side years ago, when Mrs. Kelley had her nervous breakdown."

"I always understood the nervous breakdown was from too much alcohol," said Edna.

"Well, naturally you heard Mr. Kelley's side of it, from Mr. Ewing."

"Mr. Ewing never spoke to me about Mr. or Mrs. Kelley. He died soon after we were married," said Edna.

"Uh-huh. Well, naturally Mr. Kelley is grateful to Bill Ewing, more so than he ever would be to Bob Hotchkiss," said Priscilla. "He recommended Bill to Jack McNair, and that was quite a promotion. But let's not have that make any difference between us, Edna. I consider you my closest friend in Cleveland. I've lived here four years, and it seems to me I could have made more friends in Cleveland, but I came here from Springfield, Mass., and you talk about Boston being snobbish. I'll give you Cleveland any time. My father manufactured bicycles. The Lightning. You may have heard of it. It was very successful."

"Oh, yes. My father had a Lightning," said Edna.

"He manufactured the Lightning till one of the big companies bought him out and he retired. We had plenty of money and I went to Smith College for a year before I married Bob. Bob was going to the Yale Law School, having been to Denison University before that, a Sigma Chi. But I didn't even know where Ohio was, let alone Denison, and Cleveland was somewhere out in the tall timbers. They sure took me down a peg or two. I didn't know a soul in Cleveland, not a single, solitary soul. I used to walk along

Euclid Avenue just to be with people. One day I remember I was walking along Euclid and a man stopped me and said, 'Aren't you Priscilla Bascom?' and I said, 'Yes, but who are you?' And he said he was Kenneth Hires, used to be a foreman at the Lightning factory before my father sold out. He was working for a rubber company in Akron and was just in town for the day. I didn't know him from Adam and he wasn't very attractive but I stood and talked to him for fifteen minutes, just to have someone to talk to. I told Bob to hurry up and make me pregnant or I wouldn't be responsible. Incidentally, I wanted another baby when he left for the Border, but I just had my period so I have to wait till he gets back, whenever that will be."

"Do you like it any better here now?" said Edna.

"Oh, yes. I have the baby now, but I haven't got Bob," said Priscilla.

On an impulse Edna said, "How would you like to spend Christmas with us?"

"Oh, I couldn't," said Priscilla. "Do you mean it?"

"It'll just be Bill and I and Mrs. Ewing."

"Mrs. Ewing, Bill's mother? I know her, but—no, I don't think I'd better. She always struck me as rather strange."

"That's because she's been in mourning so long. But she blossomed out last spring. I see what you mean, but she isn't that way any more."

"Are you sure you want me?" said Priscilla.

"Of course I'm sure," said Edna.

"Can I let you know?" said Priscilla.

"You're waiting to tell Bob, is that it?" said Edna.

"Well, yes. He might not like it," said Priscilla.

"He's only got a week to find out. Why don't you let him know *after* Christmas. You want to come, Priscilla."

"Yes, I do. Very well, if you're sure it's all right. I won't be in the way," said Priscilla. "Is it all right if I bring the baby?"

"I'm counting on it," said Edna. "Come around noon and stay all day."

Mrs. Ewing said it was awfully thoughtful of Edna to have Priscilla. She knew what it was not to have a husband at Christmas-time. Bill was slightly more difficult. "It's an act of kindness, but I'm not sure it will be appreciated," said Bill.

"If you were gone, I'd expect her to have me," said Edna.

"Well, all right. It's Christmas," said Bill.

Priscilla arrived shortly after noon on Christmas Day, with presents for Edna, Bill, and Mrs. Ewing: a negligee for Edna, a handbag for Mrs. Ewing, a wallet for Bill. "You can exchange them after Christmas except Bill's wallet, that has his initials on it."

"You got me almost the same thing I got you," said Edna.

"I bought you a dozen silk stockings," said Mrs. Ewing.

"I bought you a sweater. I hope it's the right size," said Bill.

"I decided to leave the baby at home with Anna. He's still too young to appreciate Christmas, and I was afraid he'd give John-Stewart his cold. Have you noticed how many colds are around?" said Priscilla.

"It's the time of the year," said Edna. "I'm dying to know what you got from Bob."

"I should have brought it with me. It's an armadillo basket, and a Mexican silver bracelet, and a perfectly hideous beaded belt that I'll never wear. But it was all he could get. Shopping isn't easy in El Paso, as you can imagine."

At one o'clock they sat down to a turkey dinner and champagne. "Real pain to our sham friends and champagne to our real friends," said Priscilla. "That was Bob's favorite toast whenever he drank champagne."

"Well, here's to Bob and a quick and safe return to Ohio," said Bill.

"I'll certainly drink to that," said Priscilla, and did so.

"Priscilla, have another piece of mince pie," said Bill.

[117]

"There's something in it, isn't there?" said Priscilla.

"A touch of brandy, not enough to hurt you," said Bill.

"You don't know me. Champagne and brandy. Oh, all right," she said. "It doesn't affect you the way it does me, does it, Mrs. Ewing?"

"How does it affect you, Priscilla?" said Ada Ewing.

"It makes me want to go to bed with a man," said Priscilla.

"No, then it doesn't," said Ada Ewing. "Maybe if I took enough it would."

"Why, Mother," said Bill. "You shock me."

"Oh, why should I?" said Ada Ewing.

"You don't really, but you must admit I've never heard you talk this way before," said Bill.

"Then it's high time you did. Priscilla, have another glass of champagne," said Ada Ewing.

"I'll have one if you will," said Priscilla.

"No sooner said than done," said Ada, and the two women touched their glasses and drank. Edna watched them, fascinated and trying without success to force herself to smile. Her mother-in-law ignored her and smiled at Priscilla. For some reason, or possibly for no reason, Edna was reminded of Faith McCracken. That, too, had been a Christmas full of loneliness and final desperation, ending with Faith's naked body on the bathroom floor. But Edna was not sure whether Ada Ewing reminded her of Faith McCracken or if she was reminded of Faith by Priscilla and her loneliness. Priscilla's remark about wanting to go to bed with a man was Faith's unuttered cry, but Ada Ewing had been its echo. And yet there was something more to it than that. There was more to it than that.

Ada Ewing offered to help with the dishes. "I'd offer to help too, but I might break some," said Priscilla.

"Martha will attend to the dishes," said Edna.

"In that case, you'll forgive me if I have to go," said Ada Ewing.

"So soon?" said Edna.

"I have to go out to the farm and deliver some presents," said Ada. "Priscilla, why don't you come with me? We can both stand some fresh air."

"That's a good idea," said Priscilla.

With hardly more than a routine protest on the part of Edna, the two guests got in the Pierce-Arrow and were driven to the country. "I will say the fresh air should do them both some good," said Edna. "And it's snowing."

"I hope Walter has chains," said Bill. "They're going to need them. They're having a blizzard in Chicago."

"They're having one in Wingate too," said Edna. "Let's talk about the blizzard in Wingate. Let's talk about anything but our departed guests."

"All right with me," said Bill. "Mother has certainly changed."

"I thought we weren't going to talk about them," said Edna.

"Did Mother have anything to drink before she came here?" said Bill.

"How should I know? No, I don't think so. But the champagne flowed pretty freely. Two bottles for four people."

"Well, it's Christmas," said Bill. "I'm going to have to call Jack McNair sometime this afternoon. I'll bet he's at the office."

"Well, don't feel you have to go too," said Edna.

"I may have to for an hour or so. I'm sure Bob Hotchkiss doesn't stop chasing bandits on Christmas," said Bill.

Meanwhile, in the Pierce-Arrow with the side curtains snugly closed, Ada Ewing and Priscilla Hotchkiss were wrapped in buffalo robes against the cold. "It's nice and cozy in the car," said Priscilla.

"It is, but my next car will be a limousine," said Ada. "I'm getting old enough for a closed car. This car is about five or six years old, and there've been a lot of improvements since this was new. It's warm, but it isn't warm enough."

"When you get a limousine will you take me for a ride in it?" said Priscilla.

"Any time," said Ada. "You've never seen our farm, have you?"

"Not close to," said Priscilla. "Only from the road."

"I like it when the ground is covered with snow. But then I like it all the time, even when you're knee-deep in mud. I come out here almost every day in the spring and summer. I think we may be in for a blizzard," said Ada. "I wonder if we ought to turn back. Walter, do you think we ought to turn back?"

"It's coming down pretty heavy," said Walter.

"Well, we're almost there," said Ada. "You may have to spend the night on the farm, Priscilla. I'm sorry."

"That's all right, as long as I can telephone home," said Priscilla.

"You can if the wires aren't down," said Ada.

They arrived at the farm and were greeted by Lloyd and Beulah Sharpe. "You brought us a little snow," said Lloyd.

"So I did. This is Mrs. Hotchkiss. We may have to spend the night," said Ada. "Is the house ready?"

"It's always ready, Mrs. Ewing," said Beulah. "Even Walter's room. The house isn't warm yet, but it will be. Will you have supper in our house?"

"Thank you, Beulah. I brought you a few presents," said Ada.

There was a shotgun for Lloyd, a sheepskin coat for Beulah, some toys for the Sharpe children, while Beulah had knitted a sweater for Ada. "What time will supper be ready?" said Ada.

"When I get through the milking," said Lloyd. "About six."

Ada and Priscilla had supper with the Sharpes in their house, and after supper Priscilla telephoned Ann. By that time Ada's house was warm, and Ada suggested bed. "I brought you a nightgown," said Ada. "It's flannel, but I think you'll need it tonight. It's still snowing. I'm sorry I couldn't show you more of the farm, but there'll be another time. Breakfast is at seven, and we'll start back to town as soon as Walter thinks the roads are clear. Can I get you anything else before we go to bed?"

"Nothing, thank you," said Priscilla. "I'm sorry I got a little tiddly at dinner today."

"Oh, we both did, Priscilla. Goodnight."

At about eleven o'clock Priscilla came to Ada's room. "Can I sleep with you? Are you still awake?"

"Come in," said Ada. She made room for Priscilla in her bed, and they went to sleep with their arms around each other. Once, during the night, Ada awoke and kissed the sleeping girl, and she thought she must not do that. But Ada Ewing was soon asleep again.

In the morning they had breakfast in Beulah Sharpe's kitchen and Walter came in to tell them that the snowplow had been at work since six o'clock and that the road was fairly clear. "Then we'll be on our way," said Ada. They said goodbye to Beulah— Lloyd was shoveling snow—and got in the Pierce-Arrow and headed for Cleveland. "Did you have a good rest?" said Ada.

"Perfect. I even had a dream that you kissed me," said Priscilla.

"That wasn't a dream, Priscilla. I did kiss you," said Ada.

"I wasn't sure," said Priscilla.

"Is there anything wrong with that?" said Ada.

"No, no. You can kiss me any time you want to," said Priscilla. "But I'd rather you did it while I was awake."

"Hereafter I will," said Ada.

"When?" said Priscilla.

"When?" said Ada. "Why, do you want me to make a date to kiss you?"

"I could come to your house this afternoon, or we could spend the night at the farm," said Priscilla. "Let's do that, spend the night at the farm."

"Priscilla, do you know what you're saying?" said Ada.

"Yes, don't you?" said Priscilla.

"Yes, I guess I do," said Ada.

"Who'll ever know? My husband's away, and I wouldn't tell

him anyway. Shall I tell you a secret?" said Priscilla.

"What?"

"Do you know why Bob joined the national guard?"

"No," said Ada.

"He'd kill himself if he thought anybody knew. Promise you won't tell. Promise?"

"I promise," said Ada.

"Bob is very handsome and all that, and remember I told you I wanted to have another baby by him, but we couldn't. We tried everything, everything. But I guessed what the trouble was. Bob only likes men."

"Priscilla! I don't believe it," said Ada. "Bob Hotchkiss?"

"Do you know how long it's been since he had relations with me?" said Priscilla. "At least a year. He has a few drinks and wants me to get undressed, and I do, but that's as far as it goes. He looks at me, and all he does is cry. I don't think he does anything with men, either, but he likes to be with them. He sent me some snapshots and they were all pictures of naked men in swimming. He wrote on the back of one of the snapshots, 'Being faithful to you.' Faithful—well, maybe. But he's very jealous of me, especially where Bill Ewing is concerned. I asked him once what he would do if I ever had an affair with Bill Ewing, and he said he'd kill both of us. He hates Bill. He's always hated him. Bill is so much better than he is. If I so much as look at another man he threatens to beat me, and he's strong."

"You had one child by him," said Ada.

"Yes, I did, but how long ago was that? Even then he made me turn around."

"How do you mean?" said Ada.

"He pretended I was a man. He couldn't do it from the front. He likes to look at me, but it only makes him cry."

"Bob Hotchkiss, the athlete, the strong man," said Ada. "The man you'd least suspect."

"Unless you knew him," said Priscilla.

"But I've known Bob all his life," said Ada.

"Not in bed."

"No, that makes a difference," said Ada.

"Now maybe you understand why I was glad when you kissed me," said Priscilla. "It was the first sign of affection I've known in God knows how long. I need affection."

"Yes, you do, and don't we all?" said Ada. She kissed Priscilla and Priscilla kissed her in turn.

"It's not the same, is it?" said Priscilla.

"No, but it's good," said Ada. "It's affection, and who can do without that?"

"Will you take me out to the farm, tomorrow?" said Priscilla.

"Are you sure you want to?" said Ada.

"I just want to be with you. You're not afraid, are you?"

"I am, a little," said Ada.

"So am I."

"Shall we wait and see how we both feel tomorrow?" said Ada.

"Yes," said Priscilla.

They were at Priscilla's house. "Goodbye, my dear," said Ada.

"Good-bye," said Priscilla.

There was nothing in God's world that could keep them apart now. Ada telephoned Priscilla the next morning and was told by Ann that Mrs. Hotchkiss had gone to the grocery store and would be back in an hour. When Priscilla telephoned her, Ada was beside the phone. "I didn't want to call you too early," said Priscilla. "Are we going? Are you going to take me?"

"I'll be at your house in half an hour," said Ada. The excitement was almost unbearable. She had no plans, knew not what to expect, but her head was spinning with anticipation. "Go to Mrs. Hotchkiss's," she told Walter. "We're spending the day at the farm."

"Whatever you say, ma'am," said Walter. "Did you call off Mrs. Bill?"

"Oh, heavens, I forgot about Mrs. Bill," said Ada.

"You were s'pose to go there to meet her father and mother," said Walter. "I was s'pose to meet them on the twelve-thirty from Detroit."

"I'll call her and tell her," said Ada. She telephoned Edna.

"Edna, something has come up and I have to go to the farm. Will you meet your father and mother? I won't be able to have lunch with you, but I'll get there as soon as I can. It may be late this afternoon, but I'll be there. I'm sorry, dear, but you understand." She had no excuse to offer, but it was better to offer none than to offer a lame one. She would think of something when her head stopped spinning.

"Mother and Daddy will be terribly disappointed," said Edna. "Is there something the matter at the farm?"

"I'll explain it when I see you," said Ada.

There was the danger that Edna would see the Pierce-Arrow at Priscilla's house; they lived only two blocks apart. But that was a chance Ada had to take, and she took it. As good fortune would have it, Priscilla was waiting for her, arctics on, hat on, fur coat ready to be put on. "Tell Mrs. Hotchkiss I'm waiting," Ada said to Walter.

"She's coming," said Walter.

"I was waiting for you," said Priscilla.

"Never mind the lap robes, Walter. We'll put them on ourselves," said Ada. "I'm glad you were waiting, Priscilla. We mustn't let Edna see us."

"Yes, I thought of that. That's why I was ready," said Priscilla. "Are you as excited as I am?"

"Yes, and what for?" said Ada.

"That's just it. We don't know what for. I've thought about you since yesterday, you were never out of my thoughts. What shall we do when we get there? Do we have to have lunch with Mrs. Sharpe?"

"I haven't thought that far ahead," said Ada.

"We don't have to go to her house, do we? I don't really like that woman," said Priscilla. "I don't know why, but she rubs me the wrong way. What if she comes to your house to make the beds?"

"No, she won't do that. She'll have made the beds yesterday. I'll say that for her, she's a good housekeeper. We're both excited, Priscilla, and we're suspicious of everybody."

"We're like two lovers," said Priscilla.

"Exactly," said Ada.

"I can hardly wait to have you kiss me, but the chauffeur would think it's funny, two women kissing each other," said Priscilla.

"You're suspicious of Walter, and so am I," said Ada.

"There were two girls at Smith College. I never knew what they did. Maybe nothing. You always saw them together and you wondered. But they were the same age, and virgins."

"Well, we're not virgins, whatever else we are," said Ada. "How many men have you known?"

"Two. Bob, first, and one other since Bob."

"Who was that?" said Ada.

"You don't know him. He's a man I met on the train. I only saw him a few times after that. He comes from Buffalo, New York. How many have you known?"

"Two. My husband, and a man in Palm Beach," said Ada.

"That's all?"

"That's all. A wasted life, wouldn't you call it?" said Ada.

"You never slept with Clarence Kelley?"

"No, I never did."

"Bob was sure you had," said Priscilla.

"Other people thought that too, but I didn't. There's the farm. We'll go to my house and ignore Beulah Sharpe. I hope there's plenty of hot water, but there will be. Beulah's a good housekeeper. It'll seem strange, taking baths in the middle of the day, but we'll make some excuse."

"Is that what we're going to do, take baths?"

"Unless you have a better idea," said Ada.

The dominant person, the guide, was Ada Ewing. Once inside

the house they took off their coats and arctics, and Ada put her arms around Priscilla and kissed her. Priscilla responded and awaited Ada's next move in silence. Taking Priscilla by the hand, she mounted the stairs and they went to Ada's bedroom. "Let me take off your dress," said Ada. When she had done so Ada said, "You have a gorgeous little figure, Priscilla." Priscilla still said nothing, and stood in her chemise as Ada stripped her naked. "Gorgeous," said Ada. "How could any man not appreciate that figure? Now I'll join you." Ada took off her clothes and the two women stood admiring each other, but only for a moment. "I'll run the tub," said Ada.

"Aren't you going to kiss me?" said Priscilla.

"Let's wait," said Ada. "We'll prolong it," she added.

The tub was running and the women stood against each other, Ada slightly taller and with breasts fuller than Priscilla's. "What do we do now?" said Priscilla.

"You get into the tub. We'll get in together. I must have been thinking of this when I ordered a big tub," said Ada. They got into the tub, facing each other, and Ada kissed Priscilla. "Kneel up," said Ada. "Kneel up, facing me." Priscilla did so, and they kissed each other and Ada put her hands on Priscilla's buttocks, squeezing them.

"I like that," said Priscilla. "Shall I do it to you?"

"Of course, do what you want," said Ada, "Now let's get out of the tub and I'll dry you."

"And I'll dry you," said Priscilla.

They got out of the tub and Priscilla said, "It's cold. Woo, it's cold."

"Oh, you're such a baby," said Ada. "Let me dry you, and you'll soon be warm."

"Am I such a baby? It *is* cold."

"It is a bit cold, but I'll soon have you warmed up," said Ada. She took a towel and rubbed Priscilla all over her body briskly except when she came to the part between her legs, which she rubbed slowly.

"I like that too," said Priscilla. "Do it some more."

"Like this?" said Ada.

"Not with the towel, with your hand. That's better. Shall I do that to you?"

"Yes," said Ada.

"Shall I kiss you there?"

"I wish you would," said Ada. "And I'll kiss you there."

"At the same time?" said Priscilla.

"Yes," said Ada.

"This is what we wanted to do all the time, isn't it?" said Priscilla.

"I guess it must be," said Ada. She lay on the bed, and Priscilla lay beside her. "I thought you were going to kiss me, there."

"I will, and you kiss me, there," said Priscilla. "The French call it the *soixante-neuf.*"

"I know," said Ada. "Do it, and let's not talk about it."

"But I like to talk about it," said Priscilla.

"Who do you talk about it to?"

"You," said Priscilla.

They kissed each other until they were tired. "I have to stop now," said Ada.

"I have to, too," said Priscilla.

Ada changed her position and put her arm around Priscilla's shoulders. "We've done it," said Ada.

"Yes. Why is it supposed to be so wrong?" said Priscilla.

"I don't know," said Ada. "I've never done it with anyone else, but I could go on doing it to you, except that I'm tired."

"They say it's not natural, but it was natural to me," said Priscilla.

"It's as natural as Bob Hotchkiss liking only men," said Ada. "Shall we do it again sometime—I don't mean now. I think we'd better get dressed, now. But you were excited, weren't you?"

"More excited than I've ever been."

"Then we'll do it again," said Ada.

"Maybe there's something we don't know," said Priscilla.

"Yes, maybe if we did it one at a time. You to me and I to you," said Ada.

"I think that would be better," said Priscilla.

"We'll try that next time," said Ada. "Now I think we'd better get dressed. Oh, you darling girl. Why do I love you so?"

"Because I love you too."

They kissed each other and got dressed. "I have to go see Lloyd Sharpe, but I'll only be a minute. I have to have some excuse for coming out here today. Then I think we'd better be getting back to town."

"You have such dignity, you're so efficient," said Priscilla.

"The dignity is a result of a lifetime of repression, Priscilla."

They returned to town and Ada dropped Priscilla. She spent the remainder of the afternoon listening to the gossip about Wingate, and Mrs. Everett was full of that.

Nearly a year had gone by since Ada's visit to Sophie Cudlipp in Palm Beach and Will Levering's visit to her, the high point of her visit. But if Will Levering's morning call had been the high point of her sojourn in Palm Beach, it soon became insignificant. She was probably never going to see Will Levering again; a half hour of impromptu love-making with a man from Philadelphia (who may well have been sent to her room by Sophie) became in retrospect a half hour of pleasure and no more than that. Sophie Cudlipp had not been to Cleveland in all that time; New York, Newport, New York, Saratoga, Newport, and New York were the postmarks of Sophie's postcards. Then there came a letter from Palm Beach, inviting her to stay with her there, and Ada on an impulse accepted. She was, she knew, running away from Priscilla, but would not Priscilla run away from her? "I have to go to Florida for a couple of weeks," Ada told Priscilla over the telephone.

"Florida? What about me?"

"I'll be back, Priscilla," said Ada.

"But three weeks? That's forever," said Priscilla. "I thought you loved me."

"I do love you, dear, but—" There was a click on the telephone; Priscilla had hung up. Impetuous and piqued, Priscilla had hung up and given Ada an excuse for Ada to do what she wanted to do, which was to spend some time with her guilty conscience. And it was a guilty conscience. She had seduced Priscilla, and she wanted to get away for a few weeks.

Will Levering once again was in the car that met Ada at West Palm Beach, but this time he was in the back seat. "Sophie asked me to meet you," said Will. "She's getting a permanent."

"There's something I've been dying to ask you," said Ada. "Did Sophie send you to my room a year ago? Now tell me the truth, Will."

"Well, yes and no," said Will. "It was your last day, and Sophie was anxious to see that you had a good time. She suggested it. But I was willing."

"That was nice of you," said Ada.

"I'd still be willing," said Will.

"You're a sort of stallion, aren't you?" said Ada.

"I guess you could call me that," said Will. "But I don't think you'd better say anything about this conversation."

"Why not? Surely you told Sophie that you'd slept with me."

"Yes, I did, but she may have forgotten. Sophie has other stallions now. She's probably with one of them right this minute. You could have one too, you know. You're much better-looking than Sophie, and you're younger. You don't know Palm Beach, Ada. It's really depraved, and Sophie is one of the most depraved women here. She's discovered a motorcycle policeman that she sends for now and then and pays him a hundred dollars. That's in addition to her other stallions."

"I don't know whether to believe you or not," said Ada.

"You can believe me," said Will. "I'd abandon Sophie, but I've gotten very fond of the old dear. If she was ten years younger I'd marry her, but I wouldn't inherit all those millions from Cuyahoga, so I have my eye on someone else. Shall I come to your room in about an hour?"

"I guess that's why I came to Palm Beach," said Ada.

"You're honest to admit it," said Will.

"I don't know what's happened to me lately," said Ada. "I'm as depraved as Sophie."

"Why not?" said Will.

Ada did not have time to read the papers during her visit to Palm Beach; she was more pleasurably occupied with Will Levering, who made it clear to Sophie that inasmuch as she was fairly busy with her motorcycle policeman, he would entertain Ada. This did not sit too well with Sophie, but Sophie was pleased that Ada liked Will. Will was after all her idea. Ada's visit to Palm Beach was not marked by the cordiality of the previous year, and Sophie did not persuade her to linger past the second week in February. On her return to Cleveland almost the first thing she heard was that General Pershing had been ordered home from Mexico, and Bob Hotchkiss was back in Cleveland.

Tanned by the El Paso sun, Bob was now a first lieutenant, which meant silver bars instead of gold on his shoulder straps but also meant that he could no longer be called a shavetail. What else it meant was that he was sleeping with Priscilla, at least temporarily. Ada telephoned her, and Priscilla was cool toward her. "Oh, you're back," said Priscilla. "How was Florida?"

"Fine, but I missed you," said Ada.

"You'll have to go on missing me. Bob's back too."

"So I heard," said Ada.

"I said some awful things about Bob. I want you to forget them," said Priscilla.

"I'd hardly forget them, but I won't repeat them," said Ada. "It sounds as though things were all right with you two. Are they?"

"He's affectionate, if you know what I mean," said Priscilla.

"I know what you mean," said Ada. "No more baths."

"Baths? Oh, *baths*. No, no more baths."

"Well, I'll miss you, Priscilla, but if Bob is affectionate as you say, he's your husband," said Ada.

"You'll find someone else," said Priscilla.

"It looks as though I'll have to," said Ada.

"Don't call me any more," said Priscilla. "Somebody might be listening."

"Oh, don't worry your pretty head about that, Priscilla," said Ada. "But I was going to give a party for Bob."

"You don't have to."

"But I will. I want to hear all about the Mexican Border," said Ada.

She gave what turned out to be the largest party for Bob. He could not wear his uniform, but he remembered seven officers and men who had served with him and whom Ada had not included on her original invitation list. Cleveland society was well represented by the McVeaghs, the Hays, Holcombs, and the Swarzes, who also represented the board of directors of Cuyahoga. Walter Finch was there as was Christine Frogg, and they were both acquainted with the seven officers and men who were strangers to Ada, a fact which did not pass unobserved by Ada. Dr. and Mrs. Hendricks were there and stayed until after eleven o'clock. Most of the men wore white tie and tails, although some of the younger men wore Tuxedos. There were at least two hundred for dancing, and Ada had forty people in for dinner. Clarence Kelley was her escort and Jack McNair was her dancing partner. "Smiles" was the most frequently requested tune, and next to that "It's a Long Way to Tipperary." A colonel and a leftenant attached to the British Purchasing Commission dropped in by invitation of Jack McNair and behaved themselves admirably, although the leftenant had trouble believing there was such a place as Chillicothe. "My dear fellow, there must be four or five

Chillicothes," said Dr. Hendricks. To which the leftenant replied, "Isn't one enough?" Otherwise amity prevailed until two A.M. and Bob Hotchkiss, who had had that extra glass of champagne, decided he wanted to spend the rest of the evening with his army buddies. Priscilla went home with Clarence Kelley.

At eleven o'clock the next morning Clarence Kelley spoke to Ada on the telephone. "Could you possibly have lunch with me?" said Clarence. "I thought we'd go to the hotel."

Ada, with a successful party behind her, met Clarence.

"I chose the hotel because it was public and what I have to say to you is private, very private indeed," said Clarence. "It's an old trick of mine. Public place for private conversation. Ada, I want you to go away for a while. I know you've just come back from Palm Beach, but why not try California?" He cleared his throat. "Last night I took Priscilla Hotchkiss home from your party, and she unburdened herself of a lot of scandal that involves a lot of people. First, there was her husband. How much truth there is in what she told me about Bob, I have no way of knowing. But for what it's worth, she's convinced that Bob is a homosexual. He's fond of men. And I must say that that doesn't surprise me as much as it did her. I haven't got time to tell you why I suspected Bob. Suffice it to say, I had suspected him, and if what she says is true, the Lord help Bob. But then she launched into an accusation of you, Ada, that I don't even know how to repeat. Ada, will you tell me that what she said about you isn't true?"

"I don't know what she told you, but it probably is true," said Ada. "Did she tell you that we took a bath together at the farm?"

"Yes," said Kelley. "That you got undressed and took a bath together, and that you had relations together, you and Priscilla. It sounds relatively harmless when you put it that way, but can you imagine what Cleveland gossip could do to a story like that? I think you ought to go away."

"Why go away, Clarence?"

"Have you thought of Bill? Bill and Edna and the baby? Have you thought of Francis? Have you thought of yourself?"

"Yes, and I've thought of Priscilla," said Ada. "I knew it was wrong, what I did. I couldn't help myself, although that's no excuse. I went to Palm Beach, partly to think it over and partly to forget. But I didn't forget, and I did think it over. I'm past fifty, Clarence, and old enough to know better, but this girl attracted me and I attracted her, and I can't honestly say it'll never happen again. Do I make any sense to you? Do you think I'm incorrigible?"

"The workings of the female mind are mysterious to me."

"No, they're not. You understand women as well as any man I've ever known," said Ada. "You understood Bob Hotchkiss, so you ought to understand me. We have the same problem, haven't we? Bob joined the army, and I took a bath with his wife. I kissed her where a woman ought not to kiss another woman, and she kissed me in the same place. It shocks you to hear that, but we have no secrets, you and I. I'm not going away, Clarence."

"It may seem very brave of you to stay here and face the gossip, but you're not thinking of Bill."

"I've thought of Bill. If he has a degenerate mother, people aren't going to hold that against him. He's the normal son of a normal father and it's too bad about his mother. No, I'm not going away. It may interest you to learn that I had an affair with a man in Palm Beach, and enjoyed it. Maybe I am incorrigible, Clarence. Maybe I just got started late in life. But I'm not going to reform, and I'm not going away."

"On advice of counsel—you're ignoring advice of counsel," said Kelley. "In other words, do what you think best, Ada. I'd miss you if you went to California."

"Would you, Clarence? You hardly ever see me," said Ada.

"I think of you a great deal, and I think a great deal of you," said Kelley. "The two are by no means always the same. You're a strong woman, Ada. That's the word for you—strong."

"Enough about me. Are we going to get in the war?" said Ada.

"What can possibly keep us out? Wilson gets in in a few days, and then it'll be only a question of time," said Kelley. "That's all it is anyway, a question of time. Once you sever diplomatic relations, the fat's in the fire. Which may well be to your advantage. People will be so busy talking about the war that they won't be talking about you. However, don't count on it."

"I'm not counting on anything," said Ada. "Except your friendship."

The war was on. It hardly mattered that there had been nearly three years of hostilities involving England, France, Russia, Germany, Italy, Belgium, Austria-Hungary, Turkey and the yet unmade nations of Europe. Someone had taken to calling it the World War, although Luxembourg and the United States of America were not yet in it, but Woodrow Wilson in his wisdom had decided that the time had come when he could no longer stay out of it. And so the Congress, with the exception of a little old maid from Montana, concurred in his decision. In Pottsville, Pa., a company of the Pennsylvania National Guard from Scranton was billeted in the old Pershing mansion while guarding railroad bridges against the German agents, and there was an abortive effort to change the name of sauerkraut to Liberty Cabbage. The trench cap, an especially ugly article of men's headgear, with a buckled belt across the top, had a sizable sale among boys and men. Women took up rolling bandages intended for the Red Cross. There was a rash of flag-raisings, with attendant speeches on patriotism, and the first Liberty Loan lapel buttons made their appearance. Charley Brickley, the Harvard drop-kicker, booted a football as high as the Sub-Treasury Building to call attention to the Liberty Loan, and Douglas Fairbanks and Mary Pickford were reported to have raised millions by the sale of bonds. From the Pacific to the Atlantic it was impossible not to know that the war was on. "Good-bye Broadway, Hello France" was suddenly more popular than "I Didn't Raise My Boy to Be a Soldier"; "Over There" was known to millions who were just beginning to learn "The Star-Spangled Banner"; and there was a not too subtle warning in "Don't Bite the Hand That's Feeding You." The sounds of a nation newly at war, the posters of James Montgomery Flagg, the cartoons of the Dutchman Raemekers, the jokes about the Kaiser and the Crown Prince, prepared the country for the sterner realities.

"I've thought about joining the Navy," said Bill Ewing to Jack McNair.

"Why the Navy?" said Jack McNair.

"Well, frankly, it's cleaner," said Bill. "From what we hear, France is a sea of mud. It rains all the time. And in the Navy you get home once in a while. I'd like to be on a submarine chaser."

"I think I would too," said McNair. "Trench warfare has no appeal to me. But neither has any other kind of warfare. The closest I'll get will be when my kid joins the army. He's crazy to get in. He wants to get in the Signal Corps and be an aviator. That wouldn't be so bad. At least you stay out of the mud. Scotty'll get his degree at Kenyon this June, and he's applied for the Signal Corps. If his application is approved, he'll go to Texas, and then I guess that'll be the last we'll see of him till the damn thing's over."

"How long do you think that will be?"

"I don't know," said McNair. "I was talking to Colonel Abernathy about that. The British Purchasing Commission fellow. He made the point that it was a damn lucky thing we got in, or the Allies would have lost. But now that we're in, it will take about three years to lick the Germans. The Germans had been getting ready for this war too long, and they were the only ones who *were* ready for it. *We're* not ready for it, although we've known for three years that we couldn't stay out of it. Coach Wilson is to blame there."

"Coach Wilson?" said Bill.

"He coached the football team at Wesleyan before he became president of Princeton. Imagine him coaching a football team? They must have been pretty hard up. Well, at least he sent a few thousand men to the Border and that was better than nothing. It made a first lieutenant out of Bob Hotchkiss, so the Germans better look out. The Yanks are coming."

"Isn't Bob coming back to Hotchkiss, Ewing and Kelley? I haven't seen him around here much," said Bill.

"In the strictest confidence, Clarence is hoping he'll be going away soon, so he hasn't given him much to do. The firm is making a lot of money and can afford to pay Bob, but meanwhile you're doing his work. If anything happens to Clarence Kelley, Bob'll still draw pay, but if anything happens to me *and* Clarence, our best clients are going to look elsewhere for legal advice. The firm will collapse. Which brings me to a question: do you want to have Bob Hotchkiss for a partner?"

"I don't think so," said Bill. "If something happened to you and Clarence, I'd rather go out on my own."

"I thought as much," said McNair.

"I'm sure Bob would too."

"I suppose so," said McNair. "That leads me to another question. How would you like to be on the board of Cuyahoga?"

"Me on the board of Cuyahoga?" said Bill.

"That's what I said," said McNair. "You already know as much about the inner workings of Cuyahoga as any man that's now on the board. Those late nights and Sundays have paid off, Bill. They offered me a directorship and I said no, I wanted to be a lawyer. But this is something you can't turn down. They asked me who I'd recommend, and I suggested you. You're young, but that's to your advantage."

"Come to me after the war, and I'll give you an answer," said Bill.

"Unfortunately they won't wait that long. Three or four years from now isn't now. Three or four weeks from now is as long as they'll wait," said McNair.

"Then you know my answer," said Bill. "I haven't enlisted and my draft number hasn't been drawn, but any day now."

"If you were on the board of Cuyahoga you could probably get an exemption," said McNair.

"And a white feather from Bob Hotchkiss," said Bill.

"Oh, undoubtedly," said McNair. "Bill, how would you like to be a captain? You'd outrank Bob Hotchkiss."

"That would be nice. How could it be arranged?" said Bill.

"Take the job on the Cuyahoga board, and go in as a captain. Or even a major. Don't think that that can't be arranged, because it can."

"I knew there was a hitch to it," said Bill.

"Colonel Abernathy isn't a colonel. He's actually a leftenant-colonel, but when the Judge Advocate General offered me a commission back in January, I told him I'd have to have equal rank with Abernathy. That's how I know those things can be arranged. I thought it over for a while, then decided to remain a civilian. Gloves and a swagger stick look all right on Abernathy, but I like to work in shirt sleeves. But it's nice to know I could have been a lieutenant-colonel. I think of myself as a lieutenant-colonel whenever I have to do business with a captain of ordnance. Oh, I have those moments too, when I'd like to be in uniform. You're not the only one. But why don't you take the directorship on Cuyahoga? Then later on go in as a captain? You're not all that anxious to stick a bayonet in some Heinie's belly, are you? You could do more for the Allied cause as a director of Cuyahoga. What are you thinking about?"

"I was thinking about a guy named Eddie Noisrander," said

Bill. "All right, I've changed my mind. I'll be a director at Cuyahoga."

Bill was on time for dinner that evening. "I want you to go out and buy yourself something expensive. Something worth about twenty times fifty-two dollars. That's a thousand and fifty-four dollars. It can be furs or jewelry, whatever you like."

"Why the sudden generosity?" said Edna. "I'm all for it, but why?"

"Fifty-two is the number of weeks in a year, twenty is the twenty-dollar gold pieces I'll be paid for attending directors' meetings at Cuyahoga Iron & Steel. In other words, I'm to be a director of Cuyahoga."

"That's better than the two-and-a-half gold piece you'd get for being a director of the Wingate Savings Bank," said Edna. "I know, because my father used to give them all to my mother. But Cuyahoga Iron & Steel? Aren't they the ones that made you late for dinner?"

"That's why I'm giving you the director's fees," said Bill.

"Tell me all about it at dinner," said Edna.

He did so, leaving out the mention of Eddie Noisrander but including the reference to a bayonet in a Heinie's belly. "I don't know why, but that sold me," he said. "I don't think I could kill anybody. There must be some Quaker in me."

"If you were me, there's some Quaker in me on my father's side," said Edna. "My father's mother was a Quaker from down Indiana way. Anyway, I'm happy that you're not going in the army. Those that live by the sword, shall perish by the sword. And I don't mean it the way Priscilla means it."

"I'm being inconsistent, taking the job at Cuyahoga and making munitions, but Emerson said consistency is the 'hobgoblin of little minds.' I learned that from Professor Jeffries at Ann Arbor. 'The hobgoblin of little minds,' he used to say, a strange thing for a law professor to say, but it came in handy."

"What will you do as a director of Cuyahoga?" said Edna.

"Go to the meetings and listen," said Bill. "I'll be the youngest director in the history of the corporation, so I'll learn to keep my trap shut. However, after I've learned the ropes they'll hear from me. It's a step upward, Edna. Wish me luck."

"Haven't I always?"

"No, because I never asked you to before. This time I'll need luck," said Bill. "The imponderable."

"Then I wish it to you," said Edna. "The best of luck and a lot of it."

"That's the way to talk," said Bill.

His mother called him a couple of days later. "I got an announcement that you'd been made a director of Cuyahoga. Congratulations. Did you know I had stock in Cuyahoga?"

"No, I didn't. How much stock?"

"Well, now I guess it must be worth a hundred thousand or maybe more. Clarence Kelley would know," said Ada Ewing. "I inherited it from your father. Do you want it?"

"I don't think so, but I may want it later," said Bill.

"Let me know when you want it, and I'll transfer it to you," said Ada. "How did you happen to be made a director?"

"I've been working for Cuyahoga for six months or more, and Jack McNair, my boss, is in charge of their legal affairs," said Bill.

"I know the stock is coining money. I'd hate to tell you what I've been offered for my shares," said Ada.

"A hundred thousand?"

"That's what it was worth when your father died," said Ada. "I've been offered a million for it, and Clarence told me to hold on to it. I have some other stock that you may be interested in."

"What's that?"

"Akron Rubber. That's been sensational. It was worth four dollars a share when your father left it to me, and now it's worth around sixty. I have ten thousand shares. Do you know about it?"

"Everybody knows about Akron Rubber," said Bill. "But you mustn't go giving stocks away, Mother. What will you live on?"

"Clarence gives me thirty-five thousand a year to spend, and I don't really need that much. I'm not extravagant. Your father and I lived very simply, and of course I had some Bloodgood money. Your Uncle Asa and I shared that, fifty-fifty. Unfortunately, Uncle Asa spent most of his—or fortunately. He had a good time doing it, drinking and women. He went through a hundred thousand dollars by the time he was thirty, which may not seem like a great deal, but he only had nine years to spend it. Of course, he never worked, and I've had to support him since he was thirty. You're going to have to, too. Asa will probably live to be eighty."

"Why all this talk about money, Mother?" said Bill. "You haven't mentioned money to me since I went up to Ann Arbor and you sneaked me fifty dollars a month allowance."

"Yes, I thought the fifty you got from your father wasn't enough, but I never told him," said Ada. "He used to say, 'See, Ada, fifty dollars a month was enough. Teaches him to be thrifty.' Were you ever thrifty, Bill?"

"I managed to be broke on a hundred a month, so I guess I wasn't," said Bill. "But I'm learning, and Edna isn't extravagant. Mr. Everett gives her a hundred a month and she saves nearly all of it."

"That's being thrifty," said Ada.

"You didn't answer my question," said Bill. "Why are you so full of money talk?"

"Because it's really time we had some money talk. You know, Bill, I'm not going to live forever."

"I don't see why not," said Bill.

"Well, for one reason, I don't want to," said Ada.

"I'd like you to," said Bill.

"Would you? Would you really? You have Edna and John-Stewart, and you've just been made a director of Cuyahoga. It seems to me your life is full. Mine is not. I could tell you a few things about myself that you wouldn't like very much."

"I don't think you could tell me anything that would greatly surprise me," said Bill. "For instance, I hate to bring this up again, but are you sure you didn't have a love affair with Clarence Kelley?"

"No, I never did."

"I thought possibly you were going to tell me that I'm Clarence Kelley's son," said Bill.

"Well, you're not. You're the son of Francis Ewing and no one else. I was completely faithful to your father, from the time we were married till the day he died. I will tell you now that I sometimes wondered about that, why I didn't seem to be attractive to other men besides your father. A woman, any woman, finds herself thinking that if she's so attractive to one man, why shouldn't she be to someone else. Even Edna, who never looks at another man, must have moments when she secretly wishes another man would fall in love with her. It's the nature of the beast."

"I suppose it is, but I hope she never finds out it is," said Bill. "When did you find out?"

"I told you. When I was married to your father," said Ada.

"But you never did anything about it?" said Bill.

"Not while he was alive. What I've done since then is really none of your business. It wasn't while he was alive for that matter. But at least you know whose son you are, and I suppose you're entitled to that. Why did you think you might be Clarence Kelley's son?"

"He's taken such a fatherly interest in me," said Bill.

"He's taken a fatherly interest in me, too, and he's old enough to have been my father. But he wasn't. My mother and Clarence Kelley never knew each other. The Bloodgoods and the Kelleys didn't move in the same circles. Neither did the Bloodgoods and the Ewings, for that matter, but your father altered that."

"How?" said Bill.

"How? Why, he was introduced to me and he made a point of seeing me, that's how. We went on picnics together, and he made friends with your Uncle Asa, and in time we were married. He got your uncle out of a couple of scrapes. He was always getting your uncle out of scrapes."

"What kind of scrapes?" said Bill. "I'm finding out a lot about my family that I never knew before."

"Women," said Ada. "Your Uncle Asa was the kind of man who'd promise to marry any woman in order to get her to go to bed with him, and one or two of them took him seriously. Then he'd come to your father and ask him to get him out of it. Sometimes it cost Asa money, but sometimes not. Your father could be very persuasive."

"He must have been," said Bill. "A hitherto unsuspected side of him."

"The Cuyahoga and the Akron Rubber side of him were what you saw, before he died," said Ada. "The side of him that protected your uncle from blackmailing females was naturally the side he didn't reveal, but he had fun outwitting them. Your Uncle Asa adored your father, and well he might."

"He was quite a man," said Bill. "I mean—going to bat for Uncle Asa that way."

"Yes," said Ada. "He understood people's frailties."

But she wondered if Francis Ewing would have found it possible to understand her frailty with Priscilla. It was more likely that he would have understood her use of Will Levering. Francis Ewing had never mentioned the kind of relationship she had had with Priscilla, and neither had she. He had never mentioned the kind of relationship Bob Hotchkiss must have had with the men in his company, and neither had she. And yet he had somehow known about the Priscilla relationship between two women and the Bob Hotchkiss relationship with the men in his company. How did he and she know about such relationships? If people never talked about it, how did they know about them? How freely she had talked about her relations with Priscilla to Clarence Kelley, and would never have talked about them to Francis Ewing. Were there people who invited such confidences and people who did not?

Soon the National Guard would be federalized and Bob Hotchkiss would be going away to camp, and when that occurred she would know, as she did not know now, whether she was to resume the relationship with Priscilla. She had not seen Priscilla since she gave the party for Bob Hotchkiss and Clarence Kelley took Priscilla home, and there was no question that Priscilla was avoiding her. It was summer now, the weather was warm, and the dam at the farm was inviting. But Priscilla would have to make the first move, and she had not done so, and there were days when Ada did not want her to as well as days when she did. In the midst of this confusion, Bob Hotchkiss was quite suddenly sent away to camp in Georgia with his company, and Priscilla called Ada at the farm.

"I wanted to talk to you," said Priscilla.

"Come out any time," said Ada. "The farm is lovely."

"Could I come out tomorrow and maybe spend the night?" said Priscilla.

"But of course, any time," said Ada. Priscilla had made the first move.

The next day Priscilla arrived before noon, and Ada kissed her with more warmth than she was going to permit herself. "You know you've been a naughty girl," said Ada.

"I have a husband, but thank God he's gone now," said Priscilla. "I hope he gets sent over soon. That's very unpatriotic of me, but it's the truth. He got drunk the night of your party and didn't come home for two days. He didn't bother to tell me who he was with. I knew."

"Some of the boys?"

"Of course, some of the boys. He brought one of the boys home with him and made me sleep with him. How do you like that?" said Priscilla.

"You did sleep with him?" said Ada. "I thought men like that didn't like to sleep with women."

"Well, he did. And Bob wanted him to. I guess there are a lot of things you don't know about men."

"I guess there are," said Ada.

"I hate men," said Priscilla.

"So you've come back to me," said Ada.

"It looks that way," said Priscilla.

In the quiet of the country night they were together again, arms around each other, and they remembered that one, Ada, was to perform the act of kissing. "Now let me kiss you," said Priscilla.

"Do you want to?" said Ada.

"Yes," said Priscilla. "The same as you did me."

"I'm glad you want to," said Ada. "I want you to. Lie on top of me first."

"All right. Like a man?" said Priscilla.

"Just like a man," said Ada.

"Shall I do it like a man?" said Priscilla.

"Let's try that, shall we?" said Ada.

"I can't go in you, but we'll try."

"Maybe *I* can go in *you*," said Ada.

"Almost," said Priscilla. "You're almost in me. Oh, that's wonderful. Do that some more, and I'll come. Will you?"

"I think I am," said Ada. "Oh, that is wonderful. It's as good as coming."

"I came," said Priscilla. "I'm still coming. You're bigger than I am, that's why I came."

"You didn't quite come, did you?"

"Maybe not quite, but the sensation is the same," said Priscilla. "It's just as good."

"It was for me too."

"How do you feel?" said Priscilla.

"Glowing. Different from with a man, but glowing," said Ada.

"Now we must get some sleep, mustn't we? I have to be back in town at nine-thirty. I have a dentist's appointment."

"You have very nice teeth, Priscilla. You mustn't neglect them, not even for me."

"I like my bosom better," said Priscilla. "You like my bosom too."

"Yes, I do."

"That man that Bob made me sleep with, he liked my bosom," said Priscilla. "He really wasn't so awful, but Bob was. He was horrible."

"Shall we not talk about Bob tonight?" said Ada. "Or about that man? Unless you want to."

"Oh, I don't mind either way," said Priscilla.

"But you wanted to get some sleep," said Ada.

"It was Jerry Bolling," said Priscilla. "Bob put him up to it. They came in the house both pretty drunk and Bob lifted up my skirt right in front of Jerry, and the next thing I knew Jerry was doing it to me, and Bob was encouraging him."

"How do you mean, encouraging him?" said Ada.

"*Encouraging* him," said Phyllis. "Telling him what to do. Calling me names, names I wouldn't repeat even to you. Pushing Jerry's behind. Then Bob tried to do it and couldn't."

"Bob couldn't do it," said Ada.

"No. He was soft. He couldn't get an erection. All he could do was feel sorry for himself, and then he picked a fight with Jerry, and Jerry left the house in disgust. I don't blame Jerry for doing what he did. A man tells you to have your pleasure with his wife, and you lift up your wife's skirt, that's the limit. I never spent such a morning in my whole life, I never did."

The story, shocking though it was, incredible though it was, and sadly humorous though it was, was self-revealing of Priscilla and her life with Bob Hotchkiss and hardly less so of Bob Hotchkiss and his life with Priscilla. Ada wanted to be free of the girl, to get her out of the house, but she wrapped her arm around her shoulder and said, "Let's not talk about it any more. Let's get some sleep." The miserable, pretty creature. The miserable, pretty creature, whom Ada had wanted to abandon but now could not.

In the morning Priscilla had only a cup of coffee for breakfast. "I don't like to put a lot of food in my mouth before I see the dentist," she said. "I think it's very inconsiderate." She had a Scripps-Booth three-passenger roadster and looked very pretty driving away in it, waving all the way down the lane.

The Akron Tire & Rubber Company plant was only a few miles from Cleveland as the crow flies, but Bill Ewing had never seen it. "Oh, you *must* have seen it," said Jack McNair.

"I must have, but I never did," said Bill Ewing.

"Well, don't tell them that now," said Jack McNair.

"The stink kept me away," said Bill.

"Ah, then you've been to Akron?" said Jack McNair.

"Passing through," said Bill. "I was thinking of going to your alma mater, Kenyon, and I drove through Akron once or twice, but that was all. I decided on the University of Michigan instead."

"The stink is a lot worse than when you were there, but all the perfumes of Arabia won't change that now. Reason: nobody wants to change it. They'd rather have the profits from rubber."

Jack McNair and Bill Ewing were driving down to Akron because there was an important stockholder of Akron who was objecting to Bill's being made a director of the company. "This fellow Ed Lustig has made millions out of Akron Rubber, and he doesn't object to the stink. In fact, he probably doesn't even notice it. It's the breath of life to him."

"Poor man," said Bill.

"Poor man indeed," said McNair. "What he principally objects to is (a) your youth, and (b) your being a Clevelander. Not that he hasn't got four other Clevelanders on his board, but they're all older men. He wants to be told why you've been chosen."

"(A), because I'm young, and (b) because I'm a Clevelander, and (c) because I'm getting some stock from my mother," said Bill.

"He knows about the stock, all right," said McNair.

"Hold your nose, we're coming in to Akron," said Bill.

"You hold your temper, young man. This means a lot to you," said McNair.

Ed Lustig was an affable-seeming man, who wore a wing collar and a diamond stickpin. "It's very nice of you gentlemen to come all the way to Akron for lunch," he said. "Do you want to wash first?"

"We stopped on the way in," said McNair.

Lustig addressed his remarks to McNair but never took his eyes off Bill Ewing, until Bill made the discovery that he was cross-eyed. "Francis Ewing came in when our stock was selling at 4," said Lustig. "He was always optimistic as to our chances, but I doubt if even he thought it would go to where it is now. There were times when I wasn't, myself. You see that truck tire plant over there? That wasn't even built when your father passed on. Not even built."

"No, I guess it wasn't," said McNair.

"You can just bet your darn tootin' it wasn't," said Lustig. "The war wasn't even started then. That building was housing the Norka plant, bicycle tires, and losing money. Losing money hand over fist. I tried to market a clincher-type tire and almost went broke doing it. But I was right about the war. I went to work and converted the Norka plant and then I enlarged it, and it's still not big enough. Well, young man, some of our directors think there's a place for you on our board. Do you know anything about bicycle tires?"

"Bicycle tires? I know that a clincher-type tire would never sell," said Bill.

"Why?"

"People who ride bikes wouldn't take the time to change them," said Bill.

"Not even if you made the tires last twice as long?"

"Nor three times as long," said Bill. "They just wouldn't take time to change a puncture."

"But if your clincher types are all right for an automobile, why wouldn't they be all right for a bicycle?" said Lustig.

"A kid riding a bike doesn't have all day to change his tires," said Bill.

"Exactly. It took me four years to find that out. I guess because I didn't have a son. I only had my three daughters," said Lustig. "Well, gentlemen, how about some lunch?"

Luncheon, consisting of steak, mashed potatoes, lima beans, and ice cream, was served in a small dining-room adjoining Lustig's office. "I eat a steak every day of my life but Friday. Not that I'm a mackerel snatcher, but because I simply like steak. Half the time I do without my mashed potatoes, but I never do without my steak —except Friday. That one day I go without, always medium rare."

They finished their lunch and returned to the office, and Ed Lustig did not sit down. He remained standing as though the luncheon conference were over, as indeed it was. "Young man, you'll do," said Lustig.

"Is that all?" said Bill.

"I wouldn't find out any more about you if I kept you waiting an hour," said Lustig. "You can go back to Cleveland now, and I have work to do. You answered my question the right way, when I asked you about clincher types."

"What if I'd given you the wrong answer?" said Bill.

"Well, you didn't," said Lustig.

McNair and Bill Ewing got into McNair's Chalmers touring car. "It wasn't the answer you gave. It was the cut of your jib," said McNair. "Lustig is an independent cuss, and I guess you are too. I watched him when you were talking about clincher-type tires for bicycles, a pet project of his, and I thought, 'Ewing is spoiling his chances now.' But you weren't. You were enhancing them, by going against everything he was in favor of."

"It was no more than the truth," said Bill.

"Yes, but how many times would a man tell the truth in such

circumstances?" said McNair. "Now I have my eye on a directorate for you that may take a little longer. Sprague Chemical."

"What is Sprague Chemical?" said Bill.

"Sprague Chemical is a small firm that deals principally in nitrates," said McNair.

"Fertilizers?" said Bill.

"Another kind of nitrate. Explosives," said McNair. "I don't want you to say a word about this. Not even to Edna. It's very secret. The less you know about it now, the better."

"Who are the directors of Sprague Chemical?"

"George McVeagh, Alan Holcomb, Minor Hay," said McNair.

"Practically the same group as Cuyahoga," said Bill.

"The same money, but not as much of it. Not yet, anyway. It isn't listed on the New York Stock Exchange, and there isn't much trading in it. But there will be, later on. Frankly, it's considered a patriotic effort on the part of George McVeagh and the others. They've made a hell of a lot of money out of Cuyahoga and they're willing to lose some to get Sprague started. Don't ask who Sprague is. There is no such person. Sprague is actually a German chemist named Baer, B, a, e, r, Baer. Baer came from the Krupp Industries in the spring of 1914 and told our War Department about the war in Europe, but nobody paid any attention to him. He didn't speak so good the English, and for two years he had hard sledding because the Germans suspected him of being a traitor. Which, I may say, he was. Then he looked up a niece of his, who turned out to be Miss Schlatter, George McVeagh's secretary, and Miss Schlatter arranged a meeting with George. She spoke very little German, but enough to make George understand. George checked with our War Department and they asked him how he knew about Baer. They said they'd been trying to find him for a year, and George told them that they'd had him in their office in Washington but nobody paid any attention to him. By that time George had given him enough money to carry on his experiments, and Baer wouldn't go to Washington, or offer his services to the War Department. He trusted George and just about nobody else, and that's how George got first claim on his services. First and only claim."

"Where is the Sprague plant?"

"I'm not at liberty to tell you. Naturally there's a price on Baer's head," said McNair. "I haven't met Baer and neither have Minor Hay or Alan Holcomb. If you're interested in the name Sprague, by the way, that was the name of George McVeagh's old doubles partner at Harvard. He died in 1904 or '05, so it would be pretty difficult to trace any connection there. A secret chemical plant named after a dead tennis player. George could have named it Chalmers, after this car."

"The car would run better if you didn't leave your choke out so much," said Bill.

"Is that what it is?" said McNair. "I do that all the time. No wonder the carburetor's flooded. I get to talking and I forget about the car. Would you like to drive?"

"All right," said Bill. They changed seats and Bill took the wheel. "I can talk and drive at the same time, and I want to ask you something."

"Go right ahead," said McNair.

"What is the reason behind your getting me these directorships? I know you said it was because I worked so hard on Cuyahoga, but that's only part of the reason," said Bill.

McNair filled his pipe and lit it. "I was wondering when you might ask that question," he said. "Hard to keep a pipe lit in the car."

"I'll wait," said Bill.

"I'm preparing my answer," said McNair.

"I know that. That pipe comes in handy sometimes."

"Often," said McNair. "You're getting to know my habits too well. Your question was, why am I getting you these directorates, or directorships. Well, I'll tell you. First of all, because I need you. I want you to be my right-hand man, someone whose judgment I can rely upon and who knows my habits. My habits of thinking, not necessarily my habits of stalling with a pipe in my hand. Clarence Kelley was the first to bring you to my attention, because there were certain things about you that reminded him of certain things about your father. For instance, I happen to know that you were offered a good job with a New York law firm, starting as a clerk, and you turned it down because you preferred to work in Cleveland. Did you know that your father did the same thing? He did. Twenty or twenty-five years earlier your father was offered a job with Clendenning and Clendenning, which later became Edwards, Clendenning. That seemed to indicate that you were satisfied to remain in Cleveland, which pleased me, because *I've* been satisfied to remain in Cleveland. The practice of law is much the same everywhere in the United States, given certain peculiarities that make Louisiana different from, say, Rhode Island, Pennsylvania from Delaware."

"Yes," said Bill.

"Be patient, we have fifteen miles to go," said McNair. "In any case, I gave you a try, and you fitted in. And the few mistakes you made were mistakes I might have made myself. So then I thought why not make this young fellow a director of Cuyahoga? He couldn't do any harm, because there are about fifteen other directors on the Cuyahoga board and even if all his ideas were cockeyed, the other fourteen would vote them all down. Also, there was the fact that your father had been on the board of Cuyahoga, and I'm a strong believer in continuity. Cuyahoga is here to stay, and you'd be the youngest director now, but twenty years from now you wouldn't be."

"That, of course, makes sense," said Bill. "But it isn't the whole story."

"No, it isn't," said McNair. "But let me tell it my own way. Clarence Kelley was very much in favor of your being made a director, and in fact he wished it had been his idea. But Clarence isn't an envious man. If someone else has a good idea, he'll back it up. And he came to me about a month ago and suggested that inasmuch as your father had been a director of Akron Rubber, why not make you a director of Akron Rubber. And I said no. Cuyahoga was one thing, but Akron Rubber was different. Cuyahoga was mostly friends of your father's, gentlemen for the most part, who belonged to the Union Club and whose wives were friends of your mother's. Akron Rubber was a very different setup. It was run by Ed Lustig, a self-made man and a very tough customer. I could hear Ed Lustig raising the roof if they, or we, tried to put you in as a director there. Well, Clarence asked me whether I'd mind if *he* had a few words to say in your favor, and I said no, I didn't mind. So he did. And whatever Clarence said, Ed was won over."

"So that's how it was?" said Bill.

"No, not quite. There's one other directorship I want you to have, and that's Sprague," said McNair. "Oh, hell, I might as well tell you why I want you in Sprague, and you're not going to like it. I want you in Sprague for the same reason I wanted you in Cuyahoga and Akron Rubber. In plain language, I want you kept out of the army."

"So that's what you're aiming at? I should have known," said Bill. "I really should have known. Take the wheel, Mr. McNair. I don't feel like driving any more."

"I have one more thing to tell you, Bill," said McNair.

"You've told me enough for one day," said Bill.

"Will you listen to me while I tell you this? Don't stop the car, Bill," said McNair. "You've got to listen to me, you selfish kid. Do you know that I have only a year to live? Do you know that? A year, and maybe less. Ask Hendricks, he'll tell you. Ask my wife. Everybody knows it but you. I have a thing called auricular fibrillation, and that kills you, my young hero. No, everybody doesn't know. My son Scotty doesn't know. But Clarence Kelley knows, and my wife, and Dr. Hendricks. And now you."

They continued the ride back to Cleveland in silence. Bill, who was still driving, said, "Shall I let you out at the office?"

"Of course let me out at the office. It's only a little after three," said McNair. "Will you be in tomorrow?"

"Yes, I'll be in," said Bill.

"Leave the keys in the car, will you?" said McNair.

"No, I'll give them to you," said Bill. "I'm coming back with you."

On Sunday evenings in the summer Ada would sometimes send her car into town to fetch Clarence Kelley out to the farm for supper. It was a custom that had originated during a hot spell, and was repeated nearly every Sunday. "If you hadn't taken pity on me this summer, I'd have spent many evenings at the club, all by myself," said Clarence. "I don't mind it in the winter, but it gets pretty deserted along about June." They would eat their meal on the screened porch—chicken croquettes or a soufflé, out of respect for Clarence's dentures—and chat until ten o'clock, when it would be time for Clarence to go back to town. Clarence was always a good conversationalist, and if Ada suspected him of saving up topics for their Sunday evening chats, Ada did the same thing. "My dear, what is your opinion of Mr. Wilson and woman's suffrage?" he began one evening.

"Jointly?" said Ada.

"Or separately," said Clarence.

"Mr. Wilson leaves me cold. He's so professorial-looking. He leaves me cold. As for his interest in women's suffrage, how could he help it, surrounded by his wife and those daughters? His *second* wife and daughters. Mr. Baker is his secretary of war, but he's another Democrat, and I'm not for anything they're for."

"Not even woman's suffrage? Wouldn't you like to have the vote?" said Clarence.

"If I thought it would get rid of some of those Democrats. But Wilson is there till the war's over," said Ada. "I might be for it if the Republicans were in."

"They may be. It depends on when the amendment is voted in.

That may be just as Wilson is getting out. Then how would you feel about women's suffrage?" said Clarence.

"I don't think I'd vote. But I might change. Who's to say? A couple of years from now I might turn into a rabid suffragette. 'I should worry, I should fret, I should marry a suffragette.' I can't really get stirred up about it on a warm summer's evening," said Ada. "Notice those sycamores, Clarence. I wish we had more than two of them. We had three, but one was struck by lightning last spring."

But the next Sunday evening she said, "Do you remember last Sunday, asking me what I thought of women's suffrage?"

"I do," said Clarence.

"I found myself thinking about it all week," said Ada. "Why *shouldn't* women have the vote? Men have always had it, and look what condition the world is in now. You put a bee in my bonnet, Clarence. Is that what you meant to do?"

"Well, yes. All the suffragettes seem to be Democrats and you're a good Republican. Why should they have all the fun?" said Clarence.

"Now you're not proposing that I take an active interest in the suffragette movement? I couldn't do that. I wouldn't know where to begin."

"Why not begin at the beginning?" said Clarence. "Have a few women in for lunch—"

"And make a speech? Never," said Ada.

"Not a speech. But give a talk. Explain to the women that as a Republican, you're worried about the women's suffrage movement being taken over by the Democrats. And then ask them whether they're not worried too. Undoubtedly they'll say they haven't even thought about it, one way or the other. But give them a week, and they will think about it."

"Aha, the same way you did me," said Ada. "You're a sly one, Clarence."

"I've even planned your lunch for you," said Clarence. "Not more than six. I'd invite Jean McVeagh, because the McVeagh money will be necessary. Sara Holcomb, because she's active in the Junior League. Marcia Hay, because people like her. And Christine Frogg. That's four."

"Christine Frogg? She looks too much like a suffragette," said Ada. "The others I don't object to, but Christine, with her tweed suits and capes, is a bit too much."

"Then don't have her. But Christine is a worker, and she'd be very pleased to be asked. She does a great deal of charity work, you know. Not the Junior League sort of thing, but with poor people that you never heard of. Five afternoons a week. And she's a Republican."

"All right, I'll have her," said Ada. "When shall I have this get-together?"

"September sometime," said Clarence. "They're all away now, but they'll be coming back in September. Then you can have another luncheon in October, and another in November, December, January, so on."

"Why me, Clarence? Why not, for instance, Jean McVeagh or Sara Holcomb?" said Ada.

"Because I thought of you first," said Clarence.

"Well, that seems to settle it," said Ada.

Clarence did not let her forget the luncheon or its purpose, and he managed to make some mention of it every Sunday evening until the last Sunday in August. "Two weeks more," he said.

"Oh, I haven't forgotten," said Ada.

"The McVeaghs will be back the day after Labor Day, and the Holcombs sometime that week. I'm not sure about the Hays, but you can invite Christine Frogg any time. She's been in town all summer. But Jean McVeagh is your *pièce de résistance*, so invite her first."

"Whatever you say," said Ada.

The Monday after Labor Day was agreed upon, and at one o'clock the ladies arrived. They were all acquainted with each other, and they accordingly dispensed with introductions. "You're probably wondering why I invited you four to lunch," said Ada. "You were asked here because you're all Republicans."

"I'm not. My husband is, but Ah'm a dyed-in-the-cotton Dimmo-crat. Ah'm originally from Mobile, Alabama. So maybe Ah better leave," said Marcia Hay.

"You can stay, Marcia," said Ada. "Maybe we can win you over, or who knows, maybe you can win *us* over. The point is, Marcia and her Democratic friends have taken over the whole women's suffrage movement, and I've been wondering why we Republican women were content to sit idly by while they were doing it."

"Women's suffrage? It's a long way off," said Jean McVeagh.

"Ah, but is it?" said Ada. "So-called nice women, nice Republi-can women, may think so, but it's later than you think."

The luncheon lasted until two-thirty, and Christine Frogg stayed behind when the other women left. She was a rather stout woman with bobbed hair, wearing a crash suit and low-heeled shoes, and she was in her mid-thirties. "I've been interested in woman's suffrage for years," said Christine. "What got you inter-ested?"

"Clarence Kelley," said Ada.

"Dear old Clarence," said Christine. "I wonder how much we owe him. I would have gone on writing bad poetry the rest of my life if it hadn't been for Clarence. Then one day he came to my studio and saw some sculptures I had done and away went the poetry. A few kind words about my sculpture did it. If Clarence Kelly got you interested in woman's suffrage there must be some good reason, and I'm sure you have no idea what it is."

"None whatever," said Ada.

"Well, I think it's wonderful, and I just wanted to tell you so. It's a start," said Christine. "Now I have to go back to my other job. I'm a sculptress in the morning and a mission worker in the after-noon. Quite an unusual combination."

"How did you think the women enjoyed their luncheon?" said Ada.

"It was a start," said Christine, and left.

Clarence Kelley came to dinner to get a complete report on the luncheon. "I want to know everything," he said. "What they wore, what questions they asked, everything." Ada obliged him with the fullest report she could give, and added her guesses as to the individual woman's thoughts and reactions. As she finished, and they had their coffee in the library, he said, "Well, as Christine Frogg said, it's a start. Do you want to go on with it?"

"For a while, at least," said Ada.

"How did you like Christine?" said Clarence.

"Well, I've known her for quite a while but not well. Let's say I liked her better this time," said Ada.

"But leaving a lot of room for improvement," said Clarence.

"Yes, you can say that."

"You don't have to have her the next time. You don't have to have any of the women that were here today," said Clarence. "It might be interesting to see who you'd invite the second time."

"Well, of today's group, I suppose I'd invite Christine," said Ada. "I'll have to have Edna Ewing and some of the younger crowd."

"Priscilla Hotchkiss?"

"No, I don't think Priscilla would be interested," said Ada. "I'm very sorry I told you about Priscilla and me. It makes me self-conscious to mention her name."

"It makes me self-conscious too," said Clarence. "But I know what I know, and let's see if we can't turn that to our advantage. Have you wanted to see her lately?"

"Not as much, but I have her on my mind," said Ada.

"You know, of course, that at your time of life a lot depends on whom you see. A man would make a difference to you now. A man would probably drive Priscilla out of your thoughts, just as a man would probably drive you out of Priscilla's thoughts. Have you thought of that?"

"I have, but what man?" said Ada.

"Almost any man now," said Clarence.

"Walter Finch?"

"I said a man," said Clarence.

"Dr. Hendricks?"

"Well, he's a man, but he's too selfish for you. You're not suggesting anyone I think much of. I'd suggest myself if I were thirty years younger, but I'm not thirty years younger or twenty years younger. This man in Palm Beach, how old was he?"

"Forty-something."

"A good age for you."

"But he lives in Philadelphia, and he's otherwise occupied," said Ada. "The husbands of the women who were here today—George McVeagh, Minor Hay, Alan Holcomb—they're spoken for. Jack McNair."

"Jack McNair is dying," said Clarence. "He has less than a year to live."

"Oh, dear, does Bill know that?"

"He knows it now," said Clarence. "Jack had to tell him."

"His heart?" said Ada.

"Acute auricular fibrillation, it's called," said Clarence.

"Exactly what killed Francis," said Ada. "At least they go quickly."

"So I'm told," said Clarence. "I don't want to talk about Jack now. I want to talk about you, Ada. Have you wondered why I got you interested in woman's suffrage?"

"I've wondered a lot," said Ada.

"To distract you from your attachment to Priscilla. There's nothing in that for you, Ada, and I don't think you're happy in it. Priscilla is a pretty but stupid girl, very unhappy in her marriage, very unhappy in Cleveland. She'll cause trouble before she's through, mark my word."

"Yes, I know she's stupid," said Ada.

"Then get out of that liaison while you can," said Clarence. "The curious thing is, I'm sure she's looking for a man, and won't have a hard time finding one. There are always men for the Priscillas of this world."

"Women too, I guess," said Ada.

"Yes," said Clarence. "Ada, you're a woman who was faithfully married to one man for twenty-some years, and he died, a little before his time but at an age that isn't unusual for a man to die at. Then followed a period of deep mourning. That in turn was followed by the affair with Priscilla, which I can partly explain by your need for somebody while you were still unwilling to be untrue to Francis' memory. But you had an affair with the man in Palm Beach, and as you say, enjoyed it. You probably wouldn't have had the affair if you'd stayed in Cleveland, but Palm Beach was far enough away from your memory of Francis. The trouble is, you can pick up the telephone any time and continue having an affair with Priscilla, and every time you yield to that temptation you get in a bit deeper. In a few years, or even less, you'll have got in so deep with Priscilla that you won't want anyone else. But Priscilla won't be so steadfast. She'll drop you for a man, or a series of men, and you'll be left with nobody."

"I know, I know," said Ada. "I once told you that you know as much about women as any man alive, or words to that effect. How do you know so much?"

"How do you suppose?" said Clarence. "I went through the same experience that you're going through."

"But with a man?"

"With a man," said Clarence. "Instead of my wife dying, like Francis, she went on living and making my life a living hell. But I went through the same period of mourning that you went through, and then it was followed by an attachment for a man much younger than I that made up for my wife's cruelty."

"Was the man Francis Ewing?"

"Yes, it was," said Clarence. "I was content to have a kind of avuncular relationship with him. We never took baths together. But I've never known a man whose company gave me such pleasure. He was a good lawyer, if not quite a great one, and he had a hero-worship for me that I didn't quite deserve but that I tried to live up to. And I see some of the same characteristics in his son Bill. I'll do anything to keep that boy out of the army. He must go on living. And you, Ada, must help him in every way you can."

"So you loved Francis," said Ada.

"I loved both of you," said Clarence. "There, I think that'll be enough for one night. Besides, I don't want to keep faithful Walter waiting."

"What was the name of your sorority?" said Bill Ewing.

"Kappa Gamma Theta. Why?" said Edna.

"I have to fill out a paper saying what organizations I belong to, and it occurred to me that I don't know the name of your sorority," said Bill.

"Kappa Gamma Theta, also known as K. G. T., also known as Kiss George Tonight," said Edna. "I never did kiss George. In fact, the only George I knew well enough to kiss was George Shipe, from Wingate. He came up to Ann Arbor to see me one time, but it wasn't so much to see me as talk about Irma Frewling. Do you want to hear about Irma Frewling?"

"Not now," said Bill.

"You'd better hear about her now or I'll forget it. Irma was four or five years older than I was, and George couldn't decide whether to ask her to marry him or not because he'd heard stories about her. I'd heard stories too. But I knew what was the matter with Irma and George didn't, so he tried to find out from me. I couldn't tell him, or at least I wouldn't. Nice girls didn't talk about menstruating, so I didn't tell George what was the matter with Irma, but apparently she would menstruate for a month at a time."

"Why didn't you tell him she had the rag on? That's what they used to say at the Deke house," said Bill.

"He must have found out from somebody else, because he married Betty Schissler, and now they have two children," said Edna.

"So the story has a happy ending. What ever happened to Irma What's-Her-Name?" said Bill.

"Frewling. The last I heard she was working in Detroit."

"Well, I hope she doesn't have to stand on her feet all the time," said Bill.

"Poor Irma," said Edna. "What paper are you filling out now?"

"It's for the War Department records. I've been made a director of the Sprague company, subject to War Department approval."

"What is the Sprague company?"

"They're doing some work for the War Department," said Bill. "Where is it?"

"Oh, on the outskirts of Cleveland," said Bill.

"Why be secretive, Bill? If you don't want to tell me, just say so."

"I can't tell you, because I don't know myself."

"A director of the company, and you don't know where the company is?" said Edna.

"That often happens these days," said Bill. "You want to know too much."

"I'm only showing an interest in my husband's affairs," said Edna. "My husband, the big director."

They had been married over four and a half years, their son John-Stewart was three and a half years old, and it was close to the five years that they had once talked about as the limit of their residence in their present house. But wartime conditions precluded their consideration of moving, although wartime prosperity had made moving feasible. Bill was twenty-eight, making more money and known as a young man who was on his way, getting up, a fellow worth watching. His enemies—and he already had a few— were ready to say that his success was inevitable to the son of Francis Ewing, the assistant to Jack McNair, the eventual successor to Clarence Kelley. He had been made a member of the Union Club at twenty-six; he was elected to, but declined, the presidency of the Deke lunch club; and he was invariably seen in the company of older men, a reliable index of his maturity.

He was diffident and polite to the older women. "I don't think Bill Ewing likes me," said Jean McVeagh to her husband.

"And why not?" said George McVeagh. "Ought he to kiss your hand?"

"Oh, no. Hand-kissing isn't what I want."

"Arse-kissing, then?" said McVeagh.

"That neither," said Jean McVeagh, who was accustomed to her husband's vulgarities. "I'd just like him to show a little human warmth. I don't even think he likes his mother."

"Well, now, that *is* bad. Everybody knows a boy's best friend is his mother. Especially as Ada Ewing gave him all that stock."

"What stock was that, George?"

"Cuyahoga," said George McVeagh. "And Akron Rubber for good measure."

"I knew she had a lot of Cuyahoga shares. I didn't know about the Akron Rubber," said Jean.

"Well, you know now."

"Why did she give him so much stock?" said Jean.

"Because she doesn't need it, and he does. And probably because Clarence Kelley told her to."

"Is Ada rich?"

"Ada doesn't know how rich she is. That's the truth. But as long as Clarence Kelley knows, she'll be well taken care of. And as long as Clarence Kelley is looking out for Bill Ewing, he'll be all right."

"Has Ada got as much as we have?" said Jean.

"Nowhere near," said George. "But that still leaves her well off."

"She's going to want some money from me. Not right away, but the time will come. She's interested in woman's suffrage. She had me and Sara Holcomb and Marcia Hay to lunch, and for some reason, that Christine Frogg. You know what that means. Money. It was while you were in Chicago, after Labor Day."

"Well, what did you and Sara decide?"

"We decided to wait till we were asked to give, and *then* decide."

"Very wise. But of course you know that Clarence Kelley does Ada's thinking for her. Ada didn't think this up all by herself. She was never interested in politics. That brother of hers, Asa Bloodgood, tried to get a job in Columbus some years ago and asked her to help him. But she not only didn't know the governor—she didn't know who the governor was. I got that straight from Francis Ewing."

"Well, she's made up for that. She knows now. I was quite surprised," said Jean McVeagh. "That may be why Bill Ewing doesn't like his mother, she's a suffragette."

"Maybe," said McVeagh. "I'd be with him on that."

"Then I'll stay out of it," said Jean.

Sara Holcomb, a lifelong friend of Ada Ewing's, disagreed with Jean McVeagh's theory that Bill did not like his mother. "Those Bloodgoods—and Bill Ewing is half Bloodgood, don't forget—they never seemed to get along with one another, especially Ada and Asa. But there's strong family feeling there," she told Jean McVeagh. "Ada supported Asa from the time he was thirty. She'd never let him take a job that she didn't consider suitable. The result was, he never did take a job. Asa wanted to go to work managing the new hotel, and he might have been good at it. But Ada said they only wanted the Bloodgood name, and no Bloodgood had ever been in the hotel business. The hotel caught fire and burned to the ground, and Asa took that as an omen. At least he never tried to get a job after that."

"I don't see what that has to do with Bill," said Jean.

"I'm coming to that," said Sara Holcomb. "As far as I know, Bill has never asked his mother for anything. But for instance I happen to know she doubled his allowance at the University of Michigan, without his asking her to. His father gave him fifty dollars a month, and that wasn't enough for a Bloodgood, so she gave him an extra fifty, without telling Francis. And goodness knows how much Cuyahoga stock and Akron Rubber she's given him. Bill would go on not asking her, because Ada will give it to him anyway. Anything he gets from her has to be of her own volition, and I think that's nice."

Marcia Hay, who had known Ada Ewing less long than Jean McVeagh, did not participate in the discussion. "Bill isn't as loving and affectionate to Ada as my brother Robert is to my mother, but that's the way Yankee boys are," said Marcia Hay. "On top of which, Ada isn't the soul of affection herself."

Bill Ewing, whose affection or lack of it for his mother was the innocent cause of the discussion, would not have believed that any woman aside from his wife took that much interest in him. The men in his life were a different matter. Jack McNair. Clarence Kelley. Leftenant Colonel Abernathy, of the British Purchasing Commission. Stanley Nork of the Cuyahoga legal department. Ed Lustig, of Akron Rubber, George McVeagh, men whom he might see for an hour a week, but who would be in his thoughts a disproportionate length of time, made him a busy man. He was fondest of Jack McNair, the man who had told him he was dying, then never again spoken of his illness. He had the greatest admiration for Clarence Kelley, whom he had once thought to be his father. He liked, without affection, Stanley Nork. He respected, without admiration, Ed Lustig. He wanted Leftenant Colonel Abernathy to like him, without knowing why. And George McVeagh was so rich that Bill could not think of McVeagh without automatically associating him with wealth. They were good men to be doing business with. Clarence Kelley, because he was so old, could be trusted, and McNair could be trusted because he had such a short time to live. Ed Lustig could not be trusted because nobody trusted him and never had. George McVeagh could be trusted in money matters under half a million. Stanley Nork was trustworthy under fifty thousand. Leftenant Colonel Abernathy had no price but a K. B. E. at the end of the war to match his father's.

It was a personal profession, and trust was essential in it. A mutually trustworthy relationship saved time and enabled the principals to proceed with the transaction, leaving the details of legal language to be worked out later. Bill Ewing, under the influence of Jack McNair, had learned to trust most of the men he dealt with, and to tie them down by the terms of the actual contracts, which were not always exactly as the other principals had understood them to be. As a result, Bill was accused of sharp practice, but sharp practice was not dishonest practice. "You are a son of a bitch," said Stanley Nork on one occasion. "You slipped one over on me that time."

"How so?" said Bill. "We're both working for Cuyahoga."

"We are now, but I'm a union man," said Stanley.

"I know that, I've known it all along," said Bill. "If you try to slip one over on me on how much overtime you're entitled to, I won't let you get away with it. I know, for instance, that you'd like to be able to say to the union that you got them that overtime, but I'm just as anxious to be able to tell the company that I prevented it. When the war's over and you're a union lawyer, I'll fight you. But I don't like fighting you when you're being paid by the company. So who's the son of a bitch, Stanley?"

"You could have me fired," said Stanley.

"Maybe I could, but I'd rather have you where I can keep an eye on you," said Bill.

"That's very kind of you. Ruth's having another baby. But don't think that makes me forever grateful," said Stanley.

"The only thing you should be grateful for is that I caught you, but it's too late for that," said Bill.

"You're God damn right it is," said Stanley.

"You're a Catholic, aren't you? I thought they were against the Socialists," said Bill.

"I was never much of a Catholic. I guess I cared too much for poon-tang. Those girls at Ann Arbor settled my religion, and those professors changed my politics," said Stanley. "Do you remember Eddie Noisrander at Ann Arbor?"

"Yes."

"He's with the Heinies," said Stanley.

"I know," said Bill. "Have you heard from him?"

"I wouldn't hear from him. He was one of your Psi U's," said Stanley. "But I wish I could have talked to him before he joined the Heinies. He was a Psi U and one of your rich bastards, but he was as much out of it as I was, a Polack from Hamtramck with a strong back and a weak mind. That's what they used to say about us, the ones that played football. Why did Eddie Noisrander join the German army? Do you know?"

"I guess he just happened to be there at the beginning of the war," said Bill. "I don't really know."

"I think it was because he felt out of it at Ann Arbor," said Stanley. "I did too. But they were paying for my education, so I kept quiet. But I don't ever go back. They used to ask me to go back and make speeches before football games, but fuck them. Quid pro quo. I got my education out of them, and they got twenty-eight games of football out of me, plus the fact that it cost me two front teeth that they never paid for. I just wondered why Eddie Noisrander joined the German army."

"Your guess is as good as mine," said Bill.

"Yes, it could be even better, Bill. Socialists think better because they *think*," said Stanley.

"They think like Socialists, you mean," said Bill.

Bill used his own judgment about informing Jack McNair that Stanley Nork was a Socialist. He decided against telling McNair for two reasons: he could keep an eye on Nork, and he felt confident of being able to handle him; and, second, there was no use giving McNair anything extra to worry about. McNair seemed to be healthy, but Bill was more alert to signs of deterioration, and he began to detect such signs ever since McNair had told him about his heart. For one thing, McNair was short of breath. Apparently it was painless, and McNair did not complain about it, but more frequently than in the past year Bill would step into McNair's office and find him not at work. Simply not at work, as though McNair were taking a moment's rest. He would be looking out the window, seated at his desk with some papers in front of him, but paying no attention to the papers or to the people in the office building across the street. On such occasions he would seem not only dead tired but anticipating a strain that was yet to come. Upon Bill's entrance into the office McNair would take up his work, saying nothing about his condition, but faintly relieved or faintly irritated by Bill's appearance. There were other signs as well, indications that he was giving Bill more responsibility, assigning chores to Bill that he previously had taken on himself. Most significantly, McNair left the office at six o'clock every evening.

Then one day in November the inevitable occurred. It was late in the afternoon and McNair had stopped to fill his pipe while talking to Bill. A strained look came over his face and his voice was gentle as he said, "I think you'd better get me to the hospital. And call Dr. Hendricks."

Bill called Hendricks, who was making his hospital rounds, and left word with him. Then he helped McNair on with his overcoat and the two took a taxi to the hospital. "It came sooner than I expected, but I guess it always does," said McNair. He put his hand on Bill's knee. "Thanks for everything, Bill," he said. At the hospital Dr. Hendricks awaited them in the reception room.

"How're you feeling, Jack?" said Dr. Hendricks.

"Shaky," said McNair. "Shaky and weak. No pain to speak of."

"I have a private room for you," said Dr. Hendricks. "You can be quiet there. The nurse will help you get undressed. Your wife is on her way."

"Don't tell Scotty until you have to," said McNair.

"Scotty? Oh, your son. No, I'll leave that to your wife. As soon as Mrs. McNair gets here you can go home, Bill."

"The hell he can. The hell—he—can," said McNair.

"You heard what the boss said," said Bill.

It was the last speech McNair made to Bill. He died in his sleep two days later, and notwithstanding wartime conditions he was given a large funeral, larger than Bill had anticipated. Scotty was in England, learning to fly the planes of the Royal Flying Corps, and Bob Hotchkiss could not get leave; but Leftenant Colonel Abernathy was present, as were six or seven members of Alpha Delta Phi from Kenyon and four Kenyon trustees; George Mc-Veagh, Alan Holcomb, Minor Hay, Anton Czerniewicz, Stanley Nork, Edgar Ennis, representing Cuyahoga; Priscilla Hotchkiss; Heidi Schlatter, representing her uncle, Valdemar Baer; Ernie Herrick, steward at the Union Club; Mrs. Hendricks, the doctor's wife; and various fat and thin people who represented various periods of Jack McNair's life in Cleveland. After the funeral the body was put on the train for Mount Vernon, Ohio, where McNair was born and where the McNair family had a plot, and those who were able went to the home of Mrs. Francis Ewing for afternoon tea. "You'll have to tell me the names of most of these people," said Ada.

"Well, I'll try," said Clarence Kelley. "I see one you'll know."

"Priscilla. Yes, I noticed her at the church," said Ada. "She was sitting with Edna."

"Edna is going to have a busy time from now on," said Kelley.

"Why?"

"I've decided to make Bill a full partner. Why not? He's been doing Jack McNair's work, he's a director of Cuyahoga, a director of Akron Rubber, and a director of Sprague. He's not too young, although that will be the objection to him at first. But the sooner he gets used to being a full partner, the more valuable he'll be to the firm. He'll be thirty in a year and a half, and I was a full partner in the original firm when I was only thirty-two. Francis was one at thirty-three. Hotchkiss wasn't one till he was forty or thereabouts, I don't remember. This is essentially a young firm. Jack McNair was offered a full partnership when he was about thirty-five."

"Why did he turn it down?" said Ada.

"Frankly, he was afraid he might start drinking again, and he didn't want the responsibility. He was paid as much as a full partner, and heaven knows he did a full partner's work. It's settled, Ada. The announcement will be forthcoming in a month or so."

"Does Bill know?"

"No. I want you to have the pleasure of breaking the news to him," said Kelley.

"It'll come better from you," said Ada.

"I want him to hear it from your lips," said Kelley. "However, there's a fly in the ointment."

"What's that?"

"I'm going to make Bob Hotchkiss a partner," said Kelley. "I have to, to maintain the name of the firm, Hotchkiss, Ewing and Kelley. It's a whim of mine, and I hope it turns out all right, but if it doesn't I won't be around to see it fail. I can't take up any more of your time now."

"When shall I tell Bill?" said Ada.

"Tonight, this afternoon, whenever you like," said Kelley.

"One more question. Who's going to tell Bob Hotchkiss?"

"Oh, I'll write him a letter next week," said Kelley.

The gathering of the friends of Jack McNair was mercifully brief. Although Cleveland was a large city, most people went home to supper, not dinner, and did so in time for the early movie, bed by ten or ten-thirty. People got more sleep, worked longer hours, spent more time at home. There was no restaurant life in Cleveland, and the lights in the shop windows along Euclid Avenue went out at eleven o'clock. Ada's brother Asa Bloodgood had stayed for dinner after the McNair gathering, and he was so entertaining that Ada put off making her announcement to Bill until past ten o'clock. Then she said, "It's getting past my bedtime, Asa, and I want to talk to Bill."

"I was just leaving," said Asa, who was doing nothing of the kind, but he left.

"We ought to go, too," said Edna.

[169]

"Not till you hear what I have to say," said Ada. "It's for both of you, Edna. Bill, you're to be made full partner in Hotchkiss, Ewing and Kelley. Clarence told me this afternoon, and wanted me to tell you."

Bill was silent for a moment, then he looked at Edna and smiled. "I told you," said Bill. "I made it before I was thirty."

"Oh, you were expecting it?" said Ada.

"Let's say I was counting on it. Expecting it is another matter," said Bill. "Expecting it, counting on it, it's good news. How old was Dad when he became a partner?"

"Thirty-three, Clarence told me," said Ada. "I don't know whether I'm not supposed to tell you this, but Bob Hotchkiss is to be made a partner too."

"Oh, that's all right," said Bill. "As long as I got there first. Bob's thirty-three or four. Clarence and I will run things while Bob's away, and maybe by the time he gets back there'll be other changes made. Hotchkiss, Ewing and Kelley. That sounds pretty good. I assume that Bob hasn't been told."

"Clarence will let him know by letter next week," said Ada.

"I suppose there'll be one or two resignations from the firm," said Bill. "I'm pretty young to be made a partner, but Jack Mc-Nair didn't think so."

"No, and Clarence Kelley doesn't think so either," said Ada. "We ought to celebrate with some champagne."

"You haven't said a word, Edna," said Bill. "Aren't you pleased?"

"I don't see why Bob Hotchkiss is to be promoted. He hasn't done anything," said Edna.

"No, but he's a Hotchkiss, and I understand Clarence's thinking," said Bill. "If Bob were passed over, he'd no doubt resign from Hotchkiss, Ewing and Kelley."

"All right, let him," said Edna. "You've earned your promotion, while Bob was doing nothing. Now is the time to form a new firm, Ewing and Kelley. What if Clarence should die while Bob is in the army? Then it'd Hotchkiss and Ewing, without the Kelley, and Bob would come back from the army and inherit his partnership."

"I'm inclined to agree with Edna," said Ada.

"The war won't last forever," said Bill. "Let's do it Clarence's way for the present, and see what happens."

"Well, let's put off having the champagne till then," said Edna.

"Suits me," said Bill.

"That being the case, it's time we went home," said Edna. "Goodnight, Mrs. Ewing."

The reason Bob Hotchkiss could not get leave was that his division embarked for France on November 30. Priscilla went to New York to see him off, and returned to Cleveland without having slept with him. But she spent the night with Jerry Bolling, and the logical person to tell was Ada Ewing. "I think Jerry's in love with me," said Priscilla. "Wouldn't that be funny? I went to New York to sleep with Bob, but I end up in bed with Jerry."

"Why on earth are you telling me this?" said Ada.

"Well, you knew about Jerry, about how he slept with me in front of Bob. That awful experience. But it was different this time. He was sailing the day after Bob sailed, and Bob was so frightened about going to France that he simply couldn't have an erection. So he said why didn't I sleep with Jerry, and of course I said no, but I did. I hope I'm not pregnant, but if I am, Jerry's the man. It would certainly be interesting if Jerry got killed and Bob gets credit for being the father. I'm due next week, and I'm always on time, so I'll know then. When are we going to the farm again?"

"To the farm? I don't know," said Ada.

"I still like you, Ada. I hope you like me," said Priscilla. "I kept thinking about you. Do you know who else likes me? Christine Frogg."

"She does?"

"She asked me to pose for her, in the nude. I said I was afraid somebody would recognize me, but she positively assured me that

that wouldn't be necessary. She'd change my features. So I went to her studio and posed for her. Do you mind?"

"Why should I mind?"

"Well, I thought you—I don't know," said Priscilla.

"Have you told her anything about us, Priscilla?" said Ada.

"Well, I told her we took a bath together. I didn't tell her about the other time," said Priscilla. "All I told her was that we took a bath together, one hot summer's day."

"How long ago did you tell her that?"

"Oh, I guess it was a month ago," said Priscilla.

"Who else have you told?" said Ada.

"Nobody."

"Have you taken a bath with Christine?" said Ada.

"Well, yes I have. I was posing for her in the nude anyway, so she got in the tub with me. She had to stand up. There wasn't room for both of us."

"Did you kiss her?"

"No. She kissed me, but I didn't kiss her. She wanted me to, but I didn't. I'll only kiss you, down there. She practically pleaded with me, but I wouldn't."

"Does she always kiss you? When you pose for her?" said Ada.

"I guess so. Are you jealous?"

"Yes, I suppose I am," said Ada.

"You needn't be. She does things to me, but I don't do them to her," said Priscilla. "A man does things to me, but I like it better when you do. I could do without men for the rest of my life."

"I don't think I could, Priscilla."

"Well, maybe I couldn't either, not forever. Could you do without me?" said Priscilla.

"That's not a fair question, when you're sitting here and looking very pretty."

"Let's go out to the farm," said Priscilla.

"Let's go upstairs," said Ada.

"That's what I wanted you to say," said Priscilla.

They put their arms around each other and slowly climbed the stairs, and all of Ada's firm resolutions were gone. She had made up her mind not to touch the girl again, or to be touched by her, but the thought of her being kissed by Christine, and the knowledge that Christine already knew about the bath they had taken together, made her abandon caution. They got undressed and Ada kissed the girl as hungrily as though it were for the first and last time. "Men don't know, do they?" said Priscilla.

"Is that what it is?" said Ada. "I guess they don't."

"Even with their cocks they don't know," said Priscilla.

"Would you like me better if I had one?" said Ada.

"A cock? Then you wouldn't be you," said Priscilla.

"I've never said that word," said Ada.

"Cock? Do you know what Bob is? He's a cock-sucker. He's in the United States Army, but he's a cock-sucker. Think of that! So am I, but it's different with me. I don't have to be ashamed of it, the way Bob is. In a way I feel sorry for him."

"Shall we not talk about Bob?"

"O.K. with me," said Priscilla. "I could stay here forever, but it's time I got home. Will you phone me tomorrow?"

"Yes," said Ada.

She hated to see the girl go, but equally she hated to face her own thoughts when she was alone. What was she, a middle-aged woman, doing, having an affair with a young girl? What had happened to the years of contentment with Francis Ewing? What was she, a woman past middle age, doing with a girl young enough to be her daughter, when she had not even known what a woman her age did with a girl Priscilla's age? And she had not known. The heat of the summer's day had more or less dictated that they remove their clothing and take a bath together, but her lifelong habit of modesty could have prevented her from displaying her body to the girl. Was her pride in her figure so deep that she had had a desire to match her body with that of the girl? Her breasts were as firm as the girl's, her hips no broader, her legs as slender. But in truth, pride in her body had had nothing to do with what had happened to Priscilla and her. It was lust, a desire to kiss the girl and to be kissed by her. What then was the lust? Pride and curiosity might explain the first incident, but not the second. The second time was all lust, the emulation of a man by both of them, the sharing of exciting positions, and the final pathetic lies they told each other. Priscilla hated men, and not without reason; Ada still loved Francis, because he was her partner.

She would go to Clarence Kelley.

"Come to dinner tonight," she said. "Just the two of us. I'm having trouble."

"Priscilla?" said Clarence.

"Yes. I need your help," said Ada. "I'll have chicken croquettes with brown gravy. And I'll send Walter for you."

"That will be fine. Taxis are scarce," said Clarence.

He arrived at a few minutes past seven, carrying his silver-mounted, black ebony cane. "I think I'll take this in with me," he said. "It was given me by your husband, of all people, on my sixtieth birthday. It's been useful lately."

"What does it say on it?" said Ada.

"It says 'C. K.' and that's all. It's a very handsome cane, don't you think?" said Clarence. "I remember thinking when he gave it to me, 'Do I need a cane?' Well, I didn't then, but I do now. That was twenty years ago."

"Shall we go in?" said Ada.

"Yes, let's," said Clarence.

She noticed how slowly he walked on the way in to dinner. "It's very nice of you to come."

"I'd come any time you sent for me. I miss our Sundays at the farm," said Clarence. "I feel I got to know you better then than at any other time, Ada."

"And I you," said Ada. "Clarence, what's the matter with me?"

"I've been giving that a lot of thought," he said. The maid served the bouillon. "I don't know that there's anything the matter, except that you're a rich woman with too little to do. Idle hands, you know."

"The plaything of the devil," said Ada. "Here are our croquettes and little peas. That will be all, Cora. We'll have coffee in the library."

"Is that a new maid?" said Clarence.

"This week. Why?"

"She heard you ask me what was the matter with you, and she's dying of curiosity."

"She's lazy. I'm not going to keep her," said Ada. "Now we can talk."

"You're having some sort of trouble with Priscilla. What kind of trouble?"

"Trouble of my own making," said Ada. "Why does this girl excite me, Clarence? Why her, and nobody else? Edna, for instance, is prettier, but she doesn't excite me. She would die if she knew about Priscilla and me, and Bill would have me put away."

"No, he might be embarrassed, but he'd never have you put away. As to why Priscilla excites you, you have to answer that yourself," he said. "I wonder how many times this same sort of situation occurs that we never get to know about. Oftener than we think, is my guess. If a man dances too often with the same girl, we naturally conclude that he's sexually attracted to her, and we look for some overt, or covert, act on his part. But you mustn't think that you're the only woman that was ever attracted to another woman. It goes back to the island of Lesbos, at least."

"Lesbos?"

"Lesbos. Sappho. Five or six hundred years before Christ. Hence the term Lesbian, meaning a woman who is attracted sexually to another woman. According to the modern definition, you are having a Lesbian affair with Priscilla, and she with you."

"Lesbian. I've never heard the term," said Ada.

"Not many have. It isn't taught in college," said Clarence. "I doubt if one in ten thousand know what it means. Good croquettes, Ada."

"Yes, aren't they?" she said.

"When I was a young man I took a trip abroad, even before I was married. I went with another young man. and naturally we visited the bordellos. One I remember was in Naples, and there I saw for the first time the acts of perversion between two or three women. I didn't know such things existed, but apparently they not only existed but were very popular, not only in Naples but elsewhere. Berlin. Paris. London. I came back from Europe with entirely new ideas about women, and some of them never left me. I looked for places like that in New York and Chicago, but I guess I didn't look hard enough, because I never found them."

"You looked for them after you were married?" said Ada.

"Yes I did. My marriage was an unhappy one. Not that I take all the blame for that. Not that I blame my wife for it either. But she took dope and I didn't. You knew that."

"Yes," said Ada.

"So I had to look elsewhere for feminine companionship, to call it that," he said. "My wife was addicted to morphine, which finally killed her. And who's to say she didn't take an overdose deliberately? She was an unhappy woman, but I was an unhappy man. Ever since she died, which is now about fifteen years ago, I've been trying to fix the blame for our unhappy marriage, and I must say I'd make a pretty poor judge, arguing both sides of the case."

"Shall we have our coffee in the library?" said Ada.

"Yes, I like that room," said Clarence.

"Francis' law books will be Bill's any time he wants them, but that will be when he gets another house," said Ada.

"I must repair to the gentlemen's retiring room. You'll excuse me," said Clarence.

He entered the library, cane in hand, and had his coffee. "I haven't been much help to you," he said. "Let me try again. My bladder is good for an hour now, and my thoughts are a bit clearer now. Ada, your problem is not only that of a rich woman with too little to do. It's deeper than that. As I see it, you're not going to want to give up this girl—or rather let me put it this way. You're not going to give up this girl till you want to, and you're not going to want to till you have someone else to take her place. Who that will be, and when, I have no idea. But why shouldn't it be another woman? I couldn't have said that twenty years ago, but I can say it now. You're really alone in the world, Ada. Bill and Edna, and your brother Asa, if you want to include him, are not dependent on you for anything, and you're not dependent on them. Do you remember my suggesting that you go to California?"

"Yes."

"I suggest it again," he said. "If only because it will get you away from Priscilla. Go away for a couple of months, and if I know Priscilla, she'll have a man in that time. Maybe two men. Maybe three. In any event, she'll be out of your life. And you'll have found a man or a woman to take her place. Frankly, it doesn't make any difference whether it's a man or a woman, as long as it's *somebody*."

"That's quite a solution," said Ada. "And do you know what? I'm going to try it."

"Don't be too impetuous, Ada. Think it over. But it's the clear thinking of a man who's just been to the bathroom."

"Is it all right if I see Priscilla once again?" said Ada.

"What harm will that do? I never heard of a woman getting pregnant from another woman," said Clarence.

"I didn't mean that."

"I know you didn't," he said. "You're afraid she'll be irresistible. What if she is? You can make love to her and do all those Lesbian things to her, and have a tearful farewell. Just as long as you've made up your mind to spend three months away from her."

"I like the idea. For the first time I feel free," said Ada. "I may not even see her tomorrow."

"See her tomorrow, and let me know how it all comes out," said Clarence.

The old man was pleased. He sat turning his cane by his thumb and forefinger.

"What are you thinking?" said Ada.

"I was thinking that there's nothing pleases an old man so much as having his advice taken," he said.

Edna and Bill Ewing and their son John-Stewart were to spend Christmas with the Everetts in Wingate. "This'll probably be the last chance I get for a hell of a while," said Bill. "Most law offices are closed during Christmas, so I might as well go while I can. After Christmas there's no telling when I'll get any time off."

"What about your mother?" said Edna.

"She can spend Christmas with Uncle Asa. And after that she's talking about a trip to California. California! In wartime! But she has an old friend in Santa Barbara, Mrs. Shipley, whose husband just died a few months ago, and Mother would like to visit her."

"Will you make the reservations to Wingate?" said Edna.

"I'll make them through the office," said Bill.

"Get a drawing-room. John-Stewart can have his nap."

"So can William Bloodgood," said Bill.

They were met at the Wingate station by Mr. and Mrs. Everett, whom neither of them had seen since the previous summer. It was dark, but not dark enough to hide the Pierce-Arrow, which was by way of a surprise for Bill. "Well, how do you like it?" said Paul Everett. "I waited almost two months for it. It had to come from Buffalo, New York, by freight. They could have driven it, but I didn't want anybody else to handle it."

"It's a splendid car."

"The only one in Wingate, if that's any distinction," said Paul Everett. "I have about a thousand miles on it already. Do you want to drive it?"

"Oh, thank you, Mr. Everett, but I'm used to the Dodge shift," said Bill. "I might strip your gears. You'd better drive it."

"You can drive it if you like," said Paul Everett. "But the Dodge shift is a lot different."

"Is this Grandma's car?" said John-Stewart.

"Grandma Everett's car," said Bill. "Not Grandma Ewing's."

"Imagine the child knowing that," said Mrs. Everett.

"I want to sit in front with Daddy," said John-Stewart.

"All right, I'll hold him," said Bill.

"He can sit on your lap, Bill," said Paul Everett. "I'll take you for a *good* ride tomorrow, John."

"Can I blow the horn?" said John-Stewart. "*Walter* let's me."

"All right, you sit with your father and blow the horn," said Edna. "He had a nap on the train."

"Oh, then you must have had a drawing-room as far as Detroit," said her mother.

"And to Wingate," said Edna. "Bill made reservations through the office."

"We're having some people in for dinner this evening," said her mother.

"Bill has to go back the day after Christmas," said Edna.

"Not you, I hope," said her mother. "I was hoping the baby could stay for his birthday."

"Everybody ready?" said Paul Everett. "Off we go."

"Business must be good," said Bill.

"I'll say it is," said Paul Everett. "Hence the Pierce-Arrow. Government orders for a thousand desks, all made to government specifications. A thousand desks and a thousand chairs. That's the biggest order we've ever had. They sure know how to spend money in Washington, but I guess it's the same all over. Yes, we're getting our share of wartime business."

"Ah-ooh-gah, ah-ooh-gah," said John-Stewart.

"Listen to him, imitating the horn," said Mrs. Everett.

"Isn't he clever?" said Edna. "*Isn't—he—clever?*"

"Edna, I think you're tired," said her mother.

"I was the only one didn't get a nap on the train," said Edna.

"I'll take care of John while you get a few minutes' rest before our guests come. They're not expected till eight, and it's only ha' past five."

"I've been up since six o'clock this morning," said Edna. "And I didn't get much sleep last night, packing and all."

"You have a nap," said her mother.

Edna did not get her nap. What with unpacking for herself and John-Stewart, and a few minutes' conversation with Bill on how he thought Mr. and Mrs. Everett looked, and deciding who would sleep where, it was past seven o'clock by the time she undressed. Then her mother, for the fourth or fifth time, came into the bedroom and saw her in her chemise. "Are you having another baby?" said Mrs. Everett.

"Yes. Does it show that much?" said Edna.

"It does on you, you're usually so slender," said her mother. "I knew there was *something*. When are you having it?"

"Dr. Vogel says sometime in April."

"Uh-huh. You and Bill must have started it when you were here last summer," said Mrs. Everett.

"I know we did," said Edna. "I could almost tell you the night."

"Well, you don't have to go into details," said her mother.

"Oh, come on, Mother. You'd listen if I told you, only I'm not going to," said Edna.

"That's where you're wrong, Edna. Did I ever ask you anything about your private life?"

"Yes, you did."

"Only when it was necessary," said Mrs. Everett. "Only when it was necessary."

"For my own good," said Edna. "*Speaking* of Eddie Noisrander, which of course we weren't, what's the news of him?"

"I haven't heard a thing. You knew his younger brother enlisted in the marines. I'm surprised they took him, but they did. He went to camp somewhere in Virginia, and right away they shipped him overseas. Kurt. He was five or six years younger than Eddie."

"Yes, he went to Culver Military Academy, but not at the same time. We invited him to our wedding, but he couldn't come. He had to be back in school. I'll have to tell Bill, although I guess I won't. The army is a touchy subject in our household."

"I'm so glad Bill doesn't have to go."

"Well, he isn't," said Edna. "Who's going to be here tonight?"

"You'll see. Nobody you don't like," said her mother. "I hope the new baby will be a girl."

"I haven't any preference," said Edna.

"Does Bill know? Last time, you didn't tell him."

"This time I did," said Edna. "And you can tell Daddy if you like."

"It doesn't show so much," said her mother. "It's just that you're so slim-waisted. I always envied you your slim waist."

"I'm going to lie down, even if I don't get any sleep. I want to get off my feet," said Edna.

Her mother lingered on until a few minutes before eight.

Since it was the day before Christmas Eve, there was a great deal of talk about trimming the Christmas tree and Christmas presents. The Everetts had an eight-foot spruce tree, yet to be trimmed, standing bare in the corner of their livingroom. "Why don't we all pitch in and trim the tree now, and get that over with?" said Edna.

"Oh, that wouldn't be right," said her mother.

"Why not?" said Edna.

"I think everybody ought to trim their own tree," said Mrs. Everett.

"We trimmed ours this afternoon," said Bertha Linkletter Dowd. "At least I did. Harry didn't get home till too late. There was the usual party at the Elks'."

"And I was on the water-wagon," said Harry Dowd.

"You on the water-wagon? When did that happen?" said Ann Collins Pierce.

"It's my third day," said Harry Dowd.

"Oh, then you're on the water-wagon with a vengeance," said Tom Pierce. "How come you picked the holidays?"

"I didn't pick them," said Harry Dowd. "Bertha did. She said if I'd go on the water-wagon for Christmas, that would be my Christmas present to her. Fine, except that she knew damn well I'd bought her present already."

"What did you give her?" said Ann Collins Pierce. "I won't tell her."

"I'll whisper it to you," said Harry Dowd. He whispered in Ann's ear.

"Oh, you didn't!" said Ann Collins Pierce. "I happen to know it's just what she wanted, and she'll never guess."

"I had to send to Detroit for it," said Harry Dowd.

"You could have got one in town," said Ann Collins Pierce. "I saw one at Hempstead's."

"What did you see at Hempstead's?" said Tom Pierce.

"Bertha's Christmas present," said Ann Collins Pierce. "Or one like it."

"I'll bet I know what it is," said Tom Pierce. "It's an electric train, made by Lionel."

"No, but that's close," said Harry Dowd. "Isn't it, Ann?"

"Sort of," said Ann. "But not really."

"Can I join this conversation?" said Edna.

"You can, but Bertha can't," said Harry Dowd. "We're talking about Bertha's Christmas present."

"Does she know what it is?" said Edna.

"She thinks she does, but she doesn't," said Harry.

"Don't tell her, don't tell her," said Mrs. Everett.

"Tom says it's an electric train," said Harry.

"An electric *train?*" said Mrs. Everett. "What kind of a—oh, you're joking. Well, dinner's ready. Bill, you sit next to me, please."

The dinner lasted too long, and when the guests left, which they did together, Bill announced that he was going to bed. Edna followed him. "You could have stayed and talked to Daddy," she said.

"I don't mind talking to your father, but two hours of your mother is enough for one evening," said Bill. "Two hours of gossip about people I don't know and don't care about. I don't see how your father stands it."

"He loves her, that's how," said Edna. "And you can put up with her for a few days. She had everything you like for dinner, and God knows your mother isn't the easiest person to talk to."

"For God's sake leave my mother out of it," said Bill. "You've been cranky ever since we came to Wingate, and I'm going to bed. Just because you're pregnant is no excuse."

The next day, after a ten o'clock breakfast, Bill joined Paul Everett in an inspection of the furniture factory and its thousand desks and chairs. "I thought I might take you to lunch at the hotel," said Paul Everett. "Our wives are going to be busy most of the day. Is that all right with you?"

"Yes, of course," said Bill.

"There's a good bunch of fellows eat at the hotel every day," said Paul Everett. "It's Monday, but they'll be there, most of them. And most of them will be working Christmas Eve. That's the war for you. By the way, it isn't Rotary."

"I've never been to a Rotary Club meeting," said Bill.

"This is different," said Paul Everett. "I belong to Rotary, but this is a whole lot different."

Bill could see that Paul Everett had come up in the world by the company he kept at the Round Table. They were not much different from the Union Club. Eight of them, out of twelve, sat down to lunch that day, and by their clothes, their manners, their conversation, they demonstrated that they were the elite of Wingate. "Gentlemen, I'd like to introduce my son-in-law, Bill Ewing," said Everett. "Bill is from Cleveland." Some of them had been to Edna and Bill's wedding, and said so. Then they took their seats and ordered lunch. "You went to Ann Arbor, didn't you?" said the man on Bill's right. "Did you know my son?"

"I'm sorry, I didn't get your name," said Bill.

"Van Nostrand, my son's name was Philip."

"Oh, Phil Van Nostrand. Of course I knew him. He was a class behind me. What's he doing now?" said Bill.

"Right now he's in the army, waiting to be sent overseas," said Van Nostrand. "He's with the Medical Corps. I suppose you knew he studied medicine, although there's no reason why you should."

"I did see it in the alumni magazine," said Bill. "Phil would make a good doctor."

"Well, I thought so. I'm glad you agree with me," said Van Nostrand. "You studied law, didn't you? I'm a lawyer myself."

From Van Nostrand, Bill's attention went to Stephen Linkletter, the uncle of Bertha, and from Linkletter to a man named Logan, who had just shot his fourth moose, and from Logan to a man named Eldridge, who had just sold his five hundredth Buick. They were all men of affluence, including Logan, who was currently planning to go to Alaska and hunt for the Kodiak bear.

"How did you like my friends?" said Paul Everett.

"I like them just fine," said Bill.

"I've known them all my life, but I'd hardly say they were always friends of mine. Then one day two years ago Logan invited me to sit with them at the Round Table, and I knew I'd begun to amount to something. They just about run things in this town. It's funny, I'm the only member of Rotary that was ever invited to the Round Table. But I still go to Rotary."

"Why not?" said Bill.

"You know why not, Bill," said Everett. "But there was a time when I was lucky to get in Rotary, and I don't forget that," said Everett. "Shall we put a little mileage on the Pierce-Arrow? You sure you don't want to take the wheel?"

"No, you drive," said Bill.

They went to the garage back of the hotel and got the car. Everett was silent for the first few minutes. "You know, for the sheer pleasure of driving you can't beat a Pierce-Arrow," he said. "It's a lot of car, mind you. It takes careful handling, and it sure eats up gas. But you expect that. I haven't had her on any long rides so far, but I get somewhere around six or seven miles to the gallon and I won't get much more, even when the car's broken in. The man from the factory told me that. He said to me, 'Don't expect a Pierce-Arrow to set any economy records, Mr. Everett.' He said it'd be the same whether I had a Packard or a Winton or any other big car. They're just not engineered to save gas and oil . . . We'll drive out to where they're planning to build the new country club. They have enough land for an eighteen-hole course but they're planning to start with nine. They didn't show much originality with the name, the Wingate Country Club, but some of these Dutchmen wanted to call it the Utrecht Country Club, and that was worse than Wingate. There aren't that many Dutchmen around here anyway . . . Notice a few snowflakes? The paper was right. This looks as if it might last. The wind is from the west, and this time of year that usually means snow. Comes all the way from Lake Michigan, and let me tell you, it can be no laughing matter. But you knew that, from your four years at Ann Arbor . . . There, now, you see where those woods are? That's the western boundary of the country club. A fine stand of oak, mostly. Any time the club likes to sell, I'll be in the market, but I don't look for that to happen soon. Besides, the owner isn't anxious to sell, and he has plenty of money. Whitehill is his name, J. Clinton Whitehill, the only Yale graduate in Wingate. He has a son, J. Clinton Junior, living on

Long Island. Whitehill made his money in copper, and I'll bet he's coining it now. Coining money in copper. I almost made a joke. But it's no joke the amount of money Clinton Whitehill's making. He used to be the richest man in Wingate, and now he must be one of the richest men in the whole of Michigan."

"Edna mentioned him to me," said Bill. "They sent us a wedding present."

"Oh, I'm sure they did," said Everett. "He took sort of a liking to me, through fishing, I guess it was. He's a great friend of Sterling Logan, that you met at lunch today, and it wouldn't surprise me if Clinton Whitehill was behind Logan inviting me to the Round Table. Well, there you see the site of the new country club, and now I guess it was time we started back."

Paul Everett put the car in the garage and closed the double-doors. "Well, I enjoyed our day," he said. "There's one thing more I wanted to mention, Bill. Be nice to Edna. Not because she's pregnant, but Christmas in this house—the year before you were married she had a friend visit her over Christmas, Faith McCracken. They came home from a dance and retired for the night. But we found Faith lying on the bathroom floor, naked as a jaybird, asphyxiated. Christmas here always brings back Edna's memory of that unfortunate incident, and I'll tell you something I've never told Edna or Mrs. Everett. Faith was pregnant. So be nice to Edna, will you?"

"I will," said Bill. "I knew about Faith McCracken, but I didn't know she was pregnant. You know, Mr. Everett, you're a hell of a nice man."

"Oh, well," said Paul Everett. "Anyway, I'm not all business and making money, the way some would have you believe." The Christmas spirit was a time for understanding, and Bill was sure he understood.

He had made up his mind to be especially nice to Edna, but it was not hard. A night's sleep, and possibly a day with Mrs. Everett, had made her less cranky. In any event, she was glad to see him when he returned from the ride with her father. "Where did you have lunch?" she said.

"At the Round Table," said Bill.

"Where's that?" said Edna.

"Oh, you don't know about the Round Table," said her mother. "That's a big event in your father's day, lunch at the Round Table. It's a group of men who meet at the Wingate Hotel. Your father thinks they're important, so I guess they are."

"Who are they?" said Edna.

"Oh, I didn't mean they weren't important. It's just that your father seems to think they're the twelve Apostles, and I won't go that far," said Mrs. Everett. "They're a bunch of rich men who think they're better than anyone else."

"Like the Union Club in Cleveland," said Edna.

"I guess so," said her mother.

"Quite a lot like the Union Club," said Bill. "Of course, Edna has never been inside the Union Club."

"No, but I know what it's like," said Edna. "A bunch of old men—"

"And young men trying to be old men. I'm one of those," said Bill. "I said that before you did."

Edna's mood was a bantering one; she could adopt the mood when she was free of her mother. It occurred to him, for the first time in the dozen times they must have visited this house, that he had never seen a gas burner in the bathroom. He wondered if Paul Everett had had it removed. It would be just like Paul Everett. In any case, he had never seen the instrument of Faith McCracken's suicide, and he liked to think that Paul Everett had had it removed during Edna's second semester at Ann Arbor, with or without consulting Mrs. Everett. It occurred to him, too, that he had grown enormously fond of his father-in-law. Why was that so? The relationship between a man and his father-in-law could be strained and unnatural by virtue of the fact that the sexual relationship between the man and the father-in-law's daughter could never be mentioned. You got used to it, you took it for granted. But it was always there, closer to the surface than the man or his father-in-law permitted. And Bill wondered whether the subtle strangeness that had come between himself and his mother did not have something to do with it. What *was* the subtle strangeness? He did not know, but he admitted it was there. He loved his mother, and she loved him, but they were no longer as close as they once had been. Was that a natural consequence of his happy marriage to Edna?

"What are you thinking of?" said Edna.

"I'm thinking of myself trying to be an old man," said Bill.

"You weren't thinking anything of the kind," said Edna. "I know you, Bill Ewing."

"Then tell me what I was thinking," said Bill.

She whispered to him: "You were thinking how you couldn't stand my mother. Am I right?"

"Oddly enough, you were very close," said Bill.

"I have to put up with her, she's my mother," said Edna. "But if I had to spend another day at Hempstead's Emporium, buying last-minute Christmas presents, I don't think I could. Anyway, I bought you a nice present. I hope it fits you. Do you want me to give it to you now?"

"Of course," said Bill.

"All right, I will," she said. "And I paid for it myself. I'll get it."

She went to the hall and came back with a large package. "Open it," she said.

He did so, and it turned out to be a sheepskin coat. "By God, it's just what I wanted. It really is," he said.

"Oh, you *didn't* go and give him his *present*," said Mrs. Everett. "It isn't Christmas yet."

"It is in Greenland or Spain," said Edna. "Try it on, Bill."

"Oh, I just don't think it's right to open your Christmas presents before it's Christmas," said Mrs. Everett. With that they proceeded to open all the presents except those for John-Stewart, which they saved for morning: a pair of fur-lined gloves for Paul Everett, a

Persian lamb coat and matching hat for Edna, a sealskin muff for Mrs. Everett, a pair of ice skates for Bill, a copy of *Who's Who in America* for Paul Everett, a pair of snowshoes for Paul Everett, a silver-mounted fountain pen for Bill, another silver-mounted fountain pen for Bill, a cigar humidor for Paul Everett, a pair of silver peacocks for Mrs. Everett, a year's subscription to *The Delineator* for Mrs. Everett, three sweaters for Edna, a diamond wristwatch for Edna, a diamond bracelet for Mrs. Everett . . . They all stayed up until one o'clock in the morning. "Oh, dear, I forgot about Midnight Mass," said Mrs. Everett. "I told Margaret Brady I'd meet her there. I hope she didn't wait for me. She was going to save me a seat in her pew."

"What on earth would you be doing in a Catholic church?" said Edna. "And who is Margaret Brady?"

"Margaret Brady, a very nice woman moved here from Grand Rapids," said Mrs. Everett.

"Her husband came to work for me last summer," said Paul Everett. "He's an expert on finishes. John Brady. I got him from the Ottawa Furniture Company."

They retired, and when Bill got in bed with Edna she said, "Thank God, you're not Christmas."

"Why?" said Bill.

"Christmas comes but once a year," said Edna.

In the morning John-Stewart was out of bed before sunrise, the first member of the household to be up. The hall light was on and he made his way to his parents' room. "Mummy, I want to go to the bathroom," he said.

His mother was sleeping soundly, but his father got awake. "Go back to bed," said Bill.

"I wanta go to the bathroom," said John-Stewart. "I don't know where it is."

"Oh, Christ," said Bill. He got out of bed and led John-Stewart to the bathroom, where he urinated.

"Is Santa Claus here yet?" said John-Stewart.

"Oh, that's what you want," said Bill. "Yes, he's been here. Let me take a leak first." The boy watched fascinated while his father urinated, then put on his bathrobe and slippers and the two went downstairs.

"Where are my presents?" said John-Stewart.

"Under the tree, you dumbkopf," said Bill. "Be quiet or you'll wake up your mother. What do you want to open first?"

"Did I get an electric train?" said John-Stewart.

"You got a train, but not electric," said Bill. "Here, I think this is a flashlight. Yes, it's a flashlight. That should come in handy when you can't find the bathroom." The boy took the flashlight, then wound up his mechanical train, then played with the wooden animals under the circus tent, then watched his father releasing the cowboys and Indians that were held by an elastic cord to a piece of cardboard.

"Didn't I get a bicycle?" said John-Stewart.

"A tricycle. I think it's in the hall," said Bill.

Edna came downstairs. "Young man, it's not even five o'clock yet. You go back to bed."

"Aw, Mummy, must I?"

"Let him stay up," said Bill. "He's wide awake, and I'm getting there."

"Do you want a cup of coffee?" said Edna.

"Might as well," said Bill. She sat on his lap and they watched their son playing with the cowboys and Indians. "Merry Christmas, little mother," said Bill.

"Merry Christmas to you, big father," said Edna. "I'll get your coffee."

"One of my cowboys broke his arm," said John-Stewart. "Can you fix it, Daddy?"

"No, you'll have to pretend he's a cowboy with a broken arm," said Bill.

"Quick thinking," said Edna.

[190]

"What else did you expect?" said Bill. "This boy has a real smart father. Didn't I always tell you? How about that coffee?"

The smell of the coffee brewing must have carried to Paul Everett's bedroom. He came downstairs, wished Bill and Edna a Merry Christmas, and was ignored by John-Stewart, who was playing with the caboose. "You didn't get much sleep," he said to Edna.

"I think I'll go back to bed, soon as I've made your coffee," said Edna. "I hope you don't mind it without the eggshells. Mother always puts eggshells in the pot, and I never knew why. Maybe you can tell me."

"I don't see that it makes the slightest difference," said Paul Everett. "The best coffee I ever drank was on fishing trips, and I don't put any eggshells in it. Bill, you didn't get much sleep."

"Your grandson saw to that," said Bill.

"Santa Claus appears to have been very good to him," said Paul Everett. "I remember one Christmas I had when I was a boy, a little past his age. Santa gave me a pair of gum boots, and even they were too big for me. A pair of gum boots and a twenty-five-cent piece. Things certainly have changed, although I guess they didn't change so much for you."

"Well, not as much, I guess," said Bill. "I always remember a Flobert rifle my father gave me. He took it away from me Christmas Day, because I pointed it at my mother."

"It's funny what we remember about Christmas," said Paul Everett.

"Tell me something, while Edna's in the kitchen. Did you get rid of the gas heater in the bathroom?"

"You mean the one Faith McCracken committed suicide with? Yes, I got rid of it. No use having that around to remind Edna. She was upset enough without that to remind her. Why? You never even saw it."

"I know I didn't, but I was wondering," said Bill.

"I put in a radiator. I should have done that in the first place, but gas seemed all right," said Paul Everett. "Not that I ever blamed myself for Faith McCracken. She would have found a way to do away with herself."

"Two coffees coming up," said Edna. "Now I think I'll go back to bed, and leave you two to entertain my son."

"You go on upstairs," said Paul Everett.

"My three men," said Edna. "I'd like to have a picture of you, but I left my Brownie at home." She left them.

"Too bad you have to go back tomorrow," said Paul Everett.

"I'm sorry too," said Bill. "But since Jack McNair died . . . But I want to tell you, Mr. Everett, it's been a good Christmas."

"For me, too," said Paul Everett. "In a way, my best."

Clarence Kelley and Bill saw Ada Ewing off on the Chicago train. "Edna was sorry she couldn't see you off," said Bill.

"Oh, I understand," said Ada. "And I'll be back in plenty of time for her baby."

There were some Cleveland people on the train, whom she had lunch with. She spent the night in Chicago, and boarded the Los Angeles train the next day and made herself comfortable for the long journey. She bought *The Saturday Evening Post, The Literary Digest, Everybody's,* and *Life,* and a collection of John Galsworthy's short stories called *The Sheaf.* She passed a good deal of the time looking out the window of her drawing-room. She had never been to California and had never been as much as two nights on a sleeping car. She knew none of her fellow-passengers and did not wish to know them. This train ride was to be a rest as was her stay with her friend Rhoda Shipley. She did not anticipate the Lesbian adventure that had been suggested by Clarence Kelley, and as the train put hundreds of miles between her and Priscilla Hotchkiss she found herself thinking oftener of Rhoda than of Priscilla.

Rhoda met her at the Los Angeles station in a chauffeur-driven Packard. "Have you been waiting long?" said Ada.

"Not me," said Rhoda. "I telephoned and found out the train was two hours late, so I knew when to leave. Let me look at you."

"I had a good rest on the train," said Ada.

"No strange men making overtures?" said Rhoda.

"I stayed in my drawing-room most of the time," said Ada.

"You're still a handsome woman, Ada," said Rhoda. "Let Michael take care of your luggage. Did you bring a trunk?"

"It's coming by Adams Express. I have a large suitcase and a small overnight bag. It's good to see you, Rhoda."

"It's been a long time since we've seen each other," said Rhoda. When they got in the car Rhoda said, "How is Asa?"

"He spent Christmas Day with me. He's about the same. Looks a little older, but don't we all?"

"All except you," said Rhoda. "I'm a very rich woman, Ada. Why doesn't Asa come out here and marry me?"

"Well, maybe that can be arranged," said Ada. "Are you that rich, Rhoda?"

"When Arthur died he left me close to ten million dollars. I had no idea he was worth that much, and I'm thinking of ways to spend it."

"Asa could help you there," said Ada.

"I'll be darned if I turn it all over to some Californian. I like the climate, and there are a few people from back East that I like, but the Californians are just not my dish of tea. I always liked Asa, but he was younger than I and nothing ever happened there. Well, if you must know, something did happen before I married Arthur, but I don't suppose Asa remembers."

"Why, Rhoda, tell me about it," said Ada.

"Why not? I was noted for having a large bust, and Asa every chance he got used to squeeze it, and I liked him to. But he was only about sixteen then and I was past twenty, so nothing ever came of it."

"He had a weakness for large busts," said Ada.

"Most men have," said Rhoda. "Arthur certainly did. But

Arthur's gone now, and I don't care for Californians. Now there's your first giant palm tree."

On the way to Santa Barbara the two women exchanged bits of information on relatives and friends—Rhoda was childless—and finally drew up to the Shipley house, a large Monterey-style structure that was still short of being the home of a ten-times millionaire. "You're probably dying for a tub," said Rhoda. "If you want anything, this is Monica. Lunch will be at one o'clock."

Rhoda was a tall woman, half a head taller than Ada, who had never lost her Eastern Seaboard accent. Her parents had brought her to Cleveland when she was five years old, and as they talked well-bred New Yorkese, and she had been sent to a defunct New York boarding school, her speech was that of a well-bred New Yorker. She was very nearly homely, but she escaped it by the animation of her brown eyes and the extraordinary beauty of her teeth. Her frank conversation in the Packard was so characteristic of her that Ada had forgotten about it until she heard it again. She was, for instance, the first girl of Ada's acquaintance to use the word fuck, which she had done when they were about ten years old. "It means when a man puts his piddle thing in a girl's piddle thing," said Rhoda.

"Why would he do that?" said Ada.

"To have a baby," said Rhoda.

"Oh," said Ada, pretending to understand, and vaguely comprehending from her limited knowledge of animals. It was Rhoda and not Ada's mother who at thirteen or fourteen explained the mystery of menstruation to Ada, and years later it was Rhoda who prepared Ada for the pain and pleasure of intimacy with Francis Ewing. It was more or less inevitable that Ada should want to ask Rhoda about Priscilla Hotchkiss, but that might take some time.

Lunch at one o'clock was to be followed by some shopping in Santa Barbara. "Can you drive a car?" said Rhoda.

"Yes," said Ada.

"Good, then you can use my little car. It's a Chevrolet, one of those sporty little cars with the divided seat in front and room for two in back. I only drive it with the top down. When it rains I use the Packard. I'm thinking of buying a Rolls-Royce, but it takes so long to have one delivered."

"You ought to have a Rolls-Royce, with all that money," said Ada.

"Oh, I'm considering it," said Rhoda. "Arthur always wanted one. If I'd known he had all that money I'd have insisted on his getting one. Tell me, Ada, you've been a widow for four years—"

"Five."

"Yes, it is five, isn't it? When did you stop actively missing Francis? I mean actively."

"If I know what you mean, two years ago," said Ada.

"That means I have three years to go, less four months. Were you always faithful to Francis?"

"Yes, I was."

"I wasn't, to Arthur. I had a couple of flings, one when we'd been married for two years, and the second when I was in my forties. The first was when I found out that Arthur'd been having an affair with an old girl of his. You know her, she's from Cleveland. So I packed my things and had an affair with a man in New York. The second was here in Santa Barbara, with a much younger man, and Arthur never found out about it, but it was quite serious for a while."

"I slept with a man in Palm Beach. He was younger too. I slept with him again, a year ago."

"Nobody in between?" said Rhoda.

The temptation was almost overwhelming, but the time nad not yet come to tell Rhoda about Priscilla. Ada herself was ready, but Rhoda was not. "No," said Ada.

"You wouldn't lie to me, Ada?" said Rhoda.

"I might," said Ada.

"That's more like it," said Rhoda. "You didn't come all the way to California to comfort the afflicted widow. Have you fallen in love with a married man?"

"No, but that's all I'll tell you now, Rhoda," said Ada.

The days in Santa Barbara slipped by, one into another, until they became one, not a Tuesday or a Friday but a Daytime. There was a lot of rain, and on those days there was no polo to watch, but on days when it did not rain there *was* polo to watch, there were drives to take, the sun to bask in, idle talks to be had. And whether it was sunny or the rain was pelting down, there was always the companionship of Rhoda Shipley, the newness of her after so many years of not seeing her, the oldness of her friendship that seemed to have gone on forever. "Do you realize that I've known you over fifty years?" said Ada.

"A lifetime," said Rhoda. "Yes, it has been that long, and a little longer. I came to Cleveland when I was five years old and except for the time I was at boarding school in New York, I must have seen you every day. I was sorry I couldn't get back for Francis' funeral. But it was the same thing when Arthur died. You couldn't be here for his, either. It's an odd thing about being a continent away. You write a letter to someone in Cleveland and it's two weeks before you get an answer, and by that time you've forgotten what you said in your original letter. Think what it must be like for an Englishwoman whose husband is in the army in India."

"Especially now, with the war on," said Ada.

"Do you realize that that's the first time we've mentioned the war?" said Rhoda.

"It can't be. The first time?"

"The first time," said Rhoda. "I purposely hadn't mentioned it, that's why I noticed that you did. I thought you must be tired of talking about the war, in Cleveland. You're somehow much closer to it there."

"We're close enough, heaven knows," said Ada. "My son Bill's been wanting to get into it since it started, but every time he wants to enlist they pile more work on him. He's a director of Cuyahoga and Akron Rubber, and a mysterious firm called the Sprague company, all having to do with the war. His last chance to enlist came when Jack McNair died."

"Jack McNair was my first lover," said Rhoda.

"Jack McNair?"

"He was just starting his legal career then, and he almost ended it with his drinking," said Rhoda. "But he was gay and reckless and didn't give a darn, and Arthur was quite the opposite. Jack and I used to meet in out-of-the-way places, such as George Mc-Veagh's yacht, the *Thistle*. Nobody would ever think of looking for us there. Then Jack stopped drinking and I had nobody. But I found somebody, in New York."

"Then there were *three?*"

"Oh, don't hold me to facts, Ada," said Rhoda. "There was Jack McNair and there was the man in New York, and there was also a man on the train from New York to Cleveland. I could turn out to have been an awful slut if you count everybody. I *was* a slut, till Arthur stopped seeing his old girl. But I was faithful to him till years later and I met this younger man. He was a bachelor and treated me abominably, because he knew I was crazy about him. I didn't love him. How could I love anyone like him? But he was what I wanted at the time, which was after Arthur had had his first stroke. I would go to his house, a huge place up the hill from here, and present my fair white body to him. He would pretend to interrupt his piano-playing while I ministered to him tenderly. He was really hateful. When I'd start down the hill he'd pound the piano, to show how much he didn't need me. Chopin's Polonaise, he'd always play. *Dum*-de-dum, da-da *dum*-de-dum—dum-dum. He was mocking me. But I'd go back up the hill, because he had what I needed. And of course he was beautiful. Not handsome, beautiful. He could make me do things I'd never do with anyone else."

"Such as?" said Ada.

"Oh, perverted things," said Rhoda. "Pretend he was the woman and I was the man. I suppose they were things I'd always secretly wanted to do, but it took him to discover them. I was fascinated by him. Have you ever known anyone like that?"

"Yes, I have," said Ada. The time had come.

"Who was the man?" said Rhoda.

"It wasn't a man. It was a girl," said Ada, and proceeded to tell her all about her affair with Priscilla. She spared herself nothing, and Rhoda listened in silence. The only measure of the time it took to tell her about Priscilla was the number of cigarettes in Rhoda's ashtray. There were four.

"I've been wondering what was on your mind," said Rhoda. "And that's it."

"I'd have gone away without telling you, but you spoke of perverted things," said Ada. "There's no use my pretending I'm not perverted. Do you want me to leave?"

Rhoda smiled. "Hasn't it occurred to you that I might be the same way? Hasn't that ever occurred to you?"

"I don't think so," said Ada.

"You mean it has," said Rhoda.

"Yes, I guess it has," said Ada. "You always knew so much more than I did."

"And I haven't told you everything," said Rhoda. "Ada, you're very innocent. I want to kiss you."

"I want you to," said Ada.

"What's to stop us?" said Rhoda. She took Ada's hand and they went upstairs to Rhoda's bedroom. "You must never leave me."

"Never?"

"Never," said Rhoda.

"All right, I won't," said Ada.

"I think Mother must be sick," said Bill. "Read this letter. It was addressed to me at the office."

"Funny she should write to you at the office," said Edna. "But then your mother is a funny woman."

The letter read:

Dear Bill:

I had planned to return to Cleveland in time for the birth of Edna's new baby, but there has been a drastic change in my plans. I do not know when I shall return, but it will not be for some time. I am putting the house up for sale and I am transferring ownership of the farm to you. (Clarence Kelley will be so informed.)

I am sorry that I will not be in Cleveland when the baby comes, but as the child already has one grandmother I do not feel it will be neglected in that respect. Mrs. Everett will undoubtedly be pleased to take over this responsibility; I feel that the new baby will be in safe hands. As for Edna, she will have her mother to see her through the accouchement instead of a mother-in-law.

Do not worry about me, please. Mrs. Shipley is taking good care of me. She is, as you know, my oldest and dearest friend. As we grow older we come to realize how precious they are.

My love to Edna and to you.

Sincerely,
Mother

"Well, that about tells it all, except it doesn't really tell us anything," said Edna.

"I showed the letter to Clarence, and he'd had two letters. One to the office, and one at the club. The letter to the office contained her instructions about the house and the farm. The one at the club was private and personal, and he didn't show it to me. That's the one I'd like to read, but I don't suppose I ever shall."

" 'Not for some time,' she says. Do you suppose she means forever?" said Edna. "I don't know Mrs. Shipley, but she sounds like the answer for a lonely woman—and your mother was a lonely woman, Bill. She never got over the death of your father."

"And I guess I wasn't much good to her. The day we got home from our wedding trip, he died. Remember?"

"I should say I do," said Edna. "Will I ever forget it?"

"I've had a feeling about Mother that she was going to do something like this," said Bill. "That house must have been dreary after my father died, and I don't know why she didn't sell it right away. She had no real friends. Mrs. Cudlipp was hardly an intimate friend, and Mrs. McVeagh and Mrs. Hay had their husbands to keep them busy. I think I'll write a letter and tell her to stay in California, if it's all right with you."

"Of course it is," said Edna. "I'll tell Mother to come keep house for me and take care of John-Stewart. She bores the hell out of him, as she does some other people I know, but you can put up with her for a couple of weeks. You'll be at the office in the daytime, and spending your evenings at the hospital with me and the baby, so you'll hardly ever have to see her."

And so it was.

A family named Berg bought the big house. Samuel Berg wanted to rent the house, with an option to buy, but Clarence Kelley would not listen to Berg's proposition; he insisted upon a straight sale for $125,000. Walter Scroggs, who was given a life pension of $100 a month, bought the Pierce-Arrow for $50 and let it be known that he and the car could be hired through the Union Club for $10 a day or any part thereof, and Clarence Kelley, who seldom needed a car, made a counter offer of $100 a month for Walter's full-time services, which was accepted. The farm became Bill's property, with Ada paying the upkeep and the taxes, including Lloyd Sharpe's salary. Bill and Edna had their pick of the furniture, etc., in the big house, and they kept Francis Ewing's desk, his easy chair, his books (including the eleventh edition of the *Encyclopaedia Britannica*), his trophies. Many of Francis Ewing's possessions were already at the farm, and the same was true of Ada's belongings. The farm had become for her her real home; the town house, after Francis Ewing's death, a *pied-à-terre,* and now it was not even that. Samuel Berg was invited to make a bid for the contents of the town house, and he offered $25,000. To his surprise and consternation the first bid was accepted. "Maybe I should have offered you ten thousand," he told Clarence Kelley.

"The rugs alone are worth that," said Kelley. "Twenty-five thousand was for a quick sale. I doubt if Mrs. Ewing will ever come back to Cleveland."

Bill, who heard that conversation, later asked Kelley if he was sure of that.

"Reasonably sure," said Kelley.

"Then tell me," said Bill. "Is Mother ill?"

"Not that I know of," said Kelley. "She made her decision to stay in California, and she acted on it. It may have seemed impulsive, impetuous, but I assure you it wasn't. Only the act itself was impulsive. The thinking behind it took a long time."

"Well, Mother is old enough to know what she wants to do," said Bill. "She may be burning her bridges behind her, but they're her bridges."

"And she can build new ones," said Kelley. "What's the news of Edna?"

"We had one false alarm, but the baby's due any minute. Mrs. Everett arrives tomorrow, and Edna wouldn't dare have the baby before that."

"You've never seemed to care for Mrs. Everett, or am I wrong?" said Kelley.

"Lila Everett, as someone once said, is her own worst enemy— but not while I'm alive."

"I think that was said by Oliver Herford at the Players Club in New York," said Kelley. "I might be wrong. I've never been to the Players Club and I've never met Oliver Herford."

"I've never even heard of him, but you're usually right. Mrs. Everett, Lila, is one of those women who's the salt of the earth, whatever that means. What *does* it mean? I know that salt used to be considered legal tender in the Roman army, hence the expression a man is worth his salt."

"Well, Bill, this is all very interesting, but let's get to work, shall we?" said Kelley. "The Sprague company, meaning Valdemar Baer, are going ahead with Plan B, which is the War Department's euphemism for poison gas."

"Is that so surprising?" said Bill.

"Not at all. It was offered to our army back in 1908. It was ruled against during the Hague Conference of 1899. It was used by the Germans at Ypres in 1915, with great effect. And last year they began using mustard gas, and they're still using it. It isn't a bit surprising that with a man like Valdemar Baer on our side, his chief interest should be in poison gas. Valdemar Baer is an expert on poison gas. The Sprague company is a cover-up, not to hide him from the Germans. They have good reason to know all about Valdemar, and they're not fooled by the Sprague company and nitrates. However, it has taken all this time to get the go-ahead sign from our War Department. They didn't quite trust Baer, and Congress has always been squeamish about chemical warfare. I'm squeamish about manufacturing bayonets, myself, but that's neither here nor there. The Sprague company has been given the go-ahead signal and you, as a director of Sprague, are being given your chance to get out. George McVeagh doesn't want anybody on the board who has scruples against making poison gas, so he told me to ask you."

"I have no scruples," said Bill. "War is war, and as you say, I'm squeamish about making bayonets, but the Germans make them and they make poison gas. So we might as well."

"That's what I was sure you'd say, but George told me to ask you, and now I have," said Kelley. "Now I must tell you a little more about the gas that Baer proposes to make. It's worse than the mustard gas that they've been using. It's practically odorless, but the minimum quantity of it, the size of a drop of water, destroys a man's eyesight, permanently. Think what that means, Bill. I know a man who lost his leg at the Battle of Gettysburg. He's actually younger than I am, and he gets around very well on his one leg. But to have been blinded at Gettysburg is quite a different story. Eighteen plus thirty-seven, that's fifty-five years of total blindness. The Baer gas, being practically odorless, also has an instantaneous effect, so that a regiment of men would be blinded and confused and ready for slaughter, completely defenseless. Does that change your mind about the Baer gas?"

Bill did not answer immediately. "It could," he said. "Have the Germans got this gas?"

"We don't know," said Kelley. "But it's only a question of time before they do have. As soon as we use it, the Germans will use their version of it. Or they'll start using an even more horrible gas. We have reason to believe that the Germans have a gas that affects the nervous system. It's similar to the Baer gas, but where the Baer gas affects the eyesight, the German gas paralyzes the entire nervous system."

"How?"

"You may well ask that," said Kelley. "Valdemar Baer told us that the Germans were working on the nerve gas, and he urged us to get to work on his gas while there was still time. That was almost a year ago, and the Germans have had a year to perfect their nerve gas. Meanwhile we've lost a year. The advantage of the Baer gas is that the merest drop, or the equivalent of a drop in vapor, will blind a man and blind him permanently. But as I understand it, the German nerve gas is effective only if a larger quantity of it enters the lungs. The human body, for instance, can resist a drop of chloroform, and it can resist a drop of the nerve gas. But how *much* of the nerve gas can it resist? We don't know. Presumably about as much as it takes to anesthetize a person with chloroform."

"It's so much simpler to make bayonets, isn't it?" said Bill. "You're not bothered with ethical questions."

"There really isn't an ethical question here," said Kelley. "You committed yourself to the Baer gas when you said you had no scruples."

"Then why did you ask me if I'd changed my mind?" said Bill.

"Because I wanted you to know what you meant when you said, 'No scruples.' I'm deeper in this than you are, Bill. I know a lot more about it than I've told you today, partly because I've met Valdemar Baer and I speak German, the German of Schiller and Goethe, not the German of Baer."

"Now I never knew you spoke German."

"I took it up about forty years ago, but that's before you were born, isn't it?" said Kelley. "You'll have to meet Baer. He pretends he can't speak English, but that's a device. He speaks it with a thick accent and a limited vocabulary, but he makes himself understood. *There's* a man without scruples. There's *really* a man without scruples. I find him fascinating, and you will too. You won't like him, but he has no desire to be liked, one of the few men that that's true of."

"Well, he's in the right line of work," said Bill.

"Indeed he is," said Kelley. "He left a wife and two children in Germany, knowing what might happen to them when his defection became known. Did that affect him? No, not a bit. *Geschlechtich* is his word for it. Sexual. He can get that anywhere in the world, he says. He's hard-headed, and I may say that that's not the only thing about him that gets hard. He's only about forty-five, you know. He's already had an affair with Louise Schlatter, George Mc-Veagh's secretary, who happens to be his niece. How did I know that? He told me. He asked me if I had had an affair with her, and when I told him how old I was, he said he expected to be having affairs when he was my age, if the Germans didn't assassinate him first. He's a man without a soul."

"Maybe I am too," said Bill. "This war has made me wonder about that. I began to wonder when I took the job with Cuyahoga, which was about the time I was most eager to get in the army— actually the Navy. Then I took the job with Akron Rubber and al-

most immediately with Sprague. Jack McNair admitted that he—
and probably you—were trying to keep me out of the army.
Whereas if I'd had a soul I would have enlisted. That's what my
soul told me to do."

"You can still do those things, resign from your directorates. But
the army will have you working in the Judge Advocate's office.
You could be a captain and wear boots and spurs, the spurs to
keep your feet from rolling off your desk, as the saying goes. But
you'd be in uniform. And what would you be doing for your country? Well, we have a man from our office who is a major in the
Judge Advocate's department, Jim Williams. He has his boots and
spurs, and the last I heard he was going over the contracts for
some dredging they were doing in the lower Mississippi. The Corps
of Engineers does the actual work, but Jim has to read those contracts. How would you like to do that?"

"I hope the fishing is good on the lower Mississippi. Jim likes to
fish," said Bill.

"Don't you think that what you're doing is more important, more
patriotic, than whatever you'd be doing in the Judge Advocate's
department? I do. Jim Williams could be spared, Bob Hotchkiss
could be spared. Two of the young men we took on a year ago have
been ordered to report to their draft boards, and they can be
spared. But you can't be. You're my right-hand man, Bill. And this
war isn't going to last forever. Two years at the most."

"Long enough to use the Baer gas?" said Bill.

"Who can tell?" said Kelley.

Abby Clay, Kelley's secretary, entered the office without telephoning beforehand. "Now what, Miss Clay?" said Kelley.

"It's Mrs. Ewing, Mrs. Bill Ewing," said Miss Clay.

"And?" said Kelley.

"She's on her way to the hospital," said Miss Clay.

"I don't think this is a false alarm," said Bill.

The baby, a seven-pound girl, was delivered at three o'clock in
the afternoon, and Edna went to sleep shortly after that. She was

asleep when he noticed that she was wearing his Deke badge, and that made him cry. "She didn't want to take it off," said Dr. Fogel.

"I guess it brought her luck," said Bill. "I didn't know she still had it."

The baby was immediately named Mary, after nobody. "I always hated the name Edna," said Edna. "And I don't want to name her after either of our mothers. We have a John and now we have a Mary, and that takes care of names."

"What if we have another baby?" said Bill.

"We'll give it a number. Number Three," said Edna. "But I don't want another . . . Is my mother on her way?"

"Yes, and I sent my mother a telegram," said Bill. "It turned out that you could have a baby without either of them."

"Oh, I knew that," said Edna. "All I need is you, that's really all I need."

"And my Deke pin to bring you luck," said Bill.

She smiled. "You saw that?"

"I cried," said Bill.

The troop trains bound for the East and the South would stop at the Union Depot long enough for the Canteen Division of the Red Cross to distribute coffee, doughnuts, cigarettes, and chocolate bars, then the trains would head for Buffalo or Pittsburgh, north-easterly or southeasterly. The soldiers stayed aboard the trains, windows open, making flattering or rude remarks at the civilian passers-by, and watched carefully by the Military Police with .45 automatics at the hip. Sometimes the trains would change engines, which meant a longer stopover, but sometimes they pulled out in five minutes, which meant no coffee and doughnuts.

Asa Bloodgood, wearing a Red Cross brassard, was often the only male among the Canteen Division contingent. It was woman's work, but there were seldom enough women. Almost every day, including Sundays, a troop train would stop at Cleveland between ten and eleven in the morning, but as the war went on, trains were added, and the additional trains would pull in to the Depot at any hour, early morning, late at night. Asa and half a dozen women would be called upon to serve doughnuts, coffee, cigarettes and chocolate bars to ten coaches full of bored and weary soldiers from the West. Without warning, the train would pull out, leaving all but a lucky few unserved, and four hundred soldiers saying, "And that was Cleveland."

Nevertheless, Asa continued to regard the task as his duty, and he had met more than two hundred trains in less than a year. He had first gone to Union Depot with Jean McVeagh, who had just been appointed head of the Canteen Division. "Come on with me, Asa," said Jean. "You're not doing anything." He had met her outside Halle Brothers and told her her uniform was becoming; it was the first time she had worn the outfit. From then on she always telephoned him when a troop train was expected, and he was there oftener than Jean McVeagh. It was rather tedious work. He assumed the responsibility for seeing that the coffee was boiled, the doughnuts ready, the cigarettes and chocolate bars and coffee mugs on hand in sufficient quantity. He had to be at the Depot an hour before the train was expected, he had to be there an hour to clean up after it departed, and it became his job, despite the fact that he was not officially a member of the Canteen Division. But he enjoyed the job; it gave him something to do. He had tried to be a Y. M. C. A. secretary and was turned down because he was too old —or so they told him; he suspected that there were other reasons that went back in his past and having to do with women. The Y. M. C. A. did not approve of men who frequented whorehouses and drank whisky and had contracted two doses of gonorrhea, whereas as Jean McVeagh had said, "You're not doing anything."

He was fifty years old when he applied for the Y. M. C. A. job, and he assumed that fifty was too old for a field secretaryship, leading the soldiers in singing "Pack Up Your Troubles" and reminding them not to forget to write home, which he had been told was part of the work of a Y.M.C.A. secretary. Well, they were right. Fifty was too old. "Jean, if it hadn't been for you, I'd have been a Y. M. C. A. secretary," he said one day at the Depot. "Actually, they turned me down. But I wouldn't have had anything to do."

"You're doing splendidly," said Jean McVeagh.

"It isn't much, but it's something," said Asa. "Last night a train came in from some camp in Missouri. It was twelve hours late. You should have seen the men devour those doughnuts. They hadn't had anything to eat since noon, and they weren't going to get anything till Erie. You'd think the army would plan better than that, but I suppose you have to get used to that in the army. I feel so sorry for those young fellows. They'll be taken to Hoboken, New Jersey, and go from the train to the ship. No leave. Hustled like so many cattle, and their next stop will be France, and God knows what. It's no wonder some of them desert. The Military Police shot a man trying to desert a week or so ago, right here in Cleveland."

"Heavens! I didn't hear about that," said Jean McVeagh.

"It wasn't in the paper," said Asa. "I looked to see if there might be something, but there wasn't. He wasn't killed, and I think what they did was put him right back on the train. He wasn't the first that tried to desert, nor will he be the last."

"Asa, what do you think of this war?" said Jean McVeagh.

"Why ask me, Jean?" said Asa. "Or do you just want to say what *you* think of it?"

"Well, all right, I do," said Jean. "I approve of it, because it's making us all so rich. Not only the steel business, but everything else is profitable. But I foresee a day of reckoning."

"How does George feel about it?" said Asa.

"The same as I do," said Jean. "Cuyahoga's been making money hand over fist for four years, and not only Cuyahoga. Akron Rubber is too, and one or two other companies. Of course, George and I don't know what it is to be poor."

"I don't either," said Asa. "I've never had to work for a living. I sponged off Ada and Francis all my life, and I had no trouble getting used to it, none whatsoever. My family had money, and I was brought up to be a gentleman—in Cleveland, of all places, where you're supposed to work for a living. But it took the war to make me realize what a wasted life I've led. I went to Kenyon, where I was taken into the select brotherhood of the Psi Upsilon fraternity, and I believe that was the high point of my career. But you don't see many Psi U's on those troop trains. There may be some, but they're not identifiable. And of course there are no members of the Union Club on those trains. And yet when you say that, Psi U and the Union Club, you've said it all, as far as I'm concerned. I'm chief cook and bottle washer for a trainload of men who are on their way to France, and that's the only worthwhile thing I've ever done. Apart from giving various females the pleasure of my company."

"Well, Asa, I'm sure it was a pleasure," said Jean.

"Now why do you say that?" said Asa. "I always had the feeling that you disapproved of me."

"Oh, I disapproved of you, or your chasing after women all the time," said Jean. "But I confess I used to wonder what it would be like to have you hold me in your arms."

"Now why didn't you ever let me know?"

"Oh, you were too busy, and besides, I love George," said Jean.

"There's still time," said Asa.

"At my age? No. Stop flirting with me, Asa. I told you I love George."

"But what George doesn't know won't hurt him," said Asa.

"You're still too busy, even now," said Jean.

"How old are you, Jean?"

"Old enough to know better," said Jean. "A lot older than your sister Ada. By the way, Ada has sold her house. Does that mean she's staying in California for good?"

"Changing the subject, yes, I guess it does. She's going to live with Rhoda Shipley. Do you approve of that?"

"It doesn't make the slightest difference whether I approve or disapprove," said Jean.

"No, I suppose it doesn't," said Asa. "But you *don't* approve, do you?"

"Well, two middle-aged ladies—oh, Ada has apparently made up her mind."

"That Rhoda will be more companionable than someone much younger?"

"I didn't say that, Asa," said Jean.

"No, but we both know what I'm talking about," said Asa. "Gossip gets around."

"And I think it's awful. You're gossiping now," said Jean. "And about your own sister."

"I haven't really said a word, have I?" said Asa. "Where did you hear about Ada and a certain young person?"

"Indirectly, from that certain young person," said Jean. "She is *rumored* to have said that Ada Ewing would be back with her. Where did you hear it?"

"Indirectly, from the same source," said Asa. "A lot of people don't know that I'm Ada's brother, you know. New people in Cleveland. I just hope that none of this reaches young Bill Ewing, but I guess that's too much to hope."

"If the stories I heard are true, that certain young person will see that they reach Edna Ewing, if not Bill," said Jean.

"Shall we call that certain young person Priscilla?"

"Yes," said Jean.

"Shall we call her Priscilla Hotchkiss?"

"Why not?" said Jean. "There are stories enough about her, without dragging Ada into it, but she takes some delight in talking about Ada. I don't see that she comes out so well in the stories she tells, but an older woman is somehow guiltier than the young woman. I think Priscilla is slightly mad. She's certainly vicious."

"She's vicious," said Asa. "She has nothing to lose. You know about Bob Hotchkiss?"

"Only rumors," said Jean.

"They're more than rumors," said Asa.

At that moment they were joined by Marcia Hay. "Ah do declare," said Marcia. "Jean McVeagh, and lookin' more like the angel of mercy than Flo'nce Nightingale herself. Asa honey, how late do you expect the train to be today? Ah'm afred Ah can't stay past twelve o'clock."

The very first word that Priscilla Hotchkiss had had an affair with Ada Ewing reached Bill Ewing in a brutal way. Bill and Priscilla encountered each other on Ninth Street and Bill asked Priscilla if there was any news of Bob. "Oh, he never writes to me," said Priscilla.

"What do you mean, never writes to you?" said Bill. "You write him, don't you?"

"When necessary," she said. "He gave a what-do-you-call, power of attorney to Clarence Kelley, and that takes care of business matters. But I have to write him once in a while about—well, such things as shall I plant rose bushes in the garden this year. Things like that. He never answered that letter, by the way, so I went ahead and planted them. Tell me, how's your mother?"

"You knew, of course, that she's living in California. She has a friend in Santa Barbara, Mrs. Shipley—"

"I know about Mrs. Shipley. Does your mother give her her bath?

"What ever are you talking about?" said Bill.

"Why, poor old innocent Bill. Don't you know about your mother and baths?"

"I haven't the faintest idea what you're talking about," said Bill.

"No, I guess you haven't," said Priscilla. "Well, next time you write your mother tell her I miss our baths. I'll leave you here. I suppose you're going to the Union Club."

"Not before you tell me about my mother and baths," said Bill.

"Let me know what she says," said Priscilla, and dashed across the street.

Bill was having lunch with Clarence Kelley, and toward the end of the meal Bill said, "I had a strange conversation with Priscilla Hotchkiss." He then related the encounter with Priscilla, and when he had finished, Clarence said, "That . . . bitch. Let's go where we can talk."

"Your office?"

"All right, I guess we won't be interrupted there." said Kelley.

On the way back to the office Clarence Kelley said not a word, and Bill respected the silence. "Miss Clay, I don't want to be disturbed," said Kelley. "Sit down, Bill. You'd better have a cigarette. Give me one, too." They lit their cigarettes and Kelley put his out immediately and folded his hands. "I hoped I might die and be spared this, but I didn't get my wish. However, I'm an old man and a good friend, and old men and good friends have their uses at a time like this. Bill, do you know what a Lesbian is?"

"Yes," said Bill.

"Your mother is a Lesbian."

"Mother? She was happily married to my father for over twenty years. I don't believe it."

"She was married, I don't know how happily. But that's neither here nor there. At all events, your father died and your mother was a widow for three years, three years in which she mourned your father deeply. But during those three years something happened to her, and the first person she was attracted to happened to be Priscilla Hotchkiss. To state the facts as I know them, your mother seduced Priscilla. The first time was in the bathtub, out at the farm. The second time was at your house in town."

"You've known this all along?" said Bill.

"And possibly a great deal more," said Clarence Kelley. "You know that I've loved your mother for years, platonically, I suppose you'd call it. But understandingly. I recommended the trip to California, in the hope that she would get over her attraction to Priscilla, which apparently she's done. But I reckoned without

Priscilla's attraction to her. I'm sure Priscilla has had affairs with men, but she hates to give up her hold on your mother. I believe your mother is happy with Mrs. Shipley, and the longer she stays in California, the better. They're mature women. Priscilla is a little bitch, and I've never called a woman that before. Well, there I've told you, God help me."

"So my mother is a—Lesbian, you say?" said Bill. "I don't quite understand what women do to each other."

"Well, they haven't got a penis, so that eliminates that," said Kelley. "I must say, you're taking this quite calmly."

"Outwardly, maybe," said Bill. "Inside me I'm all confused. You see, no matter what my mother has done, she had me. I'm proof that she wasn't always a Lesbian. And my son and daughter are extra proof."

"You're not shocked?" said Clarence Kelley. "Except for your first indignant denial, you don't seem to be."

"I've known for some time that Mother wasn't herself," said Bill.

"But she is herself, Bill. Probably more so than she's ever been. What made you think she wasn't herself?"

"Little things, mostly. She hasn't been as close to Edna and me, but I assumed that that was because she didn't really like Edna. The old mother-in-law problem," said Bill.

"The fact is that she likes Edna very much, but it wasn't Edna who excited her. It was Priscilla," said Kelley. "Your mother is like a gentleman who is attracted to a prostitute, and I can't help but think of Priscilla as a prostitute."

"Exactly," said Bill. "I've known plenty of men who were attracted to prostitutes . . . I knew there must be some reason why Mother didn't get here for the birth of my daughter."

"Possibly two reasons. She was happy with Mrs. Shipley, and she was a little afraid of Priscilla," said Kelley. "I hope you'll keep both these facts in mind and make it easier for your mother to stay in California. Also, I think for the time being it would be better if you didn't mention Priscilla to your mother. Your mother is the kind of person who'd feel she had to face the music, meaning Priscilla, if there was any music to face. When the war is over, Priscilla will get a divorce from Bob, and Cleveland will see no more of her. She hates Cleveland. So I suggest, I *urge* you, to say nothing to your mother about baths. Let's keep those three thousand miles between your mother and Cleveland."

"I agree with you," said Bill. "What shall I tell Edna?"

"By all means tell her about your mother, and tell her right away," said Kelley.

"That's not going to be easy, but of course you're right," said Bill.

"None of this is easy," said Kelley. "Edna is a fine girl, a fine girl, and you may discover that she has a great deal more understanding than you credited her with. This whole thing is a matter between women. It really isn't a matter between men. Therefore, Edna will be either more tolerant of your mother's conduct, or she'll be completely *in*tolerant. My guess is that she'll be tolerant."

"I hope so," said Bill.

"You know so," said Kelley. "The new baby getting along all right?"

"She's fat as a pig. I think she weighs ten pounds," said Bill. He stood up. "Thank you, Clarence, for everything."

"You're more than welcome, Bill," said Kelley.

It was evening, past nine o'clock, before Bill could talk to Edna. "I'm going to make a long speech, and it has to do with my mother," he began. "So please listen." He then proceeded to tell Edna the whole story about Ada Ewing, drawing on his interview with Clarence Kelley for the most part. As he concluded he said, "Thank you for listening."

"Have you finished?" said Edna.

"I believe so," he said.

"Well, I must say you're lucky to have Clarence Kelley as a friend—and so is your mother. I guess you have to be eighty-some to have such understanding, to know so much about human weaknesses," said Edna. "While I was listening to the part about the bathtub I was reminded of Faith McCracken, the girl who committed suicide in my house. And then I was reminded of an altogether different girl, Ruth Velie. As far as I know, neither one of them was queer, although I did always think that Faith wanted to get intimate with me. There were other girls at Ann Arbor that had crushes on one another. They were always doing favors for each other, acting as servants, giving each other presents. But the only one that I ever felt uneasy with was Ruth Velie, and that was strange because she hated me. You know how cold it could get in Ann Arbor, and oftentimes girls would get into bed with each other to keep warm. I know I did. But one girl I'd never get in bed with was Ruth Velie. Granted that I was sure she hated me, and she didn't live anywhere near me, but I had that feeling about her, that that was one girl I could never bear to touch me. And then one night—I've never told you this—she came to my room, after Faith killed herself, and first she said she knew how much I missed Faith and so on. And then she said, 'I could make you feel good too.' I didn't know quite what she meant, but I *did* know, and when she put her hand on my bosom I was sure. 'Don't do that,' I said, and she said, 'Oh, playing innocent?' And I got her out of my room as quickly as I could. Then she *really* hated me. Anyway, that was as close as I ever came to being like your mother and Priscilla, but I know that one woman can be attracted to another, physically. And I can see why your mother would be attracted to Priscilla. She's pretty and has a good figure, and she has a way of looking at you that—I don't know. You know she's a woman, but she flirts with you like a man. She looks at your eyes, and then your bosom, and then down below, and back to your bosom. She must have looked at your mother that way, and your mother was highly susceptible. The only person I'm susceptible to is you."

"Thank God for that," said Bill.

"I forgive your mother for not coming East when the baby was born," said Edna. "I didn't at the time, but Clarence Kelley is right. She's better off in California. She's even better off with Mrs. Shipley. We're better off, too, because as long as she stays in California there'll only be gossip about her, and I don't think people pay much attention to Priscilla's gossip."

"Maybe not," said Bill.

"Bill?"

"What?"

"Do you know what a woman does to another woman?" said Edna.

"Well, I guess they sort of kiss each other," said Bill.

"Down below?" said Edna.

"I imagine so."

"But you and I do that," said Edna. "If that's all they do, what great harm is done? I like it when you do it to me."

"But you wouldn't want Priscilla to do it," said Bill.

"I wouldn't like you to do it if you didn't put your sword in me."

"Sword. That makes me think of Priscilla," said Bill. "It doesn't even look like a sword. This conversation is making me horny."

"In another two weeks, Dr. Fogel says. We can wait that long," said Edna.

"If we have to," said Bill.

"It's just as hard on me," said Edna.

"A hard-on is what we call it when our peckers get stiff, so let's not mention hard-ons for two more weeks," said Bill.

"You've been very good, Bill. It was longer this time because Dr. Fogel had to take some stitches, but two weeks and I'll be ready."

George McVeagh was a man who had twice reached a plateau of financial security. The first time was when his father died in 1883 and left him in control of the Duncan McVeagh Iron & Steel

Works, which was worth well over a million dollars. The second time was in 1902, when he had formed the Cuyahoga company, and George McVeagh, if he wished, could claim to be worth ten million. After that, knowing he was rich, he could take small chances with his money, and frequently did so. He put up $50,000 to manufacture an automobile that was cooled by air, but in Syracuse, New York, some people were already working on an air-cooled car and McVeagh took his loss. He backed a man who had invented a fountain pen which had possibilities, but when they tried to mass-produce it, it leaked in warm weather, and he wrote that off at a loss of $25,000. He then became interested in a resort hotel in Niagara Falls, New York, and that cost him $100,-000, mainly because young newlyweds could seldom afford the rates the hotel had to charge. Meanwhile George's personal fortune had been increasing, but his comparatively minor losses had taught him that there was no fun in investing his money in ventures he knew nothing about. The air-cooled car, the fountain pen, the resort hotel were such ventures. There was fun as well as profit in Cuyahoga, and though he knew nothing about the rubber business, Akron Rubber was highly profitable and Ed Lustig was an entertaining individual. The Sprague company had begun as a patriotic gesture, mainly at the suggestion of the War Department, and he rather enjoyed the secrecy attending its formation. But Valdemar Baer was not the kind of man George McVeagh would ordinarily have chosen to do business with. He could deal with crooks, and had had to; he could deal with forgetful men and men whose forgetfulness was strategic; he could deal with honorable gentlemen and gentlemen whose sense of honor was subjected to suspension; he could deal with all of them and find himself liking them. But Valdemar Baer was an unprincipled scoundrel, who had been forced upon George McVeagh by the exigencies of patriotism. He had been a traitor to Germany, the enemy country, but he had come to the United States to engage in the same nefarious work that he had been performing for the enemy, so the nefarious work was clearly not the reason for his betrayal of Germany. Baer's desertion of his wife and two children made him untrustworthy: either the desertion was false, or Baer was a cold-blooded, selfish man. McVeagh inclined to the latter belief.

There was also Baer's specialty, poison gas. The War Department showed McVeagh numerous photographs of the victims of chemical warfare, beginning with Ypres, and they had won him over to the support of a counter-offensive with gas. War was war. Nevertheless, McVeagh remained squeamish about its use, and he privately abhorred that phase of war-making. The fact was that McVeagh abhorred his association with Baer. "I finally found a man who is a complete son of a bitch," he told Clarence Kelley one day at the club. "Not one redeeming feature."

"Except that he's on our side," said Kelley.

"Yes, and I have my doubts about that," said McVeagh. "He is now, but he could turn against us."

"Where would he go?" said Kelley. "What other countries are there?"

"Well, this war has the world pretty evenly divided between us and the Germans, but look what's happening in Russia. This fellow Lenin is bound to be a troublemaker. He said himself that a new phase of Russian history is just beginning."

"I read that too, but he has his hands full in Russia," said Kelley. "It'll be a long time before Russia is ready to engage the services of Valdemar Baer. Our war will be over by then."

"Yes, I hope so," said George McVeagh. "And maybe Lenin will be disposed of before then. But there'll be others to take his place."

"And maybe the Germans will dispose of Valdemar Baer," said Kelley.

"Valdemar Baer will be disposed of by an outraged father, right here in Ohio," said McVeagh. "He likes sixteen-year-old girls."

"I didn't know about that, although it doesn't surprise me," said Kelley.

"Oh, I've had him watched," said McVeagh. "For his own protection, of course."

"Of course," said Kelley.

"But just incidentally, mind you, just incidentally, the detective agency has reported to me that Valdemar Baer, in spite of the fact that he lives in fear of his life from the Germans, likes young girls. Very young girls."

"Do *they* like *him?*" said Kelley.

"I don't know whether it's him they like or his money. Both, probably. Some of these farm girls have never seen a five-dollar bill. He's had two of them out at the farm he rents, at different times, of course. I suppose a sixteen-year-old girl is safer than a mature woman. A mature woman might turn out to be a German agent."

"And probably not as much fun," said Kelley.

"Why, Clarence!"

"Hearsay, George," said Kelley. "So you've been having Baer watched?"

"From the very beginning," said McVeagh. "I didn't put up five hundred thousand dollars without taking some precautions. That's what Sprague cost me originally. More than that, since then."

"I know that, I'm your lawyer," said Kelley.

"Thank God you are," said McVeagh.

"Since you've been having Baer watched, you must know about Heidi Schlatter."

"She's his niece," said McVeagh.

"That's not all she is," said Kelley. "She *has* been his mistress."

"How in God's name did you know that?" said McVeagh.

"He told me," said Kelley. "He wanted to know my relations with Miss Schlatter and even seemed a bit surprised when I told him I'd had none."

"Nor have I," said McVeagh. "I thought you'd like to know that, Clarence."

"That's very reassuring, George," said Kelley. "Propinquity in the office, I'm told, often leads to other things. Miss Schlatter is a beanpole of a woman—and so, for that matter, is my secretary, Alma Clay. But you must have heard that old expression, 'The nearer the bone, the sweeter the meat.' Besides, it didn't make that much difference to Valdemar. It's difficult to imagine Miss Schlatter in bed with anyone, but it's just as difficult to imagine Valdemar Baer carrying on with sixteen-year-olds. I guess my memory doesn't go back that far."

"Your memory's as good as mine, Clarence," said McVeagh. "The question is, ought I to report Miss Schlatter to the War Department?"

"Are you asking for legal advice?"

"Well, legal advice to begin with," said McVeagh.

"Legally, you ought to report her for having had an affair with Valdemar. You'll probably discover that the War Department is way ahead of you. They don't tell you everything they know, rest assured of that. But they like *you* to tell *them* everything *you* know. If you should report Heidi Schlatter, it'll still be a better-kept secret than Valdemar Baer has kept it. Yes, I'd tell the War Department that it has come to your knowledge that Louise has had intimate relations with her uncle. Then you'll be in the clear. You should also tell them that you have no intention of discharging Miss Schlatter. She's been your secretary since before the war started, and in spite of her German name and background, you've had no reason to be suspicious of her. A lot of confidential information has gone across her desk since 1914, and there've been no leaks, have there?"

"Absolutely none," said McVeagh. "I'm sure the British Purchasing Commission investigated her thoroughly. Those fellows even had me fire a foreman in our shipping department. O'Malley, his name was. He was pro-German. Used to get drunk and curse out the British, so I guess he wasn't a proper man to be in charge of our shipments overseas. They're very thorough, the British."

"Therefore, you'd consider her trustworthy," said Kelley.

"You make it sound as though I were in court," said McVeagh.

"I'm just trying to be as thorough as the British," said Kelley. "But you don't want to lose a good secretary because she fell for her uncle."

"No, and I don't intend to lose her," said McVeagh.

"Report her, just to be on the safe side," said Kelley. "Baer talks too much, but he has no shame."

"What about my sense of shame, Clarence? I wish the War Department hadn't talked me into backing Sprague. I'd much rather they'd talked me into making something clean, like bayonets. Instead, I'm making poison gas. And I've gotten other people into making it. Bill Ewing, for instance. He and Minor Hay and Alan Holcomb went in on my say-so."

"Minor Hay and Alan Holcomb are old hands at knowing how to deal with you," said Kelley. "But Bill Ewing—it's about time he was learning. You're so rich that he thinks you can do no wrong, and it's time he was learning to say no to you. I remember that hotel you had in Niagara Falls. Bill was too young to get in on that, but he would have if you'd suggested it."

"You remember that, do you? Cost me a hundred thousand dollars. The only thing wrong with it was that people couldn't afford it."

"Yes, I know," said Kelley. "You couldn't have afforded it, either, if you'd been making twenty-five dollars a week, and that's about the average salary of people who go to Niagara Falls. You get carried away with your enthusiasms, George, and you make it difficult for people to say no to you. You're a damn good salesman."

"Yes, I am, aren't I?" said McVeagh. "People don't realize that, either. They think, steel is steel and iron is iron, and it sells itself or it doesn't. But I manage to get a good price for my steel and I always have, and that's where the salesmanship comes in. Charley Schwab isn't the only salesman in our business."

"No, by no means," said Kelley. "Speaking of Bill Ewing, what's going to happen to him when I die?"

"Why, I suppose he'll be a partner in Hotchkiss, Ewing and Kelley, just as he is now."

"Ah, but will he?" said Kelley. "If the war's still on, will he want to continue having Bob Hotchkiss as a partner? Jim Williams is a good, reliable man, but he's getting on. With me dead, and Hotchkiss in the army, and Jim Williams working for the Judge Advocate, you'll have to give some thought to who's going to be your counsel."

"I have. It'll be Bill Ewing," said McVeagh.

"That's what I wanted to hear you say," said Kelley.

"He can get whoever he likes to take Jim Williams' place. As for Bob Hotchkiss, he never did quite fit in, and if the truth be told, I wasn't too keen on his father either. Francis Ewing and Clarence Kelley were my men. You know that."

"I should, but every once in a while I like to be told," said Kelley. "Yes, I know that, George, and I believe Francis Ewing knew it too."

"The thought of Hotchkiss, Ewing and Kelley without you is something I'll never get used to. Why, you *are* Cuyahoga. There wouldn't have been a Cuyahoga without you, and I mean that sincerely."

"Before there was a Cuyahoga, there was a Duncan McVeagh Iron & Steel. We had something to work with," said Kelley. "But you've satisfied my vanity, and now let's return to Bill Ewing."

"I have plans for him," said McVeagh.

"What plans, George?" said Kelley.

"Well, when you're past sixty and you have as much money as I have, and no children to leave it to, you begin to look around. Are you having any dessert, Clarence?"

"Rice pudding," said Kelley.

"I'll have that too," said McVeagh. "Do you ever eat anything else for dessert?"

"Custard," said Kelley.

"Mr. Kelley will have the rice pudding, and so will I," McVeagh told the waiter. Then, "A little cinnamon on mine, if you please."

"You may go ahead, George. The waiter's gone," said Kelley.

"Hovering, as usual. Waiters like to pick up scraps of information," said McVeagh. "Well, it goes without saying that Bill Ewing has my confidence. And yours. Ever since he's been a director of Cuyahoga he's been going to those meetings, keeping his mouth shut, but always learning something. He has learned, for instance, that Minor Hay is a sort of devil's advocate, opposes everything new, constructive or otherwise, but in the end votes for everything I suggest. There's nothing wrong with that, since I almost always have my way. But it's Minor Hay who gets things out in the open, and promotes discussion, which is healthy. Bill Ewing found that out by watching Minor Hay's tactics, and not from anything he was told. For instance, when we had some trouble with the ore boats, Minor suggested that we bring them in two at a time. We'd have to pay the men a certain amount of overtime, but we'd make up for that by not paying them when they weren't working. I was against the idea, but I didn't say so at the time. When it came to a vote, I noticed that Bill Ewing voted against it, and afterwards I asked him why. He said, 'Mr. McVeagh, I've noticed that Mr. Hay is your sacrificial goat. Whenever you don't like an idea, you get him to introduce it, then you vote against it.' And of course he was right. But some of our other directors have taken a long time to get wise to that. Some of them never will. He's a smart boy, and he's not such a boy any more. Bill Ewing could run this town ten years from now, as long as he stays out of politics."

"Why do you say that?" said Kelley.

"Well, it's natural for a lawyer to want to get into politics. Judgeships. District attorney. That sort of thing. But what do you get out of politics? Twenty-five thousand a year—and Bill is making that now. There really is no limit to what a man can make if he doesn't restrict his activity by going into politics. How much can an honest politician make? Let's say he is appointed to a receivership, a big fat receivership. Let's say the Bar Association is generous and allows him a hundred thousand or two hundred thousand dollars. All right, let's say that the two hundred thousand is all clear, which of course it isn't, but let's say it is. All right, how many of those receiverships does he get appointed to? One. One. Because don't forget, the next time it has to be someone else's turn. Or, forgetting about receiverships, suppose a politician is interested in the insurance business, which I understand is one way a politician can make money and stay honest. Suppose he has friends in Columbus who give him a lot of state business. That cuts out the insurance dealers in Cincinnati and Sandusky, but let's suppose he does extremely well, as much as a hundred thousand a year. Of course he has to donate at least twenty-five thousand to the party in power, making his gross income seventy-five thousand, and when the administration changes he'll probably get nothing. Do I make my point?"

"Your point, of course, is that Bill Ewing had better stay out of politics."

"All right, Clarence. I know when to stop," said George Mc-Veagh. "Incidentally, I don't see a single politician having lunch here today. Where are they all?"

"In Columbus, probably. Out politicking, or selling insurance. I don't know where they are," said Clarence Kelley.

"Not that I miss them. They'll come to me when they need money, and when I need them to do me a favor I'll know where to find them. That's really my point, my dear Clarence. Steer clear of politicians, whether they're amiable men like Warren Harding or cold-blooded aristocrats like Henry Cabot Lodge. But steer clear of them."

"I manage to," said Kelley.

"Well, then you agree with me that Bill Ewing is better off

having nothing to do with them?" said McVeagh.

"In principle, yes," said Kelley. "But how is he going to run this town, as you put it, ten years from now?"

"Cuyahoga," said McVeagh.

"Ah," said Kelley.

"Cuyahoga. The orchestra. The museum. The art gallery. This club. His wife and two children. His ability. His personality. All the things about him that you like and respect, and that I've learned to like and respect."

"Tell me a little more about Cuyahoga, George," said Kelley. "Just a little more."

"In confidence?" said McVeagh.

"Everything you've said is in confidence," said Kelley.

"Very well," said McVeagh. "It's my intention to make some arrangement whereby Jean inherits my stock in Cuyahoga, but the voting rights go to Bill Ewing. That can be done, can't it?"

"Offhand, I'd say yes," said Kelley. "It'll be complicated, but I think it can be done."

"I want it done fairly soon, Clarence. I'd rest easier if I knew that my Cuyahoga stock was in good hands. I mean, of course, that the income went to Jean and the voting rights went to Bill Ewing, in some kind of a trust. Will you work it out?"

"Haven't you made a will?" said Kelley.

"I made a will the year Jean and I got married, but that's a long time ago."

"Does Jean know this?" said Kelley.

"Jean doesn't know anything about money, my money or hers," said McVeagh. "But she does know that I have great confidence in Bill."

"That wouldn't mean a thing in court," said Kelley. "Here we are, two old men, deciding the future of a young man we both like. I'd better start working on a new will for you. But first I'd better relieve my bladder. How's your bladder, George?"

"Filled to capacity. It must be the cinnamon," said McVeagh.

"Odd. I didn't have any," said Kelley.

They signed the chits for lunch and made their way to the lavatory. Kelley, with his walking stick, stood at the urinal alongside McVeagh. "This may take a little time," said Kelley. "My bladder tells me to go, but nothing comes for a while."

"Have you had your prostate out?" said McVeagh.

"Long ago," said Kelley. "*There* it comes."

"I haven't had mine out, but I suppose it's only a question of time."

"You're still a comparatively young man," said Kelley.

"After sixty you can expect anything," said McVeagh.

"Yes, you can even expect to live twenty years longer, as I have. Without my prostate," said Kelley.

They went to the door of the club. "Can I give you a lift back to your office?" said McVeagh.

"Thanks, I'll walk. It's within walking distance for me," said Kelley. "Isn't that a new car?"

"Oh, I decided to buy a Winton this time. Do you like it?"

"Well, it's a home-town car, so I musn't say anything against it," said Kelley. "I hardly know one car from another. I can tell a Pierce-Arrow because it has its headlights on the fender, and that's about all. I have one because Francis Ewing's Walter works for me, but I get very little use out of it. I'll get to work on the will, George."

"Do that," said George McVeagh.

It took not only a great deal of work to prepare George Mc-Veagh's will, but a great deal of tactful handling to keep Bill Ewing in the dark about its contents. McVeagh had not specifically stated that Kelley was not to say anything about the will, but he inferred that Bill was not to be told. "I'm not saying anything to Bill Ewing about your will," said Clarence at their next meeting.

"Good God, I hope not," said McVeagh.

"You ought not to take those things for granted, George."

"I guess I relied on your discretion," said McVeagh.

"Well, that's what you pay me for, but my natural instinct was to tell Bill the good news. Fortunately I was discreet," said Kelley.

"Are you bawling me out, Clarence?"

"Not quite, but I'm not getting any younger, George. And your next lawyer may not be able to read your mind as well as I do," said Kelley.

"There you're wrong. My next lawyer will be Bill Ewing himself, and he can read my mind as well as you can."

"Then why don't you take Bill into your confidence?" said Kelley. "Tell him that you're changing your will, and all the rest of it?"

"I'm not ready to do that," said McVeagh.

"I think you ought to—unless you haven't quite made up your mind."

"Maybe that's it. It's an awful lot of money, Clarence. I have no idea how much," said McVeagh.

"George, are you being frank with me?"

"Frank with you? No, Clarence, I'm not. And the hell of it is, I don't know how to be now," said McVeagh.

"Well, I'm not going to help you," said Kelley.

"No, I guess you're not," said McVeagh. "I have to get out of this myself." They were again at the Union Club, where Clarence Kelley had lunch frequently but George McVeagh only sporadically. "You know, Clarence, I've known you a long time, but in all that time we've seldom talked about our women friends, our wives, the female sex generally."

"A matter of taste, as a rule," said Kelley. "I belong to the old school that believes a gentlemen's club is a place where you can get away from women, either their presence or as a topic of conversation. I seem to be in the minority there, but I'm too old to change."

"Don't change," said McVeagh. "It's a good rule. But I'm going to have to break it."

"Go ahead," said Kelley.

"I have your permission? All right. The lady in question is Ada Ewing. Ordinarily, she has every right to do as she pleases, have her own friends, live where she pleases and all the rest of it. But I don't understand this moving to California and taking up residence with Rhoda Shipley. A handsome woman, by the way, and I was sorry to see her leave Cleveland. But why did Ada suddenly move to California and not even come back for the birth of her grandchild? The reason I ask is that I know you're a great friend of Ada's and won't repeat any idle gossip. But more than that, I propose to leave her son my voting interest in the Cuyahoga corporation, and that's a big step. I happen to know that Rhoda Shipley is a very rich woman, and Ada Ewing isn't exactly poor. And the two of them have no sinister designs on Cuyahoga. But suppose I make a will leaving my voting interest in Cuyahoga to Ada's son, and suppose some crackpot has designs on Cuyahoga. Or not a crackpot. A smart fellow who finds out that Bill has this voting interest. There's an awful lot of money in Cuyahoga, just the voting interest. Are you listening, Clarence?"

"Oh, yes," said Kelley.

"You don't seem to be," said McVeagh.

"Oh, but I am," said Kelley. "George, I'm afraid I have to bow out of the job of preparing your will. Somewhat late in the day I realize that I can't do it. In the first place, it wouldn't be fair to Bill Ewing, to prepare the will as you want it, and then to have you change your mind. And I have a feeling you're going to change your mind, if you haven't already. At least you're not as *sold* on the idea as you were when we last discussed it. In the second place, I couldn't do all the work myself, and yet I'd have to, to keep Bill from knowing your plans. And let me remind you that the one man I'd trust to do the work I *can't* do is Bill himself. I'm not getting any younger. I'm tired of saying that. What I should be saying is that I'm getting older. It's possible that I wouldn't be able to finish the preparation of your new will. But the one thing more than any other that has made me decide not to work on the will is the involvement with Ada Ewing. At my time of life—or at any other time of life, but particularly now—I don't want to do anything that might complicate my relationship with Ada. For instance, I don't want to continue working on the will, only to have you change your mind about leaving all that power to Bill. That would be disastrous to my friendship with Ada, and she'd know about it. Bill would know about it, too. Those things get around—that you had planned to change your will in favor of Bill, and then decided against it. I should have thought of all this before, and to be honest with you, I had. But as long as it was only a legal problem, I could handle it. I could handle it, or advise you against it. But it's become a personal problem, involving Ada and Bill and millions of dollars, and the lives of quite a few other people. So as of today you must consider me as having withdrawn as counsel. I'm sorry, George, but at the same time greatly relieved."

McVeagh listened in silence. "Knowing you, I'd say your decision is final," he said.

"Final, and permanent and unequivocal," said Kelley. "And not even Miss Clay is aware that I've been working on your will. The only people who know anything about it are you and I and your wife Jean."

"I notice you didn't leave out Jean."

"No, I didn't leave out Jean," said Kelley.

"Well, you're right," said McVeagh. "Jean, as an interested party, raised the question of Bill Ewing voting her stock, and in effect controlling the destinies of Cuyahoga."

"Mm-hmm," murmured Kelley.

"Oh, all right, Clarence. I'll be frank with you this time," said McVeagh. "She also brought up the question of Ada and Rhoda Shipley, and their strange friendship."

"Why is it so strange? They've been friends since they were five years old. It's an *old* friendship, if that's strange. One of them lived in California and the other in Cleveland, and they're both widows."

"Now, Clarence, you know what I'm talking about."

"Cunnilingus?"

"I don't know what that means," said McVeagh.

"No, I was sure you didn't."

"One of your legal words, I suppose, like writ of mandamus," said McVeagh. "Siny die. You learn Latin only to mispronounce it."

"Pulling a heat isn't exactly plain English," said Kelley.

"It is to me," said McVeagh.

"And that's what matters, isn't it?" said Kelley.

"To me, yes," said McVeagh. "What was that word you used, ending with ingus?"

"Never mind."

"I think you're trying to change the subject," said McVeagh.

"Far from it, but it's a good idea," said Kelley.

"Well, let's get back to it," said McVeigh. "You're giving up the task of changing my will, and I'm sorry. But I'll look around for someone else. Meanwhile, of course, you'll go on handling Cuyahoga."

"If you wish," said Kelley.

"I do wish. You and Bill Ewing and the firm as a whole will still be in charge of Cuyahoga's legal affairs. And to show you my heart's in the right place, if you want to raise your fee, you'll find me in a receptive mood."

"That's very nice of you," said Kelley.

"The board will have to approve, but even Minor Hay won't object to that," said McVeagh. "We'll say no more about changing my will."

"Suits me," said Kelley. "This, of course, means that you *have* changed your mind about leaving Bill Ewing the power to vote your stock?"

"For the time being," said McVeagh. "I may change it back again, but I'll have to give the matter a lot of thought. I don't want to go off half-cocked again."

"You ready for your rice pudding, Clarence?" said McVeagh.

"I had rice pudding yesterday. Today I'll have custard," said Kelley.

He had managed to avoid bringing Jean McVeagh into the conversation, beyond letting McVeagh know that he had guessed it was her influence that was the deciding factor. He was curious about what Jean had said and where she had participated in the gossip about Ada and Rhoda Shipley, but not so curious as to prolong the discussion with George. George McVeagh was not a man who was interested in his wife's gossip, and his account of what Jean had said and where she had said it was probably unreliable. Besides, Clarence was tired, and instead of returning to the office he went upstairs to his room. He had done enough for one day.

Priscilla Hotchkiss was not expecting a telegram, but a telegram had been received by the mother of Jerry Bolling announcing his death, and Priscilla was not totally unprepared for one. It arrived the next day. NOTE: GET WORDING OF TELEGRAM ANNOUNCING BOB HOTCHKISS'S DEATH AT CHATEAU-THIERRY. She decided to be brave, and though she did not know Jerry Bolling's mother, she went to call on her that afternoon. To say that Mrs. Bolling was not expecting her was putting it mildly. "What did you say your name was?" said Mrs. Bolling.

"Priscilla Hotchkiss. My husband must have been killed in the same battle as Jerry."

"Oh, yes, I've heard Jerry speak of Bob Hotchkiss. They were in the same company," said Mrs. Bolling. "They were down at the Mexican Border together. Could I get you anything?"

"No thank you," said Priscilla.

"Let me get you a cup of tea," said Mrs. Bolling. "It won't take but a minute."

"All right," said Priscilla.

"A man telephoned from the *Plain Dealer,* asking if I had a photograph of Jerry. I have one taken at the Border, but it's the only one I have. He's in uniform, with one of those hats they wore."

"I have one like that of Bob," said Priscilla.

"I can't decide whether to let them have it or not. It's the only one I have, except some snapshots that were taken of Jerry in a bathing suit. What do you advise me to do?"

"Let them have it, if they promise to return it."

"It was taken almost two years ago," said Mrs. Bolling.

"Yes, so was Bob's," said Priscilla.

"Mr. Blackwell, that's the man from the *Plain Dealer*. I guess I'll let him have it. I wish I knew more about how Jerry lost his life."

"I guess the chaplain will write you a letter when he gets time," said Priscilla.

"Did you get a letter?" said Mrs. Bolling.

"No, I think they must have been killed at the same time."

"Do you get insurance?" said Mrs. Bolling.

"I don't know. I haven't even thought about it."

"I understand we get ten thousand dollars. That's a lot. Do you take cream with your tea, or lemon?"

"Either one. Whichever you're having."

"Wasn't your husband a lawyer?" said Mrs. Bolling.

"Yes, he was," said Priscilla.

"Jerry wanted to be a lawyer too, but he didn't finish college," said Mrs. Bolling. "My husband was killed in a railway accident. I get a forty-a-month pension, but that isn't enough. He was a brakeman on the Nickel Plate. You probably remember that terrible accident they had. The New York, Chicago & St. Louis, it was called, but everybody called it the Nickel Plate. They had this terrible accident just outside of Buffalo, New York. I'll never forget it if I live to be a hundred. You wouldn't want a drop of something stronger?"

"What, for instance?" said Priscilla.

"Well, I have gin, if you don't mind the taste of gin," said Mrs. Bolling. "It's a little early, but . . ."

"All right," said Priscilla.

"I take it with a drop of those Angostura Bitters. It makes a nice appetizer. Did you ever have that?"

"No," said Priscilla.

"Just a drop. Try it and see how you like it," said Mrs. Bolling. "It makes all the difference in the taste." She produced two shot glasses and poured the gin and bitters, and watched Priscilla's reaction. "Notice how different the taste is?"

"Yes, I do."

"I almost forgot. Here's to your husband and my son. May they rest in peace," said Mrs. Bolling.

"Rest in peace," repeated Priscilla.

"Are you a Catholic?"

"No, I'm not."

"I am. Or you might say, I was," said Mrs. Bolling. "I turned when Jerry was born. So I was wondering whether I ought to have a Mass said. Your husband wasn't a Catholic, was he?"

"No," said Priscilla.

"I raised Jerry a Catholic till he was about fifteen, but when his father was killed I stopped going to Mass and so did Jerry. The Catholic Church never brought me any luck. But I guess I ought to have a Mass said for him. The priest was here this morning, Father Sheehan. I will say *that* for them. They don't forget you when you're in trouble. I don't know how he found out about it so soon, but there he was, offering sympathy and wanting to know when they should say a Mass for Jerry. I put him off. I just told him I'd let him know. It isn't as if there was a body that they had to have a funeral. Jerry would have been twenty-eight on the sixteenth of January, but that's too long to put it off." While she was talking Mrs. Bolling refilled the glasses with gin and bitters. "Twenty-eight. He was born the sixteenth of January, Eighteen-and-Ninety-one. How did you get to know Jerry?"

"Through my husband. They knew each other in the National Guard and later the army," said Priscilla.

"Yes, Jerry was very fond of your husband," said Mrs. Bolling.

"He was fond of me, too," said Priscilla.

"You don't mean there was anything between you? You don't have to tell me if you don't want to, but the way you said that. Jerry was fond of the girls. That's why he never got married. I used to say to him, 'Jerry, one of these days some girl's going to take you seriously.'"

"Oh, I wouldn't say he took me seriously," said Priscilla.

"No, and of course you were married, although that didn't always stop Jerry Bolling. There was a young married woman living upstairs that Jerry would wait for her husband to leave the apartment, and like a shot Jerry'd be up there. Her husband was a printer on the Eyetalian paper and worked at night. He got a job on the Eyetalian paper in New York and she went along with him, but she always sent him a Christmas card. Oh, that Jerry was a devil. Not that he was mean or anything. He just couldn't leave the girls alone, and I will say he got plenty of encouragement. This apartment is going to seem lonely without him."

"Yes, I'll bet," said Priscilla.

"First I had to go and lose his father, then Jerry. Now I don't know what I'll do," said Mrs. Bolling. "I had a couple of friends used to come in and play poker Saturday night and we'd have a few beers. But this summer in the hot weather they gave it up, and I have the feeling they gave it up for good. The only one left of the old poker crowd is Vince Bondy, and him and I fight all the time. We always make up, but one of these nights he'll go just a little too far with his remarks about my weight and that'll be the end. A woman knows when she's putting on weight. Do you think I'm too stout? Tell me truthfully."

"I'd say you were pleasingly plump," said Priscilla.

"I could take off a few pounds, but that Vince Bondy forgets that I weighed ten pounds more when he first met me," said Mrs. Bolling.

"Mrs. Bolling, I really have to go now," said Priscilla, rising.

"Well, it was very nice of you to come. I wish I knew Bob Hotch-kiss when he was alive. He came here one time and blew his horn for Jerry, but he didn't come upstairs. I said to Jerry, why didn't he ask him to come up? Was he ashamed of his mother? But Jerry was never ashamed of me, no matter what Vince Bondy said. I'll be sure and let you know if I have a Mass for Jerry."

"Don't come down with me," said Priscilla. "I know the way out."

"Goodbye, dear," said Mrs. Bolling.

Goodbye, dear!

If there was any grief to be shared by Priscilla it was her small grief over the death of Jerry Bolling, and that had vanished in her conversation with his mother. She was a slob, and thank God she had not told her any more about Jerry and herself. But that was dead as Jerry was dead, as Bob was dead, as Cleveland was dead. There were things to be discussed with Clarence Kelley, legal things and money things, but thank God there was no reason for her staying in Cleveland much longer. There were things to be discussed with Bob's mother, the Widow Hotchkiss, whom she rather liked because Mrs. Hotchkiss had never been popular in Cleveland, but for no other reason. Thank God she was almost free of Cleveland. Thank God for the German bullet or whatever it was that had set her free from Bob Hotchkiss and Cleveland.

Her maid, Tillie, was on the telephone when she got home. "Who was that?" said Priscilla.

"Mrs. Ewing, but she hung up," said Tillie. "She called twice."

"Did she leave any message?" said Priscilla.

"Just to express her condolence and say if there was anything she could do. You got several of those calls. I wrote them all down. Mrs. McVeagh called, and Mrs. Hay called you long distance from out of town. There was several called and didn't leave their name. I been busy answering the phone all afternoon. I'd no sooner hang up than there'd be another call. And Mr. Barr called, Mr. George Barr. I wrote them all down."

"Did Mr. Barr leave a message?" said Priscilla.

"Just wanted to know where you were," said Tillie. "But I reckon he'll call again. You know how he is. I told him youse at Mrs. Bolling's and he said, 'What Mrs. Bolling?' How could I tell him if I didn't know?"

"Did he say where I could reach him?" said Priscilla.

"Yes, he said he'd be at the store till ha'past five."

"Why didn't you tell me that?" said Priscilla.

"Honey, I can't tell you everything at once," said Tillie. "Give me time."

Priscilla waited for Tillie to leave, then telephoned George Barr at his shop. "Hello, you," said Priscilla.

"I've been trying to reach you all day. Who is Mrs. Bolling?" said George.

"She's a fat old woman, her son was killed with Bob, or I *guess* he was killed with Bob. Jerry Bolling's mother, if that's any help to you."

"None whatever. I thought your maid got the name wrong," said George Barr. "Are you being the brave little widow?"

"Yes, I am. The brave little widow. And I'm tired of it already. Why don't you come out here and play?"

"Too many people will be dropping in on you," said George. "I could come out later, around midnight."

"Do I have to wait that long?" said Priscilla.

"You don't want a lot of people interrupting, do you? Twelve midnight. All right?"

"All right," said Priscilla.

Mrs. Arthur Pinkham Hotchkiss, the last of Priscilla's callers, stayed on and on until it was nearly half-past eleven, and Priscilla was afraid she would have to ask her to spend the night, but that she was determined not to do. "Goodness, look what time it is," said Mrs. Hotchkiss.

"It's quite late," said Priscilla. "I'd ask you to stay, but I must get some sleep."

"You must be tired," said Mrs. Hotchkiss. "You get a good night's sleep. And *I* have to go to Shaker Heights. You're not afraid to be alone?"

"What's there to be afraid of?" said Priscilla. And so, ten minutes later, Priscilla was alone at last. She put on her negligee and awaited her lover.

George Barr was about forty and looked every bit of it. He had pouches under his eyes and a deep, rather musical voice and a cigarette cough. "You almost had to entertain my mother-in-law," said Priscilla.

"No thanks," said George. "I get enough of those old bags at the shop. *You're* bearing up well under the strain."

"The strain is over," said Priscilla.

"Then let me see your little pussy," said George.

"How do you know I'm ready?"

"You're always ready to show me your pussy," said George. "I've never had any trouble in that direction. It's a good thing I'm so fond of it."

"It's just like any other," said Priscilla.

"Come on, you don't believe that," said George. "Is it like Ada Ewing's?"

"She has more hair than I have," said Priscilla.

"And hers is darker," said George.

"Much darker, practically black," said Priscilla. "Where it isn't grey."

"I've never seen a grey-haired pussy," said George.

"I have. Two. Christine Frogg has some grey hair," said Priscilla. "*You* have a *lot* of grey hair."

"Mine doesn't count. I started to get grey when I was eighteen," said George.

"Get undressed and stop talking," said Priscilla.

"I'll get undressed, but stop talking? Me?" said George Barr. He took off his clothes, chattering as he did. "Don't you know that I talk so much to cover up my nervousness? Especially now, when you're not paying any attention to a thing I'm saying, but all your attention is focused on one part of my anatomy. Did you hear what I said?"

"Something about your anatomy," said Priscilla. "I really wasn't listening."

"Just looking? Stare at it, and see what happens," said George. "Nothing."

"Maybe if you hypnotize it," said George.

"There. Something's happening," said Priscilla.

"Let's see how long it takes," said George. "Don't touch it."

"But I want to touch it."

"All right, if you must. Now let me be Ada Ewing."

"All right," said Priscilla. "You be Ada, and I'll be me." . . .

"Now I want to be me," said George.

"Be Ada some more," said Priscilla.

"I'm tired of being Ada," said George.

"Just a little more," said Priscilla . . . "Oh, Ada. That was delicious. Now you can be you. Go in me."

"I'll go in you, but you'll be Ada," said George.

"All right," said Priscilla . . . "Who was I then? Ada or me?"

"I think you were Ada."

"I think I was, too," said Priscilla.

"Well, I must have a cigarette," said George.

"Let me light it for you," said Priscilla. "Did I really seem like Ada?"

"Considering that the only times I ever saw Ada Ewing she had all her clothes on, at the concerts, you gave a very good imitation," said George. He had the cigarette, Priscilla lighting it for him as George gently fondled her breasts. "They're nice," he said.

"I like them," said Priscilla. "What else do you like about me?"

"Here," said George, putting his finger on her vagina. "And here," gently pressing her buttocks.

"What *don't* you like about me?" said Priscilla.

"Your elbows," said George.

[248]

"Kiss them," said Priscilla.

"But I told you I didn't like them," said George.

"Kiss them anyway," said Priscilla.

"Why?"

"Because I told you to," said Priscilla.

"Would it make you happy if I did? Or because I obeyed you?" said George.

"Because you obeyed me," said Priscilla.

"Then I don't know that I will," said George. "I have to draw the line somewhere."

"Do you want to know why I wanted you to kiss my elbows?" said Priscilla. "Because the first date I had with Bob, he kissed my elbows."

"Funny I should pick them as the part I didn't like."

"Not so funny when you think of Bob," said Priscilla.

"No, if you put it that way," said George.

"No, he really didn't like women."

"And men have elbows," said George. "Elbows and asses. There's a saying, 'He didn't know his ass from his elbow.' *I* could always tell the difference. Are we through playing for the night?"

"I'm not, but I guess you are," said Priscilla.

"Unless I can spend the night," said George. "But your maid gets here early in the morning, doesn't she?"

"Seven, seven-thirty," said Priscilla.

"Then we're through for the night. Thank you for a delightful evening, Priscilla."

"The pleasure was all mine," she said. "Well, not all."

"Not by any means," he said. He began putting on his clothes. "What are you going to do? What are your plans?"

"Getting out of Cleveland as soon as I can," said Priscilla.

"Yes, I guessed that," said George. "I'd get out too, but I have the shop, and let's face it, all my friends are here. Where will you go? Not back to Springfield, Massachusetts?"

"I thought I'd try New York."

"I had an idea you might try California," said George.

"No, she's through with me—if you mean Ada."

"Yes, but are you through with her?"

"As long as California's as far away as it is. I still like her, though. I keep thinking about her."

"And her black hair, where it isn't grey," said George.

"You shouldn't have said that. Maybe if you had a little nap we could do it again? Do you think you could?" said Priscilla.

"I'm willing to try," said George. "It's one o'clock. Six hours' sleep."

"No, I don't have to be up at seven, and you do. See, I can be nice. You go home and we'll save it for tonight," said Priscilla.

"That would really be better," said George. "When do you think you'll get out of Cleveland?"

"Oh, several months, I guess. Why?" said Priscilla. "Are you going back to the boys?"

"What makes you think I ever left them?"

"You left Walter Finch, didn't you?" said Priscilla.

"We had a falling-out. But he'll be back. I saw him on Euclid Avenue the other day and he was very friendly. He asked about you, and I said you were fine. He didn't get anything out of me, but *he* knows. Christine tells him everything. By the way, what do you know about a girl named Ruth Nork?"

"I never heard of her."

"She has a husband that beats her and she's become very friendly with Christine. I thought you might know her because her husband's a lawyer. Dark-haired girl."

"Do you want me to find out about her?" said Priscilla.

"Well, keep your ears open," said George. "When you go to New York I'll *have* to have *somebody*. And a girl whose husband beats her sounds interesting. Maybe *he's* interesting. You never know. I'll try to make it tonight, dearie. If I don't I'm sure you'll understand."

"I'll understand, but try to make it," said Priscilla. "I'll be lonely after all those sympathetic wives telling me how wonderful Bob was and what a good husband. The thought of him makes me puke."

She went to bed and slept soundly after her exertions. In the morning the phone began ringing at eight o'clock, but Tillie said she was not taking any calls before ten. She thereby did not have to answer calls from Edna Ewing and Mrs. Bolling, but at ten-fifteen she took a call from Clarence Kelley.

"There was a nice article in the *Plain Dealer*," said Kelley. "Have you seen it?"

"No, I haven't had a chance to read the paper," said Priscilla.

"It was all about where he went to school and the usual biographical material. His father. His tennis career," said Kelley.

"I'll read it when I have more time. The phone's been ringing incessantly," said Priscilla.

"Well, I called to let you know we're at your service here," said Kelley. "How are you bearing up?"

"Mr. Kelley, I don't have to lie to you."

"Meaning?"

"Meaning that Bob Hotchkiss is dead and that's the only good thing that's come out of this war."

"I wouldn't repeat that if I were you," said Kelley. "There are a lot of people in Cleveland who think of Bob as a war hero and before that as a nice tennis player. Anyone who was killed in the war achieves the status of a hero, and then people more or less forget him."

"Oh, I know," said Priscilla.

"*De mortuis nil nisi bonum*, as you must have learned at Smith College," said Kelley. "Of the dead, speak nothing but good, and I hope they'll remember that when my time comes. True, you may remember unpleasant things about Bob Hotchkiss, but most people are going to remember that he played tennis and was killed in the war. And that's all they'll remember unless you give them something else to remember, something that'll keep his memory alive. Do you see what I mean?"

"I guess so," said Priscilla.

"You see, you'll be alive to remind them of the unpleasant things he did. But without you to remind them, he'll descend into merciful obscurity. And you're a young woman, Priscilla. You'll marry again and have another identity."

"Why do you care what I do?" said Priscilla.

"I'm an old man, Priscilla. Past eighty. It doesn't make much difference to me what you do. But if I can persuade you to put your bitterness aside, you may remember me for just that. Do you plan to go on living in Cleveland?"

"God, no."

"Good. Get a new start," said Kelley. "You never did like Cleveland, did you?"

"No, and Cleveland never liked me, so we're even," said Priscilla.

"Next stop New York?" said Kelley.

"I think so," said Priscilla.

"Good. New York is a good place to make a new start," said Kelley. "Meanwhile, as I said, we're at your service here. You can always reach me at the office or the Union Club."

The next call was from Edna Ewing. "Are you receiving callers?" said Edna. "I know you're receiving telephone calls, because I've been trying to reach you."

"Why don't you just drop in any time?" said Priscilla.

"Oh, I guess you didn't know, Bill and I and the children are all at the farm. Bill drives in every morning."

"Oh, the farm," said Priscilla.

"It's nice out here," said Edna. "There always seems to be a little breeze stirring, and the children love it. I swim twice a day. We're thinking of staying here through the winter. It's only ten miles from town, and the township school is pretty good, so I hear. How about you coming out here?"

"Maybe I will when things quiet down," said Priscilla.

"You know where it is, don't you?"

"Oh, yes. I've been there with Mrs. Ewing," said Priscilla.

"Ada?"

"Yes, I spent the night there once," said Priscilla. "And I went there another time."

"The telephone is 44-J. Are you having any kind of a memorial service?"

"I haven't planned to, but I'm leaving that up to Mrs. Hotchkiss. There's no hurry."

"Poor Priscilla. I wish there was something I could do, but I don't suppose there is. I thought it was a nice article in the *Plain Dealer*, didn't you?"

"I haven't had time to read it, but Clarence Kelley told me it was nice. I must go, there's somebody at the front door," said Priscilla.

"Goodbye," said Edna.

That was Edna, the housewife, the little mother; pretty Edna, who probably had never *seen* another man but her husband, whose mind was on the township school and her twice-daily swim, who had fulfilled her duty the moment the telephone call was concluded. Priscilla rather enjoyed thinking about the farm and what had gone on there, and what smug little Edna would have to say about *that*. Somehow she knew she would have to contrive to tell Edna before she left Cleveland. Smug little Edna. It would give *her* something to think about. And smug Bill Ewing, the smuggest of them all. Until now she had not realized how much she hated Bill Ewing, and even now she did not know why. But hate him she did, and it was enough to know that she did. She would find a reason, and it would be a good one, even if it turned out to be the fact that he had never been susceptible to her charms. *That* was almost the *best* reason. Which reminded her that George Barr had not telephoned her. Who did he think he was? Who the *hell* did he think he was? She knew enough about *him* to have him arrested.

The telephone rang. "Tillie, will you answer that, and if it's Mrs. Bolling tell her I'm out," said Priscilla.

"Just *out?*" said Tillie.

"Yes, just out, and you don't know when I'll be back," said Priscilla.

"Mrs. Hotchkiss' residence," said Tillie. "She's out, and I do' know when she be back."

"Good," said Priscilla.

"That was Mrs. Bolling, all right," said Tillie. The phone rang again. "That's her again."

"It may be somebody else. Answer it," said Priscilla.

"Mrs. Hotchkiss' residence," said Tillie. "Oh, it's you, Mr. Barr."

"I'll talk to him," said Priscilla. "Hello, you. Did you get enough sleep?"

"Enough for our purposes, anyway," said George. "Midnight all right?"

"All right," said Priscilla. "You can bring a friend if you like."

"Who, for instance?" said George.

"I'll leave that up to you." said Priscilla. "I thought if you were tired."

"Priscilla is thinking of a little orgy," said George. "Well, it may be a little late to get someone now, but I'll try. Would you prefer a male or a female? I could probably get Christine, if she's in town."

"No, not Christine. I don't feel like her," said Priscilla.

"I have an idea. You know that friend of Christine's, Ruth Nork? The one whose husband beats her? I was saving her for myself, but she might be just right. The only trouble is, midnight, and she's married. Too short notice. But it's an idea."

"Couldn't we go to your apartment?" said Priscilla.

"You like my idea? You want to play this afternoon?" said George.

"I do now," said Priscilla.

"I'll telephone Ruth and see what can be arranged," said George.

Priscilla hung up and waited while George called Ruth. In about twenty minutes he called Priscilla. "It's no use, she doesn't answer her telephone. Some people go on vacation this time of year," he said. "Do you still want to play this afternoon?"

"Yes, I couldn't stand waiting till midnight," said Priscilla. "I'll be at your apartment at ha' past four."

She was actually there at four-twenty and he was playing the Victrola. "What have you got on?" she said.

"*Ein Heldenleben,*" he said, and took it off.

"What's that?" said Priscilla.

"It's by Richard Strauss," he said. "I just got it."

"Oh, it's one of your twelve-inch records. They take forever," said Priscilla. "I like your pajamas. They almost match your eyes."

"And yours. That's why I wore them," said George.

"You did, George?"

"Oh yes, I have my sentimental side," he said.

"It doesn't show very often. You're usually very cynical," she said.

"That's because I've been disillusioned. I was disillusioned at a tender age."

"How old?" said Priscilla.

"Three," he said. "That was when my mother took her teat away and put me on the bottle."

"Well, I'll put the teat right back," she said. "Do you want the right one or the left one?"

"Whichever one is strawberry," said George.

"They're both strawberry," said Priscilla.

"Then I'll take both," he said.

She took off her dress and bared her breasts. "Notice I'm not wearing a brazeer. I had to wear a slip because you can see through my dress, but that's all I'm wearing. I might as well take that off, too. What about your pajamas? Are you going to keep them on all day?"

"Oh, I guess not," he said. "I've tortured you long enough," he said. He took off his pajamas and stood before her and she embraced him at the waist so that his penis touched one, then the other, breast. "What do you want to do now?" he said.

"Let's do this some more," she said. She held his penis so that it kissed her nipples and pressed into them. "I like that," she said. "Do you?"

"Of course I like it. But I'd rather you put it in your mouth. Or someplace."

"I'm ready," she said.

"To put it in your mouth—or someplace?" he said.

"Both," she said . . .

"We seem to be fucking," he said.

"What's wrong with that?" she said. She raised her knees high, then wrapped her legs around his waist.

"You got really in me that time," she said. " 'Way in."

"I know I did. You came twice, didn't you?"

"Three times. The first time was when your sword pressed against my bosom. Sometimes I like that, and other times it has no effect. Look at my nipples. They're still big."

"But my pecker isn't," said George. "I have to have a cigarette now."

"I'll light it for you," she said.

"You spoil me. You did that last night, too," he said. "Have you given any more thought to Ruth Nork? I talked to her later in the afternoon, and she was interested. Not for today, but sometime."

"If she was here now—but you want her first, don't you?"

"I don't think she'd do anything now," said George. "I think she has to be played with a little."

"But you don't *know* that, George. I've had some experience with women when no else was there."

"All right, you're welcome to try her. But be careful."

"She likes Christine Frogg, and I'm nicer than Christine," she said. "Don't you think I am?"

"Oh, I think so, but I'm not Ruth Nork. And *you* may not like *her*, don't forget."

"Well, she has dark hair and Christine likes her, and so do you. I'll trust your judgment, and if it's only the one time, she can go back to her husband and let him beat her. But I've also had experience with husbands that beat you."

"Did Bob Hotchkiss beat you?"

"*Did* he! Why do you think I hate him so? I was ashamed to tell anybody when he was alive, but now I don't care who knows. The God damned war hero. The son of a bitch," said Priscilla. "What time is it?"

"It's only about quarter after five," said George.

"I'd like to stay here."

"You might as well. I've closed the shop," said George. "There aren't any customers this time of year, so I let everybody go home."

"I'll call Tillie and tell her she can go home. Then we can spend the night here. Is that all right with you? I'm so tired of being the war widow. We can have some spaghetti here, and you can play the Victrola. You're just about the only person I like to be with, of all the people in Cleveland. That's true, George. The only person I like to be with. I'll be glad to get out of here. I think another year of this and I'd commit suicide."

"That makes two of us," said George Barr. "Oh, yes, I've thought of doing the Dutch act. What on earth is there for me to live for? I have an older brother that hardly speaks to me because he knows what I am. Of course he started me on the downward path, but he forgets that. Then he straightened himself out and married a girl from Cincinnati and they have two children, boys, and he keeps them out of my sight, afraid I'll corrupt them. Well, maybe I would."

"Is Chauncey Barr your brother?"

"That's him, all right. The pillar of society with the fairy brother, that runs an interior decorator shop."

[247]

"He rides to hounds. That's all I know about him. Mr. and Mrs. Chauncey Barr. She rides, too," said Priscilla.

"And on top of everything else, I'm terrified of horses. Simply terrified. I break out in a rash whenever I go near one. They have one boy that's as afraid of horses as I am, but Chauncey makes him ride, and he's a terrible rider. Always falling off or getting thrown. Chauncey won't be satisfied till he breaks his neck. When I warn him—even *I* know the boy's a terrible rider—Chauncey tells me to mind my own business."

"Where does all the money come from?" said Priscilla.

"Inherited from my father, who never rode a horse in his life. My father was over fifty when I was born, and Chauncey is ten years older than I am. He was about fifteen when he began to sleep with me, with predictable results."

"Your father must have worn out a couple of wives," said Priscilla.

"Oh, indeed he did. My mother was my father's third wife, and she didn't last much longer. I was brought up by an aunt. A great-aunt."

"Your father must have been one of the first settlers of dear old Cleveland."

"He was not. He was born in Stonington, Connecticut, and didn't come to Cleveland till he was twenty-five or so. He was in the tanning and hide business. But he got out of that and opened up a little store, and from that he went into banking, which is where he stayed and how my brother got into it. Do you want to know all about the Barr family? I'll tell you if you're dying to hear about them."

"I don't feel that there's any urgent necessity to know your father," said Priscilla.

"There's even less to know my brother, although he may surprise you. He's at the dangerous age now, you know. And those horsey people, you never can tell about them."

"What's his age? Fifty?"

"Ten years older than I am," said George.

"Clarence Kelley is in his eighties," she said.

"I don't think you can expect anything there. He's either had his prostate out or else he's lost interest."

"What is his prostrate?"

"His prostate. It's a gland that gives you trouble and you have to have it taken out. It isn't the same as castration, but one's as bad as the other, so I'm told."

"Castration is your balls, isn't it?"

"Don't *talk* about it. Yes," said George.

"Is it like when a woman has her ovaries removed?" said Priscilla. "I'm thinking of having that done."

"First be sure what they're taking out of you," said George.

"I just don't want to have any babies. But I want them to leave the thing in that causes me to get a thrill. That's all I want."

"Explain that to the doctor. In other words, you want the playpen but not the nursery."

"Oh, that's cute. Did you think that up?" said Priscilla.

"Heavens, no. I first heard that from a prostitute," said George. "Let's go for a ride in your car? It'll be cooler and then we can have supper. Do you mind taking me for a ride?"

"All right," said Priscilla.

"Will you drive, or shall I?"

"You drive," said Priscilla. "I'm supposed to be in mourning," she said.

"Then we might as well take my car. Then I'll need gas. My Marmon eats up gas but it's such a *beautiful* car. Such chaste lines, reminds you of a woman's bosom. That's why I bought it. It's the *only* reason why I bought it. If only it weren't so fat. My brother's Pierce-Arrow has a horn on it that sounds as if he were having an attack of flatulence, if you know what I mean. The chauffeur blows the horn twice for flatulence, then follows it once, ah-*oogah*, that sounds like puking. A most unbecoming sound. You don't hear any such noises from my Marmon."

They stopped at a farmers' inn along the way and had a chicken-and-waffle supper, and they were back at George's apartment before eleven o'clock. "Wait here while I put my car away," said George.

"I'll go with you," said Priscilla. She went with him to the garage and accompanied him while the Marmon was stored by the night man. She put her arm in George's and walked in step with him to the apartment. "I'm tired, are you?" she said.

"Can hardly keep my eyes open," he said.

"Me, too," she said. "I'll sleep in the small bed."

She kissed him goodnight and covered her nakedness with a sheet. She waited for him to get in bed with her, but he stumbled and groped his way into the other bed, and presently they were both asleep. She was awake at five o'clock in the morning and he was still asleep. She crept into bed with him and began to play with him. Scarcely opening his eyes, he said, "Priscilla, you're insatiable, insatiable."

"It didn't take you so long," she said.

Paul Everett was discouraged by Lila. Her birthday, the Fourth of July, had been a very unsatisfactory holiday for her this year. It was a Thursday, ordinarily a good time to set out for the week-end at the Lake, but somehow everything seemed to go wrong. Edna, for instance, was not coming for July this year, and it did not look as if she would make any part of it. Now there were two children, not one, and it was that much more inconvenient to travel. And Bill and Edna had elected to spend all summer on Mrs. Ewing's farm, which had a swimming pool and tennis court and was only ten miles from Cleveland. Paul Everett was busier than ever at the furniture factory, doing a rush job on the government order for a thousand desks, which meant working overtime for him and the possibility for Lila that he would have to postpone his trip to the Lake. "Will you kindly tell me what's the use of making all that money if you don't get any pleasure out of it?" Lila asked him.

"The government needs those desks, Lila," said Paul Everett. He did not add that there was a rumor going around that the government was planning or at least considering the cancellation of the wartime emergency contracts, which they had the right to do. Which in turn would mean trying to unload his surplus desks at the best price he could get for them, in addition to his uncertainty about making plans for a medium-priced line of furniture sometime in the late fall. It was all very well to have those government contracts, but the steady bread-and-butter line consisted of something to take the place of the old Mission line. Everyone agreed that the Mission line was through, passé, out of style. Everywhere you went the salesmen were saying that the Mission line was such old stuff that you couldn't *give* it away, an exaggeration that Paul Everett did not quite go along with. But that the designers of the coming furniture were ready to go to work was beyond any doubt, and Paul had been talking to them. The question was when, and how soon? The answer was easy: as soon as this damn war was over and you could start manufacturing again. Anything that would sell.

But you could not talk to Lila about furniture design in the mood she had been in since the Fourth of July. He had gone up to the Lake for one night, the night of the Fourth, and had returned to Wingate next day because he was fed up with her complaining. He attended the Round Table lunch that day, and was somewhat surprised to see that only one other member, Stephen Linkletter, was there. "Hello, there, Steve. How did you happen to be working today?" said Paul Everett.

"I could ask you the same thing," said Linkletter.

"Oh, we have that big order for desks, I must have told you," said Paul. "The biggest order we ever had. But I thought this would give me a good chance to talk to one of our designers."

"Paul, you're one of the busiest men I ever knew. You must be making a mint of money."

"Well, we're working double shift now. I hope these workmen are saving a little of their overtime. I'd hate to think it all went into silk shirts. They tell me some of the men at Ford's wear their silk shirts to work."

"I *saw* them, I actually *saw* them," said Linkletter. "How is Edna these days?"

"Fine, fine," said Paul. "They're spending the summer on her mother-in-law's farm, just outside of Cleveland. She moved to California."

"Nice for Edna," said Linkletter.

"Yes, she has a swimming pool and a tennis court, and in this hot weather . . ."

"Very quiet here today," said Linkletter. "Sterling Logan showed up the other day, having his guns looked over for his trip to Alaska. Van Nostrand had a letter from his son, and that must make him feel better. He hadn't had a letter from him since he went overseas, and then three or four letters arrived all at once. Phil is with a base hospital somewhere near Paris. I guess that's all the news this week. Try the fish chowder, Paul. I recommend it."

"If you recommend it, I'll give it a try," said Paul.

"You staying up at the Lake for the summer?" said Linkletter.

"Well, I don't believe I can. It's a little far to drive back and forth every day, so I think I'll be taking my meals here. The help are all with Lila at the Lake."

"Batching it, eh?"

"For July, anyway," said Paul. "Maybe I'll get some time off in August, but it doesn't look that way now."

"Does Lila enjoy summering at the Lake?" said Linkletter.

"Well, she has her little group of friends that she sees every summer. We've been going up there almost twenty years now. I added a new wing to the cottage the summer before last, and now that I have two grandchildren I thought we'd need the extra space. But it looks as though Edna will be spending her summers on the farm. I don't blame her." Paul came close to complaining about Lila, but Stephen Linkletter was not interested in finding out why Edna liked the farm. It occurred to Paul that Linkletter might be slightly deaf. In any event, the men of the Round Table, like the old-fashioned members of the Union Club, avoided discussing their wives.

"Yes," said Linkletter. "Well, Edna's married long enough to have a life of her own now. It must be five years."

"Five and a half. Five years in January," said Paul.

"The time goes by," said Linkletter.

"It certainly does," said Paul. "Yes, it certainly does."

Linkletter pushed back his chair. "Hope you enjoy your chowder," he said.

"Oh, you leaving?" said Paul.

"Somebody has to be at the bank," said Linkletter. "Somebody at your factory may want to open up a new account, and I like to be there to shake hands with him. We have forty-five new accounts from the factory, so they're not all buying silk shirts. So long, Paul. Probably see you here tomorrow."

Linkletter was not one of the interesting members of the Round Table, but his departure left Paul alone to finish his fish chowder. He was almost sorry he had left Lila, but a few days alone would do her no harm. He thought of Edna and wondered why she had not inherited more of Lila's personality. The girl had always resisted her mother. As a young girl up at the Lake she had always shown her preference for her father's company. Fishing with him. Swimming with him. Going for rides in the old Hudson with him. Telling him things she did not tell her mother. It must have been kind of a lonely life for Lila, but Lila had only herself to blame. If she had been a little less strict with Edna it might have made a difference. There was the time when Eddie Noisrander had invited her down to Culver for some military ball, and Lila acted as if he had insulted her. "I should say not," Lila had declared when Edna asked her permission. "I guess everybody knows what Culver is like." But everybody did not know what Culver was like, least of all Lila Everett.

"Are you sure it's not Culver but Eddie Noisrander you're objecting to?" said Paul.

"*That* impudent snotnose!" said Lila. "Strutting about in his uniform. Smoking cigarettes in front of the drug store and passing remarks about the girls that go by."

"The Noisranders are good customers of ours," said Paul.

"Don't remind me," said Lila.

"I have to remind you every once in a while," said Paul.

There were times when it seemed as if Lila had a hate on for everybody, and July of that year seemed to be one of those times. She had taken the train up to the Lake on Monday, the first of July, in order to get the cottage ready. Most of the July people were already in residence by that time and had caused a shortage of butter at the Lake store, so that there was none to be had until Tuesday afternoon. On Tuesday, when Lila was able to buy butter, there was a shortage of kerosene for light and fuel. She sent the servants to borrow kerosene but that put her in the position of having had to borrow it, which was almost as bad as not having it. There was no hot water until long past suppertime and Lila could not take her bath. In the morning, Wednesday, a copperhead was discovered lying on the porch, and one of the maids quit her job to go back to Wingate. "How do I know the place isn't full of them?" said the maid.

"You don't know," said Lila. "But you have to get used to them. I've been coming here twenty years and they never bit anybody."

"There's always the first time, and I'll be it," said the maid. "I'm very sorry, Mrs. Everett, but I can't stay."

Paul arrived in the Pierce-Arrow Thursday morning. "I got up at five o'clock this morning and I made it in just under two hours," he said. "I call that pretty good time."

"You must have broken the speed limit," said Lila.

"I went forty most of the time," he said. "The speed cops don't mind if you go forty. What are we doing today?"

"I don't know. What do you want to do?" said Lila.

"Go for a sail, if that's all right with you."

"I don't know if the boat's ready. In fact, I know it isn't," said Lila.

"Oh, come on, Lila."

"Come on yourself. Don't expect me to have the boat ready for His Majesty. I had too many other things to do. We ran out of kerosene. We had no butter. One of the maids quit and went back to Wingate because she saw a copperhead. We had no hot water. And you arrive up here the morning of the Fourth and expect me to have everything in readiness for His Majesty. Well, it's time you thought of somebody else. I'm good and sick and tired of waiting on you hand and foot."

"Well, why don't you go visit Edna for a while?"

"Because I wasn't invited, that's why. I know better than to go where I'm not wanted."

"All right, all *right.*"

"And don't shout at me. I'm not used to being shouted at," said Lila.

"You make me wish I hadn't come up here," he said.

"Well, why did you? All you've done since you arrived was complain about your boat not being ready. How was I to know it was supposed to be ready? You didn't say anything. Was I supposed to read your mind?"

"It's a good thing you can't now," he said. "Where we having lunch?"

"At the Shack," said Lila. "I asked the Osborns to meet us there at ha' past twelve."

"The Osborns? I come all the way up here to have lunch with the Osborns? Great. Just great. I thought they weren't coming back this summer."

"Well, they're back, and they're having lunch with us."

"Who else are we having lunch with?" said Paul.

"Nobody, just the Osborns," said Lila.

"Well, I hope he stays awake. He has a habit of falling asleep during a meal. I guess that's because she never stops talking," said Paul.

"Mimi Osborn is a very entertaining conversationalist, and one of my closest friends," said Lila.

"Well, we'll hear all about the suffragette movement," said Paul.

"I hope we do. I hope we do," said Lila. "A heck of a lot more interesting than your Round Table conversation. Are we going in the Pierce-Arrow?"

"Either that or walking," said Paul.

"We *could* go in the Osborns' car," said Lila.

It turned out that they *all* went in the Pierce-Arrow because that was the car Mrs. Osborn liked to ride in. She sat in front, next to Paul; Osborn sat in back with Lila. But Mrs. Osborn turned half around to converse with Lila and Osborn. Lunch at the Shack offered a choice between the minute steak, the Spanish omelette, and the liver-and-bacon. The waitress, after hearing the orders, announced that she was sorry, no more minute steak. "Then why did you tell us you had it?" said Mrs. Osborn.

"Because if only one of you ordered it you'd have been all right. But the four of you ordered it," said the waitress.

Politeness decreed that each of the four should volunteer to take something other than the lone minute steak. The upshot of the discussion that ensued was that Mrs. Osborn said, "Well, I'll eat it if nobody else is going to." The others ate the Spanish omelette. When it came time to order dessert, Paul made an announcement of his own. "If anybody else doesn't want the lemon meringue, I notice there's only one piece left."

"Oh, dear," said Mrs. Osborn. "Well, I guess I'll take the coconut custard."

"Why? Did you want the lemon meringue?" said Lila.

"It's a favorite of mine," said Mrs. Osborn. "But I know Paul wanted the minute steak, so he can have the lemon meringue."

"Thank you," said Paul.

"I think we ought to go Dutch on the check," said Osborn.

"All right," said Paul.

"Oh, Paul!" said Lila.

"I think going Dutch is a good idea. We ought to do it all summer," said Paul.

The women were silent, and the men paid the bill. They went back to the Everetts' and got the Osborns' car, and Paul took his seat on the porch. "Well, at least we established one precedent," he said.

"You mean Dutch Treat? I think it was disgusting, if you want to know what *I* think."

"It was Osborn's idea. Maybe he turned over a new leaf. He never paid a single check all last summer. All—last—summer," said Paul. "A couple of times he even let me pay the check when I wasn't having lunch with him. Force of habit. And it isn't as if he bought my lunch in the wintertime. Where is it he lives? Petoskey. I live in Wingate and he lives in Petoskey. Not much chance of my having lunch in Petoskey."

"Oh, you're just being disagreeable," said Lila, and went inside.

She came out a little before three o'clock. "I'm going over to Alice Pflug's to play 500. I'll walk," she said.

"A whole block? Be careful you don't strain yourself," he said. He waited until he saw her turn in at Alice Pflug's, then drove the Pierce-Arrow to the boatyard and killed some time there with the owner. It turned out that the yard owner had automatically put his boat in shape and launched it for the summer.

"I figured you might be needing her over the Fourth," said the owner. "But there isn't much of a breeze now." So they talked about the war, and the difficulty of getting labor to work in a boatyard and a furniture factory, and Paul enjoyed himself. When he got home, Lila was on the telephone.

"Thought you were going to play cards with Alice Pflug," he said.

"It's tomorrow," said Lila. It was not necessary to tell him that she had the date wrong.

"It just isn't your week, is it, Lila?" said Paul.

"You're hateful," she said.

For her it was strong language, and for him it required, demanded, a strong reaction. He left the next day for Wingate, pausing in their bedroom—it was not yet six o'clock—only long enough to tell her he was leaving but not to say goodbye. She was still in bed but awake. All the way down to Wingate he kept telling himself that he did not give a damn, and it was not until he was alone at the Round Table that he began to feel regret. And his regret was partly self-pity. He did not ask her to do much, but she might at least have remembered his boat (the owner of the boatyard had). She knew he did not like the Osborns. He was not hateful. He was, in fact, a devoted, faithful husband. And it was not his fault if Edna liked him better than her.

He suddenly decided to go see Edna.

There was a six-something train leaving Detroit for Cleveland, and it got into Cleveland somewhere around eight. Say nine. It was ten miles to the Ewing farm. It might be better if he telephoned Edna in advance. It might even be better if he arrived in Cleveland in the morning or if he arrived at night and telephoned Edna in the morning. That was the better idea: to telephone Edna at the farm and spend the day with her there. He would not telephone Lila.

He accordingly took the six-something train for Cleveland, had dinner on the train, checked into the hotel, and had a good night's rest and was awake, as usual, at six o'clock in the morning. He had breakfast in his room and at eight-thirty he was telephoning 44-J, Edna's number. Bill Ewing answered the phone.

"Hello, Bill. This is your father-in-law. I hope I didn't get you up."

"Mr. Everett! No, I was just leaving. How are things in Wingate, or are you up at the Lake?"

"I'm in Cleveland, seeing a man about some furniture."

"I'll come and get you," said Bill.

"Oh, that won't be necessary. You're working too, and I understand. I'll hire a car, and maybe you'll be coming home for lunch," said Paul.

It was so arranged, and Paul was at the farm at nine-thirty. "Well, what a pleasant surprise," said Edna. "Didn't Mother come with you?"

"No, she's up at the Lake. It's just a quick trip," said Paul. "And look at this young man. Say hello to your grandfather, John."

"Hello," said John.

"He's as brown as a berry. He must spend a lot of time in the pool. You're quite brown too, Edna. And here's little Mary."

"She's had the croup. I took her to the doctor yesterday and he doesn't like the look of it. He wants to keep an eye on her. The doctor is a young man, and I don't think he's had much experience with babies. She's had trouble breathing. Oh, Daddy, if anything happened to her . . ."

"Well, children have to go through these things, Edna. When you were Mary's age you had the croup too, and you survived," said Paul. "My goodness, you had the croup, and measles, and just about everything a child could have when you were little. Old Doctor Meiklejohn was always coming to our house."

"I wish we had him now," said Edna. "At least you had the feeling that he knew what he was doing . . . You've had your breakfast, a good breakfast, I hope?"

"I had corn flakes, two fried eggs and bacon, toast and coffee.

That's a pretty good breakfast for the sixth day of July. I usually manage to have a good breakfast because I eat it early and don't eat again till twelve-thirty or one. Nothing in between. The men at the factory have a second breakfast around nine o'clock—just some coffee and cake. But they've usually been up since six o'clock, so they need it. Also, it gives them a little time out. The kind of work they do for me gets monotonous, doing the same thing over and over again, like building a desk drawer. I know I'd get tired of it . . . Come here, Edna. Cry on my shoulder. *I* know you're worried about little Mary."

"It isn't only the baby that makes me cry," said Edna.

"What else? Bill? You having some kind of trouble with him?"

"Not Bill," said Edna. "I can't tell you, not even you. It's a family secret. Not Bill or me or the children, and don't ask me any more because I wouldn't know how to tell you even if I were free to. Which I'm not."

"Take my handkerchief," said Paul.

"I'll get you one of Bill's," said Edna. "And don't let on to Mother." She wiped her eyes and gave her nose a slight blow.

"Considering I don't know what your secret is about, you're safe there," said Paul.

"I know Mother would try to worm it out of me, but you won't, will you?"

"As long as you have Bill to share it with, that's enough," said Paul.

"You're a good Daddy."

"I remember when you used to say that when you were little. And not so little, too. You may be an old married woman to some, but you're still a girl with a pony cart to me," said Paul.

"Well, I'm not a girl in a pony cart. I'm a lot older than that," said Edna. "I expect Bill back about noon. Do you want to sit and talk to me, or do you want to go down to the pool with John-Stewart? It's all right, he's playing with the farmer's children at the pool."

"Then I'll stay here and keep you company," said Paul.

"That's good," said Edna. She put the baby in her crib and sat with her father.

"Well, you certainly have a nice place here," said Paul. "What do you have? About two hundred acres?"

"You know, I never found out. But I think it must be that. Yes, it must be. Mrs. Ewing bought it about fifteen years ago, and I think she added to it once or twice. It's still legally hers. The papers haven't been signed. But she's giving up her residence in Ohio and settling in California, so I guess it'll soon be ours."

"I guess the weather in California is a lot better than here, although I don't hear any complaints about the weather this summer. Not having been to California, I still like Michigan weather. I like winter to be winter and summer summer. Of course, some of those forty-below temperatures make me wish I was in California, but we've had it go to a hundred-and-five in Wingate, so I guess it evens up in the end."

"Tell me some more about the Michigan weather, Daddy," said Edna. "Or didn't you know I was born there?"

"I'm sorry, Edna," said Paul. "Just making conversation. Do you want me to stop talking?"

"Well, about the weather," said Edna. "What made you come here the weekend of the Fourth?"

"I had some business in Cleveland. It wouldn't wait," said Paul.

"Is your business a woman?"

"Good heavens, no, Edna. What ever made you think that?"

"Because I had a phone call from Mother this morning. She's very upset. I couldn't talk to her very long, but she didn't know you were here. She didn't know *where* you were, and neither did I, then," said Edna.

"So, in addition to your other troubles, you were worried about your father?" said Paul.

"A little. Mother telephoned you in Wingate, and when you didn't answer, she thought of all sorts of things," said Edna.

"Including another woman," said Paul. "I wonder who she thought of. It would have to be a prostitute, I guess, and I don't know any. Your mother and I—let's put it this way: our life has been an open book since I proposed to her, almost thirty years ago. When I was a very young man, before I asked her to marry me, I sowed my wild oats. There was a house I used to go to down near the Michigan Central freight station. That's where all us young fellows used to go, and pretend we were hell-raisers. But we didn't raise much hell. For the usual two dollars you could go upstairs and have a woman, and that, I guess, would be that. It was really rather nasty, and I gave it up. And now I suppose I ought to call your mother and let her know where I am. Let her know I'm in safe hands."

"Yes, I guess it's mean to keep her in suspense," said Edna.

Paul telephoned Lila at the Lake and explained his whereabouts. "I spent the night in Cleveland, and now I'm out here, at the farm. I'll be back in Wingate on Monday."

"Monday? That leaves today and all day Sunday," said Lila.

"I know it," said Paul. "I'm hoping Edna and Bill will ask me to spend it with them, but if they don't, I'll go back to Cleveland."

"But what about me, Paul?" said Lila.

"You're the one that called me hateful, Lila. Maybe you forget, but I remember, and I'm not used to that."

"Is that all you're going to say?"

"That's all I have time for now. The worm has turned," said Paul, and hung up.

Edna entered the room. "I overheard that last remark," she said. "About the worm?"

"Yes, and it's about time," she said. "Mother's been taking advantage of you for years, years. She's never had enough to do, that's her trouble. It isn't that she's really mean, but she's gotten so used to leading you around by the nose. The factory is yours, and she stays out of that, but everything else she had her say in. I just hope she hasn't learned her lesson too late."

"What makes you think she's learned a lesson? A week back in Wingate and she'll be leading me around by the nose again," said Paul.

"Well, it'll be your fault if she does," said Edna. "Do you love her? Really love her?"

"Love? It's so long since I've thought about love that—yes, I guess I do, when you come right down to it."

"Don't be afraid to say you don't," said Edna. "There are times when I don't love Bill. And I'm sure there are plenty of times when he doesn't love me. He went out this morning without a word about the baby, not a word."

"But you may be sure she was on his mind," said Paul.

"Now don't you start taking his side. I took your side against Mother," said Edna. "All he thinks about is Cuyahoga, and Clarence Kelley, and the Akron Rubber Company, and the Sprague Chemical Company."

"The Sprague Chemical Company? Is that something new?"

"Oh, it's supposed to be secret, and I guess it is. He doesn't tell me much about it," said Edna.

There was a silence. "Why don't you show me around the farm?" said Paul.

"All right, I will," said Edna. She took him on a tour of inspection, and it was apparent that she was beginning to enjoy herself. She introduced him to Lloyd Sharpe, who was doing some work on the tractor. Paul met Beulah Sharpe, who was collecting eggs from the hens' nests, and asked about Mary. "They seemed like a nice couple," said Paul.

"Oh, they are. They have a son named Bruce and a daughter named Esther. Lloyd wants Bruce to be a doctor. I don't know what Esther will be, but she's very bright . . . Now this is the corn crib, pretty empty now, but it'll soon be full to overflowing . . . I love it here . . . I'm learning to ride, English style. Post to the trot, sit to the canter. Here's my horse—and what do you think his name is? It's Prince, the same as my pony. But believe me the resemblance ends there. He's a handful. This is Bill's horse, that he doesn't get much chance to ride, so I exercise him. His name is Satan, and he's a devil all right. He threw me once, but you mustn't tell Bill. It was my own fault for riding with such a loose rein . . . This is my pride and joy, it's called a station wagon. I'd rather have it than your Pierce-Arrow, although it's only a Ford. The side curtains come down when it rains, but so far I've left them up . . . And here is the only thing I'm afraid of, Mrs. Ewing's prize bull. His name is Nobleman of St. Mary's the *Second*, and let me tell you, he's fierce. The only thing *he's* afraid of is Lloyd's collie Shep. When we water him we have to make sure the gates are closed, and then he comes charging out. If there's a cow to be serviced—you know what that means—she's let out at the same time, and sometimes he ignores her, but not for long. I'd never seen a bull service a cow. It's a frightening sight, that long sharp thing of the bull's, and his mounting her. John-Stewart calls it stabbing her, and he's asked a lot of questions about it."

"What do you tell him?" said Paul.

"I tell him the bull is giving the cow a calf. He's just reached the age where he's curious about such things. Oh, he's aware of the difference between a bull and a cow," said Edna.

"It'll probably save you a lot of explanations later on," said Paul.

"It should. He calls his own thing his stabber," she said.

"You like being a farmer's wife," said Paul.

"Well, you'd hardly call me a farmer's wife *yet*, but I'm getting there," said Edna. "It was hard getting to know the Sharpes at first. They'd had the run of the farm pretty much to themselves, till we came along. But we're thinking of living here the year round. It's only ten miles from Cleveland, and they tell me the country school is pretty good. Bill likes it here now. The question is, will he like it when cold weather comes? Well, we'll just have to see. It's hard to decide where to bring up your children, but I'm in favor of the country."

"Wingate was practically country," said Paul.

"Oh, but this'll be very different. Wingate had a social life, next-door neighbors, church. This is *farm,* Daddy. I've come to a stage in my life where I don't need other people as much as I once did. Back in Wingate I used to see people every day. Bertha Linkletter, Ann Collins, the boys that hung around the drug store. Not any more, though. I have my husband and my children, and they're really all that matter to me. The question is, getting John-Stewart someone to play with, and then later Mary. Bruce Sharpe is so much older than John-Stewart, and we haven't been here long enough for John-Stewart to meet children his own age."

"Maybe when school starts he'll meet children his own age," said Paul.

"Well, yes, I hadn't really thought of that. I guess I'm in too much of a hurry. But I like it here. This is where I want to live."

"You give me that impression, I'll say that. In fact, you give me the impression of a very happy young woman. I'm very pleased. And you mustn't worry too much about Mary. Croup isn't anything to worry about. You had it, I think you had it twice. You get all these things when you're an infant and build up a sort of immunity, a resistance."

"Well, John-Stewart had croup but it was a different kind of croup. They gave him anti-toxin, twenty thousand units. It sounds like such a lot, twenty thousand units, but I don't know whether it is or isn't. I know he had an awfully sore little shoulder for several days. Let's go back and see how Mary is. She must be awake, I heard her coughing."

The doctor arrived while the baby was coughing. "Good morning, Mrs. Ewing."

"This is my father, Mr. Everett," said Edna. "Dr. Wilson."

"*Mister* Everett? I thought you'd got another doctor," said the

[265]

doctor. "Has the baby been coughing that way long?"

"Off and on, all night," said Edna.

"Then I think we'll give her some anti-toxin. And just to be on the safe side, keep her little brother away from her. Keep him out of the same room. This may be diphtheria. I didn't say it *is* diphtheria, but let's not take any chances. Are there any other children around?"

"Two."

"Then all three should have anti-toxin," said the doctor.

"Should the farmer and his wife have it?"

"Only the children," said the doctor.

"Mary's brother had anti-toxin several years ago," said Edna.

"Then he won't have to have it now. How about the other children? By the way, how old are they?"

"About eighteen and fourteen," said Edna.

"The fourteen-year-old will have to have it. Diphtheria is usually a children's disease, Mrs. Ewing, but let's not take any chances."

The administration of the anti-toxin was accompanied by screeches on the part of the baby. Esther Sharpe was away on a picnic. Dr. Wilson was glad to leave the Ewing household. "Well, that's over," said Paul.

"I can't help it, I just don't like that man," said Edna. "How would you like to have a swim before lunch? Bill is due back any minute."

"I'll have to borrow a bathing suit," said Paul.

"Bill's won't fit you, but it'll cover you."

"That's all that's necessary," said Paul.

They were both good swimmers. "Do you remember when I taught you to swim?" said Paul.

"I'll never forget it. The water was freezing cold and Mother wouldn't go in. Is that right?"

"Yes. She'd never go in in July. She still won't. The water's just as cold in August, but you can't tell her that. If anything it may be a few degrees warmer in July."

"I'm enjoying this, Daddy. I wanted to tell you before Bill got here."

"Why before Bill got here?" said Paul.

"Oh—because I won't get a chance to after he does."

"I guess I understand. I *think* I do," said Paul. "It's really the first time we've been together in I don't know how long."

"Ever," said Edna.

"Yes, I guess it is."

"This close," said Edna.

"Yes," said Paul.

"I don't know whether it was you having the fight with Mother, or Mary being sick, or what it was, but I'm glad I had this moment with you. And that's all I'll say."

"That's all you have to say," said Paul.

"The sun is just about overhead. It must be close to noon," said Edna.

"Just about," said Paul.

"Do you notice the difference between here and Wingate?"

"Well, Michigan is that much farther north than Ohio," said Paul.

"*Here's Bill*," said Edna.

Bill Ewing, in a blue linen suit, shook hands with Paul Everett. "I hope you notice my bathing suit," said Paul.

"I thought it looked familiar," said Bill. "Did I see Dr. Wilson's car in the lane?"

"He's been giving the baby anti-toxin," said Edna.

"Does that mean she has diphtheria?" said Bill.

"He said he wanted to be on the safe side," said Edna.

"You're staying for lunch, I hope?" said Bill to Paul Everett.

"If it's not any trouble," said Paul.

"No trouble. I'm sorry the baby had to be sick, your first visit to the farm. Is Mrs. Everett joining you?"

"No, not this trip. I had to see a man on business, and this was the first chance I got."

"You'll stay the night, won't you?" said Edna.

"Well, if you're sure I won't be in the way," said Paul.

"Excuse me while I have a look at the baby," said Bill.

He left them to go inside. "Do you think I ought to stay?" said Paul.

"Stay, by all means," said Edna.

The Bill Ewings had a couple drop in for supper that evening. They were a Mr. and Mrs. Teshmacker, and he was a lawyer with Hotchkiss, Ewing and Kelley. He was about forty and apparently had been with the firm about twenty years. His wife, whose name was Crystal—"People think my name is Christine, because I'm nicknamed Cris"—was a fairly recent second wife of Teshmacker's, and the mother of his two-year-old son. She was not much older than Edna, and they talked about their children. "Now you're Edna's father, is that right?" she said.

"I'm Edna's father, that's right," said Paul.

"And where are you from?" said Cris Teshmacker.

"Wingate, Michigan," said Paul.

"Is that anywhere near Detroit?"

"Not very. Detroit is a couple of hours by train."

"And what do you do in Wingate?"

"I run a furniture factory."

"Oh, you're not a lawyer?" said Cris Teshmacker. "I somehow thought you were a lawyer."

"Do I look like a lawyer?" said Paul.

"A lawyer, or a doctor," said Cris Teshmacker. "That may be because I've never known a man who runs a furniture factory. Do you know Clarence Kelley?"

"I've heard of him, but I don't know him."

"Did you know Francis Ewing?"

"I met him at Edna's wedding," said Paul.

"He was a wonderful man," said Cris Teshmacker. "I was almost his secretary, but he died. Then I married Tesh."

"Tesh? Oh, Mr. Teshmacker."

"Everybody calls him Tesh. Teshmacker is too long," she said. "His name, that is. I don't want you to get the impression that *he's* too long. He's just right, for me."

"That's good," said Paul.

He wanted to get away from her. He wanted Edna to be warned away from her. For this woman, from having started by asking him the dullest questions she could ask, had suddenly changed to making the dirtiest remark he had ever heard a woman make. He had to sit beside her at dinner, but he ignored her as much as he could and talked to Edna. He never had a chance to talk to her husband because the Teshmackers had to go back to Cleveland and their two-year-old son.

"I'm going up and have a look at Mary," said Edna, and left them.

"Well, how did you like the Teshmackers?" said Bill.

"She's rather outspoken," said Paul.

"Yes, she is," said Bill. "She only does it with men, never with women. Consequently the women don't believe it when a man says she talks dirty. What did she say, or would you rather not repeat it?"

"Something about his not being too long for her. I've never heard a woman make a remark like that before, a remark about her husband's privates."

"She was Teshmacker's lady friend before he married her, while his wife was still alive. She was a stenographer in the office of Hotchkiss, Ewing and Kelley, and after the original Mrs. Teshmacker died she had a baby by him. But I don't think they're getting along too well now. I think Teshmacker is getting tired of her, or she of him, or both. Also, I suspect she likes the bottle. I'm always surprised when I hear that. That was the trouble with Clarence Kelley's wife, but she also took dope, and I guess that was worse."

"Yes, from what I hear," said Paul. "Morphine. A minister's wife in Wingate died of it."

"It's just booze with Cris, but that can be bad enough," said

Bill. "Teshmacker spends a lot of time in Washington. Two, three weeks at a time. Kelley has suggested that he move there, but she says it's too hot. That *may* be her reason. Anyway it's her excuse."

Edna returned. "It looks as if I'll be up all night with her," she said. "I took her temperature, and it's a hundred and two. I called Dr. Wilson and left word with him to call me, soon as he gets in."

"I heard her coughing," said Bill. "Why don't you ask Beulah to sit with you?"

"Oh, no. There's no use doing that," said Edna. "If I need her later I'll ask her to, but let's not get her now."

"Is there anything I can do?" said Paul.

"Yes, just sit here and talk to me and Bill, and wait for Dr. Wilson's call. They didn't say when he'd be back. His sister answered the phone, and I hope she remembers."

The phone rang. "She remembered," said Bill. "Will you answer it or shall I?"

"Both of us," said Edna.

They went inside for a few minutes, then came out. "He's coming right over," said Bill. "Right over means fifteen minutes."

"Well, at least we know he's coming," said Edna. "I'll go upstairs and wait for him. You stay here with Daddy."

"All right," said Bill.

He waited with Paul. "Does he live far?" said Paul.

"Oh, about two miles," said Bill. "It shouldn't take long, if he starts right out."

"No, it just seems long," said Paul. "The one that's waiting . . . time weighs heavy."

"And this time it's Edna," said Bill. "Poor Edna. If anything happens to that baby . . ."

"It won't, Bill. I have a feeling."

"Mr. Everett, I don't count on your feeling. I want to hear what the doctor has to say," said Bill. "I think that may be his car. Yes, it is."

Dr. Wilson's Ford roadster drove into the lane, and the doctor got out. "Hello, Mr. Ewing, Mrs. Ewing upstairs?"

"With the baby," said Bill.

"Mr. Everett," said Dr. Wilson. "Let's have a look at the baby."

"Me too?" said Paul.

"No," said Dr. Wilson. "You stay where you are."

Bill accompanied Dr. Wilson upstairs, and they were gone for an hour. Paul heard Dr. Wilson say ". . . for a tracheotomy . . ." But that was all he heard. Then Dr. Wilson came downstairs, and by the heaviness of his footsteps on the stairs he told Paul what he had to know.

"The baby's gone?" said Paul.

"Yes, it was too late for a tracheotomy. Actually it's a fairly simple operation if you do it in time."

"But you didn't do it in time?" said Paul. "Thank you, Doctor."

"Good night, Mr. Everett," said Dr. Wilson.

"Good night, Doctor," said Paul.

Bill came downstairs, but the doctor had gone into the night leaving a strange, empty death behind him, or even taking a strange, empty death with him. For the death of the baby was a cause of sadness for Edna, but beyond Edna's sadness, none for Paul. Vicarious sadness, it was. He had not known the baby except as his daughter's tiny daughter, and it was only by feeling sadness for his daughter that he was able to feel sadness at the baby's death. And that was not enough. The small, short life of Mary Ewing had ended before it had a chance to begin, and there was no use pretending otherwise. But his love for Edna intensified, whether through guilt or not it did not matter.

Edna came down and sat on the porch with her father. "Well, that's that," said Edna, and allowed her father to put his arm around her and sit close to her on the swing. "I guess we ought to call Mother," said Edna. "At least it's over, and we won't have her making a fuss. Bill's going to telephone his mother in the morning."

"It's three hours earlier out there," said Paul.

"I know, but he doesn't want her to come East. The baby will be buried Monday in the Ewings' family plot. I wonder if I ought to have another baby. I don't think so, not right away. Maybe never. Bill was an only child, I'm an only child, and now John-Stewart's an only child."

"Your mother will come down for the funeral, of course."

"Yes, but try to get her to leave Monday. I really don't want her to stay here. Bill doesn't either. It'd almost be better if she stayed away, but I guess that's asking too much."

"I'll take her back to Wingate Monday afternoon."

"The sooner Bill and I start to lead a normal life . . ."

It was decided that Edna should be the one to announce the baby's death, at nine o'clock the next morning. It was Sunday, and Lila Everett could not get a train from Detroit until four o'clock. "Your father's there, isn't he?"

"He and Bill are attending to the undertaker."

"You're going to have it simple, of course," said Lila. "Just the family and a few friends?"

"Just the family, Mother. No friends," said Edna.

"Well, people like—"

"No, Mother! No friends! Is that understood? No flowers, no friends. There's really no need for you to come to Cleveland."

"Well, if you'd rather I didn't . . ."

"All right, then, you stay up at the Lake. You'd have to go back tomorrow anyway."

"*Tomorrow?*"

"With Daddy. Bill and I want to be by ourselves, and the sooner the better."

"Well, if that's the case, I won't come," said Lila.

"All right, that's settled," said Edna.

"Is it all right if we send flowers?"

"No," said Edna. "I must hang up now, there's somebody at the door."

The people at the door were Bill and her father. "Well, I took care of Mother. She's not coming," said Edna.

"How did you stop her?" said Bill.

"She'll probably never forgive me, but stop her I did," said Edna. "Is there any reason why I can't go for a swim?"

"No, we'll all four go. You and I and John-Stewart and his grandfather," said Bill. "You can wear my other suit, Mr. Everett. I think they're both dry anyway."

"Then we can have some lunch, just as if nothing happened," said Edna.

A week had passed since the funeral of Mary Ewing. It was Monday, the first normal Monday since Mary Ewing had died, and though only a week had passed, it could have been a year since Edna Ewing and her husband and her father and—uninvited —Clarence Kelley had gathered at the little Church of the Redeemer. There were no pallbearers. The tiny casket was driven in a Winton hearse and two men from the undertaker's carried the casket up the aisle and rested it on a wheeled collapsible stand that was still too large for the casket. The clergyman was very young, wore a cassock and surplice, and kept his voice down low, as if he were aware of the unsuitability of the mature sentiments of the funeral service. Edna thanked him, still not knowing his name, and introduced her father to Clarence Kelley. She forgot to invite Kelley to lunch, but got in the undertaker's Winton limousine with her husband and father, and in ten minutes she was back at the farm. "Does dead mean I'm not going to see Mary any more?" said John-Stewart.

"Just what it means," said Edna. "Will you miss her?"

"No. She cried too much," said John-Stewart.

"Well, she won't bother you any more," said Edna. "Daddy, I don't want to rush you, but you can take a one-thirty train for Detroit. I can drive you to the station in my Ford, and Bill can go to the office in his car."

"Whatever you say, Edna. The sooner you and Bill start to lead a normal life. I have to check out of the hotel, so we'd better get started," said Paul.

There were so many small things to be done that had to be done. The headstone for Mary's grave took just as much time as a monument for a grown person, because it involved an exchange of letters with Ada Ewing. "Are you going to write to your mother, or shall I?" said Edna.

"I'll do it, although I don't want to," said Bill.

"I'll do it if you tell me what to say," said Edna.

"No, I'll do it, but you tell *me* what to say," said Bill. "Or what not to say."

"Well, one thing not to say is that we know about Priscilla Hotchkiss."

"I'm not so sure. I've been thinking it over, and I've been wondering about that," said Bill. "It's even hard for me to tell you. But in a way Mother's living with Rhoda Shipley makes it easier. What would you think if I wrote her a long letter and told her that we'd found out about Priscilla Hotchkiss, and then went on to say that we understood about Rhoda Shipley? In other words, killed two birds with one stone? It's going to be a hell of a hard letter to write, but we're going to have to face it sooner or later. You know, I feel that Mother is dead. Her affair with Priscilla was something I'll never understand, but her affair with Rhoda Shipley is almost natural. She had that inclination to go to bed with women, and I wish it hadn't been with Priscilla. But I remember Rhoda Shipley pretty well, and I can remember that they were always quite close, good friends. Companionable. I don't think there was ever anything between Mother and Rhoda in Cleveland. Nothing like taking baths together or sleeping together, the way there was with Priscilla. That came later, I guess."

"You may be sure," said Edna.

"I am sure. Rhoda Shipley was what I'd call a passionate woman, and my mother must have been too, although it's hard for me to imagine. It's still hard. What ever possessed her to do those things with Priscilla? No matter. She did them, and we know she did them. Priscilla didn't imagine them. She hasn't got that much imagination."

"It doesn't take much imagination," said Edna.

"What do you mean?" said Bill.

"You and I do those things. Why does it take more imagination for a man and woman to do those things than it does for two women? If anything, it takes less. Women are together all the time, rooming together before they get married, sleeping in the same bed, getting undressed together, and so on."

"But you never did anything," said Bill.

"No, I didn't. But Faith McCracken wanted me to. I know she did. And you remember Ruth Velie. And before that, Bertha Linkletter used to come to my house and we'd look at each other's private parts. I was so pleased when I finally got a little hair to show her, because she had hair before I did. And Ann Collins had hair at least a year before I did. Ann had a lot of hair. The point is, girls and women have a lot better opportunity and temptation than men and boys have. So imagination has nothing to do with it. Besides, who knows that your mother was the first to ever do things with her? How did we first find out about Priscilla?"

"She told me," he said. "At least she dropped a hint."

"She told you? She bragged about it, and you had to get poor old Clarence Kelley to do the actual telling," said Edna. "I don't know. I think maybe you ought to write that letter. Our mothers give us such trouble."

It was decided that Edna should write the letter about Mary's grave, and she did. It was the first letter Edna had ever written to Ada, and it was noncommittal. It avoided the use of the word love. Bill's letter took longer to write, but after two attempts he completed it.

Dear Mother:

Edna has written you that we have buried Mary in the family

plot, but it is not about that which I wish to write you. The occasion for this letter is perhaps equally sad. I shall proceed at once with the facts as I know them and you will see what I mean.

Several weeks ago I ran into Priscilla Hotchkiss on Ninth Street and in the course of our brief conversation she asked me to tell you that she "missed our baths." Later, when I reported this mysterious conversation to Clarence Kelley, his reaction was to disclose the true nature of your relations with Priscilla, which I need hardly go into. Clarence did not condemn your actions with Priscilla, but he realized that if she was capable of such a casual reference to them to me, it was time that I knew about them. Obviously you yourself had confided in Clarence, and he in turn revealed that he had originally suggested that you go to California. It is also just as obvious that you have confided in him as to your relations with Mrs. Shipley, but if Clarence did not condemn your behavior with Priscilla, he strongly approves of your relations with Mrs. Shipley.

This could have been a much longer letter. In fact it was. But I have kept myself out of this draft (my third) as I see no reason to inject my personal feelings into a matter which concerns you. It is apparently your intention to make California your permanent residence, a decision with which I concur.

Your loving son,
Bill

"That about tells the story," said Edna.

"It's cold, but as I told you, she's dead to me," said Bill. "I didn't mention you, but she'll know you read it."

"I'll be curious to see how she answers it," said Edna. "She didn't answer my letter."

"She may not answer this one either," said Bill. "Maybe she's dropped us before we dropped her."

"You haven't dropped her, Bill. She's still your mother," said Edna.

But Ada answered Bill's letter by special delivery, addressed to him at the farm, within two weeks, which gave her only a day or two to compose her answer.

Dear Bill:

I am very sorry that you finally had to learn the no doubt painful truth about your mother, but it is fortunate that it was Clarence who had to be your informant and it is a relief to me that the truth be known. Yes, I intend to remain in California. The farm is already yours and the money from the sale of the house in town will be given to you. I will keep the securities that were left me by your father so that I will have enough to live on until I die, then they will go to you. Clarence has all the details, including my will, which I give him permission to show you.

Mrs. Shipley and I are happy together, which I do not expect you to understand; but I could not be happy unless I knew that you and Edna and John-Stewart were happy, too. I send all three of you my love.

Mother

"A good letter," said Edna. "She didn't say anything she didn't mean."

"No, I guess not," said Bill. "It's strange, but now she's more dead than ever. I wonder if she plans to be buried in the family plot."

"Good heavens, she's just starting a new life. She's only about fifty-three, isn't she?" said Edna.

"I think so," said Bill.

"She has a lot of years ahead of her," said Edna. "*She* won't get diphtheria."

Clarence Kelley had not been to the farm in 1918, and already half the summer was gone. "One year ago tomorrow I had supper in this house," he said. "Your mother and I talked about the

Eighteenth Amendment to the Constitution, which had just passed the Senate. I should say that *I* talked about it. Your mother was fond of champagne, but she didn't think they were going to prohibit that. Well, they haven't prohibited it yet, but I'm afraid they will."

"Who are you?" said John-Stewart.

"Me? I'm a very old man who works in your father's office," said Kelley.

"You have a big nose," said John-Stewart.

"John-Stewart!" said Edna.

"Do you want to tweak it?" said Kelley. "Not hard, now."

"Fortunately he doesn't know what tweak means," said Bill. "Sit down and stop being fresh."

The boy sat down but did not take his eyes off Clarence Kelley's nose.

"I'm very glad you asked me for supper. I was afraid the summer would pass without my coming out here," said Kelley. "Sunday at the club is very quiet, especially in the summer."

"My father goes to the club," said John-Stewart.

"And so did his father, and I hope you'll go there too," said Kelley.

"I know who you are," said John-Stewart. "You're Mr. Kelley."

"That's right. How did you guess who I was?"

"I didn't guess. I remembered, you silly. Mother said you were Mr. Kelley. Don't you remember?"

"Not as well as I used to," said Kelley. "But I remember that you said I had a big nose. Which I may say I have."

"But I like you," said John-Stewart.

"In spite of my big nose?" said Kelley.

"Look here, boy, you be quiet or upstairs you'll go," said Bill.

"Oh, he doesn't bother me. Besides, he broke down and admitted that he liked me," said Kelley. "I haven't had such a forthright declaration in thirty years."

"Nevertheless, it's time he went to bed," said Edna.

[278]

"Aw, Mother, can't I stay up a little while?" said John-Stewart.
"Bed. Bed," said Edna. "It's long past your bedtime. I said he could stay up till you got here. Say goodnight to Mr. Kelley and your father, and I'll be up in a few minutes."

"Goodnight, Mr. Kelley, goodnight Daddy," said John-Stewart. The boy shuffled off.

"He can hardly keep his eyes open," said Edna.

"You spoil him, Edna," said Bill.

"Oh, what if I do?" said Edna, and followed the boy upstairs.

"The baby died a month ago yesterday," said Bill. "You can imagine how much discipline there's been here since then."

"He's a charming little boy," said Kelley.

"He is, but I don't want him to get too fresh," said Bill. "And I don't want him to become a mama's boy. Edna swims with him twice a day, which is all right except that he's not used to it. Before the baby died he was lucky to swim with her once a day, and he's not used to all this attention. I'll be glad when school starts. That'll be about a month from now, I think."

"Is he old enough to go to school?"

"Kindergarten," said Bill. "I think I told you, we're planning to live here all winter. If the weather gets too bad, we'll move into town, but we're going to give it a try. Edna loves it here, and I do too. The farm is the right place to bring children up, especially a boy."

"I've never lived on a farm, so I don't know," said Kelley.

"Well, I never have either, but I've taken to this place. I bought a horse and one for Edna, and I'm thinking of buying a pony for John-Stewart. Not a Shetland. They're mean little bastards. I'll get him a pony about twelve hands high, preferably a gelding that's been broken to the saddle, and I'm hoping John-Stewart gets to like him."

"Have you heard any more from your mother?"

"Only that one letter. I don't expect to be hearing from her. You'll be more likely to hear from her than I will."

"Yes, I suppose so," said Kelley.

Edna appeared. "He was off to sleep the moment his head touched the pillow," she said. "Would you care for something to drink, Mr. Kelley?"

"I might have a little libation. A finger of rye whiskey would do the trick," said Kelley.

"I'll have one with you," said Edna. "Bill, will you do the honors?"

"I'll join you," said Bill.

"Make mine half water," said Edna.

"Not mine. Make mine all whiskey," said Kelley. "Bill, I've been waiting for Edna to join us so that I could present a proposition to you. I don't have to have an answer now, unless it's in the negative. But I wanted Edna to hear it."

"Shoot," said Bill.

"Well, I had a talk with George McVeagh on Friday, Friday afternoon, and George has an idea that he'd like to make you general counsel of Cuyahoga."

"What would that mean?" said Edna.

"Succeeding whom?" said Bill. "Anybody?"

"Succeeding nobody," said Kelley. "The general counsel for Cuyahoga is and has been the firm of Hotchkiss, Ewing and Kelley. The work was done by me and you and, until he died, Jack Mc-Nair."

"Whose idea was this?" said Bill.

"George McVeagh's," said Kelley. "He arrived at this proposition independently, completely on his own. I assure you I had nothing to do with it. Unless, of course, you rule out telepathy, and I do. We don't do business by telepathy. We're lawyers."

"Well, of course I knew that Cuyahoga hasn't got a general counsel. After all, I'm a director, and they'd have a hard time slipping one over on me. But seriously, Clarence, this comes as such a complete surprise—tell me more," said Bill.

"There really isn't so much to tell," said Kelley. "McVeagh and

I had lunch at the club on Friday and somehow or other the conversation turned to the subject of old age. A very delicate subject when I'm present but one that keeps coming up. And oddly enough, it keeps cropping up when George and I have lunch together. George isn't nearly as old as I am, but he's more conscious of his advancing years than I am. I said advancing. Mine have been advancing for so long that I don't pay attention to them any more. I wake up in the morning, find that I'm still breathing, get out of bed, and by the time I've finished shaving I've gotten used to the same old nose and the same old bones all over again. Somebody brings me my first cup of coffee and my day has begun. Contrast my day with George McVeagh's."

"I don't know anything about George McVeagh's," said Bill.

"Well, I don't either," said Kelley. "But I can imagine what it's like without too much trouble. I'm sure he wakes up about the same time I do—five-thirty or six o'clock. He's careful not to disturb Jean, who's just getting her beauty sleep, and I do happen to know they sleep in the same room. That gives George an hour or so till Jean is ready for her morning tea, which they both have at the same time. I know, because I've stayed at their house in the country, and you can't get a cup of coffee before seven-thirty. One reason why I no longer visit them. At least the night man at the club brings me my coffee at half past six. You'd think with all that money and all those servants—well, never mind. So we have George fully awake and given his tea, but only after two hours of. being kept waiting for it. One of the richest men in Cleveland, mind you, but he's made disagreeable every morning because—*because*—his wife must get her beauty sleep. And I know that for a fact. A good third of the morning wasted. Tyrannized by his wife and their lazy servants. You didn't know that, did you? You didn't know that George is put in a bad humor by his wife, who must have her beauty sleep? Well, I'm telling you, and you remember it, Edna. When Bill gets to be the head of Cuyahoga, be sure he gets his coffee first thing in the morning."

"Head of Cuyahoga? You mean general counsel," said Edna.

"No, I was looking beyond the general counsel job. Bill will be chairman of the board of Cuyahoga," said Kelley. "If general counsel was all Bill had to look forward to, I'd tell him to stay with Hotchkiss, Ewing and Kelley. But Bill will be chairman of the board. However, we first have to make him general counsel. Bill, how do you feel about it?"

"I'd like to know more about it, but my answer is certainly not in the negative," said Bill.

"Then we can go on with it?" said Kelley.

"I'd be foolish to say no," said Bill.

"You would indeed," said Kelley. "You would indeed. Ten years or less, as general counsel and director for Cuyahoga, the chairmanship will be inevitable. I have only one piece of advice for you."

"And that is?" said Bill.

"Stay in Cleveland. Stay in Cleveland," said Kelley. "Those New York fellows will make tempting offers, but how many of those fellows will have made as much money as you will by the time you're forty? Not many, if any at all. And what on earth can you do in New York that you can't do in Cleveland?"

"Supper's ready," said Edna, rising. "Mr. Kelley, would this mean that Bill has to resign from Hotchkiss, Ewing and Kelley?"

"In due course," said Kelley. "But pretty soon there won't be a Hotchkiss or a Kelley left anyway. There'll be a Williams and a Teshmacker and half a dozen junior partners, but when I go there'll only be a Ewing left, or when Ewing goes there'll only be a Kelley left. And that won't be for long. For that reason I suggest we go about the business of disbanding."

"Goodness! Isn't this rather sudden?" said Edna.

"Yes, very," said Kelley. "But last Thursday I had no idea that Bill was going to be general counsel for Cuyahoga, and now I know that he is. We have a lot of days to think it all over, but we haven't got a lot of months. Let's use the days to proceed in orderly fashion."

The warm summer's evening was really not the time for a prolonged discussion of Bill's future, and they settled down to a quiet supper. Jellied consommé. Chicken hash. Ice cream. "Edna, this supper was just right for my dental equipment," said Kelley. "I assume that that was not accidental."

"I had some help from Bill," said Edna.

Kelley telephoned McVeagh.

"You've had a week to think it over," said Kelley.

"Think what over?" said George McVeagh.

"The proposition to make Bill Ewing your general counsel," said Kelley.

"What's the matter with you, man?" said McVeagh. "Haven't you spoken to Ewing?"

"I have, but I was waiting for you to speak to me again," said Kelley.

"What was his answer?"

"He's all for it," said Kelley.

"That's all that's necessary," said McVeagh. "I leave the details up to you."

"You're dumping a rather important thing in my lap, George," said Kelley.

"Well, you're a rather important man," said McVeagh. "All right, we'll have lunch."

They met for lunch.

"Clarence, I don't want you to think I was slipshod or haphazard about this. Anything but. However, when you ask a man to do something, and the man has as good a record as yours, you leave it up to him to get things done. You don't pester him with the details. You say you want something done and he goes ahead and does it. Now what is it you want to know?"

"I'm very touched by your confidence in me, George. And I
didn't think you were slipshod or haphazard. But the firm of Hotchkiss, Ewing and Kelley has been in business a long time, and I object to its being dissolved so unceremoniously. And that's what
you're planning to do. By taking Bill Ewing as your general counsel,
you leave only me in the firm, and I need not point out to you that
I'm about done for. Oh, yes I am. I'll never see ninety. And even if
I should, I'll be of little use to anybody. Only the other day I
couldn't remember the Rule in Shelley's Case, and once you've
forgotten the Rule in Shelley's Case you're done for as a lawyer."

"I never did understand it," said McVeagh. "I know it has
nothing to do with Shelley the poet."

"Oh, I understand it. The trouble is remembering it," said
Kelley. "Where were we?"

"Trying to remember the Rule in Shelley's Case," said McVeagh.

"Oh, yes," said Kelley. "But before that?"

"You were talking about the dissolution of your law firm."

"Yes," said Kelley. "Well, I'm in favor of your making Bill Ewing
your general counsel, and Bill wants to do it. But what else happens
to Bill? Does he resign from the board of Akron Rubber? And what
about his membership on the board of Sprague?"

"He can keep his job with Akron Rubber. There'll be no conflict
there. In fact, I can see occasions when it would be useful for him
to be on both boards, Cuyahoga *and* Akron. Of course, he won't be
their general counsel. Ed Lustig retains McIlhenny and Cohen for
his general counsel. He has to have one Jew in there, besides himself. As for Sprague, Bill can get out of that. Resign. It's not making
any money and it isn't likely to."

"That will please Bill. He doesn't like being connected with
Sprague *or* with Valdemar Baer. He only took that job because of
you," said Kelley.

"And I'm in it only because the War Department suggested I be
in it. I don't know how much Newton D. Baker had to do with my
getting in it, but I know that Baker is a Democrat and I'm a Re-

publican. Anyway, it's a losing proposition and probably always will be, so Bill is well out of it."

"Oh, what about Edgar Ennis? How is the head of your legal department going to like it when he hears that Bill Ewing is to be your general counsel?"

"I hope he doesn't like it a bit," said McVeagh. "Aside from being Sophie Cudlipp's brother, he's nothing. I hope he'll resign, and if he doesn't take the hint, I'll ask him to. I passed over him when I made Bill a director of Cuyahoga, but he has the hide of an elephant. He naturally likes the salary I pay him, so he swallowed his pride, along with the dozen oysters he eats at the Club every day."

"You seem to have taken care of Edgar Ennis. Jack McNair would thank you for that," said Kelley.

"Good old Jack. He and Rhoda Carstairs were the most unlikely pair you could ever imagine, but they used to get together on my boat and nobody had any idea. Not even Jean. That was before Rhoda married Arthur Shipley, and my boat was the last place anybody'd expect to find them. The funny thing was, I kind of had an idea that Rhoda liked *me*, and it came as quite a surprise to learn that she was squiggling McNair."

"It comes as rather a surprise to me—not that I ever entertained carnal thoughts about Rhoda," said Kelley. "You know, of course, that she has Ada Ewing as her house guest."

"So I gather," said McVeagh. "So I gather."

"Jean told you?"

"Yes. I guess it's all over Cleveland by this time. It's not supposed to be a secret, is it?" said McVeagh. "Ada sold the house to a fellow named Berg, Samuel Berg. You knew that. Of course you did. You're Ada's lawyer."

"Yes, I knew that. But I didn't know it was, as you say, all over Cleveland."

"Jean heard it from Marcia Hay, or maybe it was Blandina Holcomb. What one of them knows, all three know. So I know it and Minor Hay knows it and Alan Holcomb knows it. That about takes care of Cleveland, at least the people who count in Cleveland."

"I'll bet you could go outside to Ninth and Euclid and ask John Temple if he knows about Rhoda Shipley and Ada Ewing, and he wouldn't know who you were talking about," said Kelley.

"He might, he just might," said McVeagh.

"I doubt if you know who John Temple is," said Kelley.

"Is that so? Well, I give him ten dollars every Christmas. He's the cop on the corner, and I know him as well as you do. He counts for ten dollars at Christmas time. Don't be so democratic, Clarence. It ill becomes you, with your Greek and Latin and all the rest of it. You're no more democratic than I am."

"Oh, I'd say considerably less so," said Kelley. "I've never given John Temple a Christmas present, and now I probably won't."

"Then he won't miss it," said McVeagh. "To get back to Bill Ewing. I have high hopes for that young man, Clarence. When I made him a director of Cuyahoga, I confess it was largely because of your influence. True, he was his father's son, but so was Bob Hotchkiss, and I didn't want him to be a director of Cuyahoga."

"You didn't make any mistake about Bill Ewing."

"No, but I had to find that out," said McVeagh. "So after I made him a director, I watched him very carefully. At our board meetings he didn't hesitate to oppose me, even when it put him on the losing side. He still spoke his mind. And I think I told you right at this table that Bill Ewing caught on to the little scheme that Minor Hay and I worked out, whereby Minor would introduce an idea that I wasn't going to like, and we'd hear him out but I'd vote no."

"Yes, you told me, and it was at this table," said Kelley.

"There are members of my board at Cuyahoga who still haven't caught on to Minor's and my scheme. But Bill Ewing caught on because he *listens*, he *listens*. He even listens to Minor Hay's crazy schemes, because some of them aren't so crazy. Oh, Minor's no fool. For instance, he brought up an idea a couple of weeks ago that beginning the first of October, Cuyahoga would discontinue extra shifts. 'Discontinue?' said some directors. 'Yes, discontinue,' said Minor. Well, I knew what he had in mind, although I couldn't say so. You see, Minor has been seeing a great deal of Colonel Abernathy, of the British Purchasing Commission. They play golf together, and I guess golf gives them a good chance to say things that they wouldn't say for fear of being overheard. They have the golf course all to themselves, except Tuesday, which is ladies' day. Anyway, they were playing golf a few weeks ago and Minor asked Abernathy to go duck-shooting with him in October, and Abernathy said he thought he'd be back in England by that time. The head of the British Purchasing Commission back in England by October? What did that mean? Well, it meant one thing to Minor Hay. It meant the end of the war. A chance remark like that. Minor didn't say anything more to Abernathy, but he came and told me that the war would be over next winter, and he told me why he thought so. I wasn't as convinced as Minor, but we get reports from Switzerland that the German morale is very low, and I believe it. The Allies have pushed the Germans back from the Marne, and it's only August. It would take a miracle for them to get through the winter, especially with almost two million Americans lined up against them. And so that was one time I voted with Minor Hay. But do you know who else voted with him? Bill Ewing."

"Good. Good," said Kelley.

"Good hell, it's perfect," said McVeagh. "Because when I asked Bill why he voted to discontinue the extra shifts—this was privately —he gave me the best possible answer. He said—and I always vote last—that October is usually the time when our big ore boats stop shipping. That young fellow is not only a good lawyer, Clarence. He's beginning to know the steel business."

"Ah, so you're going to make a steel man of him," said Kelley.

"Well, I'll begin by making him our general counsel," said McVeagh. "Come on, have something besides the same old rice pudding or custard."

"All right. I'll have strawberry ice cream," said Kelley.

"Good idea, Clarence. I haven't had strawberry ice cream all summer."

"That's nothing. I haven't had it for at least five years," said Kelley. "Maybe ten. And I used to be very fond of it."

"It's funny how you get out of the habit of something you like," said McVeagh.

"Well, I could wish everything was as simple as a plate of strawberry ice cream," said Kelley.

Edna was staring at her husband in a way that he was not accustomed to.

"You've been staring at me for five minutes," said Bill.

"Have I? I didn't realize it was that long," said Edna. "How old was your father when he first got grey hair?"

"My father? Well, we've been married five and a half years, and he was about fifty-two or three then. Mother was forty-seven, which makes her fifty-two or three now. Now, I remember hearing Mother say that my father was getting grey hairs when I was in my first year at Ann Arbor. Subtracting four from fifty-two, leaves forty-eight. So he must have been forty-eight when he first got grey hairs. Why?"

"Because you have a patch of grey hair behind your right ear. I just noticed it. It's only a small patch, but you're getting grey at a very early age for a Ewing. My father was always a little grey and his hair was thinner than yours, but he's never gotten really bald. I hope you don't get bald."

"They say that bald men are concupiscent," said Bill.

"Concupiscent? What on earth does that mean?" said Edna.

"That's a word I came across in the dictionary when I was looking up concurrence. It means lusty."

"Well, you're concupiscent, especially on Sunday mornings," said Edna.

"So are you," said Bill.

[288]

"I wonder how many people are concupiscent on Sunday morning. I don't think my father and mother were. They nearly always went to church on Sunday morning."

"Well, we have something better to do," said Bill.

"Do you think this is where your mother and Priscilla did whatever they did?"

"I suppose so," said Bill. "Here and the bathtub. How many times do you think we've done it?"

"What we do? I'd guess about—oh, fifty-two weeks in a year, times five and a half. That's two hundred and eighty-six weeks. Times three times a week. That's roughly seven-hundred and fifty-eight. Subtracting the times I was pregnant. Twenty weeks every time I was pregnant. Forty from seven hundred and fifty-eight leaves seven hundred and eighteen."

"Don't forget the times we did it twice. Not to mention the times we did it three times."

"I'd say we've probably done it about seven hundred and fifty times," said Edna. "God, when you think of all the girls that have never done it even once."

"It's quite a lot of fucking."

"You never say that unless you want to make me concupiscent," she said. "Well, I'm ready whenever you are."

"Concupiscent Edna," said Bill.

"That's because I like you to fuck me," she said. "The magic word."

It was a Sunday morning in September, and when they had had their breakfast and said good morning to their son, Edna said, "Do you realize he starts school Tuesday?"

"Yes. Are you taking him to school?" said Bill.

"The first couple of days, I am. But I'm going to let him get accustomed to walking. It isn't very far, and he's *not* going to be the only child to have his mama take him to school. Or bring him home. The whole point of having him go to school in the country is to let him get better acquainted with the farmers' kids."

"Oh, I agree with you completely," said Bill. "He has to begin sometime. How far is it to school?"

"Eight tenths of a mile by your speedometer. I clocked it, figuring your speedometer would be more accurate than mine. It's not too far."

"To think he'll be five the first of February," said Bill.

"And he can read. His writing could stand improvement, but so could yours."

"It's not one of my strong points, but it never was. At school I used to print everything, and since I've been with Hotchkiss, Ewing and Kelley, I've mostly dictated. No, my handwriting is nothing to brag about. Have you ever noticed Clarence Kelley's handwriting? It's what they call a fine Spencerian hand. I said to him once, 'Do I have to write that way? If I do, I'm going to have to get another job.' He said no, I wrote the same uneducated hand as my father, and my father had turned out well."

"At least he turned out better than your mother," said Edna.

"Who's to say he did?" said Bill.

"Well, that's true," said Edna. "I spend a lot of time thinking about your mother, her life with her friend Mrs. Shipley. What if I hadn't met you? Suppose I had been more attracted to Faith McCracken? I've been thinking a lot about her, too. I sometimes think that if I'd been nicer to Faith, she wouldn't have turned on the gas. And what would it have cost me?"

"Me, for one thing."

"But would you have had to know? I'd more or less put her out of my mind till we found out about your mother, and that changed things."

"How?" said Bill.

"Well, first I was furious at your mother, furious. But then I began thinking of how close I'd come to being just like her. God knows I was a virgin when I married you, and I might have stayed one if Faith McCracken had been more attractive. So I began wondering about myself, and the more I wondered, the more I understood your mother's point of view, if you can call it that. Your mother was married to your father all those years, but was she ever really happy with him?"

"*He* was happy with *her*," said Bill.

"Yes, but was she happy with him? After he died, she went into mourning for him, but when she got out of mourning her interest was in women. First Priscilla, and then Mrs. Shipley, and maybe somebody in between."

"It's possible," said Bill. "There may have been others during that mourning period, so-called. I don't think you wait till you're middle-aged to give in to that instinct. I've been thinking that Mother was always rather strange. She used to go to concerts by herself, preferably by herself. She could always have gotten someone else to go with her, but she preferred being alone. That didn't strike me as strange at the time, but it fits in with the things we know about her now. At least I think it does."

"I don't know about that," said Edna. "I could imagine wanting to be alone, to listen to the music, uninterrupted by the chatter of another woman. However, I agree with your theory that there probably were others besides Priscilla and Mrs. Shipley. On the other hand, I don't believe your mother was like Ruth Velie."

"That's because you don't like Ruth Velie," said Bill.

"Well, that's true," said Edna.

"Do you want to know what I believe? I believe that my mother was capable of anything. That she was perverted and kept it secret as long as she could, and finally went to California and there she's stayed. And there I hope she stays. I meant it when I said I consider her dead. I just wonder when she died, that's all. I've put her out of *my* life."

"I don't think you can do that so easily," said Edna. "I put my mother out of my life a long time ago, but she keeps coming back in. You can't put a woman out of your life because she's a gossip and she's mean, and you can't pretend a woman is dead because she likes to kiss other women."

"Oh, can't I? You just see if I can't," said Bill. "She's spoiled my entire memory of her, all the nice things she used to do when I was a boy. And the worst thing is what she's done to my memory of her and my father. How would he feel about the way things have turned out? Suppose he were still alive and discovered her taking baths with Priscilla Hotchkiss?"

"That's what makes me think she waited till she got out of mourning," said Edna. "Her grief, her loneliness . . ."

"No," said Bill. "Her grief and loneliness turned into something nasty, and that's what *she* is, something nasty. My father died thinking she was something good and decent, but she wasn't. What you don't seem to understand is how I've had to change the entire picture of my boyhood and my youth, to include this perverted woman. Everything I've learned about her these past few months has soured me on her. If she suddenly turned into Florence Nightingale she'd make me turn against Florence Nightingale. I haven't said anything to you, because it wasn't clear in my mind how much I detested her, but lately I've come to realize that if I rejected her, put her completely out of my life, she'd lose the power to hurt me, to do me harm. Well, she can't harm me any more."

"If only it was that easy," said Edna. "You won't know till you see her again."

It took time to accomplish the formalities of the appointment of William Bloodgood Ewing to the post of general counsel of Cuyahoga. But George McVeagh became rather impatient at the delays, and he set a date, November 1, which happened to be a Friday, as the day on which Bill could move into his new office. "That will give you plenty of time to wind up your affairs with Hotchkiss, Ewing and Kelley," he said. "I have a feeling that Clarence Kelley may be dragging his feet, and if you're moved in on the first that will show we mean business."

"He knows we mean business," said Bill. "I've resigned from the firm. I resigned a week ago, and there are already half a dozen guys hoping to get my job. If it looks as though Clarence is dragging his feet, that's why. He isn't going to give anyone else my job."

"Say, what exactly was your job?"

"Well, I guess you'd call me head confidential assistant to Clarence Kelley. That's as good a description as I can give you. I was a partner too, of course. I was the Ewing of Hotchkiss, Ewing and Kelley, although most people assumed that the Ewing was my father. But that's because they left my father's name on the letterhead, and never bothered to put my name on, down among the junior partners. Now they'll have to take my name off."

"We'll see if they do that," said McVeagh. "Clarence wanted a Ewing in the firm, and he'll keep your name there as long as he can . . . I'd like you to resign from the board of the Sprague Company. Write me a letter, saying that pressure of other business makes it necessary, et cetera, et cetera, and I'll write you a letter accepting your resignation. It's just a formality, but I don't want anybody on the board of Cuyahoga to be on the board of Sprague. Minor Hay is resigning from Sprague and so is Alan Holcomb."

"Why are they all deserting the sinking ship?" said Bill.

"Because that's exactly what it is, a sinking ship. It was really never anything else," said McVeagh. "I don't mind taking my loss. I backed a hotel in Niagara Falls and one or two other ventures. But Sprague was a money-loser from the very beginning, and nobody ever had his heart in it. So I'm giving you a chance to get out of it."

"And you never liked Valdemar Baer," said Bill.

"No, but I could have learned to like him, or at least tolerate him, if I saw he was making money for us. But not that fellow. I'll tell you some things about him that would curl your hair. Do you know what a flagellant is?"

"Vaguely. It has to do with whips."

"You're damn right it has to do with whips," said McVeagh. "I've had two or three agents keeping their eye on Baer for a couple

of years, and in the course of this investigation there wasn't much
I didn't find out about him. One thing was this flagellation business,
which is beyond me. How does a man get pleasure out of being
beaten with whips? But Baer enjoyed it. He must have, because he
had the same woman come to his farm once a week this summer
and she took off her clothes and whaled the hell out of him. And
you'll never guess who that woman was."

"Never."

"It was Priscilla Hotchkiss," said McVeagh.

"Oh, I don't believe it," said Bill.

"Priscilla Hotchkiss," said McVeagh. "None of my men recognized her at first, but one followed her home, and that's who it
was. Is there anything that girl won't do?"

"How did your man happen to see her without any clothes on?"
said Bill.

"I'll let you in on a secret, Bill. My agent wasn't a man. It was a
woman, a prostitute. She arrived at Baer's house with Priscilla and
they both got undressed. Then the woman stayed all night with
Baer, and another of my men followed Priscilla home."

"It's fantastic," said Bill.

"You bet it is," said McVeagh.

"Do you trust the detectives?"

"I don't trust them, but I believe them. I'd believe anything
about Baer, and that's one of the reasons I want you to resign. I
didn't tell this to Minor Hay or Alan Holcomb. But there's a certain
obvious connection between Priscilla and a member of your family,
if you know what I mean."

"Say it—my mother," said Bill.

"I understand Priscilla's left Cleveland," said McVeagh. "Well,
Cleveland's loss is New York's gain."

"Meanwhile, what happens to Baer?" said Bill.

McVeagh's expression was cold and executive. "I think we'll
know how to take care of him," he said. "Naturally, I'll need your
advice."

"I'll be glad to give it," said Bill.

And so on the first of November 1918, William Bloodgood Ewing arrived at his new office in the Cuyahoga Building. It was ten minutes of nine, a clear day, and to his pleased surprise he was greeted by George McVeagh, who welcomed him with a little speech in the presence of Heidi Schlatter, George's secretary; Dorothy Chase, who was to be Bill's secretary; Stanley Nork, of the Cuyahoga legal department; and Charles Folsom, who was five months out of the University of Michigan Law School. (Edgar Ennis, nominally the head of the Cuyahoga legal department, was detained by business in Columbus.) There was a large bouquet of cornflowers and yellow roses on Bill's desk. "I hope you notice the flowers," said McVeagh. "They're the colors of the University of Michigan, maize and blue, and I had a hard time getting them. Well, ladies and gentlemen, you all know what we're here for. To welcome Bill Ewing as the general counsel of Cuyahoga Iron & Steel. Bill's father was associated with us for many years till he passed on, and I'm very glad to have Bill carry on the tradition. As general counsel Bill will be working with Stanley Nork and Charley Folsom and of course Edgar Ennis, who had to be in Columbus today. I don't know that I have anything else to say except that Cuyahoga is delighted to have Bill with us. And now I suppose we can all get back to work." There was no applause, although Charley Folsom beat his hands together two or three times in an abortive attempt at politeness, and they all departed for their various offices, leaving Bill alone. It was nine o'clock on the dot.

Bill spoke into the telephone. "Now that that's over, will you ask Mr. Nork to come in?"

"Yes sir," said Dorothy Chase. "He's right here."

Stanley Nork entered Bill's office. "Well, you finally made it," said Nork.

"Yes. Didn't you think I would?"

"Does it make any difference what I think?" said Nork.

"Not a hell of a lot, unless you intend to work with me. If you don't, you might as well quit now, Stanley. I detect an air of hostility that I can do without, and I'm not going to waste time finding out what caused it. This is going to be a tough enough job as it is, without your having a fig up your ass."

"Do you want me to quit now?" said Nork.

"I didn't *say* that," said Bill. "You're a good lawyer, and you know the ropes here. But I'm boss now, and you're going to take orders from me, not Edgar Ennis. Who, I noticed, wasn't here to welcome me in the new job. So let's cut the shit, Stanley. We've known each other too long."

"I'm sorry if I seemed hostile this morning. It had nothing to do with you. I'm sore at Ruth. She didn't get home till three o'clock this morning. If I weren't a Catholic I'd get a divorce. It's not the first time she was out half the night. I took a swing at her."

"That's too bad," said Bill. "Did you hit her?"

"Not this time, I didn't. But I have before. She was too quick for me," said Nork.

"You have a powerful build, Stanley. If you connect with her, she'll feel it. Or maybe she won't feel *anything*. Well, I'm sorry if you're having trouble at home. Come in Monday and we'll talk some more," said Bill.

"I want to work with you, Bill. Ennis doesn't know anything, and I'd say this to his face," said Nork.

"Come in Monday," said Bill.

He made a note on his memorandum pad: "S. Nork—any time Monday." Stanley was ordinarily a quiet man, almost to the point of lethargy, but Bill had seen him play footfall at Ann Arbor. He had a reputation for being a savage tackler who was put out of at least one game against Wisconsin for "unnecessary roughness." There was even some talk of terminating athletic relations between Michigan and Wisconsin, but it did not amount to anything. Away from the football field, Stanley was a studious man and determined to use his Polish background to advance his career. The large Polish population of Cleveland offered him as many advantages as Hamtramck, Michigan, and Bill suspected that Stanley supplemented his income by giving legal advice to the Poles. Well, that was all right; the man in charge of labor relations at Cuyahoga was Anton Czerniewicz, and the two worked together.

On Monday Bill noticed the memorandum concerning S. Nork, but dismissed it as having no urgency. He had lunch with McVeagh and Clarence Kelley and let them do the talking, and from force of habit he found himself heading back to the office of Hotchkiss, Ewing and Kelley with Clarence. "I was wondering if you'd do that," said McVeagh.

"Well, I did," said Bill.

Clarence Kelley was amused. "I should hate to think Bill would forget us so soon," he said.

"I'll *never* forget you," said Bill, and fell in step with George McVeagh as the old man headed for his own office.

In the Cuyahoga Building, Dorothy Chase was on the telephone. "Never mind, here he is," she said. "I was trying to reach you at the Union Club. Something awful has happened. The police . . ." She burst into tears.

"It can't be as bad as all that, Miss Chase. What is it?" said Bill.

The woman was less lachrymose than hysterical, and he waited for her to calm down. "I'm all right now—at least I think I am," she said. Speaking slowly, to make every word distinct, she continued: "Mr. Nork—has murdered—his wife—and the police—are coming." Then she had hysterics again, and Bill called Miss Schlatter.

"What's this about Stanley Nork killing his wife?" said Bill.

"I guess it's true," said Miss Schlatter.

"When? How?" said Bill.

"Sometime last night," said Miss Schlatter. "He struck her with a hammer, repeatedly. The police have all the details."

"Where is Stanley now?" said Bill.

"They don't know where he is, but they're looking for him," said Miss Schlatter.

"Yes, I should think they would be," said Bill.

"I must tend to Dorothy. She's in the rest room," said Miss Schlatter.

"Yes, you tend to Miss Chase," said Bill. He was alone for only a moment. Two men came in unannounced.

"Mr. Ewing? I'm Lieutenant Berk, that's B,e,r,k. And this is Sergeant Smigly. We're from Police Headquarters. Do you mind if I smoke my cigar?"

"Go right ahead," said Bill. "Tell me about Stanley Nork."

"Well, according to the information we received, Mrs. Nork came home shortly after eleven o'clock last night and right away she and Mr. Nork had words. They live in a two-family house, a very respectable neighborhood on Iuka Avenue, and they made such a disturbance that their next-door neighbors were going to complain to the police. But as near as I can make out, it must of been somewheres after twelve midnight when the noise quieted down. Then the neighbors heard Nork start the car, a 1916 Chevrolet touring, and drive away. Then Mrs. Goff, the next-door neighbor, her suspicions were aroused by all the lights being on at that late hour, and she decided to investigate. First she tried to reach the Norks by telephone, but when there was no answer she and her husband decided to investigate further. I ought to say here that Mr. and Mrs. Goff were worried, because Nork on two occasions had beaten up Mrs. Nork, although no report was made to the police. So anyway, Mr. and Mrs. Goff went inside and found Mrs. Nork on the dining-room floor, her skull fractured and various other injuries. She was dead. Fully clothed, except for her shoes."

"Where is Nork now?"

"Oh, we'll get him," said Berk. "Is it all right if I use your phone?"

"Go right ahead," said Bill.

"I want to tell them where we are," said Berk. He telephoned Police Headquarters. "Lieutenant Berk speaking. Let me talk to Captain Weems . . . Hello, Sam. We're at Mr. Ewing's office in the Cuyahoga Building . . . Uh-huh. Uh-huh . . . Okay, Sam. See you later . . . Well, that was quick work." Berk hung up the telephone. "Stanley Nork shot himself. He was found dead in his car about nine o'clock this morning, on the road to Lorain."

"He was probably on his way to Hamtramck, Michigan," said Bill.

"Do you have a match? My cigar's out," said Berk. "He was quite a football player, wasn't he? I remember seeing him play against State, must of been six or seven years ago, at Columbus."

"Six or seven," said Sergeant Smigly, his only utterance during the interview.

"Well, I won't take up any more of your time, Mr. Ewing. We may want your help later, but that's all for now."

The end of Stanley Nork depressed Bill; the death of Ruth Velie Nork depressed him not at all. But Stanley Nork was a man for his future, a man whom he was ready to like and trust and to have patience with and to understand. These things would have taken time, and now there was no time except for liking and understanding, and for that there was all the time in the world, or none at all. Bill telephoned Clarence Kelley. "You heard about Stanley Nork?"

"Yes, I tried to reach you but your line was busy," said Kelley. "You knew he committed suicide?"

"No, but I'm not a bit surprised."

"On the Lorain road. He shot himself," said Bill. "They found him in his car."

"Well, there was really nothing else for him to do, was there?" said Kelley. "You can look upon his suicide as anticlimactic, but it was the logical Part Two of killing his wife . . . The Austrian army has surrendered."

"I haven't seen the ticker," said Bill.

"Oh, things are moving fast," said Kelley. "Things are happening all at once, just as though they hadn't heard about Stanley Nork. Of course I'm joking. But you're more concerned with what happened to Stanley Nork than you are with what happens to the Kaiser. I'm more interested in what happens to the Kaiser, because I hardly knew Stanley Nork and I'll *never* know the Kaiser. Do you see what I mean?"

"Not quite," said Bill.

"I've only got time for the larger issues," said Kelley. "Peace. War. Abdication. No time for a young lawyer in Cleveland, Ohio, who kills his wife and commits suicide. I have to think of God, you know. I'll be seeing Him soon, and I don't want to go into His court unprepared. Unfortunately I may be preparing rather late . . . Miss Clay has just come in and told me it's time for me to take a nap, so I must lie down for half an hour."

"Goodbye, Clarence," said Bill.

It was the fourth of November, a Monday. Three days later the United Press made its slightly premature announcement of the Armistice, which the War Department denied a couple of hours later. "Our old friend Newton D. Baker must have everything right and proper," said George McVeagh. "But I suppose he's right."

"There are probably thousands of contracts that expire automatically on the day the war ends. But this is only an armistice. They *could* start fighting again tomorrow," said Bill.

"The bloodthirsty ones will go right on fighting up to the very end," said McVeagh. "It's now supposed to end on the eleventh hour of the eleventh day of the eleventh month. How would you like to be ordered to attack on the *tenth* hour of the eleventh day of the eleventh month?"

"I don't think I'd like it a bit," said Bill.

"What if you were an artillery officer, in command of a battery of French Seventy-fives—would you wait until ten fifty-nine, one minute before the armistice, and then fire, just to get in the last shot of the war?"

"I'd want to make sure the range was right," said Bill.

"What if your watch was slow and you fired at one minute past eleven?" said McVeagh. "Wouldn't that be awkward?"

"As one who went through this whole war without firing so much as a BB shot . . ." said Bill.

"That will be to your advantage now," said McVeagh. "They won't be able to call you militaristic."

"I'm going to be sorry for the rest of my life that I wasn't in it," said Bill.

"Bill, there were two million Americans in France, more or less. How many of them actually fired a shot or were anywhere near the fighting?"

"No matter how many there were, I wasn't one of them, and I'll always regret it," said Bill.

"Do you know why you weren't? Clarence Kelley was saving you for better things," said McVeagh.

"I'll say no more about it," said Bill.

The Monday of the Armistice began for the Ewings in darkness, but joyfully. Edna was awake before five o'clock and silently inserted herself between the covers of Bill's bed, so that he was awakened by her hand between his legs. "It's Armistice Day," she said. "Shall we celebrate?"

"I don't see why not," said Bill. He put his hand between her legs. "Hmm. *You're* ready," he said. "You're nice and juicy. How long have you been here?"

"Hours," she said.

They made good love, and then she said, "There's no school today, so our young man will be home all day. I think he's up already. *John-Stewart, is that you? You can come in.*"

The boy opened their door and kissed them good morning. "No school today," he said. "After breakfast can I go with Lloyd and feed the pigs?"

"If you won't be in the way," said Edna.

"If I don't spill the swill? That's what Lloyd says. 'Don't spill the swill.'"

"He's a poet and doesn't know it," said Edna.

"A poet and doesn't know it. That's good, Mother," said John-Stewart. "Fuck a duck. That's a rhyme too."

"I like spill the swill better," said Edna.

"The charm of the farm," said Bill.

"Yes, I see," said Edna. "Well, I'll get you two your breakfast."

"I could go back to sleep for a few more hours," said Bill.

"All right, you've earned it," said Edna.

"Fuck a duck," said John-Stewart.

"Maybe instead of going back to sleep you should clean up your offspring's vocabulary," said Edna.

"I'll see what I can do, but not this morning," said Bill.

"In other words, Edna, *you* take care of that," said Edna.

"Well, that's a good idea," said Bill. "You take care of it till the offspring reaches the age of ten."

"Thanks, thanks," said Edna.

She took the boy to the kitchen and prepared his oatmeal, and he immediately left for the pigsty. She had her own oatmeal and coffee and busied herself with the dishes and had a moment's peace in the kitchen. So the war was over, and now Bill would no longer have to be bothered at not being in uniform. It was indeed a moment's peace.

At ten o'clock she awakened Bill, and he was rested. "It's Armistice Day, and we ought to celebrate," he said.

"Again?"

"Well, not the same way," said Bill. "Let's have the Sharpes in and give them a drink of champagne."

"All right," said Edna. She called Beulah Sharpe and she readily agreed to have a drink with the Ewings. "Lloyd is somewhere around, but I'll get him," said Beulah.

The Sharpes, accompanied by their collie, Shep, turned up in about ten minutes. "Well, Beulah, Lloyd, we thought we'd offer you a glass of champagne," said Bill. "It's quite an occasion, the Armistice."

"That's very nice of you," said Beulah. "We were thinking of having some dandelion wine, but my goodness, champagne. I've never had champagne."

"I don't hardly drink wine, only beer," said Lloyd.

"Well, this is an occasion. Eleven o'clock is when the shooting stops," said Bill. "I'll open the champagne now, so we'll be ready."

Lloyd looked at his watch. "I make it ten-forty-two," he said. "I think your clock may be a little fast, Mrs. Ewing. This potato of mine was left me by my uncle, a conductor on the Nickel Plate, and it keeps pretty good time."

"I have ten-forty-four," said Bill, looking at his watch.

"There goes the church bells from the United Presbyterian," said Lloyd. "They're way ahead of time."

"Maybe they're not waiting till eleven o'clock," said Bill.

"I guess that's it," said Lloyd.

"Well, let's open the champagne," said Bill.

"We haven't got any champagne glasses," said Edna.

"There's the stem kind, and there's the other kind, called Delmonicos," said Bill. "Ordinary wine glasses will have to do."

"But not sherry glasses," said Edna.

"Well, here goes. I hope it pops," said Bill. He opened the champagne and there was an audible pop, and some of the wine spilled out.

"Did you hear a cannon go off?" said Beulah. "Yes, that was a cannon. I wonder where it was from."

"Right on time," said Lloyd, showing his watch to Edna and Bill.

"Here's to the Armistice," said Bill.

"Here's to peace," said Edna.

"To peace," said Beulah.

"And to prosperity," said Lloyd.

They drank the rest of the champagne, and the Sharpes departed. "Well, let's have them again sometime. Next Armistice Day," said Edna. "What did he mean—here's to prosperity?"

"I was more interested in his watch," said Bill. "Do you suppose he winds it twice a day?"

"Oh, well, dull as they are, they're reliable," said Edna. "What do you want to do now?"

"Listen to the church bells and then do some work," said Bill. "God knows I have plenty of that to do. And we mustn't forget about prosperity."

"Yes, and we mustn't forget, I married you for your money," said Edna.

"If you did, so far you've been robbed. But things will begin to look a lot better from now on," said Bill. "Cuyahoga, Cuyahoga ..."

The day after the Armistice George McVeagh called together an informal meeting of the directors of Cuyahoga. Minor Hay was present and Alan Holcomb, and Edgar Ennis, who almost never attended board meetings, was there to represent his sister, Mrs. Cudlipp. The meeting was held in McVeagh's office instead of the large board room. "I called this meeting because although our Chicago and St. Louis members couldn't be present, and we have no idea what the future holds for Cuyahoga, I didn't want any feeling of panic to exist. Our stock went off three points yesterday and it's off another two this morning, and I expect it to go lower. But you all remember that it went off a few points when we announced that we were going to discontinue overtime, and it crept back up a few days later. So I don't think we'll be in a bad way. And if anybody would care to unload his stock, I don't think he'd have much trouble finding a buyer. We've known all along that the war had to end before winter, and as I say, it's too early to make any predictions about what will happen to Cuyahoga. But let there be no doubt that after a period of trial and error, good things are ahead. As soon as the automobile industry begins to build automobiles again, Cuyahoga will be getting its share of that business, if not more. Structural steel will offer us another source of income that we haven't been getting these past four years, and I for one see almost unlimited possibilities there. Don't forget that it's cheaper to make structural steel than to build automobiles, and I'm in favor of going after the structural business. The question is, of course, how soon the automobile business will get back on its feet, and putting out new models every year. But while the automobile business is tooling up, I'm of the opinion that we ought to go after the structural business. If I were a doctor, I'd say the prognosis is good. Any questions?"

Edgar Ennis raised his hand.

"Oh, you have a question, Edgar? Or did you wish to be excused?" There was laughter.

"I have a question," said Ennis. "When can we expect the auto industry to start tooling up again, and when will we be getting orders for structural steel?"

"I'd call that two questions, Edgar, neither of which I can answer. Any damn fool could say 'Next year sometime.' But you're dealing with the two largest industries in the United States, steel and automobiles, and we've only had one day of peace. Next question."

"I have a question," said Alan Holcomb.

"Let's have it," said McVeagh.

"Since this is an informal meeting, does the company pay for our lunch?"

"Now that's a very good question," said McVeagh. "Technically, legally, I don't suppose the company should pay for our lunch. However, I invite you all to repair with me to the Union Club, and I'll foot the bill. That will save our new general counsel the trouble of looking up the rule on informal meetings."

They repaired to the Union Club, where a table had been reserved for them. When the luncheon was over the manager of the club, Louis Mueller, spoke to McVeagh, who was with Hay, Holcomb and Bill Ewing. "Have you heard anything about Mr. Kelley's condition?"

"His condition? Is there something wrong?" said McVeagh.

"Oh, I thought you knew," said Mueller. "Mr. Kelley was taken to the hospital this morning, in an ambulance. St. Luke's Hospital."

"Did you hear that?" said McVeagh. "Clarence Kelley was taken to the hospital this morning. What time this morning?"

"Before I came to work, about eight-thirty," said Mueller.

"It was his heart, of course," said McVeagh.

"So they said," said Mueller.

"Who's his doctor?" said McVeagh. "Hendricks, I think."

"Yes, Hendricks," said Bill.

"Let's call up right away," said McVeagh. "Bill, you call the hospital and I'll call Dr. Hendricks."

Bill called the hospital. "This is William Ewing. I called to inquire about Mr. Clarence Kelley."

"Yes, Mr. Ewing. This is Dr. Rice. Mr. Kelley died at ten o'clock this morning. The family have been notified. Do you wish to speak to Dr. Hendricks?"

"Will that bring him back? No, thanks," said Bill.

He hung up and waited for McVeagh to finish his conversation with, presumably, Dr. Hendricks. It was a long conversation; George McVeagh was George McVeagh, and Dr. Hendricks was Dr. Hendricks; George McVeagh wanted to know all the details, and Dr. Hendricks was eager to supply them.

McVeagh, Hay, Holcomb and Bill Ewing went into the bar, and McVeagh consulted his penciled notes. "Clarence passed on shortly before ten o'clock this morning," said McVeagh. "He'd apparently had a stroke early this morning, and when the man came to bring his coffee he was lying on the floor, but he was still alive. Breathing, but unconscious. The man then telephoned Dr. Hendricks, whose telephone number was written on the blotter of Clarence's desk. Shows how Clarence was prepared. Dr. Hendricks sent for the ambulance and meanwhile went to the hospital to be there when Clarence got there. But it was too late to do anything. Clarence might as well have stayed here in the club and died here, which he would have liked. He'd had the same room for a hell of a long time, and he might as well have died here. Anyway he just stopped breathing at about a quarter to ten. I think he was eighty-four, but I'm not sure."

"I think they should have let him die here," said Bill.

"So do I," said Minor Hay.

"You were very close to him, George. Will you see about the funeral?" said Alan Holcomb.

"There isn't going to *be* any funeral," said McVeagh. "In accordance with his wishes, he's to be cremated as soon after his death as possible, and his ashes, as he said, scattered to the four winds. This is all contained in a letter he wrote to one of his daughters, about a month ago, and which Dr. Hendricks saw. He wanted no funeral service of any kind, especially no religious service. His will ought to make interesting reading. I know what's in it, and so does Dr. Hendricks. Two thousand dollars to Dr. Hendricks for every year he stays alive after 1916 . . . The choice of all his law books to Bill Ewing . . . A thousand dollars to the man who brings him coffee in the morning . . . I think he had a certain amount of fun writing that will . . . Five thousand dollars to the employees' pension fund of the Union Club . . . The bulk of his estate is to be divided between his two daughters, provided they carry out his wishes about no funeral . . . Oh, Clarence was a sly one, all right."

"At this moment he's probably in the furnace," said Bill.

"I shouldn't be surprised," said McVeagh.

"Yes, it's all over for Clarence," said Minor Hay. "And yet, having no funeral keeps his memory alive, if you know what I mean. I wonder if he thought of that."

"He thought of everything," said Bill. "He even waited till the Armistice to die. He could just as well have died Sunday, but he waited."

"That's very true," said McVeagh. "He was anxious to have you get started with Cuyahoga, Bill. He wanted that all straightened out. Let's go upstairs and have a look at his room, shall we? I don't think he'd object to that."

"All right," said Bill.

"You fellows go," said Alan Holcomb. "I have to meet a train. Blandina's sister arrives from Chicago on the three-fifteen."

McVeagh, Hay and Bill, accompanied by Louis Mueller, went to Clarence Kelley's room. "I've never been here," said McVeagh.

"Neither have I," said Minor Hay.

"I have, but I've never *seen* it. You didn't look at *things* if Clarence was in the room, fixing you with those sad eyes," said Bill.

There were hardly any law books in the room, but the walls were lined with reading matter, some beautifully bound, some unbound. There were the six volumes of Havelock Ellis's *Studies in the Psychology of Sex;* Krafft-Ebing's *Psycopathia Sexualis,* in English and French; Whitman's *Leaves of Grass,* alongside William D. O'Connor's *The Good Gray Poet;* Freud's *Three Contributions to the Theory of Sex,* and *The Interpretation of Dreams;* Carl Jung's *Psychology of the Unconscious;* Sir Arthur Conan Doyle's *The Memoirs of Sherlock Holmes* . . ."I haven't read one of those books," said McVeagh. "Not even *Sherlock Holmes.*"

"Well, here's one you must have read, George," said Minor Hay.

"What's that?" said McVeagh.

"*Uncle Tom's Cabin,*" said Hay.

"No, I went to see the play twice, but I never read the book," said McVeagh. "Oh, here are some books I've read. *Life on the Mississippi. Huckleberry Finn. The Adventures of Tom Sawyer.* He kept those books separate from those others. *A Lume Spento,* by Ezra Pound. Anybody ever heard of him? *Mr. Dooley in Peace and War,* by Finley Peter Dunne. I always thought his name was Peter Finley Dunne. You could spend hours looking through these books if you had the time, and I'm sure Clarence read them all. What a lonely life he must have led."

"I don't know," said Bill. "It was by his own choice."

"You only knew him as an old man, Bill," said McVeagh. "He didn't always spend his time reading books. Isn't that true, Minor?"

"In his quiet way, I guess Clarence had his share of the opposite sex," said Minor Hay. "There was never anything more than gossip that I knew of. But, George, you remember that opera singer. What was her name?"

"Ida Bertelli," said George.

"Ida Bertelli, that's right," said Hay. "And Charlotte Healy, the vaudeville actress. Clarence was partial to actresses. They'd only be in town a week or two. And I guess his wife didn't care much what he did. She was too busy hitting the bottle."

"The less said about her, the better," said George.

"I never knew about that side of him," said Bill. "The women."

"You were much too young," said Minor. "This was thirty, forty years ago. You weren't even born yet."

"Well, at least Clarence had his memories," said Bill.

"And I suppose when you're in your eighties, that's enough," said McVeagh. "Is this a picture of his wife? I don't remember her looking like that."

"Yes, that's his wife," said Hay. "That was when they were first married, before the booze got to her. The two little girls are his daughters."

"Here's a picture you ought to recognize, Bill. It's your mother and father, taken on my boat, around 1902 or '03. I remember because that was the last year I had that boat. *The Wanderer.*"

"I never saw that picture before," said Bill. "You'd have thought I'd have recognized a picture of my mother and father, or Clarence would have said something about it. I wonder why he didn't."

"Well, that we'll never know," said George. "I guess we've been here long enough. Mr. Mueller, thank you for showing us Mr. Kelley's room."

"You're very welcome, I'm sure," said Mr. Mueller. "You know, Mr. Ewing, I never saw that picture before either, and I've been in this room hundreds of times."

"Only adding to the mystery," said Bill. "Goodbye, Louis."

Bill sent a telegram to his mother, with the news of Clarence Kelley's death and the information that Kelley did not want a funeral. He sent the telegram from his office in the Cuyahoga Building, as though the Cuyahoga Building were not any closer to his mother than the Western Union office in the railroad station. But Clarence's death made him feel closer to his mother than he had in a long, long time; and so had the discovery of the snapshot on *The Wanderer.* He did some quick arithmetic and satisfied himself that he could not have been Clarence Kelley's son; thirty from 1918 was 1888, when his mother was twenty years old and did not know Clarence. But somewhere in the years after 1888 his mother could have had an affair with Clarence, and somehow he hoped she had, if only for Clarence's sake. Clarence must have taken out that snapshot the night before he died, perhaps for a last look at it.

What difference did it make now? He would never know from his mother, and she was the only one who could tell him.

George McVeagh came to his office. "You busy?" said McVeagh.

"It'll keep," said Bill. "I'm getting ready a letter to the staff. Actually it's about Stanley Nork. So much has been happening that we haven't had much chance to do anything about Stanley."

"Do it later," said McVeagh. "I just want to talk."

"About Clarence?" said Bill.

"Oh, about Clarence, and your future, and this and that," said McVeagh. "You must have times when you wonder what the hell it's all about."

"Indeed I do," said Bill.

"I know I do. But I can't talk to Minor Hay, and Alan Holcomb always wants to talk about Blandina. I'm going to miss Clarence," said McVeagh.

"Yes," said Bill.

"We used to have lunch together. I'd always joke with him about what dessert he was having. Custard or rice pudding, on account of his teeth. And I used to make remarks about his cane. But I think he was sensitive about that, so I stopped."

"Yes, I think he was a little sensitive about that," said Bill.

"How's that nice wife of yours?" said McVeagh.

"She's fine," said Bill.

"Jean wants to get to know her better, and so do I. After all, Bill, you're part of the family now. You know that, don't you?"

"Yes, I think I am," said Bill.

"Good, good," said McVeagh. "Well, I won't keep you from your letter. Just wanted to chat a little. Oh, are you free for lunch tomorrow?"

"If I'm not, I will be," said Bill.

THE END

11 P.M., 9 Feb. 1970

About the Author

Son of a doctor and the eldest of eight children, John O'Hara was born in Pottsville, Pennsylvania, January 31, 1905; he died at his home in Princeton, New Jersey, on April 11, 1970, two months after he finished *The Ewings*.

After graduation from Niagara Prep School, he worked at a great variety of jobs. His career as a reporter was also varied. He worked first for two Pennsylvania papers and then for three in New York, where he covered everything from sports to religion. He also was on the staff of *Newsweek* and *Time*, and over the years, wrote columns for *Collier's*, the Trenton *Times-Advertiser*, *Newsday* and *Holiday*.

His first novel was *Appointment in Samarra*, published in 1934, and with its appearance he became, and continued to be throughout his life, a major figure on the American literary scene. He published seventeen novels and eleven volumes of short stories, in addition to plays, essays and sketches, many of which he never got around to collecting for books. Because of his prodigious energy and productivity, he left behind a considerable body of finished work not yet published in any form.

His novel *Ten North Frederick* (1955) received the National Book Award for 1956, and in 1964 the American Academy of Arts and Letters presented to him the Gold Medal Award of Merit.